THE ARK

BEN JEAPES

THE ARK

BEN JEAPES

SCHOLASTIC INC.
New York Toronto London Auckland Sydney
Mexico City New Delhi Hong Kong

*To Jamie
and Thomas*

No part of this publication may be reproduced in whole or in part, or stored in a retrieval system, or transmitted in any form or by any means, electronic, mechanical, photocopying, recording, or otherwise, without written permission of the publisher. For information regarding permission, write to Scholastic Inc., Attention: Permissions Department, 555 Broadway, New York, NY 10012.

ISBN 0-439-21917-5

Text copyright © 1998 by Ben Jeapes. All rights reserved. Published by Scholastic Inc., 555 Broadway, New York, NY 10012, by arrangement with Scholastic Ltd. SCHOLASTIC and associated logos are trademarks and/or registered trademarks of Scholastic Inc.

12 11 10 9 8 7 6 5 4 3 2 1   0 1 2 3 4 5/0

Printed in the U.S.A.   01

First Scholastic printing, November 2000

Prologue

To: All heads of state in Sol system
       All parties in Sol system with spacefaring capacity
       All press agencies in Sol system

From: Senior of the First Breed Earth Mission
       First Breed residence, Manhattan

FOR IMMEDIATE RELEASE

Manhattan, 23 August 2148: Following communication with the home world of the First Breed, I am authorized to announce the following.

We have been made welcome as guests in your solar system for over a year and have closely observed your ways and your history. We have concluded that our histories are very similar; your world's development has paralleled our own, and of all the species that we have discovered, you are the closest to us in technological development. On our world, too, natural resources have been plundered; our environment has been dealt a grievous blow; we have known the pain of the extinction of species. We, too, within the last ten decades, have finally begun to make good the harm done by those who came before us. With sympathy and amusement, we have observed your efforts to hide from us your warlike past and the damage that you have done to your own world. Had you made contact with us first, we would doubtless have made the same efforts.

There is no need for two such similar races to continue their development separately; indeed, we are convinced that if we try it will only result in future conflict, as our interests will inevitably clash.

Therefore, we extend to the human race this invitation.

We have a world which we would like to share with you: the second planet of a star that is not visible from Earth but which lies in the direction of the southern constellation of Pavo. The world (appendix 1) is very similar to Earth. It is over 1000 light years away but we can help you cover that distance quickly. There is room for both our races there. We call it the Roving.

The First Breed have only one nation; you have many. We therefore invite all interested parties with spacefaring capacity to tender for the joint development of this world. Together, as a partnership, our two races will go out into space, side by side as friends.

All interested parties will provide one (1) delegate authorized to represent their interests fully; and a spaceship, capable of supporting its crew for at least one month to transport that delegate to the

Roving. Consumable supplies will be renewable upon arrival. Each ship must have the minimum technical specifications noted in appendix 2. The First Breed reserve the right to refuse entry into the delegation. Our decision is final and no correspondence will be entered into. Once accepted into the delegation, all delegates will be treated as equals.

The delegation ships will rendezvous at a place and date to be announced. A First Breed prideship will be responsible for escorting the delegation fleet to and from the Roving. We guarantee the safety of all humans in the fleet until they have returned to this system, and we take responsibility for their well-being for all the time that they are our guests. Each delegation ship will have a member of the First Breed appointed to it, to help liaise with the delegate and to accustom the ship's crew to dealing with our species.

Upon arrival, delegates will have a chance to study the Roving at firsthand, and will then attend a Convocation. There they will state the case for their party's bid to take charge of the human side of our alliance. Precise rules and a timetable for the Convocation are laid out in appendix 3. Each case will be considered carefully and an alliance will be made with that party whose interests most closely match our own.

This is a chance for both our species to make a fresh start. We of the First Breed hope that you will take it.

For further information, instruct your aide to consult the Invitation Helpdesk at the First Breed Mission.

Verbatim Bald
First Breed residence, Manhattan
23 August 2148 CE

One
20 March 2149

The alarm sounded when the cluster of M-type asteroids was two hundred miles ahead, visible as small pebbles through the viewports and as massive, slowly rotating mountains on the displays.

Michael Gilmore airswam into HMSS *Australasia*'s cramped flight deck, a boxy little space at the front of the boxy little ship. His mind was still full of the baffling dispatch he had left in his cabin. He pulled himself into his couch at the command desk with a practiced twist of his body, and the autostraps slid out and held him in place. "Status," he said.

"Just a brief echo, Captain," Hannah Dereshev said. His first officer was calm and matter-of-fact. "The gas detector picked it up. A couple of molecules —"

"And again, sir," said Adrian Nichol. The young pilot twisted round to look at them and his eyes shone. He wasn't much older than Gilmore's own son, who was still in his teens, and his shock of hair and freckles made him look even younger. "Definite contact. Must be a scuttler."

Of course, there was nothing but asteroids in the viewports. It always amazed Gilmore that non-spacers couldn't grasp the concept of hiding in space: if something was in direct line of sight with nothing in between, they would reason, it must be visible. They had no sense of the scale of things. A small object like a ship, using stealth so radar couldn't lock on to it, in the vastness of space . . . what did they expect? Anyway, the Rusties had been lurking in space undetected for years, or so it was widely believed, and their vessels were a lot bigger than the average scuttler.

But all ships had to maneuver at some point, as this one had done. It would have baffles over its thrusters to hide the glare from prying eyes like those on *Australasia,* but even they couldn't stop the fact that gas was being ejected into the void. Gas that *Australasia's* scanners had picked up, and now the chase was on.

"I confirm that, sir," said Hannah, consulting her own instruments.

"Flares," Gilmore said. There was a muffled thud from outside the flight deck.

"Flares away," Hannah said.

"Fire us up, point three gee."

"Aye-aye, sir," Nichol said. His fingers flickered over his desk.

A muffled roar came from astern as *Australasia's* main engine fired and a faint semblance of weight returned to the flight deck. The small ship began to move towards the asteroids, and the flares that had been fired off from the ship seconds earlier exploded, bathing the cluster in their white glare. The viewports and visual displays dimmed automatically but the ship's sensors were taking everything in. No shadows were cast against the mottled surface of the rocks.

"Nothing, sir." Hannah's voice was flat.

"Damn!" The last scuttler of the patrol was going to be a hard one. It was somewhere inside the cluster. Gilmore looked at the cluster's radar image and fought off the temptation to go home. He had every excuse, with the recently received dispatch still fresh in his astonished mind:

"*HMSS* Australasia *will return to UK-1 with utmost haste —*"

So, he could just walk away from this. But he couldn't live with an unfinished job on his conscience. As always happened at times like this, the black spectre of failure swam in front of his eyes; and as always, he banished it by conjuring up a mental picture of exactly what he needed to do. All the necessary actions, laid out before him with the precision and detail of a technical diagram.

"Bring us up to point five gee, cut burn and bring us over Number One Rock's north pole. Tell the hands to brace for indefinite maneuvering."

"Aye-aye, sir," Nichol and Hannah said.

Outside, seven asteroids had been nudged together into a cluster by surveyors from UK-1, *Australasia*'s parent vessel. The surveyors had staked provisional mining claims and left them in the route of UK-1, which would roll up in its own good time and begin exploitation.

But the clustering had signalled to every freelance miner in the system that those rocks were worth working. So, as UK-1 drew near, so did the scuttlers, earning their name by scuttling in to stake their own claims. All they had to do was actually process some ore and the claim was automatically theirs. UK-1 had the legal right to prevent trespassers approaching its provisional claims, but once a claim had actually been worked by someone else, then it belonged to that person and there was nothing anyone could do about it.

In his capacity as a private citizen, Michael Gilmore had to admire the cheek and the enthusiasm of the scuttlers; as a holder of the king's commission and commander of one of UK-1's sweep ships, he was a legalized bully boy, whose duty was to deter them so that UK-1 wouldn't have to share its provisional claims with anyone. There was no reason why there couldn't be several mines with different owners all on one rock, but that offended UK-1's sense of tidiness and — Gilmore had to be blunt — greed.

And now there was a scuttler out there. Gilmore could already picture it in his mind. It would be painted matte black, and fitted with the latest stealth tech and a host of gadgets for absorbing or deflecting as many forms of electromagnetic radiation as possible. Scuttlers might start their journey months, even years earlier, maybe with the crew going into cryo, coasting silently through the solar system up to the chosen cluster to stake their claim.

On patrol, in the waiting stage of the game, *Australasia* had been on silent running, using exactly the same tricks as the scuttler to stay hidden in the void. All that was over now as the sweep hurtled over the north pole of the nearest rock. At the same time, under Adrian Nichol's careful piloting, some thrusters flared, others did not and the ship oriented itself so it was pointing into the heart of the cluster: a few hundred tons of ship, a small ferropolymer bubble of warmth and air and light in the deep dark, surrounded by a ring of harsh mountains.

There had been no sign of fusion burn from the scuttler: no glare and no radiation. So, it wasn't using its fusion engine, if it even had one. It couldn't be moving very fast. With a bit of luck it, too, was still in this bottomless valley in space, still heading for the hills.

"Flares," Gilmore said again. "Three-hundred-and-sixty-degree spread."

"Aye-aye, sir," said Hannah. "Flares away."

The flares streaked from *Australasia* in all directions and now white light was reflected off seven pitted surfaces; a vista of small craters and shadows to the left and right, above and below, giving a brief and terrible sense of vertigo. Gilmore narrowed his eyes, trying to beat the sensors: were any of those shadows moving? Were —

"Got 'im!" Nichol said. His voice cracked and he coughed. "Um, scuttler sighted, sir, 320 degrees, pitch down 13 —"

Australasia's sensors were zooming in on the co-ordinates. Still nothing showed on the radar — the scuttler's stealth tech was good — but searchlights mounted on the ship's hull reached out and speared the intruder. It was 70 miles above the surface of Number Three Rock and dropping. An ugly, functional collection of boxes and pipes, painted night-black. With visible contact made it would find it hard to shake off *Australasia*'s sensors.

"Concentrate flares in that area," Gilmore said. "Bring us to that bearing and burn —"

Hannah and Nichol were already doing their jobs. *Australasia* turned towards the scuttler, now clearly picked out, and her main engine fired.

Gilmore told the comms AI to open a channel. "This is HMSS *Australasia* to unidentified craft," he said. "Provisional claims have been staked on these asteroids by UK-1 and you are in violation —"

"Come and get us." It was a male voice, taunting. Accent impossible to trace. "We're on our way down and we're gonna make a claim, like it or not."

"We are empowered to prevent —" Gilmore began.

"Yeah? How?"

How indeed? Gilmore thought glumly. *And why*? The *why* was easier to answer: it was his job.

He glanced quickly at the scanners and absorbed their data. At its present rate of fall the scuttler would touch down on the rock in just over five minutes, though before then it would have slowed

down. However suicidal the scuttler captain was
feeling, the ship would have automatic safeties to
stop itself being dashed to pieces —

Safeties. He checked *Australasia*'s heading: the
sweep was pointing straight at the rock. Excellent.

"Full burn," he said. "Take us to one gee —"

Nichol's eyes were round. "Sir?" he said.

"Full burn, Mr. Nichol," said Hannah, still calm but
somehow suggesting torments beyond imagination
if the pilot didn't do as he was told. It was a knack
Gilmore had always wished he had.

"Aye-aye, sir!" The main engine fired and again
weight returned to the flight deck: this time a full
one Earth gravity. After so long in micro-gee, it felt
heavier.

There hadn't been time to set this up with the
computer — it would have to be manual, relying on
Nichol's reactions. Gilmore outlined his plan to the
other two and after that there was nothing more to
do but watch Number Three Rock come ever closer.
Millions of tons of rock, falling on top of them.

Gilmore's mind went back to the dispatch in his
cabin. "Number One," he said, as if to make conversation.

"Captain?"

"It appears I've been given command of the *Ark
Royal*."

Hannah stared at him but the scuttler's comms interrupted anything she might have been about to
say.

"It won't work." Was there a hint of uncertainty? If there was it didn't come close to matching the uncertainty Gilmore felt: *Australasia* was charging on full flame straight at the little ship. "You won't ram us and we're on manual."

Gilmore gave a grim smile: they had guessed his game. If the scuttler had been on auto, its collision safeties would have moved it out of *Australasia*'s way and hence away from the rock.

"Now," Gilmore said. Nichol fired the thrusters — and *Australasia* flipped head over tail, engine still burning. A minor correction and again the sweep was heading straight at the scuttler, preceded by an invisible beam of nuclei blasted by the fusion engine directly at the intruder. Thrusters flared on the scuttler and the little black ship fled to one side.

Gilmore grinned. Collision safeties were one thing, but some safeties just couldn't be overridden in a hurry, and the safeties that prevented a ship from straying into another's fusion flame were one of them.

"You —" the scuttler's comms crackled with anger, before someone on that end had the sense to break contact.

"*Yes!*" Nichol shouted. Gilmore and Hannah both scowled at him. "Sorry, sirs," he said, only slightly abashed.

The scuttler's neatly planned approach arc had been spoiled and thrusters blazed against the dark as the scuttler crew fought to reestablish an arc to another point on the rock.

"Bring us round as soon as you can," Gilmore said.

"Aye-aye, sir."

"*Ark Royal*, Captain?" said Hannah.

"So it seems. It means promotion to Commander."

"Um . . . congratulations . . ."

"I'll need a first officer, of course," Gilmore added.

This time Hannah was spared from answering by the weight as *Australasia* slowed and the flight deck crew were crushed into their couches. The ship's fusion engine gave her more power than the scuttler but with it came 200 more tons worth of momentum and inertia. She couldn't be hurled around the heavens the same way as the other ship, which had already reestablished its approach. It was coming down to Number Three Rock with a lot more urgency than before and in a few minutes it would be over the rock's horizon.

Australasia came round and gave chase. What next? Gilmore thought. The trick wouldn't work twice. He ran figures through his control desk. If he trusted the flight computer and Nichol's piloting they could bring the ship in between the scuttler and the rock. . . .

He gave the orders and the ship came round slightly, poised to boost again.

"Scuttler is ninety-two miles ahead," Hannah said. "Probable touchdown in two minutes." She frowned. "What's that? They can't be abandoning ship."

Gilmore glanced at the display. A small blip was slowly making its way from the larger blip that represented the scuttler. *Australasia*'s new course meant the blip would miss it by over a hundred miles.

The blip changed direction, to head straight for them, and a silent alarm began to ring in Gilmore's mind. He had read something about —

"My God, get the laser on it!" Gilmore shouted. "Do it n —"

A blinding flash through the viewports, and all the displays went fuzzy.

"They fired at us!" Hannah said, shocked. "They fired a torpedo at us!"

Glib answers ran through Gilmore's mind. *A first time for everything*. *So it seems*. So the rumours were true. Ships were arming themselves.

"Yes," he said, "they fired at us. A nuclear warhead, it appears."

More to the point, he felt, someone had fired a nuclear warhead *at him*. He was in a small ship whose only defenses were the standard anti-meteor laser and passive radiation shielding, and he suddenly felt very vulnerable. Even more so, since his ship was now blinded by the electromagnetic pulse of the explosion and headed straight for a giant mountain in space.

"How long before we can get the systems on-line again?" he said.

"A couple of minutes, sir," Nichol said, not looking up as his hands moved rapidly over the controls.

"How long before we hit the rock?"

Nichol glanced up at the viewport. "A couple of minutes, sir," he said.

After that there wasn't much to say and no point in saying it, as they worked to get the ship up and running again. The rock was visibly closer.

"We have control," Nichol said at last.

"Then get us away from that thing!" Gilmore said.

"Aye-aye, sir." The weight came back, as Nichol brought the ship round again and fired the main engine. As *Australasia* slowed, Gilmore called up the display for a last view of the scuttler. It was approaching the rock's terminator, out of the light of the sun and *Australasia*'s dying flares, and would be invisible again in a few more moments. He glared at the smaller ship in a white fury: okay, they weren't taking any chances with this maniac who played chicken with asteroids and spaceships, but a *torpedo* —

Then Gilmore saw it and his eyes widened in horror.

"Scuttler, pull up!" he yelled. "Fire everything and pull up!"

The scuttler saw it, too, and started to maneuver, but too late. The mountain that had been waiting on the rock's dark side loomed ahead, carried round by the rock's natural rotation. The yells over the radio belied the apparent calm dignity with which the scuttler ship met its fate. Almost delicately the mountain seemed to reach out for the black ship and stroke it with a rough tentacle of rock. Over the radio came screams and the sudden, terrible roar of explosive decompression which stopped just as abruptly as it began.

"Oh, Christ," Nichol murmured. On the displays, small fragments of the scuttler floated gently out of the cloud of vapour, some moving off into space, some bouncing featherlike off the rock's surface.

"Match orbits," Gilmore muttered. "Get a team down there." Returning to port could wait a bit longer. It was possible, just possible, someone on board had been suited up, and their suit hadn't been punctured by debris, and . . .

It wouldn't have happened, but it was possible.

Two
26 March 2149

The foreshortened perspective of space made UK-1 seem to be only a few feet away from *Australasia*. It always looked like just some other ship or station and Gilmore still had to make the necessary adjustment with his eyes and senses to appreciate just how big it was. It was the largest spaceship ever built — seventeen massive wheels in space, spinning around a common axis. The last redoubt of the exiled House of Windsor.

"Engineer to flight deck. The engines are powered down," said a voice from the engine room.

Gilmore thumbed the contact to make the return message. "That's exactly what it says on my display here, Mr. Loonat, but thank you for the courtesy."

"You're welcome, Captain."

Australasia was coasting on its own momentum, a minnow to UK-1's whale, as grapples reached out to snare it and drag it into its cradle on the stationary docking strake that ran the length of the great ship. Then HMSS *Australasia* was safely docked at its home port and another patrol was over.

The satisfied smile vanished from Gilmore's face as he caught his reflection in the panel in front of him — just a dim image but he knew too well the resigned look of gloom that tended to be his expression of default. A long-ago love had told him that his face was fragile, and that his eyes seemed larger than usual, which gave them more emotion and hence made his thoughts easier to read. The sad thing was, she had meant it as a compliment. He had been wary of showing his thoughts through his too-large eyes ever since. Thoughts were a dangerous thing to show.

"Ship secured, sir," said the pilot of the watch.

"Fine." Gilmore sat back in his couch. "Let's take a look at our neighbours."

It was something he usually did, just to see which old friends might be in the vicinity. Several other ships of the Royal Space Fleet were docked as well: two liners, some freighters and a couple of sweeps.

And a Rustie ship — not one of the seven starships of the First Breed that had burst into the solar system nearly two years ago, but a smaller, interplanetary job. At first sight it was unremarkable and not obviously alien, but gradually you realized that the proportions were all wrong. It was built for a race that thought humans were too tall.

Gilmore had never caught Rusticmania, and privately wished they had never come. They were going to share the secrets of their ships and (everyone else hoped) the rest of their tech. Soon there would be no room for an average ship's captain like him, raised on the old ways. Sail was giving way to steam all over again.

"The overhaul team asks permission to come on board, sir."

"Fine." *Australasia* — Gilmore was still finding it hard to accept — had been fired at with a nuclear weapon: it needed the once-over by a better team of engineers than he had on board to check for damage from heat or radiation.

Even more annoying was that he suspected the Admiralty were delighted one of their ships had actually been fired upon. *Torpedo* was probably too grand a word for it — a nuclear bomb tied to a small booster engine, obviously with thrusters so that it could alter course to a certain extent, but still far from being a proper guided weapon. Crude, no doubt, compared with what was to come. If he had been quick enough, he could have hit it with the ship's laser and that would have been the end of the threat.

But that wasn't the point. Gilmore had heard rumours of space weaponry being developed in secret, as space gradually lost the neutrality it had enjoyed for two hundred years, and human interests took over. And now it had happened. Someone had fired a torpedo in anger. He had been ordered to send on every scrap of data from *Australasia*'s sensors relating to the incident, as well as to make a separate report giving his own impressions. And he had no doubt where all that data was going: straight into the Admiralty's own weapons development programme.

"Dispatches are ready for downloading, sir," said the comms officer.

"I'll take them in my cabin."

"Very good, sir."

As Gilmore airswam down *Australasia*'s central passage towards his cabin, a snippet of conversation drifted out of the wardroom.

"Hey, you know there's Rusties in town?"

"Come to see His Highness, I suppose —" That was Adrian Nichol. He stopped when he saw Gilmore looking in. "Afternoon, sir."

"Carry on," Gilmore murmured. He turned to go. "Oh, and the king is His Majesty, Mr. Nichol. Worth remembering."

Gilmore sat in his cabin, but he was looking into infinity and seeing the *Ark Royal* at the end of it.

The ship wasn't even in service yet and was already a legend in the Royal Space Fleet. State of the art, fast and manoeuvrable, with systems a generation ahead of any other human-built ship in space. Word was that she wasn't even an official Admiralty project but was funded by the king, which immediately made her ten times more interesting. The king kept a number of privately funded projects going all the time, with varying degrees of secrecy: sometimes they would produce something beneficial and the product would be released into the public domain; sometimes word of the project only got out in the form of rumours.

But what did the king want the *Ark Royal* for? There was one obvious answer, even though it hadn't been confirmed officially, and if it was true it meant—

"You wanted to see me, sir?"

Hannah Dereshev stood in the entrance to his cabin. Gilmore smiled and beckoned her in. He was holding an aide in his hands, carefully not letting the display point in her direction.

"Yes," he said. "I mentioned the *Ark Royal* a while back —"

"Yes, sir, I —"

"Please," Gilmore said, holding up a hand. "I don't want your decision yet. For a start, I'm convinced they've got the wrong Captain Gilmore."

"There aren't any other Captain Gilmores in the Fleet," Hannah said. "I checked."

"Whatever. Anyway, I want you to see this first." He passed the aide over and watched her eyes widen. "Congratulations, Number One."

She couldn't take her eyes off the aide and the words it was displaying. A corner of Gilmore's mouth turned in a smile when he remembered the first time he had received a similar message: brief and toneless, but oh so important. It had been one of the dispatches waiting for them when *Australasia* returned to UK-1.

"*You are instructed to take command . . .*"

"It's the *Antarctica*," she said. Her first command, and promotion to lieutenant commander with it.

"The Earth run."

"That's right."

"You'll want Samad as Chief Engineer?" Gilmore
said.

She smiled broadly. "I wouldn't have it any other
way."

Hannah was married to Samad Loonat, *Australasia*'s chief engineer. The two of them hired out their
joint services to the space lines: it was a common
means for married couples to get around the long
separations of space travel. Where Hannah went,
Samad went.

And where Hannah was going was one of the
Royal Space Fleet's freighters, shipping goods between Earth and UK-1. Definitely one up from a
sweep ship like *Australasia*. Gilmore had been
there once.

"I'm glad for you," he said.

"Mike —"

"No, I am." And he was. Hannah deserved better
than him.

She looked at the display again, then slowly raised
her eyes to his. "Going back to the *Ark Royal* . . ."
she said.

"What about it?"

"Do you know anything more about it?"

"Not yet. I'm ordered to report to the palace once
I'm done here."

"The palace? Not the Admiralty?" she said.

"Correct. I'm going to hear it from the horse's mouth."

"Can I give you my decision when you know more about it?" Hannah said.

Gilmore smiled. "I wouldn't have it any other way," he said. However much he wanted her as his first officer, he wanted her to make the decision fully informed.

"And I might not get the choice anyway," she pointed out. "I'm *instructed* to take command."

"If I'm to be captain of *Ark Royal*," Gilmore said, "I'll be doing the instructing."

Being inside UK-1 was meant to be like being back on Earth. The laser images projected on the ceiling gave the feeling of the infinite vault of a real Earth sky. Live flora and even fauna were loose in the open areas, all native to the British Isles. The air had a clean, piney smell which Gilmore always felt to be tacky, being so blatantly artificial.

His legs were wobbly: he had been on a two-month patrol in a ship without a centrifuge, and working out in the ship's gym had only just kept muscular atrophy at bay. Now those wobbly legs were trying to carry him through a crowd, which he hated at the best of times, and his eyes were fixed firmly ahead, trying to navigate a passage through the jostling people. In this way he almost stumbled over a cluster of three Rusties.

They were gazing into a shop window, for all the world like tourists out on a buying spree. Gilmore fought to regain his balance and suddenly he discovered he wasn't quite so uninterested in the stumpy, four-legged creatures after all. Still only a tiny percentage of people had seen one in the flesh and until now he hadn't been one of them. He tried to look at them without staring.

"Mike!" A powerful hand slapped him on the back and drove the breath out of his lungs. "How are you?"

"Hello, John," Gilmore muttered after a couple of breaths. "Have you seen the Rus —"

"Yeah, yeah, they're old hat." John Chase was a large man in all directions. He and Gilmore had started in space together but Chase had shot ahead and now, while Gilmore languished as a lieutenant commander — well, only just made commander — and was called a captain by virtue of commanding a ship, Chase was a captain by rank. And that meant he was able to draw Gilmore away from the three aliens and carry on chatting, and Gilmore couldn't do a thing about it except to cast a final look back as the Rusties were swallowed by the crowd. "Heard the darndest thing about them," Chase continued. "Did you know they make their ships out of pottery?"

"Yes," Gilmore said. A plastic-ceramic compound, to be accurate, but not ferro-polymer, like the ships made by humans.

"Say, Mike . . ." Chase looked about them and drew him to one side. "Rumour says you've been given command of *Ark Royal*. That true?"

"I'm on my way to the palace now," Gilmore said hopefully. Chase drew back quickly.

"Then why are you talking to me? Get on, Mike! I'll catch you at the Captain's Club."

He backed away into the crowd and Gilmore gratefully headed for the transport tube.

Straphanging on the way down to the palace — the colloquial name for F-wheel, the sixth wheel of UK-1, occupied exclusively by the king, his family and staff — Gilmore pieced together his brief impression of the Rusties. Quadrupeds, the largest of them coming up to his chest. Flesh covered by a ruddy, fuzzy substance that could be hair, could be feathers, could be something with no analogue on Earth. It was the colour of oxidized iron, and even close up, it really did look like patches of rust were flaking off the creatures. Now Gilmore thought about it, he could remember a smell which he realized had been coming from the aliens. It was as if they had splashed on too much aftershave: not displeasing but not pleasing either.

The jokes about telling them apart weren't fair: he had seen they were all of slightly different sizes and shapes. The only identical thing about them was the translator units hanging around their necks. They also had harnesses around their necks and over their bodies, on which hung things that might have been tools or decoration or both, and were as varied as human clothes.

And that was the sum of Gilmore's impression of the aliens. He thought dark thoughts about John Chase, a man so accustomed to them that he thought they were old hat, but he shook the thoughts away as the tube reached F-wheel. He still had his appointment with the king and if His Majesty had in mind what Gilmore suspected, he was going to see a lot more of the Rusties than John Chase ever would.

Three
27 September 2148

"This is a chance for both our species to make a fresh start. We of the First Breed hope that you will take it."

The entire text of the Rusties' invitation was burned into his mind: he had memorized it and looked at it backwards, forwards, left to right, right to left and upside down.

They wanted something. Nothing was so simple, so straightforward as the invitation made out: life wasn't like that. In the opinion of R.V. Krishnamurthy, life was far too short for riddles and far too short for being expected to answer them. He believed in taking the simplest solution, and with solving riddles the simplest solution was to ask someone already in the know. This was precisely what he expected to do here, in this remote lodge in the Himalayas, with no one as yet but his loyal assistant and 20 elite NVN soldiers for company.

"We have them on radar, Excellency." The speaker was a slim, nervous man in his mid-thirties — twenty years younger than his master.

"Thank you, Subhas," Krishnamurthy said.

Subhas Ranjitsinhji was one of those people who was permanently making Krishnamurthy ask himself why he tolerated them. And yet tolerate him he did: the man had been by his side for years. Ranjitsinhji could handle Krishnamurthy's network of spies and informers, and all the other fiddling but necessary details that frankly bored his master. A useful subordinate and occasionally a handy scapegoat or just plain kicking stool.

Krishnamurthy deliberately did not get out of his chair but turned another page in his book. A shame about the appearance he had to keep up, he thought, because outside the great studio windows of the lodge the view of the Himalayas gleaming in the sun was stupendous. He had spent many happy holidays here and he was well aware of its isolation, so when he had heard that a party of Rusties visiting Katmandu wanted to look at Everest . . .

Now he could hear the engines of their flyer, echoing along the valley. He slowly put down his book and got up, stretched and wandered over to the balcony. Someone handed him a pair of binoculars and he put them to his eyes. His paid-for, tame pilot was flying down this particular valley with no questions asked, which was as well because the man would have taken much more persuading if he had known about the bomb.

A puff of smoke and flame burst out from one of the flyer's engines and the whole craft yawed, dropping out of the circle of vision of the binoculars. Krishnamurthy followed the trail of smoke down until he had it again and set the binoculars to auto-focus, holding the plunging flyer in the middle of his circle of vision. At the same time, the sound of the explosion reached them in the lodge, with the noise of the tortured engines that were trying to hold the flyer up.

"Recovery team, stand by," said the NVN major.

The flyer came down on to the valley floor in an exploding cloud of smoke and sparks and dust. It skidded along the ground, still wavering from side to side, ploughing out a scorched furrow behind it, until it slammed sideways into a boulder. It tilted up and for a moment looked as if it might somersault over the boulder, but then it fell back down and settled right way up with a mighty crash. It was directly below the lodge on the floor of the valley, two hundred yards away. It couldn't have been better.

The recovery team was already scrambling down towards it. Much as he regretted it, Krishnamurthy turned away from the scene — image was everything — and returned to his chair. "Time to finish my chapter, I think," he said. "Get the ski masks ready."

Armed men in masks stood around the mangled four-legged form on the floor. Krishnamurthy had ordered that only one survivor be left but it looked as if he had been lucky to get even that one. The flyer had come down more heavily than intended.

He squatted down by its head and poked it. The Rustie shuddered in pain.

"Can you hear me?" he said.

No answer, except a rattling noise which could have been its usual speech or could have been a gasp of pain that its translator unit couldn't handle. He hoped it hadn't lost the power of speech; he wasn't going to be able to repeat this trick and secure himself another captive. They might believe *one* flyer full of visiting Rusties could be struck down by some natural cause, but two?

He prodded it harder. "I can't understand you. Speak clearly."

Or maybe the translator was smashed—

The creature spoke. ". . . Hear," it said.

"You are a prisoner of the Movement for Free Nepal," Krishnamurthy said. The Movement was his current bugbear and deserved a few more enemies. "Your friends are dead and you are badly injured. If you want to live you will answer my questions."

". . . Help," the alien said.

"Are you asking for it or saying that you will?" Krishnamurthy chuckled. "Never mind, I will soon find out. Now, what is the real purpose of the invitation?"

The creature was hurt but it wasn't stupid, and it took a lot of encouraging to answer. Water deprivation, pain, keeping it out of the healing coma that was its natural response to its injuries. Much of what it said didn't make sense but he took it all down for later playback.

Five hours later the creature was dead, naturally,

of its own injuries. So, no need for the freedom fighters story. Krishnamurthy pulled his mask off and stood over the body, hefting in his hand his aide with the recording of the session. He would find out. He would piece it all together. Oh, yes. . . .

"The Rusties have asked us," said Manohar Chandwani, secretary to the Prime Minister of the Confederation of South-East Asia, "to pass on to you their appreciation of your efforts in trying to save their colleagues. They regret the effort was wasted."

Krishnamurthy shrugged expansively. "One does what one can," he said.

Chandwani had Pathan blood in him somewhere: the shrewd look he gave Krishnamurthy could have frozen a lesser man in his tracks. Krishnamurthy had long become inured to what others thought of him, however, particularly lukewarm wishy-washy liberal Progressives like Chandwani. *For a while*, he thought, *for a brief while, for a glorious couple of decades, we had begun to reclaim our country's heritage once more. And now people like you would throw it all away again.*

"It was convenient the flyer came down so close to your lodge, Krishnamurthy. And convenient you and your NVN friends were holding your security conference there," Chandwani said.

Another shrug. "Fate."

"Yes. Of course." Chandwani touched a button on his aide and the display changed: Krishnamurthy couldn't see what it was. "To business, Krishna-murthy. The Prime Minister has studied your pro-posal most carefully."

"That is very good of him."

"And he has decided . . ." Chandwani gave a heavy sigh and glared up at him. "He has agreed."

"Agreed?" Krishnamurthy's blood pounded in his ears.

"Every detail. The budget, the procurements, the overall strategy, everything." Chandwani sat back and put his hands behind his head. "You can even keep that idiot Ranjitsinhji as your assistant, though goodness knows why you want him. Every detail."

Every detail, Krishnamurthy wanted to sing. It was all coming true.

For years, he had been laying out the case for why the Confederation had to have a presence in space. The one gap in his country's defences was so sadly obvious. For the last century, Delhi had been too ob-sessed with expanding its empire sideways to bother with upwards, and as a result the Confedera-tion was a world power with no space presence. The logic was that there was plenty of room down below on Earth; but Krishnamurthy, who had spent most of his career helping his country acquire and retain its empire, knew otherwise. Afghanistan, Tibet, Bangladesh, Burma . . . there wasn't much further they could expand before they clashed with the interests of other nations that it would be best not to antagonize.

But now the Confederation was going on the delegation, and he would be in charge. . . .

"They're giving me rope," he murmured.

Chandwani gave a thin smile. "How can we lose? At best, your plan succeeds, we win the bid for this world of theirs, and you will no doubt remain as administrator or whatever. You're out of our hair. At worst, we lose the bid and you return in disgrace, defeated, finished. You're out of our hair."

"The administration's gratitude for my past efforts is almost overwhelming."

Chandwani's smile vanished. He stood up, pushing the chair back, and crossed to the window to look out at the bicentenary monument in the square outside — a fifty-foot statue of the Mahatma.

"The Indian republic is two hundred years old," he said. "And in that time I think we've occasionally drifted somewhat from the principles on which it was founded." He nodded at the statue. "Every now and then a country goes mad. It happened to the fascist and communist states of the twentieth century, the combines of the twenty-first . . . and it happened to us in the twenty-second. We were rich and powerful but we were peaceful. We founded the Confederation because economically and technologically we dominated Asia and we wanted to use that power for the good of all. And we did, for a while, until you and your kind came along with your talk of Greater India and your dreams of the bad old days. Conquest, war, glory."

"You have to admit it is more interesting than parliamentary democracy," Krishnamurthy said.

Chandwani glared at him.

"I know how you despise the Progressives," he said, "but we are healing India, and hence the Confederation. We came close to the Mahatma's ideals once, and people like you drew us away. Now we're having a second chance."

"What goes around comes around," Krishnamurthy said. "Very karmic. And in the process you weaken our borders, dilute our power —"

"Our border acquisitions were justified at the time as necessary for our security. Now that we are confident in our security, we no longer need the acquisitions. Thus, the administration shows its consistency and sense of purpose." Chandwani strolled back to his desk and sat down again. "We are getting off the point. The Rusties are grateful, your plan is approved, now go."

Krishnamurthy turned to leave, slowly, showing that he was leaving because he chose to and not because he had been dismissed.

"The crew *will* all be citizens, of course?" Chandwani said behind him. Krishnamurthy smiled to himself: so, even Chandwani had an ounce of patriotism inside him.

"Of course," said Krishnamurthy. The Rusties had specified that all delegates provide their own ship — a stipulation doubtless intended to separate the men from the boys — and it had almost ex-

cluded the Confederation, except that one of the
procurements the Prime Minister had just approved
was for a spaceship adequate to the task in hand.
The crew would have to be picked from the trained
spacers of other spacelines, but—

"May I suggest the *Gandhi* as a suitable name?"
Chandwani said.

"It had occurred to me." If it kept the man
quiet . . .

But not Gandhi, no — for all Krishnamurthy's admiration of the way the man had stood up to the
British. Krishnamurthy worked for the Confederation but at heart he was an Indian, and the ship's
name would be from an earlier and darker part of
India's history: a man for whom Krishnamurthy's
admiration was unbridled and unconditional.
Founder of the Maratha state, protector of his
people and owner of a name that had struck fear
into the hearts of his enemies.

"*Shivaji!*" he murmured, but only to himself.

Four
26 March 2149

An amboid was waiting for Gilmore when he reached the palace. The icon that glowed on the amboid's faceplate told the world that the artificial intelligence occupying it was called Plantagenet: the intelligence itself was contained in a ROM-crystal somewhere else on UK-1, but its attention was concentrated here. Such high-level AIs were rare, especially for running mundane errands, and Gilmore wondered if he should feel flattered that one had come to meet him. He presumed that the design of the icon was based on the Plantagenet arms.

"Did the king have any reason for calling you Plantagenet?" he said, on a whim, as the amboid guided him through the palace.

"His Majesty calls us all after Britain's royal dynasties, Commander Gilmore."

"I can't wait to meet Saxe-Coburg-Gotha," Gilmore muttered, thinking: one more example of the Pretender to the throne of Great Britain's eccentricities.

"That AI is simply called Saxe-Coburg," Plantagenet said helpfully. Gilmore stopped making conversation.

It was the first time Gilmore had stepped in

an F-wheel, and with his first chance to look around he began to revise his opinion of the king. It was as one felt a palace should be: quiet, calm, ornate. Somehow he didn't doubt that the carpets and paintings and tapestries were genuine . . . and that was just it. Mad kings hid in pianos and let their realms go to pot; King Richard had put a lot of love and care into this. He was obsessive about his kingdom, certainly. But maybe — just maybe — he wasn't as mad as rumour suggested.

"This way, Commander," said a voice at his elbow, and he suddenly remembered where he was. He followed Plantagenet.

"Please wait in here, Commander," Plantagenet said. Gilmore was led into a room lined with books. "His Majesty will be with you shortly," Plantagenet said, and left.

As was no doubt expected of him, Gilmore began to inspect the books. Few surprises there. Churchill's *History of the English-Speaking Peoples*. The complete works of Shakespeare, every play individually bound. How much had shipping all this out from Earth cost?

"Impressed?"

Gilmore didn't jump: naturally the king would have a sense of theatre and he would have to show up just now. So he turned round slowly.

Richard Windsor was a thickset man in his early sixties. He wore a suit which looked quite casual but which Gilmore suspected was well out of his price range. He seemed quite friendly and his eyes were very shrewd.

This man, Gilmore decided, *is not in the least bit mad*.

"I would come a long way to see a library like this, sir," he said. His reply was meant to be to the point, abrupt, showing the king he wasn't here to take nonsense. Then he ruined it by adding a "sir" at the end.

The king nodded, absorbing the information without acknowledging it. "Can I offer you tea?" he said.

A slim man with a moustache was waiting for them in the v-room where tea was served.

"Have you met my son?" the king asked. "James, Lieutenant Commander Michael Gilmore."

"How do you do," said James, Prince of Wales. He and Gilmore shook hands. Gilmore knew the man by sight, of course, as he knew his two younger sisters and their mother. One princess was an actor, the other worked for a space company — not the RSF — and the Queen spent most of her time on Earth. None of them played a part in UK-1 affairs.

"Please, sit down," the king said. "What do you think, Commander?"

Gilmore sat and looked with interest at the virtual display all around them. It was as though they sat at a point in the central axis of UK-1, and the great ship's walls and ceilings were transparent. They could look down at anything in the ship, anywhere. It was the closest thing the king could find to standing on a mountain and looking out over his kingdom. There were even people moving about in the corridors and plazas.

"If you were to zoom in on this room," the king said, "you would find three simulacra there, watching a similar scene. Of course, at that level the resolution begins to get fuzzy. Other than that, it's just made up. The people cycle through the same set of activities every three minutes."

"Nice toy," Gilmore said. It was impressive, even if it was just a show. There was no flicker, no disjuncture between cycles. Beginning and end merged seamlessly into each other. It did annoy him slightly that the king felt he had to call attention to everything. If you're king, he thought, you shouldn't have anything to prove.

A woman came in carrying a tea tray and Gilmore was trying to place her — not any of the senior politicians, not a member of the Fleet — when it finally dawned on him that she was here purely to serve the tea. After that he couldn't take his eyes off her: he couldn't believe that in somewhere like UK-1, where everyone paid their way, there were people whose sole function was to pour tea.

"So, do you like my kingdom?" the king asked. He

did lower himself to passing the cups himself once the servant had gone. They sat in chairs side by side and looked out at his realm. Prince James sat opposite them and drank silently, rarely taking his eyes off Gilmore.

Gilmore wondered why the king seemed so anxious to get his approval. He was like a small child, constantly drawing attention to his new toy. "It's a grand achievement," he said. "It's been something to look forward to at the end of each voyage."

"I'm glad. I enjoy it, too, you know. More than I would if I still had my ancestral throne, I suspect. I have a kingdom of seven thousand four hundred and thirty-seven subjects, which is quite a comfortable size to rule. Of course, everyone thinks I'm mad. You think I'm mad."

"Not anymore."

"Really? How kind." The king sipped his tea. "And if you don't think I'm mad anymore, what do you think?"

"I think you know exactly what you're doing."

The king beamed. "Then we'll get to business. I heard about your last mission, by the way — that run-in with the scuttler. Shame it ended that way."

"Yes," Gilmore said. An enquiry had been held while *Australasia* was on its homeward voyage and he had been cleared of all blame, which still didn't make it easy. Lives had been lost, and wouldn't have been if he had just left things alone.

And neglected your job. He was used to having

the two halves of his intellect slug out the different sides of an argument, and he was able to relegate them to the back of his mind while he listened to the king.

"But that stunt you pulled to make the scuttler back off — that was inspired, Captain. And not the first time you've pulled something that isn't in any of the books."

"Maybe I should write a book," Gilmore said.

The king chuckled as he pulled out an aide and flipped it on. "Maybe. And I heard about the torpedo, of course. Is your ship okay?"

"Our radiation shielding held up, so no crew exposure. The ship was blinded for a couple of minutes but that was all. No blast damage."

"Excellent," the king said. Even nuclear weapons weren't that effective in space, with no air to carry the shockwave of the explosion: heat and radiation were the killers, and they were dissipated over space distances. But they were good enough to hold an enemy at bay, which was what the scuttler had been doing. "You know, there's a lot of theoretical work going on about space warfare. Fascinating stuff. Nuclear weapons for long range combat, lasers and solid objects for close quarters. Early days yet, of course."

"So far," Gilmore said. He couldn't help thinking that if even scuttlers now had access to weaponry, it was more than early days.

The king changed the subject.

"Now, let's see." His eyes scanned the display as he spoke. "You've commanded the *Australasia* for three years, doing sweep duty. Prior to that you were chief executive officer on the *Oceania*, which was your first job in the Royal Space Fleet. My spies report that you run a happy ship and none of your crew members ever have any complaints about you. You've worked for the Fleet for seven years in all."

Gilmore sipped his tea, saying nothing.

"*Oceania* was your first job for us," the king said. "Before that, you were with the Starward Space Company, on the *Solar Sailor*." The king still smiled, but the cheer had left his eyes. This wasn't quite an interrogation, Gilmore thought, but it was damn similar.

"Correct," he said mildly.

"You worked for them ever since graduating with a blue grade. Your cadet files rated you as excellent command material."

"I wouldn't know." Gilmore knew now where this conversation was going and mentally braced himself.

"Of course not. Confidential, aren't they? Well, take it from me, they did." The king, a major shareholder in Starward, raised his cup and drained the last drops, then set it down and reached for the teapot. "Why," he said as he refilled their cups, "did said excellent command material only make it to junior exec in all those years at Starward? And how did you manage to start your career with the Fleet on a cargo ship and end on sweep patrol, rather than the other way round?"

I ought, Gilmore thought, *to throw this tea at you and storm out. And you know it.*

"I started as a junior officer on the lunar run from Earth," he said slowly. The king nodded encouragement. "The usual thing was to start there, then graduate upwards to the more prestigious jobs, like the Mars run."

"And why didn't you? Why —" *Here it comes*, Gilmore thought, "—were you instead referred for psychological evaluation? You nearly had a breakdown, Captain."

Gilmore set his cup down. It rattled in its saucer. "Mind your own damn business, King." Breathing slowly and carefully, he stood up.

"Oh, spare me the affronted walkout," the king said irritably. He held a plate of biscuits out and effectively blocked Gilmore's way. Gilmore's sense of the ridiculous was far too strong to let him push the plate aside and keep walking, so he took a biscuit and sat down again.

"I was pushing myself," he said. "I was making myself be something I wasn't. I felt I should be one of the big guns, one of the hotshots. Instead I was staring at the rapidly receding backs of my contemporaries, and then my juniors, as they all overtook me. I couldn't accept that." He took a bite from the biscuit.

They had shown him how to live with the fact

and they'd shown him how to fight the spectre of failure that loved to hang around him, but that didn't make it less painful to talk about. Gilmore was pleasantly surprised with himself that he was able to do so now.

"And you joined the Fleet," said the king.

"This is the version that Starward's psychologists threw at me," Gilmore said. "The ships I started on weren't big. They are . . ." He remembered the king's phrase, "a comfortable size to rule. Sure, I got routine promotion, but . . . I always ended up back where I was. So they recommended a transfer to the RSF. I could handle the Fleet; I just can't handle anything bigger —"

"On Starward's scale of things," the king interrupted. He was beaming, perhaps at having his words repeated back to him. "Working for a small operation like my Fleet, Captain, you excel. You have clever ideas — like charging scuttlers on full flame. Don't say you don't know it."

"Perhaps," Gilmore said. He knew it but had never really believed it. If he tried, he could remember the way things always seemed to fall into place — as they had when that last scuttler was detected — but he rarely did remember, and it didn't change how he felt. He was a good ship's captain by his current standards but only fair by the standards of the big wide world; and by the standards with which he had set out into his adult life, he was a failure. "If sweep duty is worth excelling at," he added.

Prince James finally spoke. "It's an essential contribution to our interests, Captain." He looked slightly shocked that anyone could think otherwise of sweep duty.

"Throwing people off rocks so we can mine one hundred percent of them instead of ninety. Oh yes, vital," Gilmore said. The prince began to bristle before his father interrupted him.

"So with all that in mind, Captain," the king said, "do you think you could handle the *Ark Royal?*"

At last! Gilmore had been wondering when that would come up. And since the king had researched him so thoroughly he could no longer even joke that they had got the wrong Gilmore. They meant him.

"I've only heard rumours of her, so far," he said. "I have no way of knowing."

"Sensible answer," the king said. "Diplomatic. That'll be useful on a diplomatic delegation."

Gilmore breathed out. Another rumour confirmed, and he was first to know. "So, you are going on the Rusties' delegation," he said.

"Of course I am," the king said. "Wouldn't have built the *Ark Royal* for any other reason. James will be my delegate and you will be my captain."

"Can I ask why you're going, sir?"

"Why? Same as everyone else. Can't afford not to." The king put his cup down, sat back and fixed Gilmore with his gaze. "You're a lucky man, Captain," he said. "You couldn't cut it in one system so you managed to find another one, still doing what you want. Most people don't have that choice. They don't succeed, they're out."

"Unless you're king," Gilmore said. The king laughed.

"So you would have thought," he said. "But I want to move on too. You see, this is my kingdom, and I'm proud of it. It's not just an asteroid miner, it's the biggest ship yet built and seven and a half thousand human beings are glad to call it home. Rusties have come to see it and they were impressed. The people who live here are happy and the place is flourishing. That makes me happy in my turn.

"And we're still a joke! Who out there really takes us seriously? No one. My business rivals and partners respect me, but I'm still Mad King Richard to them. I want to make us something to be reckoned with and that is why I want to send someone on the delegation."

"Do you subscribe to the trap theory?" Gilmore asked. Few took the invitation completely at face value and the most popular interpretation was that the whole thing was some elaborate trap set up by the aliens. *Why* was a completely different matter.

"I don't subscribe to theories." The king looked over at the prince. "James?"

The Prince of Wales leaned forward, putting his cup down so he could concentrate more on Gilmore. He gave the impression of seeking to convert Gilmore to a cause. "We had *Ark Royal* built because we needed a ship," he said. "You know it's a condition that delegates provide their own craft to travel in?" Gilmore nodded. "Now, we have a ship. We have several ships. But we want to do this properly. Diplomatic delegations don't travel in sweeps, do they? They have proper military escorts. Hence, His Majesty's Starship *Ark Royal*. Good name, don't you think? Traditional. Apt for the UK's first starship. Here, take a look. I'll copy it to your own aide if you like."

He passed his aide over to Gilmore, already activated. *Ark Royal*'s specs were on the display and Gilmore flipped through them.

"She's a freighter," he said at once. "A Morrison."

"Her essential frame is that of a Morrison Class 7," the king said. "It was easier to adapt than build from scratch and it seemed best to adapt a small ship."

"Why?" Gilmore said.

"Oh, there was the time frame, for one thing, and even I am subject to board agreements, shareholders. . . . I can't justify spending that limitless money on her. But I've spent more than enough. You'll find the equipment on board and the ship's AIs are state-of-the-art. With just three people in charge, two at a pinch, you could take her anywhere."

Gilmore browsed through idly, noting the brand names of the engines, the life support, the centrifuge ring. . . . The king didn't believe in false economy. He was buying quality.

"Where is she now?" he asked.

"She came out of the L5 yards a month ago and

she's presently undergoing space trials. So, Captain, what's your answer? Will you take her?"

Gilmore sat back in his chair and stared at the holographic floor overhead.

"Why me?" he said.

"You're perfect for the job," the king said. "And as you showed so recently, you can take a bad situation and make it work in ways that others haven't thought of. You're flexible."

Gilmore barely heard him. His mind was whirling with the realization that these two must actually expect him to succeed. You didn't put a man in charge of a diplomatic mission and expect him to make a balls-up.

First thing to do, he thought, *is get a good engineer and go over the ship with a fine-tooth comb* . . . Ah, yes.

"The delegation leaves in a fortnight," he said. "It doesn't give me much time to recruit a crew."

"No need," the king said. "You use *Australasia*'s existing crew."

"That shouldn't be too difficult, then," Gilmore said. "There's fifteen of them —"

"No." The king looked apologetic. "I'm sorry, but I can't let you have more than six, yourself included. Take your pick of the best of them."

"Six?" Gilmore exclaimed. "I'm expected to take a crew of six on a trip like this?"

"*Ark Royal* is years ahead of *Australasia*," the king said. "I assure you, the ship's automation sys-

tems are *par excellence*, you'll have the best quality
AIs on board . . ."

"At least ten. At least!"

"No, Captain." The king still sounded regretful but
looked quite resolute. "I've spent a large amount of
budget on providing you with a state-of-the-art ship
and I only have funds left for six crew. I'm sorry, but
there it is. And I imagine you've already got two
places filled, no?"

The king knew every detail of Gilmore's career
but still Gilmore was irritated at being taken for
granted: even more irritated that the king was absolutely right. Hannah Dereshev would be his
choice for first officer, and that meant Samad Loonat
as chief engineer. Two places filled.

"Commander Dereshev has just been offered
command of her own ship," he said, careful to include Hannah's new rank.

"But surely you'll mention it to her?"

Gilmore changed the subject. "I'm not sure how
you plan to impress the Rusties with a crew of six,"
he said. "The other ships will have armies of nego-
tiators on board."

"My son is an excellent negotiator," the king said
with a smile, and looked at his watch. "Now, Captain, there are other details to brief you on and I
have appointments to keep. You'll need various au-
thorities and powers to make this work and we'll
send them through to your aide. Everything else,
James will tell you about."

He stood; Gilmore and the prince rose as well. The king took Gilmore's hand and gave it a firm squeeze. "Thank you, Captain. Now I'll leave you two together — I'm sure you'll get on just fine."

Five
6–8 April 2149

Samad Loonat left the Officers' Club with a spring in his step. He had been going over *Ark Royal*'s specs on his aide: the ship's main engine was a spanking new Saab/Messerschmidt 300 that made him salivate when he thought of working on it. He was going to a ship with the latest and best tech on board, he was going on an historic voyage and he was getting a pay rise to boot. Life was good.

It was also good, he thought, to see the change in Michael Gilmore. The man was a million miles removed from the withdrawn, downcast one who had returned with *Australasia* to UK-1. Michael Gilmore had a new challenge to take his mind off his perpetual fear of screwing up.

A lanky, straw-blond man in RSF uniform stepped straight into his path.

"Peter?" said Samad. He frowned at the other man's worried look. Lieutenant Peter Kirton, *Australasia*'s software officer, usually looked worried anyway but now it was more pronounced.

"Erm, may I have a word, sir?" Kirton said.

They could have gone back into the club but Samad had things to be getting on with. "Certainly," he said, and stepped to one side to clear the sidewalk. "How can I help?"

"I'd, um, like your advice, sir. You are my line officer, even if we're off duty, and they want an answer
soon, and —"

"Wait, wait." Samad held up his hands. "Start at the
beginning. Who are *they*? Loan sharks? Ex-wives?
Missionaries?"

Kirton didn't seem to appreciate the humour and
Samad remembered he hailed from Mars, where
jokes about missionaries — or ex-wives, or probably loan sharks, or just about anything — just
weren't funny. *Oops.*

"I've been offered a job," Kirton said.

"Small world," Samad said.

Kirton's eyes widened. "You, too, sir?"

"*Ark Royal*?" said Samad.

"Sir?"

They looked at each other with the blankness
that comes from a complete lack of communication. Samad broke the silence. "Tell me about this
job, Lieutenant."

"I'm not sure if I should take it, sir. I wondered if
you'd heard of it? It's in N-wheel and the code name
is Woodcut."

"Oh." N-wheel — that was where the power systems were. Samad hadn't heard of any new projects
to do with the power systems, either officially or
through the grapevine. "No, never heard of it. Why
did you apply for it in the first place?"

"I didn't, sir. They contacted me."

"They contacted you? My advice is take it! It

sounds like you've been headhunted, and that's a compliment."

"Sir, can I show you something?" Kirton handed Samad his aide. "This is the waiver they want me to sign."

Samad's eyes scanned over the text and grew rounder. "Wow! No talking about it, no writing home, no mentioning of it to partners or diaries or goldfish or . . . Oh, look, you can dream about it. That's okay, then." He looked up hopefully: no, that joke hadn't worked either. "Seriously, you shouldn't be talking about this to anyone." Abruptly he handed the aide back to Kirton. "Including me."

"I know, sir. But . . ."

"Does all the secrecy bother you?"

"I'm . . . I'm just not sure what my rights are in this situation, sir."

"Nuts to rights," Samad said. "No one ever got anywhere by standing on their rights." He smiled: Senior Officer's Reassuring Smile No. 3. "I doubt there's anything dodgy in this, so go for it."

Kirton actually smiled. "Thank you, sir. Thank you."

He hurried off; Samad turned in his own direction. On a whim he took out his aide and ran a query on Woodcut: nothing. He shrugged, put it back at his belt and set off home.

"Good day, dear? Yes, thanks, nice day, lovely." Samad had come up to the door to the apartment he and

Hannah lived in, and he tapped in the access code.
"Oh, and did I mention I helped a young lieutenant
work out all his problems . . ." The door slid open
and he went in. ". . . and learnt all about the
mysterious Woodcut."

"So I heard," said a man's voice by his ear. Samad
yelled. The newcomer was leaning against the wall
next to the door, arms folded and a look of cold
amusement on his face. He had dark shaggy hair
and a pronounced five o'clock shadow: quite reasonable, Samad thought, it being five o'clock. "I was
wondering if you could tell me a bit about it, Mr.
Loonat."

"You're not my wife," Samad said, recovering.

"No, I'm not the good commander. I'm just Mr.
Leroux, Head of Security Division." Leroux straightened up. "And I want to know why, twenty minutes
ago, you made an enquiry about Woodcut through
your aide."

Oops, Samad thought again. "Then it's your lucky
day," he said.

"You're going to tell me?"

"No. Everyone needs to learn at some point that
they can't always get what they want, and today is
your turn. Do you have a warrant for being here, Mr.
Leroux?"

"Let's forget about warrants, shall we?"

"No, let's not." Samad held up his aide. "Record all,
transmit copy to Hannah. Leroux, I want a warrant
or I want you out."

Leroux shrugged. "Then let's do it the hard way. I don't need a warrant to arrest you on matters related to the internal security of the Royal Space Fleet, and in that regard you, Mr. Loonat, are under arrest." His hand darted out and grabbed the aide, switching it off as he flipped it shut. "And under such terms," he added with a smirk, "I'm also allowed to impound your aide."

Gilmore sat in his apartment in C-wheel, the crystal chips that held the files of *Australasia*'s crew, on the table in front of him. Three positions filled: three to fill. Who to give them to? A lot of choice—

He had Hannah and he had Samad, as he and the king had known he would. They all knew it had been a cheek, a major cheek, for Gilmore to ask a just-qualified captain if she wouldn't mind remaining a first officer for a bit longer, but . . .

When Gilmore had transferred to the Royal Space Fleet, one step ahead of burnout, severe depression and a breakdown, it had been Hannah who in her quiet and efficient way had helped him get a crew and ship into shape, and in the process helped rebuild his own esteem. He needed her.

"A personal message," said his apartment's resident AI. Its voice was female, which was simply the voice it had had when it came from the shop. Gilmore had never seen the point of pretending AIs were people: a human was a human and a speck of crystal was a speck of crystal, so why try to compare the two?

Ships had their own personalities, of course. But then, a ship was a ship.

"Show it, House," he said, and a life-size image of the sender appeared in front of the mock fire. It was a young man and it appeared just next to a holo on the mantelpiece of the same person — taken a few years earlier as a happily grinning boy. A delighted Gilmore knew the young man's age to be 18 years and three months. *Well, well*, he thought.

"Hi, Dad," the image said. "Joel. You know, your . . . um . . . son?"

Gilmore winced. The question was not unreasonable.

"Well, I passed out, Dad. Um . . . nothing great. Grade blue." Joel grinned and it was exactly the same grin as the boy on the mantelpiece. It robbed him in a moment of his carefully acquired adulthood. "Sounds familiar. Must be in the genes, hey? Anyway, I'm now a fully qualified Middie and it seems . . . well, the one line recruiting like mad right now is the RSF, and they've taken me. So I'm off to UK-1 in a fortnight's time, ETA April 11th."

Gilmore shut his eyes and groaned. He was to leave UK-1 on the eighth.

Joel shuffled, as if uncertain what to say, then suddenly grew more confident. "Um . . . I know you've always said the RSF is a dead-end line, and believe me it's not quite what I had in mind, but . . . well, like I said, they're recruiting and I've got to start somewhere." The grin again. "'Course, that's not what I told recruitment. They think it's my life's ambition to work for the Fleet."

You think, Gilmore thought.

Now the awkwardness was back.

"Um . . . ah . . . Dad, when I registered, I had to decide what I was going to call myself from now on. Um . . . I . . . I decided on Gilmore . . . if you don't mind." Joel blinked bashfully at the camera. "So I'm Mr. Midshipman Gilmore," he said, as if he could scarcely believe it himself. "And I'm going to be King Richard's loyal subject too. Well, um . . . I thought I'd let you know I'm coming. I'll tell you my news when we see each other. If we see each other. I mean, you might be off-station all the time I'm there . . . anyway, we'll catch up, Dad. Bye."

The image froze and Gilmore stared at it, drinking in the latest picture of his son. Joel's mother — and his father — had thought she was marrying a dynamic, up-and-coming young spacer. It hadn't worked out. Joel had been a toddler when the inevitable happened and Gilmore hadn't had the heart to take him away from his mother. All he had from that time, apart from his son, was the still-fresh sense of relief at parting company.

When Gilmore had moved to UK-1, contact had become even rarer.

"House, record reply," he said. "Audio and video."

"Recording," said House. Gilmore cleared his throat.

"Ah . . . Joel. Good . . . yes, very good to hear

from you. Very good indeed. And congratulations, and I'm very pleased you've chosen Gilmore, not that the name's copyrighted or anything. Um. You're welcome to put up here when you arrive, but I won't be seeing you because I've got news of my own . . ."

"You're being obstructive, Mr. Loonat," said Leroux. They were in a private interview room in the security offices: just the two of them, Samad couldn't help noticing, which he suspected was a violation of rights it would probably be futile to try and enforce. Leroux had all the authority of the king behind him.

"You're being obnoxious, Mr. Leroux," Samad said.

Leroux got to his feet and stared down at him across the desk. It was a ploy that Samad recognized: he had been seven years old when an NVN man — an armed thug of the forces of the Confederation of South-East Asia — had glared down at him in exactly the same way as the Loonat family had left their newly appropriated home. There was no way he was going to be intimidated by it coming from an unarmed civilian.

"You're in a lot of trouble," Leroux said.

"So I gathered," Samad said. "I can count at least three of my basic rights that have been violated so far. Even you wouldn't go to all that trouble for something trivial."

"You ran a query on a highly classified project through your aide," Leroux said.

"I was curious."

"You know what they say about curiosity."

Oh great, Samad thought, *now he's going to talk to me in clichés*. "The cat got unlucky," he said. "That's all."

"So how did you hear about it?" Leroux said. That was the question they kept coming back to.

"A dicky bird told me."

"Right." Leroux sat down, fingers poised over his aide. "I want the name, rank and number of this dicky bird."

Samad had no intention of supplying it. It had been an innocent mistake and Kirton didn't deserve the treatment he would get. If you're going to offer a man a job in a top secret project, he thought, you make sure he's the right man in the first place and you certainly don't offer it to a head-in-the-clouds Martian, likely to share it with all and sundry.

"I can't tell you that," he said.

"Why not?"

"It's against my religion."

"This is some Islamic thing I don't know about?"

"I suspect there are quite a few Islamic things you don't know about."

Leroux thumped his fist down on the table: Samad had been expecting it and didn't even flinch. Leroux's interrogation style was a mixture of every set interrogation piece Samad had ever seen in the zines.

"Lieutenant —" There was a knock at the door. "What?" he bellowed. Samad looked round casually as it opened, then sat bolt upright as a crestfallen Peter Kirton was ushered in by a security man.

"Sorry, Mr. Leroux," said the man, "but this officer insists that he speak to you —"

Gilmore waited with his head in his hands as Samad finished his tale. They were in Gilmore's apartment and personnel file crystals were still scattered all over the coffee table between them. Eventually Gilmore looked up.

"So what do you want me to do?" he said.

"Pull him," Samad said. "You've got that warrant from the king, haven't you? If you say that we require Peter Kirton for the crew, Leroux can't do a thing about it."

"Supposing I don't want him for the crew?"

"You do. You know him from *Australasia*, you know he can do his job."

"I always found him a bit . . . standoffish," Gilmore said.

"You're the captain! Of course he was standoffish. I always got on with him and I was his direct superior. He shows promise, Mike."

"He's a Martian."

"That's why he shows promise. He left." Privately,

Samad had always admired the Martian puritans and he knew Gilmore felt the same way: people who would turn their back on a corrupt, decadent Earth couldn't be all bad and they had worked wonders in carving out a home on Mars when all other attempts had failed. "Mike, this could scar his record permanently and, well, I owe him. If I'd been thinking I wouldn't have run that check on my aide and they'd never have known."

"Hmph." Gilmore was silent for a moment. "How did they get him, anyway?"

"He . . ." Now Samad shook his head — he still couldn't believe it himself. "He said he heard about me through the AIs on the security network, and he thought he should turn himself in."

"Just like that?"

"Apparently."

Gilmore raised his eyebrows and looked down at the aide again. "Well, he's honest," he said. Samad said nothing: Gilmore was moving his head from side to side, ever so slightly, and Samad recognized the signs of a decision forcing its way through the maze of pros and cons to the surface.

Gilmore looked up. "We'll take him," he said. He thumbed the contact panel on his aide. "Leroux, Security Division."

"House, record," Gilmore said. He glanced around for a final look. Bags packed and at the door, with an amboid standing by ready to carry them for him. He stood in the middle of the room and clasped his hands behind his back.

"Recording," said House.

"Welcome home, Joel," Gilmore said. "I'm sorry I'm not here — I'd have liked to see you in the flesh again. I really would. Make yourself comfortable and feel free to stay here as long as you need. I've given House all the appropriate permissions.

"In half an hour I'll be on the shuttle to the L5 yards to pick up *Ark Royal*. She's already had her shaking down and we'll be taking her over from the builders. We'll get ourselves installed, then we'll pick up the prince — who's far too grand to travel with us for a second longer than necessary, it appears — and then we rendezvous with the rest of the ships.

"I'll keep plenty of notes and take plenty of pictures so you'll know what it was like, and I'll see you when we get back." He took a breath. "That's all," he said. "End recording."

"Ending," said House. "Do you wish to edit?"

Gilmore paused. He was about to say yes, because he usually did, but . . .

If this was some trap, or any kind of elaborate scheme of the Rusties that was inimical to human good health, that message might be the last Joel saw of his father. Let him see it in its raw form.

"No," he said. He left the apartment with the amboid at his heels.

Six
10–13 April 2149

The information pack came to the end of its spiel with the same image it had used to start — the invitation world, the Roving, seen from orbit. Gilmore looked at the image on his aide's display thoughtfully. Was this what Earth had once looked like? Sparkling, blue and white and green?

The Roving had two continents. There was one huge one which the pack said on Earth would have stretched from Greece to Antarctica, Senegal to the Philippines; and there was a smaller one to its west, with a long, thin strait, half the width of the Atlantic, between them. This, and assorted islands the size of Australia, was the world the Rusties wanted to share.

So much room! There were "isolated First Breed communities," the pack had said, but surely there was plenty of space for everyone, and exactly who got what would be ironed out in the negotiations.

And soon he would be seeing this world with his own eyes. *Ark Royal* was up at the L5 point in lunar orbit, undergoing final preparation, and he was here on the moon in the landing boat *Sharman*, waiting to pick up his ship's Rustie liaison.

"Sir, there's a whole crowd of them!" Adrian Nichol called from the cockpit. Gilmore put his aide in his pocket and stepped out of *Sharman* into one of *Armstrong*'s cavernous landing bays. His eyes widened at the crowd of Rusties filing in and his heart pounded with a sudden fear that there had been a misunderstanding and *Ark Royal* was meant to take all — he counted — eight of them.

But no. The Rusties huddled together, seven of them clustered around the eighth. It seemed to be an intense leave-taking. Then the crowd parted and the Rustie at the centre began to walk over to Gilmore, followed by an amboid carrying a bag. Its friends watched it go, then turned and left.

"Thank God," Gilmore muttered, watching the one approaching alien. It had the usual translator unit at its throat, and the harness and decorations, but also a couple of other things that Gilmore hadn't seen before — what looked like small gas cylinders below the ring of nostrils at the crown of its head and what at first looked like spectacles, but clearly were not because there was no glass in the frames.

"Am I in the correct place for the *Ark Royal*?" it asked. The voice of its translator unit was bland, without expression. The briefing pack had said, *The First Breed are hermaphrodites and may be referred to as "he," "she" or "it" with no offence being taken. Use of the term "Rustie" in their presence is not advised.*

It's a he, Gilmore decided at once. *If it wanted to be a she it would have set its translator to a female voice.*

"You are," he replied.

"My appellation translates as Arm Wild."

From the briefing pack: *Take care always to use a First Breed's full name. Abbreviation is an insult even between friends.*

"It's a pleasure, Arm Wild. I'm Commander Michael Gilmore, captain of the *Ark Royal*. I'm afraid I have no idea what that translates as." He held out his hand, as instructed by the pack; the Rusties were apparently happy to imitate human customs. Arm Wild's right grasping tentacle slid out of its pocket by the Rustie's mouth and wrapped around the outstretched hand, to give a slight squeeze. The inside surface of the tentacle was ribbed and quite dry, like the belly of a snake. A Rustie's graspers, Gilmore had gathered, were what it used instead of hands: they could extend in a blink to a couple of feet in length and were used for feeding, for gesturing, for manipulating.

"It is unavailing, Captain," Arm Wild said "I expect it would be as senseless in my language as my name is in yours."

Polite social repartee with an alien seemed surprisingly easy.

"Is that your bag, Arm Wild?" Gilmore said. "I'll have it taken on board. . . ."

He looked round but Nichol was already there. The sub-lieutenant stepped forward smartly and took the bag, which was half his size but quite light.

"There is not much in it," Arm Wild said. "The First

Breed do not habitually wear clothes. It does nevertheless have some private effects and a spacesuit that I can wear."

"A wise precaution, Arm Wild." Gilmore believed in making eye contact when speaking to anyone but he found he was looking at Arm Wild's nostrils. A biological cue as a human was to look at the topmost cavities in the head, but a Rustie's four nostrils went above the eyes, spaced around the dome that topped off its wedge-shaped head. He dropped his gaze to the eyes. "Will you step on board?"

Gilmore stepped aside for the alien and Arm Wild walked past him into the landing boat. Looking at him from the side, Gilmore thought he saw something flashing within the frames around the Rustie's eyes. Some kind of data display, perhaps? Arranged so that only the Rustie wearing them could read it?

There was already a Rustie couch fitted on the boat. Gilmore helped Arm Wild strap in while the whirr of the fuel pumps started up. Like all his kind, the whatever-it-was that covered Arm Wild's skin made him look as if he was disintegrating from rust and Gilmore had to fight the urge to pluck a flake off. He suspected this would be a diplomatic no-no.

From the cockpit, Nichol could be heard requesting permission to take off. While that was forthcoming, more polite conversation seemed to be in order.

"How did you come to be on this mission, Arm Wild?" Gilmore said.

"My lodge, the Wood Temple, is renowned for its diplomatic skills," the Rustie said.

"Lodge?" Gilmore said. A bizarre image of Rusties as masons — aprons, rolled-up trousers, funny handshakes — drifted across his mind.

"I am sorry — a collection of prides. Of our lodge, the pride to which I belong is the most renowned for its abilities. Therefore, we were chosen for this mission."

"I see." Arm Wild showed no sign of wanting to keep talking so Gilmore pushed his small-talk skills to their limits. "I'd heard you have only one nation. Why do you need diplomats?" he said.

"One nation," Arm Wild agreed. "Several clans, many lodges, thousands of prides. There is need for talk and negotiation amongst us."

Another silence. Gilmore plucked his final conversational thread out of the air. Arm Wild had talked about names translating . . .

"Do names have significance to the First Breed, Arm Wild?" he asked.

"No more than yours, Captain. In our mythologies, as in yours, many people received appellations with meaning which passed into the language as general designations. For example, I believe that the name Michael translates from the Hebrew language as 'Who is like God?' And that according to at least one religious belief system, Michael was the archangel who led the winning side in a war in Heaven."

"Was he?" Gilmore was impressed. He thought it might be polite, and in the interest of diplomatic relations, to study Rustie mythology in return.

"As a diplomat, it is wise to study the customs and cultures of those with whom you deal," Arm Wild said. "With your authorization, when on board I would like to interview all your crew members at times convenient to them."

"Of course."

"Countdown begins, sir," Nichol called back. "Ten, nine —"

Eight seconds later *Sharman* was spaceborne.

His Majesty's Starship *Ark Royal* was a long, sleek ferro-polymer spindle, three hundred feet long, its lines broken by the engine block at one end and the bulge of the centrifuge ring a third of the way down. At the far front of the ship was the antidebris laser turret — the only armament that *Ark Royal* possessed. Aft of the laser was the forward airlock and then a stretch of hull — studded with the sockets that had held cargo containers in the ship's previous life as a freighter — sweeping back to the wide disc of the ring compartment, ribbed by heat-dispersal fins. To Gilmore, on board the approaching *Sharman*, with the remaining two thirds of the hull hidden by the centrifuge, *Ark Royal* looked like a giant metal mushroom. The centrifuge ring held the crew quarters, the wardroom, the gym . . .

The landing boat began to brake and slowly

moved along the ship, its remaining two thirds coming into view. First came the boathouse — *Sharman* would fit snugly into its recess in the hull behind the ring, with only the wings of the arrowhead-shaped vessel protruding out into space. The boat, its reserve fuel tanks and *Ark Royal*'s engineering section accounted for all of the space between the ring and the engine block.

Finally came the engines themselves — a triangle of liquid oxygen rockets around the central core of the fusion pulse engine.

Good girl, Gilmore thought, looking out of the port. Then he remembered his guest. "She must look very quaint to you, Arm Wild," he said, wondering if the translator would pick up his slightly bitter tone.

"We still have similar craft, Captain." Arm Wild sounded quite neutral. "We are not that much ahead of you."

"A lot can happen in a century," Gilmore said. "On our world, steam completely replaced sail, then suddenly even steam was out of date."

"Our experience was akin to yours, Captain."

Everything that was said to this creature, Gilmore realized, came bouncing back neatly as "we are the same." Maybe the two races really were similar. Maybe they were destined to act together. Maybe they could, despite all the skeptics, be friends.

Sharman settled into the boathouse with barely a jar, drawn in by *Ark Royal*'s docking arm. Gilmore turned to Arm Wild to assist, but the alien was already out of its couch.

Arm Wild's bodily contortions were eye-watering to watch as he airswam through the airlock and into *Ark Royal*. He was no longer a stumpy, bulky quadruped; with four three-digit limbs, and two grasping tentacles, he was perfect for zero-gee. He could reach out at almost any angle to grab a hand-hold. A human attempting to emulate him would have needed dislocated arms and legs. Once you remembered that this was an alien behaving naturally and not a terrestrial creature undergoing torture, it was almost beautiful to watch.

Two of the ship's company were waiting as Gilmore and Arm Wild emerged from the boat: Hannah Dereshev and *Ark Royal*'s systems officer, Julia Coyne. They saluted. "Welcome on board, sir," Hannah said formally.

"Thank you, Number One. May I introduce Arm Wild of the First Breed. Arm Wild, Lieutenant Commander Hannah Dereshev."

"Very pleased," Arm Wild said. "Is that Hannah, as in the mother of the prophet Samuel?"

Hannah was nonplussed. "Um, yes, that's right," she said, with a surprised look at Gilmore, who put on the poker face he only ever wore when trying not to smile.

"Show Arm Wild to his cabin, please, Ms. Coyne," he said. "What's our status, Number One?"

"Ready to go, sir. The main engine is tested and

calibrated; we have provisions to last us all for three months; the tanks are full; watches are posted . . . all we need is the prince. Oh, and Peter Kirton brought the prince's personal AI on board. Apparently you've met Plantagenet?"

"I have," Gilmore said. He touched the nearest comms panel. "How are you, Plantagenet? Keeping busy?"

"I am very well, thank you." The AI sounded calm and unhurried. "Though there is not much for me to do until the Prince of Wales is on board, and I have to say the ship's network is very cramped compared to UK-1 and there are no other AIs of my class with whom to converse —"

"Delighted," Gilmore said and quickly broke contact. He and Hannah looked at each other. Gilmore hoped Plantagenet hadn't learned his social mannerisms from anyone close to him.

With the countdown to leaving L5 in its last half hour, the crew were assembled on the flight deck around the lozenge-shaped central console. The main desk and the officer of the watch's desk were at either end and two auxiliary desks faced each other along the short axis. Space watch was about to start and there would be someone at the main desk every second of the day until the ship reached the Roving.

"So, here we are," Gilmore said. He smiled as he looked around them. Hannah and Samad he knew well: the others, though they had all served under him, not so well.

Peter Kirton: there because Samad had felt he owed the man. And, Gilmore reminded himself, because he was good at his job. When the Martian let his reserve down, Gilmore had noticed that people liked him.

Julia Coyne: Gilmore knew she had turned down a chance to represent UK-1 in the All-System Choir Festival to come on this voyage. Yet, she hadn't been forced to come. Her sense of adventure outweighed her love for music.

Adrian Nichol: ever puppy-keen, willing to please and convinced of his own ability, even though Gilmore thought his habit of wearing his gold pilot's wings in deep space — to show he was qualified for atmospheric landing craft too — was downright immature. It was good to see young people with ambition and drive: the sad thing was, life often knocked it out of them before their prime. What awaited Nichol, only time would tell.

His crew.

"As of 1400 ship time, in about two minutes, we will be on space watch," he said. "Port watch will commence: that is, myself, Ms. Coyne and Mr. Kirton. I'm sorry the crew is on such short order, but I know we'll manage. Content yourself with the thought that when we get back you'll probably never have to work again." There was a chuckle;

they certainly would all work again, but the fact that their upward mobility would be lubricated by having served on a ship of the delegation fleet was nice to know. "Two final points, one is Arm Wild. Be polite, be courteous, be honest and do remember, even though he knows we can't be entirely representative of the whole human race, a month of close confinement with us could well colour his views. He wants to interview each one of us: we will all cooperate. And when the prince comes on board, we might all be on first-name terms, but to us he is Sir, Your Highness or Prince James." Gilmore checked his watch. "And from now on, I am Sir too. Port watch, stations."

It was only when the off-watch crew had left the flight deck that Gilmore realized Arm Wild had been waiting just beyond the hatch. He scanned mentally through the instructions he had been giving while ignorant of the alien's presence, and wondered if anything in them may have given offence.

"May I compliment you on your crew?" the Rustie said.

"Why, thank you, Arm Wild," Gilmore said. The Rustie seemed in no hurry to move on.

"I understand they all chose to follow you?"

"They all volunteered, yes. I've served with all of them before."

"Then they accept you as their captain."

Gilmore shrugged. "Apparently."

"We have a matching ceremony with our own ship seniors," said Arm Wild. "The whole pride must confirm them in their position."

Gilmore paled inwardly at the thought of having to win over a crew not of five but of something like a hundred. He could never do it, he was sure.

"That . . . must make their authority something very special," he said.

"I felt highly confident you would understand," Arm Wild replied, with what sounded through the translator like satisfaction.

Twenty minutes later the Saab/Messerschmidt 300 main engine so beloved of *Ark Royal*'s engineering officer fired and the ship pushed itself out of lunar orbit.

James Windsor took one last look around *Britannia's* drawing room. If you ignored the curving floor, the starkness of the metal ceiling and the fact that most of the paintings were holograms, it could almost pass for a room back home. He had never really appreciated the comforts of *Britannia* until there had come a time when he knew he was going to spend at least a month on board *Ark Royal*; suddenly — and more and more so, as that time drew nearer and nearer — all of the royal yacht's home comforts became a lot more apparent.

The ship was a spinner, a rotating cylinder in space; you got the feel of gravity just about anywhere on board, as compared to *Ark Royal* which just had its one spinning ring. *Britannia* was larger than *Ark Royal*; the cabins weren't exactly big but James had seen the plans for *Ark Royal* and was all too aware of the size of its cubbyholes. *Britannia* was just more comfortable, and he wished she was going on the delegation instead of Gilmore's toy ship. He knew there were good reasons why she wasn't, but that didn't stop him wishing.

The display showed *Ark Royal*, a thousand miles away and closing. A spinning top with an extended shaft: home, for the foreseeable future. Ugh. Looking on the bright side, it meant he would enjoy the occasional break from her all the more. He already had a couple of invitations to attend functions on other delegation ships during the voyage to the Roving and he meant to accept them. Mix business and pleasure.

There was a cough behind him: the ship's doctor, waiting patiently with a case in his hand. James sighed and rolled up his sleeve.

"This probably isn't necessary," he said as the doctor put an infusor together. "Free fall usually makes me chuck anyway."

The doctor pressed the infusor to James' skin and the drug hissed its way into James' bloodstream. "It's your decision," he said, with a hint of disapproval at abused medication which James ignored. The doctor wasn't the first to show disapproval of James' intentions: *Britannia*'s captain, too, had expressed reservations about what he and the ship were to do

in the near future. The spray hissed and James
winced, both at that and at a pang of prescience. If
disapproval was all he got before this business was
over, he would be lucky. He suspected he was going
to make a lot of enemies.

"Sir, a message from *Britannia*." Julia Coyne spoke
from the command desk. "Please dock —"

"Dock?" Gilmore said. He looked through the port
at *Britannia*, a quarter of a mile off. "Why can't the
prince spacewalk like any normal human being?"

"Because the prince is terribly spacesick, sir," Julia
said apologetically. "*Britannia*'s captain is afraid he
will vomit in his helmet."

"He can't be spacesick." Gilmore looked at *Britannia* again. "She's spinning! How can he be —"

As if to contradict him *Britannia*'s rotation was
slowing down, as it would have to if the two ships
were to make physical contact. But she *had* been
spinning — her crew had made the trip from UK-1
to this pickup point in one-gee — so it still didn't
answer the question of why the prince was struck
with spacesickness, an affliction that usually only
hit lubbers in free fall.

Suddenly the old ghost was back. Failure. He
couldn't manage this, his plans were falling to bits,
everyone was going to see he was no good—

Gilmore swatted it away with irritation and
waited for a moment. Crises were like this: the initial confusion and disorientation but then, if he shut

his eyes, he could normally see what needed doing. It was as if someone had laid out a plan of action for him to follow in stages: one, two, three.

But that wasn't happening either. *Grow up, Gilmore*, he thought angrily. *If you can't handle something as simple as a docking manoeuvre—*

"Very well," he said calmly. "Ask *Britannia* to extend a docking tube. Plot manoeuvres to bring the lateral lock up to —"

Julia was already looking even more apologetic.

"What?" he said.

"*Britannia*'s docking tube is non-operational, sir. They request that we dock bodily at the for'a'rd lock."

So, *Ark Royal* was going to have to stick its first ten metres of length into a hole in the front of *Britannia*. The manoeuvre would be complicated, fuel expensive and time consuming . . . but his master commanded.

"Very well," Gilmore said again, with heavy irony as though the whole affair was of no consequence. "Sound the manoeuvring bell, all loose objects to be secured."

It took half an hour for *Ark Royal* to position herself properly. Five-thousand-ton spaceships didn't respond to gentle spurts of the thrusters quite as well as personnel transport capsules — something *Britannia*'s captain knew but presumably (unbelievably) Prince James did not.

Eventually the two ships were poised nose-to-nose, with only metres between them. A burst on the thrusters moved *Ark Royal* forward, followed at once by another burst to slow her down and stop her, just as *Britannia*'s grabs took hold.

Gilmore winced at the clanging going on outside the ship. "What are they doing out there? Riveting us together?"

The noise did seem to go on for a very long time; a quite unreasonably long time. Gilmore would recommend in his log that *Britannia*'s docking equipment be given a full overhaul.

"The prince is ready to come on board, sir," Peter Kirton said at long last.

"Let's go meet him, then."

The Prince of Wales hung in midair, limp and green between two of *Britannia*'s crew. Normally a neat and dapper figure, he looked blearily up at Gilmore and moaned.

"He's well drugged, sir, and we think he's stopped vomiting," one of the newcomers said helpfully. The prince groaned. His eyes were glassy and unfocused.

"Oh, God . . . We'll get him to the ring. Give me a hand, Mr. Kirton. Leave the prince's baggage here, we'll get it stowed later."

It took another hour before everything was properly sorted out, and twenty minutes of that were taken up by *Britannia* being unable to give *Ark Royal* clearance to disengage. The clanging again went on for a very long time. Did the king really travel in that ship? Gilmore wondered. Did he have any idea of what a shower they were? It surprised him; he had always thought better of *Britannia*'s crew.

At long last, the two ships were apart. *Britannia* backed away from *Ark Royal* and slowly turned round, orienting herself to boost down the arc back to UK-1. Gilmore watched her receding blip on the radar screen with relief.

"Right!" he said, and rubbed his hands. This was finally it. *Finally* it, after all this waiting. "Ms. Coyne, plot an arc to join the delegation fleet. Half-gee boost."

"Aye-aye, sir."

Gilmore rubbed his hands together again and fought back a grin as the manoeuvring bell sounded. No more preparation, no more supplies to secure, no more last-minute worry.

They were on their way to join the delegation.

The pinging noise interrupted the reverie of His Excellency R.V. Krishnamurthy of the Department of Diplomatic Affairs, Government of the Confederation of South-East Asia (or Greater India, as he preferred to call it), and he froze the display on his aide to answer the call. "Yes?"

"Excellency." In the wall display, *Shivaji*'s captain, Surit Amijee, bowed slightly. "We've reached the rendezvous point."

"Thank you, Captain." Amijee's image vanished and Krishnamurthy stood up to look out of the porthole in the floor of his stateroom. All he could see was black beyond the port and his own reflection. But it was the rendezvous point for the delegation fleet.

"Phase One," he murmured. The countdown to Phase Two, in which the ships would travel to the point where the Rusties said they would "step-through" between solar systems, was beginning. He felt an uncharacteristic surge of excitement. Excitement was something he tried not to feel — it clouded one's judgement — but under the circumstances, perhaps he could allow himself this little luxury.

Because *he* had been the mover behind this whole scheme. *He* had stuck his neck out, insisting that the Confederation be represented on the delegation. *He* had laid out the case for why the Confederation had to have a space presence. There was a lot riding on this mission, as Manohar Chandwani had made so clear the last time they saw each other.

Well, he had eventually got his message across, though it had made him a whole fresh new crop of enemies in Delhi. Once he had got approval for his plan it had been put into operation in a very short space of time: *Shivaji* and various other items bought from the Confederation's allies; a crew (all citizens, Chandwani had said: all *Indians*, he had made sure) gathered together from other space companies. He shuddered. *Shivaji* wasn't the only ship on the delegation to be purchased or borrowed to meet the Rusties' requirements, but still, it was humiliating.

The door chime sounded. "Come," he said. It slid open and Krishnamurthy had a brief glimpse of the dark green uniforms of his NVN guards outside, before they were eclipsed by an eager Secretary Subhas Ranjitsinhji.

"Excellency," said Ranjitsinhji. "We've reached the rendezvous point."

"Thank you, Subhas. Captain Amijee has already apprised me of the situation in, I believe, precisely those words." Ranjitsinhji kept his face still, trying not to look disappointed. I don't believe it, Krishnamurthy thought. He wanted to be the one to tell me and now he's upset. Krishnamurthy pretended not to notice. "Who else is here?"

"Apart from the Rustie ship, four others," Ranjitsinhji said.

The Rustie ship. The prideship. The nearness of that triumph of alien technology, just a few hundred metres away, made Krishnamurthy's skin tingle. He had seen footage of the Rustie vessels. They were a wonder: no fusion flame, no careful balancing of action and reaction, just the playing off of one gravitational force against another. It attracted itself towards this object, repelled itself from that one. He was no spacer but still he felt it was uncanny, watching a ship move so effortlessly. Also off-putting was contrasting the size of the thing visually with the muzziness of its radar echo: its ceramic construction meant it hardly registered.

They make their ships out of pottery! Doubtless we'll find out why....

"And how is the network going, Subhas?" Krishnamurthy asked. Ranjitsinhji had been so full of his plans to install an agent on every ship that Krishnamurthy had let him go ahead, out of curiosity to see what would happen. The man did have a talent for getting his spies into the strangest places.

Ranjitsinhji's face fell. "I regret my initial plan was overoptimistic. I have recruited some agents —"

"No matter, no matter." Krishnamurthy turned back to the porthole. "The success of this mission will depend on diplomatic intrigue and the scientific application of military might. It's all very well to have some obscure, below-decks toilet cleaner in our pay, but what could he actually accomplish? Still, your agents might come in useful one day."

"Thank you, Excellency...."

Ranjitsinhji trailed off and Krishnamurthy saw his assistant was looking at the still-frozen display from his aide.

"Rustie performance art," he said. "Place Brave gave me the files and I copied them to you. Have you looked at them yet?"

"Um —"

"Fascinating. Truly fascinating. You can learn a lot from their stories of everyday Rusties. I recommend it, Subhas. Now, how long until the delegation fleet leaves?"

"Twenty-three hours, Excellency."

Krishnamurthy beamed. "It begins, Subhas. It begins."

Seven
13–15 April 2149

There was silence on *Ark Royal*'s flight deck as the countdown to Phase Two entered its final minute. Arm Wild sat in his custom-made Rustie-couch, watching. His spectacles-that-weren't gave him a vaguely owlish look that verged on the comical.

Peter Kirton had the controls. "Sixty seconds," he said.

"Very good," Gilmore said.

"Exciting, isn't it, Captain?" said a voice from the hatch, and Gilmore looked up in horror. Prince James was half in, half out of the flight deck, glancing about with interest; his spacesickness appeared to have cleared up. Gilmore looked quickly around to check that there was a spare couch available.

"Sir, we're boosting in less than a minute. Strap down!"

"Oh, don't worry about me, I'll hang on here —"

"You'll damn well strap down now!"

The prince's face grew cold. "Don't take that tone with me, Captain."

Gilmore turned round. "Ms. Coyne, make to prideship, 'Request postponement of boost due to —'"

"You wouldn't!" The prince sounded shocked.

"Forty seconds," Kirton said.

Gilmore turned back to the prince. "We'll be boosting at 1.3 gees. You could hurt yourself badly, so strap down now!"

"All right, all right," the prince said. He air-swam clumsily to the couch next to Arm Wild, who had been watching the scene without comment but who knew what thoughts, and strapped in. He was finished just as the countdown reached zero.

Fusion flames erupted from the sterns of the Earth ships. There was a distant rumble from *Ark Royal's* own stern — from *below*. *Ark Royal* had weight again: it was accelerating at a rate of 1.3 Earth-type gravities, which was the gravity of the Roving. It would take getting used to.

"Convoy status?" Gilmore said.

"All ships firing as planned, sir," said Kirton. He was grinning from ear to ear. "All systems are green. We'll be at the coordinates for Phase Three in three days, thirteen hours, twenty-three minutes."

"Very good," Gilmore said again, careful not to grin too. And it was — *very* good.

"I resented your tone on the flight deck, Captain," said Prince James, in the privacy of his cabin. The prince had asked Gilmore to see him as soon as he handed over to Hannah and the starboard watch.

Gilmore kept his voice low and calm, only hinting at his anger. "That is nothing," he said, "next to my resentment of your assumption that you are excluded from shipboard procedure. You're a prince and I'm just a lowly captain, but the laws of physics apply just as much to you as to me."

"But —"

"Shut up," Gilmore said. "I've been on ships when the boost has come on a fraction later than expected, or a fraction earlier, or not at all. It's never happened with Samad on the engines, but it might still, through no fault of his own. I've seen people break limbs because they weren't tied down, even at a very slight boost. But even that's not important. What is important is that my crew are qualified professionals and if you are told to do something by any one of them, you damn well do it."

The prince's eyes narrowed. "I'll remember your insolence, Captain."

"Oh, for . . ." Gilmore groaned. "You can't really be this stupid, can you? The king's too intelligent to let you be like this. For Christ's sake, you're going to take over his kingdom one day."

The prince bristled. "Do not take that tone with me, Captain."

"Then don't deserve it, Prince," Gilmore said.

James glared at him for a moment longer. Then: "I apologise, and I undertake to obey all instructions given by your trained professionals. That will be all, Captain."

And Gilmore found himself outside the prince's door once more. He had a feeling he had probably called the prince's bluff on something. He also felt the prince hadn't wanted it called.

Just another month and then he's out of my hands, he thought. *God give me patience*.

Samad Loonat sat at his station above the blast bulkhead in the drive compartment of HMSS *Ark Royal*. Metres away below him, a successive stream of fusion explosions was propelling the ship on its course; he paid it about as much attention as he would rain on the other side of a windowpane.

He paid far more attention to what was on his display. He frowned at it and shook his head. "Not possible," he murmured. He ran the calculations again. Then he tapped his comm panel and called up to the flight deck.

"Ade, I'm sending some figures to your station. Run them and tell me your results."

"Aye-aye, sir."

Adrian Nichol took a minute to finish and communicate the figures to Samad. His tone told Samad that the discrepancy had been spotted.

"Thanks," Samad said. "Is the captain on the flight deck?"

"Not at present. I think he's in his cabin, getting some shut-eye."

"Poor captain," Samad said.

"Captain, we're forty tons over mass," Samad said without preliminary. Michael Gilmore blinked, still a bit sleepy. His expression as he stepped off the lift had indicated that this had better be more than a misplaced decimal point. Samad hadn't disappointed him.

"What?" he said.

"I've been running the same figures over and over again, ever since we left L5," Samad said. "They were all consistent until —"

"Yes?" Gilmore said.

"Until we docked with *Britannia* and picked up the prince," Samad said.

"Ah," Gilmore said. Samad was flattered his captain didn't ask him to check the figures again. He knew Samad would have checked them into the ground. *Ark Royal* could not be forty tons over mass . . . but it was. "How does it affect fuel consumption?" Gilmore said.

"We have enough to get us there. Not enough for the return trip unless we refuel."

They looked at each other.

"I'm thinking," Samad said, "of all the racket when we docked and undocked."

Gilmore winced. "But *Britannia* would have alerted us if we were carrying off their docking mechanism . . . and we used the altitude jets to manoeuvre! Why didn't the systems pick the extra mass up then?"

"Julia was piloting us and she would have used the ship's automatic systems. And the conclusion I draw from that is that the ship is programmed to take the extra mass into account."

"Recommendations?" Gilmore said, after they had both paused to absorb the implications of the ship knowing about the extra forty tons when the crew did not.

"I'd like to suit up and conduct an external inspection."

"What do you think you'll find?"

Samad shrugged. "That will make it more of an adventure."

"True," Gilmore said. He looked grim and was heading back for the lift. "But you're not going outside while we're boosting and there may be an easier way of finding out. Come on, I need your expert testimony to support me."

Prince James slowly reached out to shut off the display of his aide and then looked up at his visitors.

"Yes," he said. "That'll be the torpedoes."

There was only what passed for silence. The muffled rumble of the engines, the whine of the centrifuge's flywheel.

"Let's hear it," Gilmore said. Prince James settled back in his chair, hands behind his head.

"When you docked with *Britannia*," he said, "you were fitted with torpedoes. You'll find that the front end of the ship, for'a'rd of the flight deck, has two casings attached, one on either side. They're curved, like the hull, and not much thicker, and they're at the point where the hull tapers."

"But how?" Samad said. "I've seen the ship's plans, there's nothing there."

"They're attached to the old cargo studs," said the prince. "When this ship was a freighter it had containers attached on either side of the flight deck. We left the studs on with the refit. Now, anyone observing the ship from a distance won't notice the difference."

"Tell me about the torpedoes," Gilmore said slowly.

"You have a mixture of types," said the prince. "Half are fusion warheads, and they're shielded so you can fire them from orbit down to the surface. The other half are what we call grapeshot — they fire clouds of solid objects at oncoming ships —"

"I know what grapeshot is," Gilmore said. He could feel the panic rising up within him and he mentally battened the hatches against it. This was outside his experience. At other times, when he saw the solution to a crisis, it was because he was trained to handle it, but this. . . . It was what he always dreaded: a situation he would not be competent to handle. A time when things would get out of control and he couldn't cope, and he would be revealed as the no-good fake that, deep down, he was.

"How do we fire them?" he asked.

"Plantagenet has the targeting software built into his code —" the prince said.

Gilmore slapped the comm panel on the wall. "Number One."

"Flight deck here, Captain." Hannah's voice sounded calm and efficient, and Samad drew in a breath. Gilmore knew why. Hannah had once told him that her earliest memory was the Flight into Egypt, when a terrified Israeli population had fled their homes as stars fell out of the night sky — and landed in neat precision along the eastern Mediterranean coast — making the land that was sacred to three religions and claimed by so many different peoples, uninhabitable by any of them.

And now she was on a ship carrying similar devices, and didn't yet know it.

"How much longer do we boost?" Gilmore said.

"Twenty minutes, Captain."

"Once we're done, prepare to roll the ship."

"Aye-aye, sir."

"What are you doing?" the prince demanded.

"I'm going to point the ship away from the convoy and fire off the torpedoes," Gilmore said.

"You are not!"

"Want to bet?"

"Captain . . ." The prince was gesturing in midair, as though trying to pluck the words he wanted out of nothing. "Those torpedoes are our insurance."

"You have knowingly violated every spacegoing convention in existence, you have mucked with my ship without my knowledge —"

"That last point, yes, guilty as charged. Believe

me, Captain, you were going to be informed. But as
for that first point. . . . It must surely have dawned
on you that we are entirely at the Rusties' mercy?
Would you throw away our one trump card?"

Gilmore sneered. "You're going to hold them up at
gunpoint, is that it? Our one ship, against God knows
how many vastly superior, armed vessels of their
own, and say, 'Right, Rusties, give us what we want'?"

"On our own, no," the prince said. "With the other
delegation ships, perhaps."

"*What*?"

Prince James took out his aide and set its display
for public viewing. Then he paused and looked at
Samad.

"I hope your crew can be trusted to keep secrets," he said. His answer was two ferocious glares
and he took the hint. "Plantagenet, display document 'gunrunner,' password 'peaches.' "

"Complying," said the AI from the speaker. A list-
ing appeared in the air above the prince's desk and
he pointed as he spoke.

"My father's intelligence agents worked hard and
spent a lot for this, Captain, and some of it is still in-
complete or unknown. But observe what we do
have. The Israeli ship, *Adonai*, we have reason to
believe, is carrying twice our number of fusion warheads. It's a bigger ship than ours, so they have
room to hide them from external view. *Algol* is pri-
marily armed for ship-to-ship combat — grapeshot
and warheads designed to give off great heat and

nothing else. Warp a ship's skin and rupture her, that's the idea. As well as carrying copious amounts of holy water, the Vatican has a meteor laser that could carve up several cities from orbit. The Americans not only have torpedoes and an enhanced laser but also a party of marines. Their two landing boats look identical and one of them is just that, but the other is a military suborbiter which can drop down from close orbit to sea level and discharge crew safely in five minutes flat —"

"I get the message," Gilmore said. He felt numb but inwardly he was shaking with anger, barely trusting himself to speak. No one likes to know he's been taken in and he had been — hook, line and sinker. He had swallowed everything and suspected nothing.

"And of course," the prince pressed on, "even if the Rusties are entirely innocent, all this proliferation puts us in an awkward spot. We really don't want to be the only unarmed humans on the delegation, do we?"

The prince had a habit of spelling out what Gilmore had already worked out for himself. Gilmore resisted the urge to hit the man and touched the comm panel again. "Number One, belay that last order. Is Arm Wild on the flight deck?"

"No sir, he's in his cabin."

"Good. Muster all hands to the flight deck but do it quietly." He looked at the prince again. "You're coming too."

*   *   *

"Perhaps it was deception," the prince said. The rest of the crew continued to say nothing, glaring at him with expressions which ranged from active dislike to sheer hatred. "If so, I'm sorry. The point is, we felt we had to tell all of you, or none of you. A crew this size can't afford secrets." He didn't sound apologetic.

Gilmore felt his anger bubbling up again, listening to this man lecture him on good shipmanship.

"If you had all known," said the prince, now looking at Hannah, "some of you would have refused to come. Now, your captain was our choice to command this ship and he was given free rein to choose the best possible crew. If some of those who were chosen had refused to come then the crew would no longer be the best possible. Therefore we did not tell the captain or anyone else." Now he looked at Gilmore. "Again, I apologize."

"How can you stand there and say that?" said Hannah. "When my native land was devastated by —"

"I'd point out, Commander, that *Adonai* is very well stocked with nuclear warheads. Perhaps the leaders of Israel in Exile have a firmer grasp of realpolitik than you."

Hannah clenched the console and Samad put a hand on her shoulder. "Easy, my love," he murmured.

"I knew feelings would run high," said the prince. "All I can do is give you my word that the torpedoes will not be used in an aggressive role. Someone will need to attack *Ark Royal* first."

"I'm afraid I don't believe you," said Hannah. Her tone was freezing cold. "You've lied to us before and you're doing it again."

"That will do, Number One," Gilmore said sharply.

The prince didn't bat an eyelid. "That's your privilege, Commander."

"I say we do what you were going to do, sir," Hannah said, looking at Gilmore. "We tilt the ship away from the convoy and we fire them off."

"A cluster of fusion bombs within a light minute of the moon, Number One?" said Gilmore, who had thought of the flaw in his original plan the moment he'd said it out loud. "They will be pleased."

"But —"

"The prince," said Gilmore, looking James in the eye, "and his father, and no doubt various other members of the Royal Space Fleet who connived in this have behaved disgracefully, and on our return I will demand a public enquiry. Sadly, for the moment it's a fact we're now stuck with. If you don't believe his word then believe mine. The torpedoes will not be fired in a first strike."

"That could warrant a tribunal," the prince said.

"I would demand a tribunal," said Gilmore, "because when this is over, I will personally see that heads roll for this." The prince shrugged as if the threat were meaningless, and indeed Gilmore himself didn't know how he would do it. He wondered how many other captains knew the truth about their ships. Those that did would doubtless be going through the same train of thought as he was: balancing the fact that every treaty in existence said space was neutral and ships should not be armed, against the reality that, like it or not, theirs were, and there was nothing to be done about it. They would draw the same conclusions. And did those captains who knew their ship was armed think that theirs was the *only* armed ship? Was Gilmore actually in an advantaged position, knowing what he did about the delegation?

"And in the meantime?" said the prince.

"In the meantime, painful as it is," Gilmore continued to stare at the prince, because it meant he was not obviously avoiding looking at Hannah, "we keep the torpedoes. We have no choice."

The prince opened his mouth as if about to say something; saw Gilmore's expression; and shut it again. He looked at his watch. "Very good," he said. "Five minutes to end of boost, I believe? I'd better tie myself down. I'll be in my cabin."

The act of climbing down the ladder from the flight deck rather spoiled his attempt at sauntering. Hannah watched him go with cold loathing and Gilmore mentally set aside a large part of the voyage for rebuilding bridges with his first officer.

James Windsor lay on his bunk with his hands behind his head. His aide was set to project a novel — text only, no interaction — at head height, and he was engrossed.

An attention-grabbing icon flashed in one corner of the display.

"Yes, Plantagenet?" he said, not taking his eyes off the text.

"I am sorry to disturb you, sir," the AI said, "but I could not help overhearing something you said to the captain."

"Yes?"

"You told him I have the targetting software for the torpedoes. I was not aware the ship had torpedoes until I heard them mentioned, and I was certainly not aware —"

"You didn't need to know, Plantagenet," James said. "As for the software, you received the upgrade before you left UK-1."

"But I only received . . ." Plantagenet began. Then: "Accessing internally." Another pause. "I see. Sir, I was misinformed. I was told that this upgrade was diplomatic data that might be needed later on in the voyage."

"That's exactly what it is."

"Sir," Plantagenet said, "as a result of this misunderstanding, Lieutenant Kirton has an inaccurate idea of my contents at the time of boarding and I am legally in a compromised position. You see, to bring something on board under false pretences is technically a felony —"

"Clever, isn't it?" said James.

"I see," said Plantagenet after another pause.

Eight
21 April 2149

Report of Arm Wild, Timbre Grey Wood Temple
Southern Plains
to Senior of the Human Operation

*I have the honour to submit for the approval of my
fellows of the delegation prideship, the following
comments on the crew of the starship (using the
term loosely) HMSS* Ark Royal, *and interviews with
the same.*

*It amuses me that when the humans first be-
came aware of our prideships, a form of hysteria
tinged with racial guilt swept over them, and they
made every effort to hide the truth of their past:
the fact that they had had wars, polluted their
planet, wiped out species and so forth. I gather
their logic was that any race which can develop
interstellar travel should by definition be beyond
such things, though this is plainly false, since all
reports I have read give the humans another century at most before they invent step-through for
themselves.*

*The relevance of this aside is that, at first, if the
humans were to be believed, they were never hap-
pier than when they were caring for and loving
one another. As they became accustomed to us,
and as we assured them of similarities in the his-*

tory of our own world, their true nature began to reveal itself. And now, here am I, travelling on what is, at least technically, a military spaceship.

Interviews follow.

Michael Gilmore, Commanding Officer
See comments made by original contact team on human psychology. The nearest First Breed equivalent to Michael Gilmore's position would be Consensual Pride Senior; indeed, the two are very similar. My understanding is that King Richard, Michael Gilmore's own chosen senior, instructed it to raise a ship's company who then chose to serve under it. By virtue of this fact, Michael Gilmore now holds total authority on board Ark Royal, *senior in ship-related matters even to Prince James, the official representative of King Richard.*

Gilmore sat at the desk in his cabin and glanced irritably at his watch. Like all spacer watches it was set to show the time transmitted by the nearest time signal, which in this case was on board *Ark Royal* herself, and gradually stretching out the ship's day to the twenty-six and a bit hours that the Roving took to spin on its axis.

But it wasn't just because the day was getting longer that the time fixed for Arm Wild's appointment seemed to be taking forever to come about. Gilmore wondered why he felt so nervous. It wasn't as if he was ambassador for the human race — Arm

Wild had asked if he could interview every crew member, and as far as Gilmore knew, similar interviews were taking place, or had already taken place, on the other ships.

But *why* were these interviews occuring at all? Perhaps that was what made Gilmore nervous. The Rusties had had plenty of chance to observe and study already. Why did they want to ask these further questions?

God, too much wondering could—

A chime interrupted him.

"Enter," Gilmore said, turning to face the door, which slid open to reveal Arm Wild.

"I trust I have not kept you waiting?" the Rustie said.

Gilmore glanced at his watch again. Spot on time. "Not at all. Come in, Arm Wild."

Gilmore normally no longer noticed the cheap aftershave smell, but here in the small cabin it was more apparent. He still had to resist the temptation to pluck rust flakes off Arm Wild's skin.

"I appreciate this chance to talk, Captain," Arm Wild said.

"My pleasure." Gilmore made himself smile. "Though I have been wondering what purpose these interviews serve."

Arm Wild was holding an instrument of some kind in one of his graspers and fiddling with it with the other. Gilmore had the feeling the Rustie glanced up to answer the question, even though his head did not physically move. The all-round vision of the Rusties was a useful tool: was it enhanced by those non-glasses Arm Wild was wearing?

"In our time on Earth we have had little chance to meet and talk with what I believe you would call 'the common man.' You are an employee. You follow the directions of your superiors. That makes you valid study material."

"I'm flattered," Gilmore said, though he could tell Arm Wild's attention was back with his instrument. Gilmore took it to be a recorder. That hadn't occurred to him — the Rusties wanted to talk to the plebs. And why not?

So was that why they insisted on this fleet, when they could have transported all the delegates together, on their own ship? There must have been several hundred humans travelling on this voyage. Several hundred humans from assorted countries, backgrounds and traditions, provided free of charge for the Rusties to study without any form of interference or bias from the humans' superiors, and a damn sight more representative than the high-ups with whom the Rusties had been forced to mix back home. The cunning sods.

Arm Wild had finished fiddling and he held the instrument up. "Perhaps we could start, Captain, with you simply giving your reasons for coming into space."

Gilmore thought, and began. "Why did I come into space? Simple. Two reasons, in fact. I'm a loner, and Earth is too small."

"Can you explain?"

"Certainly. There's too many people back home. Do the Ru — . . . First Breed know what is meant by claustrophobia?"

"We do, though we rarely suffer from it. You do not feel happy in a crowd?"

Gilmore remembered the instructions he had given the crew to be cooperative. He should follow them himself. "No," he said, "I don't. But in a small ship's crew — well, I know we're all a little alike. We've all been through common experiences, we have a common background and we all respect one another. I could never be a Captain Bligh — you'll cross-reference that name? Fine — but I can get on just by being Captain Gilmore. . . ."

Comments of Arm Wild: The story of Captain William Bligh, mentioned by Michael Gilmore, is emblematic of the differences between our races. William Bligh was the commander of a seagoing naval vessel named Bounty, *five hundred years ago. Whilst at sea on board* Bounty, *William Bligh exercised undue leniency and inept personnel management in its dealing with its crew, and this made many of them confident to challenge its authority, without due consensual undertakings. After the rebellion, William Bligh was cast adrift with a few loyal sailors and displayed superb skills of seamanship, returning to civilisation a hero. However, subsequent publicity put about by the pride of the senior rebel, Fletcher Christian, instilled the idea in the popular view that William Bligh was a harsh tyrant, thus justifying the rebellion. Contextual analysis indicates that it is this misconceived image to which Michael Gilmore refers.*

Hannah Dereshev, Executive Officer (Second in Command)
Hannah Dereshev's position has no real counterpart in the First Breed. It is necessary to the humans that the captain be somehow distant from the crew, and the Executive Officer is the one through whom captain and crew communicate with each other, though in matters not immediately related to the running of Ark Royal, neither has any hesitation in addressing the other. To make its position more complicated, all on board agree that Michael Gilmore is the one with the expertise needed to direct the ship's operations. This would imply that Hannah Dereshev is supernumerary, which plainly is not the case. I recommend further research.

The captain had been interviewed and suffered no grievous harm, which made Hannah less nervous. She looked at Arm Wild with his recorder and thought that Rusties used their graspers in much the same way as elephants used their trunks. Hannah had once seen an elephant at a zoo casually picking fruit off a pile and popping it into its mouth, while standing at right angles to the pile, not even looking at it, and nonchalantly accepting the praises of the crowd. For some reason it had both amused and impressed her. What was it like to have complete, independent control over even one extra limb, let alone two? And Rusties could use their graspers and all four feet in complete isolation from each other. . . .

"Perhaps we could talk about your cultural background, Lieutenant Commander," Arm Wild said. He either couldn't or wouldn't accept that Hannah's rank could be shortened just to commander; perhaps he felt he would be giving as much offence as if she called him just Arm. Rusties mentioned your full name or none at all; perhaps they were the same with ranks. "You describe yourself as Israeli?"

Hannah was always happy to talk about her background. "That's right," she said. "The Israelis —"

"Yet there is no longer a nation of Israel." Arm Wild, who was already aware of this fact, stated it as such for his future listeners but the blunt interruption threw Hannah slightly.

"Not anymore," Hannah said. "There's Israel in Exile, which is a very grand name for an institution with a lot of money and no land. It's like a country without anywhere to stay. A virtual nation, if you like."

"Like the United Kingdom?"

"The United Kingdom has UK-1. We have nothing except power and influence. I'm proud to be Israeli, and I have many friends in IIE — and on the *Adonai*, for that matter — but it's too unstructured for me. I feel happiest in a formal organization and so I joined the RSF."

"You like the military?"

"Don't get me wrong! I'm not a uniform-loving fascist and I don't dumbly obey orders from my superiors. Our people have suffered enough from that type in the past. If the captain gave a stupid order I'd be the first to tell him; in fact, he trusts me to do so. But it is a fact, I think, that I function best in this kind of environment . . ."

Comments of Arm Wild: The context of Hannah Dereshev's description of a "virtual nation" should alert readers of the First Breed to the fact that such a situation is in fact unusual for the humans. Most humans continue to respect political boundaries — sometimes natural, often artificial — even though there is very little degree of consensus, except in a purely passive way, as to who belongs to which nation. Though the reliance on national boundaries has decreased within the last few centuries, awareness of them appears to remain at

*an instinctive level in the human mind. Thus we
have humans who in the one grasper give
allegiance to a chosen leader — as is the case of
the crew of Ark Royal, for example — and who in
the other secretly yearn for the old days of division.*

*Samad Loonat, Chief Engineering Officer
This one's position on this ship equates very well
with the First Breed ethos. Samad Loonat holds its
position because, quite simply, it is the member of
the crew most familiar with the technological
background needed to manage the engines and
other technical systems on board. It is because of
this that it holds its present position and enjoys
supreme authority in its realm of aptitude.*

Arm Wild came straight to the point.

"You are Chief Engineering Officer of *Ark Royal*,
Lieutenant. What brings you into space?"

Samad grinned. "I'm here because of the kit."

"The kit?"

"The machines. Gadgets. Doohickies," Samad expanded. "I knew I wanted to go into an engineering
environment, and space is where all the action is. I
applied to be an officer because . . . well, because I
thought I could do it. Quite simply, I want to be the
best engineer that I can, and this seemed to be the
best way to go about it."

"You seek to optimize your natural ability?"

"That's exactly what I was saying to myself —"

Samad caught himself, remembering Gilmore's injunction that the crew would cooperate. "Yes, that is correct."

"The others have talked about their backgrounds," Arm Wild said. "Could you tell me about your own?"

"What sort of background?"

"Ethnic, religious if applicable . . ."

"Oh, that. I'm a Moslem from Bangladesh."

"I see," Arm Wild said. "I understand there is a long history of antagonism between those of the Moslem persuasion and those of Lieutenant Commander Dereshev's race and religion, and yet I believe you are pair-bonded? Married?"

"You believe correctly," Samad said.

"It is not an obstacle?"

Samad pursed his lips. "I believe there are places on Earth where we couldn't walk hand in hand down the street. Up here in space, there's room for everyone."

"Others do not share this point of view. How do you explain that?"

"They're wrong," Samad said simply. "Sorry, that's an easy and glib answer but it's the only one I have." He smiled. "And we both agree on the Christians, anyway."

Arm Wild pressed on. "You two are on separate watches. Does this interfere with your pair-bonding at all?"

Only the obvious, Samad thought. "Just say it

means we look forward to the end of the voyage all the more. On a ship this size, Arm Wild, everyone has to chip in equally. You can't afford anyone favouring anyone over anyone else. And, I'd point out that it was Hannah who drew up the watches."

"By favouring you mean sexual congress?"

"If you insist, yes."

"So there is unlikely to be sexual congress between other members of the crew during this voyage?"

Samad choked with laughter. "Not while Mike's in charge there won't be . . ."

Comments of Arm Wild: The historical context of Samad Loonat's background is important. It is the product of a culture that has fought several times for self-rule and which, the last time, lost. The humans have difficulty in accepting defeat: there is no consensual mechanism to help them accept the will of the conquerors. Samad Loonat, despite its allegiance to the United Kingdom, like Hannah Dereshev seems to owe a deeper allegiance to an intangible culture. Fortunately this culture and that of the United Kingdom are not incompatible.

(N.B. The nearest First Breed translation of 'doohickie' might be 'thingamabob'.)

Julia Coyne, Systems Officer
We come to the first human not immediately connected with the command structure of the ship.

Julia Coyne, so far as I can tell, has no particular specialty that might have led to its being selected for this crew. In terms of abilities, it is what the humans call an "all-rounder", though its specific charge is the systems on board Ark Royal.

Due to its dark skin it is the member of the crew I have the least difficulty in identifying, but amongst the humans it is gauche to point out such a distinction; although if this individual were, say, taller than the others, there would be no problem in pointing out the difference.

Like many other humans before her, Julia found herself caught out by the Rusties' 270-degree vision. Arm Wild's body and head were facing her, and her guitar was behind him, well outside the peripheral vision of a human standing in the same position. Yet—

"That is a musical instrument, is it not?" Arm Wild said, indicating with his free grasper. The gesture, and his mild tone, watered down the initial impression Julia had had of an accusation.

"Yes, it's a guitar. I gather you don't have music?" Julia had picked that fact up somewhere and it had lodged with her out of sympathy. She felt so sorry for the aliens.

"We do not have an equivalent," Arm Wild agreed.

"Do you have any form of art?"

"Most certainly, but for some reason our brains are not designed for music. Of course, a good re-

citer will make use of rhyme and rhythm to produce
an effect that I gather is similar. I have seen many an
audience greatly moved in this way. For instance, I
would challenge anyone to come away from a performance of 'The Attack of the Alpine Clan' by the
great Leaf Ruby without feeling profoundly moved."

Julia smiled. She had wondered how she would
get on with the alien, but any being that could talk
about art with appreciation would find a soulmate
in her. "I'd say the same of a performance of the Ode
to Joy," she said. "Would this Leaf Ruby be on the
Roving?"

"Where else would it be?"

Julia raised her eyebrows. "I thought the Roving
was only a colony world."

For a moment Arm Wild was silent, as though Julia had actually caught him out on something. "I see
your point," he said. "Yes, Leaf Ruby is there. It is a
native of the Roving."

"I'd like to attend one of Leaf Ruby's recitals," Julia
said. "Would that be possible?"

"It can be arranged. To this interview, Lieutenant.
You have probably gathered from your crewmates
that I usually first ask about your background, and
your reasons for being in space."

"Okay," Julia said. *Just stay off my sex life, there's
a good Rustie.* "I think I went into space because I
was after . . . after something different. On Earth,
everyone has to be exactly alike, though it wasn't always like that. Once the Italians wrote the greatest

music in the world — or say they did. Once the English were the greatest sailors. And so on. You don't get that now; you can get just as good music in England, France, Germany . . . we're one big mass of similarity. But the individuals head for the sky. That's me. Look at this ship! We're a collection of very different individuals. That's what I like about the spacer community — the diversity you get from person to person . . ."

Comments of Arm Wild: Julia Coyne came into space to seek individuality and diversity, yet it happily subsumes its identity into a crew. Such a dichotomy. Such aptitude.

Peter Kirton, Software Officer
Of the three non-command humans, Peter Kirton is most senior according to their standards; it is younger than the last interviewed, Julia Coyne, but is more experienced and has passed more tests to qualify for seniority. Such is the human way.

Peter Kirton was aware that he tended to rub his hands together nervously when talking to strangers, and was sitting on them to prevent it. His eyes were fixed firmly on Arm Wild's translator unit, slung around his neck beneath his wedge-shaped chin.

"Um — that device fascinates me, Arm Wild," he said. "How does it work?"

One place Arm Wild could not see was under his

chin. He followed the direction of Peter's gaze and his free grasper brushed the unit. "I have no idea," he said. "How would *you* make it work?"

"Some form of artificial intelligence," Peter mused. "Not necessarily sentient . . . A neural network could handle the context, the semantics . . . But it never seems to pause in making the translation, so it must think ahead to what you're about to say."

"That I do know," Arm Wild said. "We take an average of half as long in communicating the meaning of a single sentence as a human speaking Standard does. We have finished our sentence before the unit is halfway through its translation. We have to be quite patient in speaking to humans."

"I'll try not to hold you up," Peter said with a cautious smile.

"Thank you."

"You know, I've never actually heard your voice," Peter said.

For a second, a gasping hiss filled the cabin. "Now you have," Arm Wild said. "My translator is set only to pick up subvocalized speech. It is less off-putting to humans to hear just the one tongue."

"Too true," Peter said, smiling again. "Let me guess. It translates our words for you and plays them direct into your ear? Cochlea stimulation, or something."

"So I believe."

Peter looked at him thoughtfully. "You know,

we're at a disadvantage. I'll never know exactly what you say. You could deliver the vilest First Breed insult every time you refer to me, and you could set your unit to translate it as 'Peter.'"

"And why would I do that?" Arm Wild asked.

"No reason," Peter said.

Arm Wild brought the conversation round to the subject of Lieutenant Peter Kirton.

"I wanted to be an engineer, I suppose," Peter said. "Get my hands dirty. But have you ever been on Mars? Of course you have, silly question, sorry. What I meant was, did you absorb the atmosphere? The scene? The society?"

"As much as is possible for an alien. Why do you ask?"

"Because every other Martian is an engineer! We have to be. We live in a totally artificial world. Mars is still one big spaceship where a million little things can go wrong every day that could wipe a lot of people out."

"We were surprised when the government of Mars showed no interest in this delegation," Arm Wild said.

Peter laughed. "Come on! They've already spent a century trying to make Mars habitable, they've committed themselves to a programme that'll last centuries more, and then you lot turn up and announce that there's another Earth-type planet ready-made for us. They're annoyed."

"You evidently do not share this opinion."

"No, but I can tell why they do."

Arm Wild nudged the conversation back to its original course. "You said every Martian is an engineer."

"That's right. A hardware engineer. So, I decided to be different. I got into software instead. But since on Mars, that means studying the code for the air-conditioning plants and not much else, I broadened my horizons."

"To the Royal Space Fleet."

"They were the only ones recruiting at the time. This job came up, I could do it, so . . . here I am."

Comments of Arm Wild: This interview I found the most disquieting, through no fault of Peter Kirton's. This human is in charge of the ship's software, and that includes the ship's artificial intelligences. Speaking to it reminded me that as long as I am on board Ark Royal, I am surrounded by disembodied minds in the ship's fibre optics — entities that can only be discoursed with through mouthtalk or even written language: no possibility of fulltalk at all. It must be like a pride of cripples. It is not satisfactory simply to say that humans are used to it — how are they used to it? How can such a society exist?

Adrian Nichol, Assistant Engineer
After much cogitation, I am still not convinced that Adrian Nichol's arguments actually make

sense. Adrian Nichol is plainly convinced that they do. I present them for consideration.

"I'm here because what human wouldn't be?" Adrian said. He was leaning forward eagerly, twirling his thumbs around each other without realizing it.

"Many are not," Arm Wild said.

"Yeah, but I bet they wanted to. Everyone from His Highness the King down. I heard your embassy got thousands of begging calls from people who wanted to go, even though they didn't meet the requirements?"

"There were many such requests," Arm Wild agreed, "even though we had stipulated that interested parties must have their own ship. Incidentally, I had understood that the correct designation for King Richard is 'His Majesty.'"

Adrian winced. "Yeah, I should remember that. The point is, you can understand it, right? I mean, explore a new world? Yeah, yeah, it's not *new*, your people are there already, but it's new to us. It's engrained in the human psyche — explore!"

"From our own observations," Arm Wild said, "that seems only to be true of a handful of humans, even though it is a trait to which many might lay claim. The fact appears to be that explorers are a tiny minority in your race."

"Well, okay," Adrian agreed. "Okay, there are a few billion people on Earth who don't want to explore, who never have explored, who never will . . . it's lack of opportunity, is all. Most of them are tied down with the necessity of making a living, and I think that kind of drains your ambition away. House, family . . ."

"So an explorer must not be tied down?"

"Makes sense, doesn't it? I'm a spaceboy. My grandparents came from Australia but my parents were born on a habitat in Earth orbit and I was born on UK-1. I'm not tied down to a world or to a place and that means I'm free to go where I want."

"Within reason," said Arm Wild.

"Within reason, yes. I could get seriously yelled at if I made the ship go somewhere it wasn't meant to, but the point is *I'm free*. The ambition is there, given the opportunity, and here it comes!"

"If I may say so, you appear to be the only crew member with this kind of wanderlust."

"Maybe," Adrian said. "But listen: The last guy to have a continent named after him was someone called Amerigo Vespucci and he died in the sixteenth century. I looked it up. I'm not saying I'll get a continent named after me, but *I have a chance* . . . along with the couple of hundred other humans on this mission, of course."

Comments of Arm Wild: Several times Adrian Nichol emphasizes its freedom. It clearly cherishes its status as a self-determining, individual, adult human. Yet, like Julia Coyne who seeks individuality in space, it is consciously part of a social organism in which it cannot operate independently. It is difficult for the First Breed to conceptualize this, yet the humans find no inconsistency. This is not *a recommendation that we dispense with their services — far from it. I am more and more of the opinion that the human mind may be just what is required.*

Report ends

Nine
27 April 2149

Solitude at last! Strange, for a member of the First Breed to welcome it so. Since coming on board *Ark Royal*, Arm Wild Timbre Grey Wood Temple Southern Plains had worn small gas cylinders, that released First Breed pheromones into its nostrils, to give the sense of a crowd; and eye-surrounds that flashed subliminal images to give the impression of other First Breed in its peripheral vision. None of the humans had commented on the attachments, perhaps out of politeness.

Now Arm Wild was in deepest space and the nearest ship was hundreds of metres away, yet it was happy. The suit was full of pheromones, it was away from the humans and it was heading back to its own kind.

The fleet had finished boosting, and for the time being it was in free fall again, climbing high above the plane of the planets and moving through the solar system's gravitational field — searching for the correct solar alignment for the journey to the Roving system. Michael Gilmore had offered Arm Wild the use of the boat *Sharman* but it had politely declined, citing the incompatibility of docking mechanisms as a veiled excuse. Now its suit was pushing through space towards the First Breed prideship.

The only sound was the hiss of the thrusters and the hum of the suit's air-conditioning.

A voice sounded over the speakers. "This is the prideship to Arm Wild. Your suit's beacon is registered and we are bringing you in." A proper voice! Not that horrible, overloud barking of the Ganglies but the gentle, cultured tones of the First Breed; straight out of the speaker's throat, not filtered through its translator's circuitry. Mouthtalk only, of course; still inferior to the fulltalk that came from face-to-face contact, but infinitely better than nothing.

"Thank you, prideship." Arm Wild suddenly could not bear to be formal any longer. "Thank you, sibling!"

"Our pleasure, Arm Wild. Welcome home."

There to greet it in the airlock (a proper size! Gangly rooms were so cavernous!) was the Pride Senior itself, Timbre Grey. It came forward and extended its graspers, and Arm Wild twined its own graspers round them. Now they could actually see and smell each other, they could communicate properly.

<<Arm Wild>> [Welcome], the Pride Senior said. A gentle whiff of pheromones reinforced the sincerity of the greeting.

How could any race rise to civilization depending just on verbal communication? Arm Wild had often wondered. Humans recognized the existence of bodytalk, they even had the word for it, but how could they relegate it so to such negligible importance? The Pride Senior's legs were properly positioned; the slightly emphasized posture of its body showed that its welcome was genuine and glad. Arm Wild took care that the precise strength of its grasp and lowered position of its head emphasised its acknowledgement of the other's seniority.

I am noticing First Breed fulltalk! Arm Wild thought in sudden horror. *I have been among the Ganglies for too long!*

<<If you are like the others, you will be glad for the change>> [sincere, concern] the Senior added.

<<It drives me mad, Timbre Grey>> [feeling] said Arm Wild. <<I find the Ganglies fascinating and they could even be my friends, but . . . *oh*>> [pure frustration, verging on madness; subtle hint of self-control to show semi-jest]. <<It is good to be back. Even the deckplates feel different under my feet>>

[Amusement] <<They are. The humans make their ships from a different material to us. But now you can put away your eye-surrounds and your pheromone bottles, Arm Wild. You are among friends>>

<<They are effective but they are not the real thing. This break was an excellent idea, Timbre Grey>> [sincerity]

[Pleasure] said Timbre Grey. [Polite concern] <<Incidentally, I hope you do not use the word

"Gangly" to the humans. Remember we may have to learn to treat them with respect>>

<<My translator is set always to use the humans' term for themselves>> said Arm Wild. <<But I will endeavour to speak properly of them from now on, anyway>>

Timbre Grey [amusement]

<<To be fair>> [grudging respect] Arm Wild added, <<my translator is also set to distinguish between "Rustie" and "First Breed" in reverse. My Ganglies — my humans — always use the term "First Breed" in my presence>>

<<Commendable>> [approving]

Arm Wild [true]

They met in the commune-place; the First Breed liaisons from all the ships, and as many of the prideship's crew as could be spared from duties. The First Breed always felt the pain of separation, and the tales told by those liaisons who had already returned meant that by the time Arm Wild arrived, the commune-place was resonant with sympathy and healing love. Arm Wild fell into it like a fish returning to water, and for the first hour that was it. It suspected that a watching human would have seen the First Breed milling around, apparently without aim, and the first word to come to mind would probably have been *cattle*.

At long last, Arm Wild and the others felt clean

again; they were back in the pride. Food was served in small piles around the floor, beverages flooded into the drinking basins, and the proceedings finally took on a form that the humans would have recognized, as small clusters of First Breed formed out of the mass to chat amongst themselves.

[Cheerful curiosity/interrogative] <<How's the ship, Arm Wild?>> That was Tree Bright, the First Breed assigned to the Euro ship, *Bruxelles*.

[Approval] said Arm Wild. <<So far I have got on well with the crew, though I detect tension between the ship's captain and the United Kingdom's delegate. *Ark Royal*'s Michael Gilmore is a dedicated Pride Senior—>>

[Scorn/horror] <<One [general] cannot use that term for humans>>

<<One [general] can in this case. The company of Michael Gilmore's ship chose of their own volition to serve under it>>

[Uncertain challenge] <<Michael Gilmore could not be removed by the company so easily as we could remove Timbre Grey>> Tree Bright said.

<<True. But Michael Gilmore is sufficiently respected by its crew that they would not want to>> [Interrogative] <<Can you say the same of your ship?>>

[Grudging admission] <<Its captain is liked and disliked in equal measure>> Tree Bright said. <<Those of the crew who dislike it hide their feelings from it personally, but it is aware nonetheless>>

[Resignation] <<Being a human, I take it that it does not mind.>>

[Resignation reinforced] <<It does not appear to>> said Tree Bright. <<The one of us I feel most sorry for is Place Brave>>

[Interrogative] <<The delegate on his ship was probably responsible for the loss of our siblings of Roll Blank's pride in that crash. That individual is already notorious amongst the humans for a number of reasons, most recently its use of nuclear force on a city named Rangoon>>

[Loathing] Arm Wild said. <<I had forgotten Place Brave was on that ship. We can only hope they do not win the bid>>

[Minor remonstration] <<That is not our decision to make, Arm Wild>>

[Doggedness] <<Nonetheless, it is an honest hope>>

Tree Bright changed the subject. <<But to return to Michael Gilmore. I am told by my captain it is what the Ganglies call 'borderline depressive.' This is not always recommended and certainly not in a Pride Senior. In its past it has verged on what the humans call mental collapse>>

<<I do not think we are qualified to study or comment on alien psychology>> Arm Wild said. <<I did my own investigations into Michael Gilmore's career, which is on public record, and though I concede it has received more psychiatric assistance than the average human, it is now in the state in

which it functions at an optimum. One must assume Michael Gilmore's superiors know what they are doing>> [Interrogative] <<Should I or one [general] tell him about this opinion?>>

<<Inadvisable. Ganglies appear to prefer to be given information on personal mental states by specialists whom they have previously consulted>>

[Understanding] Arm Wild said. <<I have noticed that this is often the case with humans: unsolicited, unwelcome information is not welcome from someone with whom they are not well acquainted. For example, I overheard the conversation between Michael Gilmore and Prince James when the fact of *Ark Royal*'s weaponry came to light. Michael Gilmore had not been aware of the armaments—>>

[Contempt] <<Some Pride Senior>>

<<—and was most upset to hear of them from a comparative stranger>>

[Interrogative] <<They held this conversation in front of you?>>

<<I must confess I was listening in. The translator unit has a greater pickup range than the humans believe>>

[Amused interrogative] <<Did you know our scans have revealed that all the human ships have some form of armament?>> Tree Bright asked.

<<It only confirms what Prince James told Michael Gilmore>>

[Amusement] <<In the humans' position, I suppose it is the wisest thing to do>> Tree Bright said.

Arm Wild [agreement]

A formal reception on a World Administration ship! R.V. Krishnamurthy always relished irony, and this was as ironic as one could get. He wondered if David Sorhindo, the WA's delegate, had considered not inviting him to this reception, even though it was meant for all the delegates. Krishnamurthy smiled as he strolled into *U Thant*'s saloon, hands behind his back, to mingle with the others. Ah, to be a liberal! To have to be nice to everyone! It was not a problem Krishnamurthy had ever had.

Sorhindo and *U Thant*'s captain were waiting to greet guests as they came in.

"Mr. Krishnamurthy." Sorhindo's tone could have frozen warts. "Delighted you could come." They shook hands and Krishnamurthy deliberately held on long after the handshake had run its natural course.

"I'm very glad to be here," he said. "It is so important that we delegates mix together and get to know one another, wouldn't you say? I do so admire you for your work in remaining neutral."

Sorhindo managed to extract his hand. "You're very kind," he said. "Excuse me." He turned to the next delegate in line and Krishnamurthy sauntered on in. He took a glass from a steward and looked around. Not bad, he thought, not bad. *U Thant* wasn't a luxury ship but she could run to a reasonable degree of hospitality.

Then his gaze settled on a knot of three delegates together: two men and a woman. He sensed more sport and wandered over to join them. The woman was a smartly dressed blonde and the man whose face he could see had dark hair that was largely grey, and a permanent shadow on his jowls. The other, smaller man had his back turned but Krishnamurthy knew who he was. He clapped a hand on the man's shoulder.

"Your Royal Highness!" he said. "I don't believe we've met." He relished the way the expressions of the three froze, as Prince James turned to meet him.

The prince did it best, Krishnamurthy had to admit. An eyebrow went up and a look of polite disdain settled on his face. "No, I don't believe we have," he said. "Mr. Krishnamurthy, isn't it?"

"The same. Your obedient servant." *As we were your obedient servants for three hundred years, while you bled our country dry, turned us into second-class Englishmen and denied us our proper heritage.*

"Charmed," said the prince.

Krishnamurthy turned to the others. "And you are . . . don't tell me . . . Ms. duPont of the North American Federation? And Mr. Ganschow of Starward. Do tell me: What is a space company doing on this delegation? I never really gathered."

Paul Ganschow couldn't quite manage the prince's hauteur. "We have our reasons for being here."

"Of course, of course. And you, Your Royal Highness? Planning to rebuild your empire on the Roving?"

"The UK will submit its own plan for the Rusties' consideration, in due course," the prince said.

Krishnamurthy stayed jovial. "And make them all Christians? Dictate their culture? Rename their places for them?"

The prince grew even colder in contrast to Krishnamurthy's smile. "Since their place-names are all unpronounceable and mostly untranslatable, very probably," he said. "As to your other points, I really couldn't say. I like to think we've grown out of that kind of behaviour."

"Let us hope so." *And much good may it do you,* he thought, remembering the lodge in the Himalayas again, *because I know what they're up to and you don't, ha ha ha.* Krishnamurthy could have stayed and continued to annoy them, but apart from the satisfaction to be gained, there were other things he could be doing more profitably. "Well, excuse me. Business calls."

He wandered away from them, singing inside. So, those three were allies. Alliances would be bubbling up and bursting throughout this whole business. Although the invitation suggested the Rusties would only deal with one nation, that one nation would

find things far easier for itself if it had friends among
the other humans. He wondered who else would . . .

The delegate for the United Slavic Federation
drifted over to their group, and was absorbed into
the circle. Fascinating. Didn't they realize they were
broadcasting their togetherness to the world at
large? So much better to keep secrets, to keep
people guessing.

A snatch of conversation drifted across his hearing. His presence really was being felt.

"*I'm amazed he has the nerve to show himself
here.*"

"*The WA dropped the charges.*"

"*I know. I never could see why, though.*"

"*It was something like, the Burmese had voted
in an open election to remain part of the Confederation —*"

"*Sure!*"

"*—and so the Confederation was justified in
taking whatever action they felt necessary to put
down the undemocratic rebels. Rangoon was India's, so they could do what they wanted with it.*"

Precisely, Krishnamurthy thought, and we did. He
considered turning round and congratulating the
speaker defending him for his grasp of politics, but
then one of *his* circle of allies caught his eye and began to wander over. Krishnamurthy gave an imper-
ceptible shake of his head. No, don't advertise yet.
Keep them in suspense; they'll find out about us in
due course.

Ten
31 April–17 May 2149

A sphere, a strange blurry nothingness in spherical form, blossomed out of nowhere ahead of the ships. Gilmore winced as he tried to make his eyes focus on it.

"Aagh!" Samad said, puncturing the tension on the flight deck, and Gilmore knew he was feeling the same thing. How do you focus on nothing?

He noticed he was gripping the edges of his desk, and deliberately let go, one finger at a time. This, finally, was the unknown. They were about to do what no human had ever done before.

The fleet was holding position at the step-through point, eleven light minutes away from the sun. All ships were on orders to stand by for boost at a moment's notice, and Gilmore had passed the time checking with the briefing pack on what was about to happen.

The pack assured him that these passageways in space were nothing new: humans had used the theory of Quantum Gravity to predict them for two hundred years, as if that was meant to be a comfort. The Rusties called them tubules and they were constantly appearing and vanishing on very small scales: tiny tunnels through the dimensions of space-time, far too small to let anything substantial pass through, and existing only for tiny fractions of

a picosecond. The prideship had scanned for one
such tubule that connected to the Roving system,
caught it and inflated it to millions of times its normal size. Through that sphere, Roving space was
just a step away.

The command came from the prideship and one
by one, in the designated order, the Earth ships —
not without a small amount of trepidation — fired
their thrusters and advanced into the sphere. And
vanished.

Ark Royal's orders came through.

"Proceed," Gilmore said. His voice was steady, and
he determined to avoid mopping his brow, an action which would have called attention to his nervous sweating. Everyone else, perhaps using the
same logic, was carefully studying their instruments.

Adrian Nichol fired the thrusters and the ship
moved forward. There was no sense of transition.
One moment the sphere was dead ahead, almost
touching the ship, and the next there was only the
black of space around them again. Space a thousand
light-years from Earth. The ships that had gone
through ahead of them were there, waiting.

On the flight deck there was the sound of several
people suddenly starting to breathe again.

"Take up our designated position," Gilmore said.
"Don't want anyone ramming us up the stern
tubes."

Ark Royal moved aside to let the next ship, the
Vatican's *Christopher*, through. Another ten min-

utes and the last of the Earth ships had appeared. Behind it loomed the prideship, and then the sphere had vanished and the step-through was completed.

The Roving's sun was a bright marble ahead of them. They were roughly the same distance from it as they had been from Earth's sun: the briefing pack said step-throughs started and ended at the same gravitational potential, which in this case — since the two suns had roughly the same mass — meant roughly the same distance from each. And for the first time ever in space, Gilmore had a flash of agoraphobia. Even in deep space in the Sol system, he was still *home* — he was where he belonged — but now he was light-years from home, in a solar system to which humanity had a claim only by invitation of the inhabitants. One tiny human in an infinite amount of someone else's space.

He bit his tongue and ordered a status report.

The prince was on the bicycle in the ship's gym, flushed and sweating, legs pumping. Gilmore opened his mouth to speak and the prince held up a hand to silence him.

The figures on the display read 9.7, and climbing. When they reached 10 the prince stopped and let the bicycle's mechanism whirr to a standstill. Then he started peddling again at a reduced, more leisurely rate. He grinned at Gilmore. "Ten miles every day without fail, Captain. Highly recommended. What can I do for you?"

"You asked to see me when I came off watch, sir," Gilmore said.

"I did?" The prince paused with an element of theatre — just enough that Gilmore wasn't sure if he was being wound up. "I did, yes. Thank you for coming. I want to use that software officer of yours, if you can spare him."

"Mr. Kirton?"

"That's him. I've looked through your crew records. Seems he's quite a whizz with the electrons."

Gilmore held back a laugh. *Quite a whizz? Electrons?* "What would you like him for, sir?"

The prince told him and Gilmore raised an eyebrow.

"Any objections, Captain?" the prince said.

"None at all, sir." Indeed, Gilmore was delighted that for once the prince had thought of asking for something. "I think he's still on the flight deck."

Peter Kirton was indeed on the flight deck, carrying out a task on one of the auxiliary desks. Adrian Nichol was also there, at the main console, and unfortunately for Kirton they were alone.

" . . . And the Father says to the Rabbi, sir, I know the prohibitions of your religion, but there's something I must ask you." Nichol was leaning forward eagerly, awaiting every nuance of reaction. Kirton looked resigned. "Have you ever lapsed and eaten pork? And the Rabbi says, yes, yes, may the Lord forgive me, I once lapsed. But tell me, Father, I know of *your own* prohibitions, so do tell me, have you ever lapsed and . . . you know? And the Father says, well, I must confess that I once did, yes.

"And the Rabbi grins, and says —" Nichol saw Gilmore and Prince James waiting in the hatch. "Sir!"

"The Rabbi says, better than pork, isn't it?" Gilmore said. Joel had told him that one once, and had been both surprised and impressed that his father already knew it. "Mr. Kirton, a word, please."

The prince insisted that the three of them return to his cabin, where he got straight to the point. "Lieutenant, I want to be able to understand the Rusties."

Kirton frowned. "But we can, sir."

"Everything they say is filtered through their own translators, which is thoroughly unsatisfactory," the prince said. "They could be saying anything and we'd never know. Could you manage something which would do our own translating?"

Kirton rubbed his chin, eyes slightly glazed as he pondered the problem. "Well, in theory, sir," he said. "Neural technology might help . . . throw enough examples at it and it works out its own rules. So if we knew roughly what a Rustie had said from its own translation, bit by bit we could make our own translator. But then the problem is hearing a Rustie speak in its own language. Arm Wild demonstrated his translator unit for me — they subvocalize, so we don't hear their original words. Mr. Loonat may be able to devise a microphone that could hear them —"

"Good, good." The prince's cutting gesture indicated that Kirton should stop talking. "That's all I wanted to know. Actually, they have two languages. Normally they use a mixture of vocal speech and body language and even smells, but they do have what they call mouthtalk as well, which is just vocal, and that's what they use for their translators." He took out his aide. "Plantagenet, please copy to Lieutenant Kirton's archive file 'Enigma,' password 'Bletchley.' "

"Complying," said the AI's voice.

"Play file 'Enigma,' " said the prince, and a noise that Gilmore for a moment had trouble placing filled the cabin. Immediately, however, a familiar bland voice spoke. It could have been Arm Wild or any other Rustie but the voice came from a translator unit.

" . . . impressive achievement," it said. "This vessel is larger than any belonging to the First Breed."

"Thank you, you honour me." It was a human male voice now which Gilmore recognized as belonging to King Richard.

More Rustie-speak, which translated as: "Its power consumption must be —"

"Cease play," Prince James said. He looked at the other two. "They were impressed by UK-1 when they came to see us," he added conversationally, with a hint of pride.

"You could hear them speak!" Kirton said.

"Not at the time. We recorded as many conversations as we could and we enhanced the noise they made. What you have here, Lieutenant, is over fifty hours of the Rusties' own language plus their own translation into Standard, as supplied during their stay on UK-1. Will this suffice as raw data?"

Kirton's eyebrows were almost up above his fringe. "I daresay, sir. But . . ."

"But?"

"I can't believe we're the first to try, sir! In fact, I'd heard people already have, and just haven't been able —"

"Just try it yourself, that's all I ask. Will it take long?"

"*Long*?" It was only Kirton's nervous respect in speaking to the prince that stopped him from laughing out loud. He had been given a task that many others had been given — and which no one else had been able to accomplish — and asked if it would take long. "Well, sir, it might have helped if we'd got this . . ."

He stopped, remembering where he was, and Gilmore filled in the remainder of the speech: *if we'd got this data sooner and not two days out from the Roving*. In fact, why hadn't the king's people started work on this the moment they had the recording?

"Well, there it is," the prince said. "That will be all, gentlemen." They had half turned to go, when the

prince added: "Oh, on a ship this size I quite understand that you can't keep secrets from each other,
but there's no need to mention this in Arm Wild's
presence, eh?"

The Roving lay below them and it was everything
they had dreamed of. Blue oceans, wispy white
clouds, the land a patchwork of shades of green and
brown. The polar caps gleamed painfully white.

"I can breathe the air from up here," Samad said,
and the others knew what he meant. Most of them
hadn't been on Earth for years — Kirton never at
all — but still, those that had could remember the
grimy air, the endlessly recycled water . . . But here
they would have it for free — clean air, clean water,
empty open land to run free in.

After negotiation with the current occupants.

That was the variable, Gilmore thought. No one
knew anything about the Rusties' home world.
They, too, might have huddled, oppressed masses,
crying out to come and settle on the Roving. Or, like
some governments on Earth, they might want to
keep their populations at home and use the Roving's natural resources to look after them. Turn the
world into a giant mine.

What had the Rusties said in their invitation?
Something about, if two such similar races carried
on separately, sooner or later they would clash.
They had to start cooperating now. It had struck
Gilmore then, and it still did, as the wisest thing that

had been said in this whole affair. Humans and Rusties had to work together for their mutual good, and it would happen on the Roving.

The two words Gilmore had waited so long to hear were spoken by Peter Kirton, now on watch.

"Orbit established."

"Power down main engine," Gilmore said. "Disengage navigational controls. Link altitude thrusters to main computer for automatic correction."

"Aye-aye, sir."

The journey was over: they could no longer be considered to be travelling. Once orbit was established, a whole new set of paradigms took over. No one needed to be on the flight deck anymore: the automatics could keep the ship in orbit for as long as there was fuel in the tanks, and all that was needed was a crew member on board to handle emergencies or call in help.

"All delegation ships." The voice of a Rustie translator unit sounded from the comms desk. "Welcome to the Roving. Please set your scanners for visual, forward."

Kirton looked at Gilmore. "Sir?"

"Do it," Gilmore said. The view on the main display changed to dark sky with just a sliver of the Roving at the bottom right corner.

Silvery specks showed as a cluster in the centre of the display. They approached the fleet with discernible speed.

"Radar?" said Gilmore.

"Ten ships, sir," Kirton replied. "Approaching fast."

"A welcoming committee," said Arm Wild. "I dare say they have chosen to honour you with a flypast, Captain."

"How thought —" Gilmore began.

The flight of Rustie ships — small craft, much smaller than the fleet's prideship — banked suddenly, swerving to one side, then back again. Then in a flash they were past the ship and off the edge of the picture, but not before they had started a starburst manoeuvre around the fleet.

"Bloody show-offs!" exclaimed Julia.

Gilmore looked at the Rustie across the flight deck. "We're impressed, Arm Wild," he said. And, silently, he applauded the Rusties. In their inoffensive, polite way, they were making it quite clear that for the moment, the humans were guests only. Human tech could not have managed that display.

If those Rustie vessels were armed, he thought, we wouldn't have had a chance against them, torpedoes or not. Prince James, too, seemed thoughtful.

Oh, yes. Clever, clever Rusties. He pushed the thought aside.

"I want everyone in the wardroom," he said. "Will you join us, Arm Wild?"

"We are now on orbital watch," he said five minutes later. The full ship's complement was present: holding this meeting in the wardroom instead of on the flight deck was a symbolic act to show that they had indeed arrived. "Number One?"

"Sir." Hannah Dereshev consulted her aide. "The minimum legal requirement for orbital watch is one human on the ship at all times. However, we're a military ship in orbit around a new world with a hundred and one unknowns out there, so we will have two people on watch, for a period running from midday to 1159 and 59 seconds, ship time. Remember our time signal is now coordinated with the Roving day and our twenty-four hours actually last for twenty-six, so you might find yourself getting unexpectedly tired in the late evening.

"Number one watch is the captain and Ms. Coyne. Number two is myself and Mr. Nichol; number three is Messrs. Loonat and Kirton. It is now 1548 so the first watch gets a bargain. That watch is you two, Samad, Peter. Subsequent watches run in numerical order."

"Aye-aye, sir," they said with resigned grins. They knew they had already been chosen by lot.

Hannah went on. "Now, a day is a long time, and it's even longer here, but the system was chosen so that each of us can have two full days of free time between watches, to do as we will downstairs. The watches aren't writ in stone and you're welcome — at your own responsibility — to swap between yourselves. Just let me know any changes, and any problems that you have, well in advance.

"Mr. Nichol, Mr. Loonat, please ready the landing boat for atmospheric use. Mr. Nichol will be taking His Highness and Arm Wild down to the meeting place at 0800 tomorrow. Crew dismissed."

Gilmore tapped on the door to the prince's cabin, bidden by yet another summons.

"Enter."

Gilmore found the prince gazing at a live view of the Roving on his wallscreen.

"Isn't it beautiful?" the prince said. "Plantagenet, record this for my personal records, will you?"

"Certainly, sir," said the AI's voice. James was already back in his reverie.

"Look at it, Captain," he said. "Vast spaces, vast natural reserves . . . the UK deserves this place."

"Seven thousand people would rattle about a bit, sir," Gilmore said.

"Pah," said the prince. "Do you think we'll keep it all to ourselves? Of course not. There's millions, billions on Earth who'll be queuing up for a chance to come here and start again, and we'll be in charge of it. We'll clean up, Captain! Of course, we'll have to insist that they become UK citizens."

Gilmore had a sudden, horrible feeling that he knew where this was going.

"A whole new empire," he said.

"Bigger and better than ever before!" said the prince. "India, the jewel in Queen Victoria's crown?

A pebble, compared with what we'll make of this place." He gestured dramatically at the image. "The East India Company? Street traders. Wait until we start issuing shares in the Roving Company."

"Can I ask what you wanted to see me for, sir?" Gilmore said, more to shut the prince up than anything else. Didn't he realise the days of empire were gone? You couldn't have empires nowadays. People were too aware. Too free, and too accustomed to freedom. And those states that did approximate empires, for example the Confederation of South-East Asia, just served as examples of why the idea didn't work anymore.

Not that there was any chance of the prince's dreams coming true, Gilmore reminded himself. As if.

"Ah, yes." The prince pulled himself back into the real world. "Yes, Captain, I'd appreciate your presence with me at the Convocation."

"Sir, I'm on watch tomorrow," Gilmore said politely. The Convocation was what the whole mission was about: the Rusties had mentioned it in their invitation. First, the delegates would be given a whirlwind tour of the world, so as to finalize their proposals, then they would meet together, and present their respective claims to be joint masters of the Roving with the Rusties. Gilmore didn't have time for that. He had his ship to care for.

The prince looked at him as if he were mad. "Captain, we're here! We've arrived! Nothing's going to happen in orbit and I need you on the surface. All the others will be there with their hordes of advisers and assistants. Frankly, captain, you can give me face down there."

"Sir —"

"There's two of you on each watch, correct?" the prince said. "And all you have to do is be here — you don't have to work or anything?"

"Yes —"

"Then it's settled. Get one of the others to stand in for you."

"I should stand my watch, sir!" Gilmore snapped.

"What you should do, Captain, is serve the best interests of the United Kingdom, and I say that means accompanying me. This conversation is over."

The prince made sure it was over by holding the door open, even while Gilmore was trying to think of a final answer. He left the cabin, fighting the urge to kick the wall, and saw Hannah. She had the next-door cabin and she must have overheard. "We've got to rearrange the watch already, Number One," he said coldly.

"Captain, I don't think this is the last time he's going to demand your time," she said. "Either we accept that Julia will be on her own sometimes, and you join your watch when you can, or we'll be permanently rearranging."

Gilmore ground his teeth. "I suppose so," he said.

It was small consolation. For the first time the prince was actively interfering with his running of his ship, and he wondered how many more times it would happen and how long it would take them to come to blows.

Eleven
18 May 2149

The view through the ports cleared as *Ark Royal*'s docking arm moved *Sharman* away, and Gilmore got the first chance to look at his command from the outside since leaving Earth. The voyage had been shorter than many conventional trips across the Sol system but still, after such a distance he felt the ship should show something. Should be somehow battered a bit; dignified but worn, like a sailing ship of old that had just circumnavigated the globe.

Ark Royal looked just the same as when she had left the dockyard.

He heard the clunk of the docking arm releasing and felt the vibration of the boat's thrusters; he saw *Ark Royal*'s hull slide by, then the edge of the ring. He switched the display in front of him to a rear view. The ship's prow moved slowly towards the top of the image and receded as the boat dropped down out of her orbit.

Gilmore's eyes narrowed as he caught the subtle bulges on either side of the bow, which hadn't been there the last time he had had this view. Now he knew they were there they seemed to stand out a mile and he wondered how obvious the torpedo attachments looked to anyone who didn't know the ship's design.

Another, stronger vibration as the main engines fired and *Ark Royal* moved rapidly off the display. He switched it off. She had looked special. Not changed, but special. Maybe it was all in the mind but she was his command; she had carried him across lightyears to this system and now she was serene and unperturbed in her orbit, waiting for him to return.

He sat back in his seat and fidgeted. His weather-suit was stiff and unfamiliar about him.

"This is *Sharman*, complying," Nichol said from the cockpit, replying to some unheard flight direction. Then, to his passengers: "Atmosphere in two minutes, Captain, Your Majesty." He had his back to them and so didn't see the look of irritation on the prince's face. Gilmore supposed that of all the faults Nichol could have had, being unable to remember the distinction between "highness" and "majesty" was the least, but clearly the prince thought otherwise.

They flew in from the east, over the Roving's largest continent: the fleet's landers travelled in echelons towards their destination on the continent's western coast, overlooking the Great Strait. Below them was a dark, thick carpet of trees — the rain forests that covered the continent's eastern cape. They flew over a range of skyscraping mountains and came to a wooded plain that stretched into the distance.

It took another half hour to make the landing. Arm Wild had said that the capital's name was untranslatable, but because his translator was set simply to say "Capital," that was the name it had acquired among the humans. It was a sizeable community that covered the flood plain and rose up out of the valley of a large river, the width of the Mississippi. Gilmore wondered if the Rusties below were standing and looking up at the small alien invasion going on above them.

"Landing in five minutes," Nichol said. They were approaching Capital's spaceport, an ugly concrete blot on the green landscape to the north of the city. There was a roar as the verticals took over, supplementing the now meagre lift of the boat's wings. A whirr as the landing carriage dropped; and, finally, a slight bump as they touched down. The engines quietened from their high whistle to a faint murmur and *Sharman* was rolling forward at walking speed. Then it stopped and the engines died down entirely. They were on the Roving.

Gilmore grunted as he stood up. *Ark Royal's* ring had gradually been cranked up during the voyage to simulate the Roving's Earth-plus gravity but still it was an effort.

Nichol appeared from the cockpit, also wincing slightly. "They're ready when we are, sir," he said.

Gilmore nodded. "Welcome home, Arm Wild," he said, and cracked the hatch.

It was bright and sunny in Capital: a spring day for a town with a maritime climate. There was a fresh breeze blowing and Gilmore filled his lungs with sweet air.

Nichol was the last to step down on to the ground and he seemed about to make a chatty remark before finally remembering that he, *Ark Royal*'s most junior crewman, was in the presence of his captain and a prince. Prince James made the remark instead, speaking for all three humans.

"Isn't it fresh?" he said. "Uncanned, unpolluted . . ."

"Our transport," said Arm Wild, pointing. A small fleet of wheeled vehicles was approaching the landing craft. "How many of you are attending the Convocation?"

"Just the two of us for the moment," the prince said.

"Mr. Nichol, stand by for further orders," Gilmore added.

"Aye-aye, sir." Nichol looked forlorn at not being at the first formal meeting but Gilmore didn't doubt that the tedium would far outweigh the advantages. Rank didn't always have its privileges.

Capital was nowhere near as crowded as a human city. There were no tall buildings but very many large ones, much wider than they were high and completely out of proportion as far as a human's eye could tell. Though there was a vague pattern —

the typical arrangement seemed to be a palace-sized building, surrounded by open space with greenery or lakes or streams — the architecture itself was eclectic. The buildings were ornate, invariably covered with carvings. Some had pillars or flying buttresses or other architectural optional extras; others just stood alone. Some were regular and blockish; others looked like fantastic, jumbled piles of stone. The types of stone used also varied: sometimes it looked like sandstone, sometimes like granite, sometimes it was blue or purple or pink. Arm Wild said they were the pridehalls: the prides of the First Breed lived communally, on top of their work.

Gilmore decided he liked Capital. Roads curved, the pridehalls were all different shapes, nothing was predictable. There was a very organic feel to the place, as if it had been here for a long time and grown naturally, well settled into the landscape.

The convoy was moving through an open space dominated at the centre by what had to be a monument of some kind — a collection of Rusties, carved in a reddish stone. Four of them stood facing in four different directions, in an alert poise that made Gilmore think the human equivalent would be shading the eyes with one hand while scanning the horizon.

"To commemorate the prideship that first discovered an alien species," Arm Wild said.

"And how long ago was that?" Gilmore asked. The

Rusties had always clammed up when pressed for details of the other sentient aliens that they had discovered, but on their home ground he wondered if they might be more open.

"About eighty years," Arm Wild said.

"Did you invite any of them to the Roving?"

Arm Wild paused before replying. "No, Captain," he said, and Gilmore sensed the shutters coming down again on the topic. "We felt we could proceed better with your race. Once the Convocation has come to a satisfactory conclusion, then perhaps we can concern ourselves about the others. Look, we are almost there."

There was a geodesic dome standing in its own grounds just outside town. Its white panels made it look like half of a radar dome, buried in the ground, or one of the early Mars bases.

"Accommodation will be unrefined but, we hope, satisfactory," Arm Wild said. "Once we had agreed to invite you here, we had to devise something quickly to accommodate you. We hope it suffices."

The prince said he was confident that it would.

The convoy drew to a halt outside the main entrance to the dome. The humans climbed out slowly, once again having to subject their legs and backs to the Roving's gravity. A group of Rusties was there waiting for them.

"You are privileged, Captain Gilmore," Arm Wild said quietly. "That is Iron Run and the Twelve."

"The twelve what?"

"The twelve most senior Clan Seniors," Arm Wild said, "and Iron Run is the Senior of the Nation. Now please be quiet!"

And there was only one nation . . . so this was the most senior Rustie on the Roving. Gilmore did a quick count and could see fourteen Rusties: so, it was the Twelve, and Iron Run, and another.

Two Rusties stepped forward: Arm Wild said it was Iron Run and the Senior's mouthtalker, Spar Mild. The mystery of the fourteenth Rustie was solved.

"Human friends." Unlike the Rusties of the Earth mission, this one hadn't learned to subvocalize. Spar Mild's own voice could just be heard under the translated Standard. "Iron Run welcomes you to our world and to this Convocation. The nation of the First Breed looks forward to working with you. Please, come inside."

They were led into the dome along a wide corridor with — Gilmore winced — a deep-red carpet and walls of marigold and cerise, and a potted plant of some description, every few paces. They came out into a wide open space at the dome's centre. Up above was the dome's highest point, its panels translucent from the sun shining on them; around them were three circular balconies lined with doors that were refreshingly familiar: tall and narrow, human-sized. The ground floor was given over to a bar, a lounge and a refectory, each with a long side opening, facing the central lobby.

Rusties approached bearing refreshments, and the formalities began.

Three hours later, having finally escaped, Gilmore lay gratefully back on the bunk in the small room that had been allocated to him, and let the mattress take his weight. He had wondered if the Rusties would expect the humans to live together as they did, but apparently they had heard that humans were solitary creatures and had gone to the opposite extreme, providing their guests with, what were, in effect, cells. Barely six feet wide, ten long and perhaps seven high.

He took out his aide and activated it. He considered recording something for Joel to listen to one day — How I Arrived on the Roving and What it Was Like — but for the moment there were other priorities. "Get me a channel to *Ark Royal*," he said.

"Please wait," responded its semi-sentient AI, exploring all the various telecom routes available. Arm Wild had said the dome had a fully functioning network, compatible with all Earth standards, and connected to the Roving's net. Gilmore's aide cast its perception out into the network, made the acquaintance of the various Rustie protocols, bounced around several servers and satellites, and then Gilmore was hearing Hannah Dereshev's voice:

"Captain?"

"Number One. How's things?"

"Orbiting peacefully, sir. How about you?"

"Heavy," Gilmore said, meaning the gravity but happy to let Hannah draw whatever conclusions she liked. "The full programme starts tomorrow, to which I am cordially invited. What I'm calling to say is, there's no reason the off-watch crew shouldn't come down whenever you're ready." He paused and grimaced, remembering that he would have been on watch with Julia but for the prince's insistence, and he felt as if he were betraying a trust. "Accommodation is adequate, in" — he cast an eye around the cell "—a minimalist sort of way. Remember to bring my bags, and the prince's."

"Aye-aye, sir!" There was no disguising the glee in his executive officer's voice. "I'll recall Adrian straightaway."

"Don't forget your weathersuits," Gilmore said. "You'll need 'em. And when you get here, take things easy — it's surprisingly easy to overexert yourself."

"Thanks for the hint, Captain. Any further advice?"

"Yes." Gilmore looked at the floor and the walls, adorned in the same style as the lobby of the Dome. "Never ask a Rustie to do your decorating."

Arm Wild, too, was glad to get away from the reception. For the moment Prince James was the responsibility of First Breed who were far more senior than itself; its other function was to liaise with the crew of *Ark Royal*, who were not here yet.

Michael Gilmore had gone to lie down, indulging the strange human taste for solitude, so Arm Wild was free for the moment.

On the voyage it had interviewed each member of the crew and found that Julia Coyne, *Ark Royal*'s systems officer, was an advocate of that strange human art form, music. They had got to discussing the various arts on their various planets and it had made her a promise.

The Dome was fully equipped with all proper facilities and it was easy to find a communication chamber. Arm Wild entered, again wondering at the humans in one corner of its mind — how could they have taken so long to invent fully immersive, interactive virtual displays? Only a race that didn't use fulltalk could have been so tardy.

The display came up around it and it spoke a name.

<<Leaf Ruby Stone Rising Blue Table Highlands>> Arm Wild hoped Leaf Ruby was in the Stone Rising pridehall: if not, it would have to leave a message.

The image of Leaf Ruby, the Roving's greatest performer (in the opinion of Arm Wild, and of many others) appeared before it. The older First Breed was more portly around the middle than Arm Wild and its muzzle was blunter.

[Interrogative] <<Yes>> it said.

[Deferential] <<Arm Wild Timbre Grey Wood Temple Southern Plains>> Arm Wild said. Leaf

Ruby was in a different clan and Arm Wild was not
without status amongst the First Breed, being on the
Earth mission, yet he was willingly putting himself
beneath the great reciter. It read that the other First
Breed was touched by the display of reverence.
<<We have not met before>>

[Thoughtful interrogative statement] <<Wood
Temple Southern Plains>> Leaf Ruby said. <<You
are handling the human mission>>

<<Correct. You may have heard we arrived with
the humans here today>>

<<Congratulations>> said Leaf Ruby. [Interroga-
tive] <<How is the mission going?>>

[Wary optimism] said Arm Wild. <<The crew of
my ship, I feel, would understand our ways per-
fectly>>

[Expression of interest] Leaf Ruby said. [Specula-
tive hope] <<Perhaps I will meet some humans my-
self>>

<<That is why I called you, Leaf Ruby>> said Arm
Wild. <<One of mine has expressed an interest in
doing just that. It is an adherent of an art form that
the humans have developed, employing mathemati-
cally determined audible tones played at rhythmic
intervals>>

<<Sounds complicated>> Leaf Ruby said.

[Full agreement] said Arm Wild. <<I am not re-
motely able to appreciate it. However, I am a great
admirer of your work and mentioned to this human

that perhaps your recitals come closest to that art form in our culture. It asked if it could attend one>>

[Flattered, honoured] said Leaf Ruby. [Interrogative] <<Will this assist the mission as well?>>

<<It will certainly help create goodwill>> Arm Wild said.

<<Very well. I am giving a recital here in three days' time, at sunset. Bring your human. Indeed, bring yourself. I will have places of honour prepared for you>>

[Flattered, touched] said Arm Wild. <<I will, Leaf Ruby. I extend my thanks>>

<<I will see you in three days' time, Arm Wild>> Leaf Ruby said.

"Wow!" said Adrian Nichol. He stretched out his arms — he could almost touch either wall of his cubicle. "My cabin on the ship's bigger than this."

Julia Coyne, slightly taller than he was, held her own arms out and her fingertips brushed the walls. "See what you mean," she said. "Mine's the same."

They went out into the corridor where there was more room. *Ark Royal*'s crew had six rooms all together on the Dome's second level, doors facing towards the translucent white panels of the Dome's outer edge.

"I see what he meant about the decorating," Adrian said, looking back at the cubicle's garish colours.

Hannah Dereshev came out of her own room. All the cubicles were singles, which wasn't yet an issue, as Samad was on orbit watch with Peter Kirton. "I think they based it on the decoration in a typical four-star hotel on Earth," she said, "but without our own idea of what would be tasteful."

"And the cells?" Julia said.

"This place was built by Rusties who'd been told what humans were like but had never actually met any," Hannah said. "I think they did quite well, considering."

More humans were coming around the curve of the corridor, in the uniform of the American ship *Enterprise*.

"Hey, we've got the Naffies next to us," Adrian said in his most diplomatic manner, referring to the North American Federation. "You'd have thought they'd have put us in alphabetical order, or something."

"Maybe they did. Which alphabet were you thinking of?" said Hannah.

Adrian smiled at the nearest American who took the room next to his. "Hi there," he said.

"Hi," the American grunted. He was tall, broad-shouldered and had crew-cut blond hair. Adrian opened his mouth to introduce himself and the American pointedly went in and shut his door.

"Friendly," Adrian said.

"You coming with us?" Julia said. "Apparently there's a bar on the ground level."

"Sure. I'll freshen up first."

"See you later, then," she said.

Adrian went back to his room to get wash things and a change of clothes, then set out to look for the nearest washroom.

There was another *Enterprise* man in there, splashing water on his face. Adrian decided to try again. "Hi," he said. "Adrian Nichol, *Ark Royal*."

The man's appearance was identical to his comrade, down to his sour expression, but he seemed prepared to be more civil. "Carl Pieri, *Enterprise*."

"Glad to meet you." Adrian was putting two and two together. The crew cut, the muscles . . .

"You'll be one of the marines, yeah?" he said.

The next moment he was pinned against the wall, his feet off the floor and Pieri's face inches from his own.

"Who told you about that?" Pieri shook him. "Who?"

Adrian wheezed, the breath knocked out of him. The American's tight hold on his collar didn't help.

"What the hell are you doing?" said another voice, with the accent of the American Deep South.

Adrian was dropped and Pieri jumped to attention. "Sir!"

Adrian rubbed his neck and took in the newcomer. He had a captain's stripes.

"Sir! He asked if I was a marine, sir!" Pieri said.

The captain grinned. "And you wouldn't tell him if you were, would you?"

"Sir! No, sir!"

The captain waved a hand at the door. "Get out of here, Pieri."

"Sir! Yes, sir!"

The other two were left together. "McLaughlin, *Enterprise*," the captain said. "I'm sorry about that, son." He glanced around — at the mirror, at the ceiling, at the corners of the room — and put a hand on Adrian's shoulder. "Come on out, will you?"

Out in the corridor, he said, "Who are you?"

"Nichol," Adrian said, just getting his breath back. "Sir. Sub-Lieutenant Nichol, HMSS *Ark Royal*."

"Sub-Lieutenant? You could get Pieri on a charge of assaulting an officer, if you wanted. If he was a marine, that is. Which, of course, he isn't. You get the picture, Sub?"

"It's . . . um . . . common knowledge on *Ark Royal*, sir," Adrian said.

McLaughlin grinned again. "And they're convinced no one notices 'em." Again, he glanced around him: it was beginning to dawn on Adrian that he thought the area might be bugged. "Well, son, it wasn't the *humans* knowing that I'm worried about. No hard feelings, I hope?"

"No, sir." Adrian felt it was expected of him. "We're . . . well, we're all in the same boat, aren't we, sir?"

"Sure," McLaughlin said with a nod. "One happy family. Just remember that, Sub. Oh, and sorry, again."

* * *

There was an old song that Prince James had once heard and the words had stayed with him ever since. It was about Britain rising out of the sea at Heaven's command, and the chorus declared that Britannia ruled said sea and that her people would emphatically never be slaves.

At first you might have thought that the words had been written by a megalomaniac, and, granted, they were a product of the time when Britain felt it had the God-given right to conquer the rest of the world and turn everyone into little British; but the point was, they *had* been written.

James had no firm convictions on the subject of Heaven and, with space within his grasp, he was quite happy to cede rule of the waves, but nonetheless he approved of the sentiments of the song. The desire not to be slaves was a thoroughly reasonable one.

By the purely arbitrary division of the Roving time into twenty-six hours, each slightly longer than an Earth hour, it was now 2330 — well past midnight by Earth standards. Day one had gone well but James was tired and glad to have retired to his cubicle. He looked around it and half smiled, half grimaced. It wasn't exactly what he felt a prince, even a deposed prince, should be living in. All his life it had been drummed into him that he was a prince in name only; that he had to work for a living like everyone else, despite all the advantages that being the son of the richest human alive conferred. But even in this purely republican age of humanity, children were still told stories of kings and queens and princes and princesses. For as long as he could remember, James Windsor had felt vaguely cheated.

He switched his aide to voice mode. "Plantagenet."

By now, channels of communication were well established to *Ark Royal* and there was no delay before his personal AI replied. "Here, sir."

James lay back on his pillow. "Encrypt."

"Encryption on, sir."

"Good. Plantagenet, Lieutenant Kirton has a program running somewhere on the ship. He's doing a job for me, feeding our sample of Rustie-talk to a neural net to get a translation."

"I have it, sir. He has encrypted it with his own code."

"Can you break it? Discreetly, of course."

"One moment, sir," Plantagenet said. There was the silent whisper of the ether, and then: "His program is a very simple intelligence, sir. It will do what I say."

"Is it making much progress?"

"It is difficult to say at this stage, sir."

"Good. I want you to rewrite the output file with the contents of my own. File name 'U-boat,' password 'Atlantic.' "

"Complying." Another pause. "It is done, sir."

"Excellent!" James smiled, stretched luxuriously and gestured for the lights to dim. "Tidy up after yourself — keep to his protocols, don't leave foot-prints. I don't want him suspecting any more than he's going to anyway."

"Very good, sir."

"Good night, Plantagenet."

"Good night, sir."

Twelve
19 May 2149

"Good morning, sir. May we join you?" Hannah and Samad had appeared at Gilmore's table, trays laden down with breakfast.

Gilmore felt a pang of envy. Those humans not going on the grand tour had been offered a leisurely look around Capital. Granted, he was going to see a whole alien world, not just a city, but . . .

"By all means," Gilmore said, hoping they weren't feeling conversational. A 1.3 gravity and an unaccustomed mattress had made his sleep restless, and he wasn't in the mood for being nice. Then he saw Peter and Adrian lurking in the background with their own trays, clearly trying to pluck up the courage to approach their seniors. He beckoned them over, indicated they should sit.

"I wanted to ask you something, Number One," Adrian said. "Julia's asked me to swap my watch with her in two days' time. Arm Wild's arranged a visit for her to some kind of Rustie concert. Is that all right?"

"Certainly," Hannah said, with a glance at Gilmore for confirmation. He would be more affected by this than she would.

He nodded. "So we're going to share a watch, are we?" he said.

"Yes, sir," Adrian said. "And Julia will be with Number One on the watch after that."

"Fine," Gilmore said.

"Looking forward to the trip, Captain?" Prince James paused by Gilmore's table and for a moment Gilmore thought the man was going to take breakfast with him too, but James' posture indicated he was only pausing long enough to exchange compliments.

"Yes, sir," Gilmore said, not even bothering to think of something original to say.

"Good, good. Remember, we leave at 0900 sharp."

James walked off, carrying his tray across the refectory that was gradually filling up with humans. He was heading towards a group of delegates at another table.

Sitting opposite her captain, Hannah Dereshev smiled over a cup of coffee. Reading his thoughts from his expression, she said, "Well, you might have forgotten."

Gilmore grunted. The prospect of a day in the prince's company during a whistle-stop tour of the planet had never been appealing and now the first thing the man had done was get on his nerves. Not a good start.

At 0855, a crowd of about fifty humans was milling about outside the Dome, waiting for the vehicles to arrive. It had clouded over since yesterday. Then,

Gilmore had appreciated the clear air and sunshine but now humidity and windspeed had risen; looking up at what looked like looming rain clouds he was beginning to remember what weather was like, and why space was so much better without it.

Now coming out of the Dome was a short, plump man who looked vaguely familiar to Gilmore but whose identity was just out of reach, until Gilmore saw him talking to *Shivaji*'s Surit Amijee and he recognized the face at last. Was *that* the dreaded Krishnamurthy?

"Did you sleep well, Captain?" Arm Wild had appeared at his elbow. Strangely, the presence of the alien was something comforting and familiar.

"So-so," Gilmore said. He looked about him. All the other delegates had their Rustie liaisons with them and were constantly involving them in their conversation — asking for advice, suggestions, input — and yet, over there was Prince James and over here was Arm Wild.

"Shouldn't you be with the prince?" Gilmore asked.

"The prince has told me I will be called if needed," Arm Wild said. Gilmore, not for the first time, began to wonder about the wisdom of having Prince James represent the UK. Not only was the man devoid of all social graces but he seemed in no hurry at all actually to find out about the world he was meant to be making a bid for. How he expected to put together a coherent tender without Arm Wild's assistance was a mystery.

"Here you are," said Samad Loonat. He handed the small sphere to the Rustie accompanying them. "Just point, and press this button here. Can you manage?"

"I think so," the Rustie said. It was one of the ones that hadn't learned to subvocalize, and its own words in Rustie mouthtalk were audible over the translator. The problem now facing it was that the camera just wasn't designed for a Rustie to hold. One of the Rustie's graspers was wrapped around the little globe, the other poised over the button.

"Wait a moment," Samad said, and hurried over to join the rest of the crew, at the foot of the monument that commemorated the first discovery of an alien race. Four stylized Rusties each faced a different point of the compass. They appeared to have been carved to make them look domineering: their forelegs were distinctly longer than they should be, making them seem to rear up; their shoulders were bigger, their necks were longer and they leaned slightly forward, as if staring into the distance for the least hint of danger. Or looking out at new worlds to explore. Cortés on the Peak of Darien, if Cortés had been a Rustie.

Peter's aide chose that moment to beep and Samad ruined his own picture by thinking it was his own aide and looking down at it. He groaned when he heard the camera buzz and the wave of coherent light swept over them while Peter continued to hold the pose.

"Hold on, people," he begged, "one more."

"Move over, *Ark Royal*," someone said. The crew from another ship were waiting their turn, with another ship — *Shivaji* — after them. Samad reluctantly moved on to join his comrades, giving the Indians a cold glare as he did so, and they watched the next batch of humans make fools of themselves.

"God, we're a bunch of tourists," Hannah muttered. She looked around at the other Rusties, the locals from Capital, who seemed happy just to stand and watch the strange aliens. "The captain doesn't know when he's lucky."

"Ah, yes, love, but we'll have this to show our grandchildren, one day," Samad said. He was playing the picture back and studying the laser image carefully. Grinning faces from Peter and Adrian; Hannah with her arms folded and an "if I must" look on her face; and himself, staring down at his belt. Then he heard Peter exclaim.

"No! I . . . it's impossible! It's . . . it's . . ." There was such agitation in Peter's voice that the rest of the crew gathered round. He didn't notice them, he was too busy staring at his aide's display. "One hundred percent match!" he said. "One hundred per . . ."

He looked up, noticing the other humans nearby. "Over here," he muttered, and moved a few ostentatious steps away. The non–*Ark Royal* humans got the hint and kept their distance.

"What's the problem, Lieutenant?" Hannah said. The formal request helped him pull together.

"I was working on a translation program for the prince," he said. "Rustie to Standard — the prince provided the input data. My hopes weren't high, but . . . Look, say something. Anything." He held up the aide, ready to record whatever was said.

"Um . . ." the others looked hopefully at each other.

"Oh, come on!" he said. "Anything!" He looked at Hannah.

"Oh, well," she said. "Once more unto the breach, dear friends, once more, or close the wall up with our English dead."

"Uh-huh," said Peter. "Command: translate." The sound of Rustie speech came out of the aide, then the Standard word "English." "No Rustie equivalent for that," he said.

Six round eyes stared at him.

"Pete, you're a genius!" Adrian said.

"That's what's so weird," he said. "I was only doing it to oblige the prince. I can't — I couldn't — I can't believe it would have worked so quickly. I mean, the sample of Rustie speech that I had to work on was what they said on UK-1. They can't have used that many different words . . . do you really think they said 'breach,' for instance? Or 'unto'?"

"Try this," said Hannah. He held up the aide again, ready. "'Hear, O Israel, the Lord our God, the Lord is One.'"

Cough, *splutter*, Israel, *gasp*.

"Okay, my turn" said Samad. He cleared his throat. "'In the name of Allah, the Beneficent, the Merciful. Say: He is Allah, the One. Allah, the eternally Besought of all. He begetteth not, nor was begotten, and there is none comparable unto him.'"

The aide balked at "Allah", "besought" and "begetteth."

"I couldn't tell you what they mean either," said Adrian.

Peter said, "And don't tell me the Rusties, on a diplomatic visit to King Richard, used any of those words. Or 'begotten.'" He thought. "But I suppose they may have said, 'Have you met James, my first begotten son. . . .'"

"Of course," Adrian said, "all you know so far is that the translator thinks it's got a translation." The others looked at him. "I mean," he said, a bit defensively, "you can't test it against itself, can you?"

"You're right," said Peter. He squared his shoulders and walked over to the nearest Rustie.

The transporter, a converted grain freighter capable of Mach 5, was parked on the ridge up above, overlooking a deep quarry that had been visible from miles away. Gilmore, not usually given to vertigo, peeped warily over the edge. The Rusties had told them the pit was as deep as the diamond mines at Kimberley in South Africa. Gilmore had never been to Kimberley so the statistic was meaningless, but it was *big*. He held up his aide to record an image of the place for Joel's benefit, and told it to add a scale so the boy would get an idea of the size too.

The tour of the Roving was only a couple of hours old and less than a quarter of the way around the globe from Capital, zig-zagging their way across the main continent from site to site. Now they were deep in the interior, just on the eastern edge of the central desert. It was a relief to be out of the transporter; no doubt it was airworthy enough, but the Rusties' method of flying it was to point it up at about 45 degrees and put on the afterburners, taking an almost ballistic trajectory to their next destination. They were packing in as much of their world as they could in a single day.

The delegates were standing nearby, engaged in conversation with Iron Run and some of the other Rusties. The odd phrase drifted over:

"Naturally, an equitable exploitation of this world's natural resources is foremost on our minds —"

"The Confederation is unparalleled on Earth for its industrial base and its care for the natural environment —"

Blah, blah, blah.

Caterpillar-tracked trucks were climbing labori-

ously up the switchbacked road that led up from
the depths of the pit. Up close they were bulky and
looming but they looked small as beetles below.
Gilmore watched as one made it to the edge and the
flat ground with a sigh of relief from its gears. It
surely couldn't be as efficient as an antigravity device, so why didn't the Rusties use one? Gilmore ran
through the possible limiting factors in his mind
and hit on size. If an a-grav generator, or whatever it
was, were the same size as a truck . . .

"A call from Lieutenant Kirton," said his aide.
Gilmore took it.

"Gilmore," he said.

Peter Kirton seemed slightly dazed, though still
with a look of triumph. "Sir, you remember the
translation program the prince asked me to do?"

"I remember."

"Well, it . . . it works! Sir, it can translate practically anything! I've used it on some of the Rustie by-
standers here and . . . well, I think for the first time
ever I can read a Rustie expression. Very, very surprised."

Gilmore blinked. "Well done," he said. "That's
amazing."

"Not half, sir. It shouldn't work!"

Kirton went into the details of why it shouldn't
work: not enough words in the sample data, and it
had all come together far too quickly. Gilmore listened in silence.

"What now?" he said at the end.

"I'll go through it very carefully, sir. But meanwhile I think the prince should know, sir, but I thought I should go through you." Kirton twitched as though he had just been nudged from off-camera. "That is, Commander Dereshev felt I should, sir."

"Very good," Gilmore said. He glanced up over at the delegates. "The prince is busy right now, but I'll get him to call you when he's free."

The chance didn't come until the transporter was airborne again and they could get out of their seats. The prince looked annoyed.

"Why didn't you tell me earlier?" he snapped, and moved off to one corner of the lounge that was the transporter's main cabin. Gilmore shrugged and watched him take out his aide. He spoke a few words into it, listened, spoke again, listened — and his face turned to thunder. He looked around, then strode towards the washroom at the rear of the cabin. Gilmore saw his expression and decided that, if the prince was talking to one of his crew with a face like that, it was his duty to get involved.

In the washroom the prince was raging. "You . . . you *incompetent!* You *fool*, Kirton! By God, you cretin, I'll have your stripes for this, you bungling, stupid —"

Gilmore snatched the aide from the prince's hand. "That's all, Lieutenant," he said, and broke contact.

The prince's face turned a deeper shade of red. "Stay out of this, Gilmore."

"How dare you talk to one of my crew like that?" Gilmore said sharply. "They are service, you are a civilian and you will damn well keep your temper to yourself."

A sneer spread over the prince's face. "I said, stay out of this. You're captain of your toy ship but I'm —"

"The son of the man who appointed me," Gilmore said. He spoke clearly and slowly, to give the prince the benefit of every word. "You may have his ear, but let me remind you of one or two things. I was appointed directly by him. Not by Parliament, not by the Admiralty, but by the king. I was given full authority in the running of *Ark Royal* and I don't recall you being given any. You have no rank or position within the Royal Space Fleet, Prince, and your threats don't amount to anything."

"I have the rank of Rear Admiral in the Fleet, *Commander* Gilmore." The prince's grin was malicious.

"Then your behaviour is unbecoming your rank," Gilmore said. "Good officers, *sir*, do not scream and swear at subordinates, as you'd know if you'd actually earned that rank, or ever passed an exam in your life."

The prince was still breathing heavily and he held a trembling finger out to Gilmore. "I knew appointing you was a mistake, Gilmore. You're actually taking this seriously, aren't you? You think you're pretty grand. No, I'm the senior on this mission and your blockhead of a software officer —"

"Has just successfully produced the first human translation of the Rustie language. We're talking Nobel prizes here, Prince. We're talking guaranteed tenure in any AI research department the man chooses. We're talking the most amazing prestige for the Fleet and for UK-1. Do you have a problem with that?"

"He tried it on the Rusties!" the prince bellowed.

"Well, of course he did," Gilmore said, actually taken aback for the first time. "He couldn't trust the test set on its own. He had to compare it. That's basic science, Prince. Lieutenant Kirton acted on his own initiative and I back him all the way. My report to the king will endorse everything the lieutenant has done."

James shook his head. "You don't understand, Gilmore, you ass. He —"

"What's the problem, anyway?" Gilmore said. "Presumably you were . . ." He broke off as it finally dawned on him, followed by a wave of contempt. "Oh, of course. I see. He stole your thunder, didn't he? You wanted to be the first! *You* wanted to be the one who would stroll over to Iron Run and address him in his own language. What a coup for us all!"

"Now you're getting the picture, Gilmore," the prince said.

Gilmore shrugged. "So? Lieutenant Kirton is a UK citizen. He was acting on your orders, with data supplied by you, and his program belongs to the

Fleet. And Iron Run hasn't heard of it yet, has he?"
He jerked a thumb at the bulkhead, to indicate the
rest of the transporter. "As far as everyone in there's
concerned, you'll be the first. Walk out of here with
a broad smile on your face, as though everything's
dandy, go up to Iron Run and say whatever clever
phrase you want to go down in the history books."
He studied the prince's stony expression. "Unless
you want a potential triumph ruined by a little
man's petty tantrum," he added.

The prince held out his hand silently for his aide
and Gilmore gave it back. "Get me Kirton," James
said. A pause, then Kirton's voice spoke.

"Kirton?" He managed to make the statement of
his name a question: the aide would have told him
who was calling.

"I owe you an apology, Lieutenant," the prince
said, never taking his gaze off Gilmore. He put as
much inflection into his statement as if he had been
stating that water is wet.

"Ah . . . very good, sir," Kirton said.

"I commend you on your successful program design."

"Ah, actually sir, I —"

"I'd be grateful if you'd download a copy to my
aide. Now."

"Very good, sir," Kirton said again. "Coming
through." A pause of a couple of seconds. "You have
it, sir. File name 'polyglot,' password whatever you
choose."

"Thank you. Where is the original?"

"On the ship, sir."

"Secure it and delete your own copy from your aide. This is a very valuable asset. Out," said the prince. He flipped the aide shut without waiting for a reply. "Happy, Captain?"

Gilmore stood aside without answering and indicated that the prince should precede him out of the room. To join the others, to speak to Iron Run and to go down in history, however inaccurately, as the first human to speak to the First Breed through a human-made translator.

But if Kirton wasn't happy with Polyglot's suddenly perfect performance then Gilmore wasn't happy either, and he was going to get to the bottom of it.

Thirteen
19–20 May 2149

"That is one angry prince," said Adrian thoughtfully. Peter was still pale.

"Do . . . do you think he meant it?" Peter said. "About my career —"

The aide spoke. "Call from —" Peter tensed "—Captain Gilmore."

"Oh." Peter sighed in relief and took the call. "Yes, sir?"

Gilmore's expression was cold. "I'm sorry about that, Lieutenant. Ignore his threats — he can't touch you, I'll make sure of that. I'm commending you in my report."

"Thank you, sir. But there's still —"

"I know," Gilmore said. "What do you suggest?"

Peter realized, with relief, that Gilmore believed him. Peter was the software expert and in that area the captain was willing to be guided by his opinion alone.

"I'll pursue my own investigations, sir," he said. "I'll report directly to you, if I may."

"Agreed. Out."

Peter looked up at the others. Hannah looked thoughtful, Samad and Adrian puzzled. "You'll have to excuse me," he said, his mind already filling up with images of *Ark Royal*'s systems and the tests he was going to have to run. "I'm going back to the Dome."

There was silence in the lounge of the transporter. Fifty humans and several Rusties were looking at the tableau made by the prince, aide in hand, and Iron Run, standing facing him. Gilmore saw what Peter had meant by being able to read Rustie surprise.

After a long pause, Iron Run spoke to his mouthtalker.

"Iron Run congratulates you," the other Rustie said. "It enquires how you achieved this."

Prince James was basking in the respect of the Rusties and the envy of the other humans. "Data for this program, Polyglot, was compiled from recordings of the natural speech of the First Breed delegation to Earth, and from their own translations," he said. "The program was prepared by Lieutenant Peter Kirton, the software officer on the UK's ship *Ark Royal*. Captain Gilmore's ship."

The prince indicated Gilmore but only the Rusties looked over at him. The other humans were looking at the aide and, one by one, realizing just how great a coup the prince had just pulled. As well as kudos for the UK's software talent, whoever had Polyglot would be able to conduct their own negotiations with the Rusties — regardless of who won the bid.

"Captain Gilmore." As usual, Arm Wild was beside

him. "Your upper limbs are crossed, one corner of your mouth is inclined slightly upwards, and your head is in motion from side to side around your vertical axis. Forgive me, but this is a stance I have learned to equate with amused disbelief in your species."

Gilmore quickly uncrossed his arms and straightened up. "If you want to learn human body language," he said, "look at that lot."

"What will I see?"

"Naked greed."

"How interesting."

The prince's cabal were gathered together, awaiting a moment to be alone with their colleague. When he and Iron Run had finally finished speaking, the prince turned away and they intercepted him before any of the other humans had a chance. James had his own arms folded and he held his head high: every now and then he would nod or shake his head or say something brief.

The tables had suddenly turned. Prince James had been the poor man of that little clique, his membership based on pure expedience and his father's clout back home. Even *Ark Royal*'s armaments were a minimal contribution to what the other ships could offer. But now . . . now the others were coming cap in hand to him, and he could name his price.

"Caution," said the aide. "The limited memory capacity of this unit will greatly increase the time taken for your program to execute."

Sitting in his cramped little room in the Dome, Peter Kirton thought wistfully of the vistas of memory space up on the ship. "Execute," he said.

"Complying."

A long-range diagnostic of the entire ship's systems, conducted through an aide on a signal that bounced around the Roving's communication network . . . it was going to take hours.

On the way back to the Dome, he had had time to think. Polyglot's output was too perfect and three possible reasons came to mind: Someone had substituted the program's output with their own; someone had rewritten the neural net that generated it; or someone had substituted the *input* data that the neural net filtered.

All seemed equally unlikely and it came perilously close to being just a problem to be solved out of intellectual curiosity, but for one thing: Peter Kirton was convinced that some entity had got into *Ark Royal*'s net undetected and tampered with his program, and that made it personal. He would leave the whys and wherefores until later: *who* was most important now.

But entities capable of interfering seamlessly with other people's programs didn't just appear out of nowhere. They had to know precisely what they were doing, which meant being familiar with the style of the person who had written the program in the first place, and they also had to be *in situ*. Peter could only think of one entity fitting this description.

Thankful for multitasking, Peter picked up his aide and called Gilmore, to ask permission to return to the ship.

Julia Coyne slowly reached out a finger to the display that glowed in front of her over the watch desk on *Ark Royal*'s flight deck. It was divided into a grid of eight squares, and her finger hovered over a symbol in one of them.

She touched it, then touched another blank square.

"Knight to king five. Checkmate in fourteen," said Plantagenet.

"Rats." Julia touched another square.

"Checkmate in nine," said the prince's AI. "Strictly speaking, Lieutenant, once you have made your initial move you cannot undo it. When playing with real pieces, a player is committed if she removes her hand."

"I'm not surprised," Julia said. "Anyway, who's the human?"

"You are."

"Thank you." Julia repeated her initial manoeuvre: she didn't doubt it would be checkmate in fourteen but at least it gave her slightly more of a chance of finding a way out. Some way. Any way.

The game was going the same way as the last seven, when suddenly the collision alarm sounded and everything else was forgotten.

"Show emergency."

A schematic of the delegation fleet orbiting around the Roving appeared over the board, and the nature of the emergency wasn't difficult to spot: four ships were all converging on *Ark Royal*. Just as she was opening her mouth to demand thruster control and an audio link, the readouts by the four ship icons changed. They were no longer moving but they had undeniably changed position. They were the Americans' *Enterprise*, the Russians' *Nikolai*, the Euros' *Bruxelles* and Starward's *Algol*, and they were now above, below and to either side of *Ark Royal*, enclosing the smaller ship like a shell.

"Who's the most senior captain of the four ships that have just moved?" she demanded.

"Based on length of service, Captain Andrew McLaughlin of the *Enterprise* has seniority by four months," the ship said.

"Get me a link to *Enterprise*," she said.

A moment later a man's voice spoke: "This is *Enterprise*, First Officer Davis. Captain McLaughlin is on the planet's surface. How may I help, *Ark Royal*?"

"Coyne, officer of the watch. What the hell are you lot playing at?"

"Sorry, *Ark Royal*." The American sounded genuinely surprised. "We received orders to move in around you."

"Without asking?"

"Hey, space is free, *Ark Royal*! We're not within your blast distance, are we?"

In other words, because the ships hadn't come so close to *Ark Royal* that it would be unable to fire its main engine, they had simply repositioned themselves without letting *Ark Royal* know — as they had every right to do.

"*Ark Royal* out," Julia said ungraciously, and called her own captain.

"Wait there," he said when she had explained the situation, and his image was replaced with a red glowing "Hold." He reappeared after a minute, looking furious. "Communications breakdown, Lieutenant," he said. "*Ark Royal* has some valuable property on board and the prince's allies want to safeguard it. I'm sorry you weren't told. I'm sorry I wasn't told."

"Are you sure they're allies, sir?" Julia said, glancing again at the orbit schematic. It really did look quite menacing. Purely tacit, but the menace was there.

One corner of the captain's mouth twitched in a vague smile. "So I'm told," he said. "The prince says, ask Plantagenet to show you the file 'tontine' from his archives. It's authorized for the most senior officer on board and the other ships all have copies, too. I'm sorry I'm not there, Lieutenant."

"No problem, sir," Julia said. There very definitely was a problem, but neither of them could do anything about it. "*Ark Royal* out. Plantagenet, what is file 'tontine'?"

Plantagenet spoke for the first time since the game of chess. "File 'tontine' is an agreement between Prince James and the delegates for Starward, the North American Federation, the European Union and the United Slavic Federation. In summary, it says that if any of the above wins the bid for the Roving, the other four will receive preferential terms. It also incorporates a mutual defence pact, to the extent that their five ships will form a single defensive unit if necessary, and that if one ship is imperilled, all the others will come to its aid. The defensive unit will be commanded by the most senior officer on board a ship present."

"Well, nice of them to let us know," Julia said. She let her mind linger on the implication that *Ark Royal* was, or might be, imperilled.

"We are being hailed by the landing boat from *Christopher*," said the ship.

In all the excitement, Julia had almost forgotten her relief was due. "At last," she muttered. She pushed herself over to the command desk. "*Ark Royal* here."

"*Loyola*, tender to *Christopher*," said a voice. "We have your relief on board. Request permission to dock."

"Granted, *Loyola*. Please come to the for'a'rd lock. I'll put the beacon on for you."

"Thank you, *Ark Royal*. *Loyola* out."

Five minutes later came the clunking noise of a

ship docking, and Julia airswam for'a'rd. The green
light glowed on the lock door to show pressures
equalized. When it opened, Hannah and Adrian
were waiting on the other side.

"Permission to come on board?" Hannah said.

"Granted. Come in, Hannah, Ade . . . Pete!" Julia
had just seen Peter Kirton waiting behind them.

Peter looked preoccupied as he pushed himself
into *Ark Royal* behind the others. "There's work
I've got to do," he said.

"It's a long story," Hannah added.

One of *Christopher*'s crew waited behind Peter,
not coming on board. "Do you need a return trip?"
the man called.

"Um . . . yes," Julia said. "Thanks. Wait — I'll get
my things."

"Five minutes, *Ark Royal*."

"No problem." Julia went back to the flight deck.
Peter had pulled himself into the chair at the
watch desk and had seen the display. "Chess?
Who're you playing with?" he said.

"Plantagenet." Julia was surprised to see Peter
frown slightly.

"Is he any good?"

Julia shrugged. "Not bad. He's won a few."

"Hmm."

"Something you want to tell us, Lieutenant?" Hannah asked.

Julia started. "Oh — you have the watch, sir."

"I have the watch," Hannah said. The formula absolved Julia of responsibility for the ship from that moment on. "Anything to report?"

"Standard orbital correction at 0647," Julia said, "and one other thing." She told them about the sudden maneuver of the other ships. "Apparently we've got something important on board?"

"We have," Hannah said.

Peter sat at his desk. He had already forgotten the presence of the other two.

"Would you like to complete Lieutenant Coyne's game?" Plantagenet asked.

"No thanks," Peter said. "I'm going to run some tests on the ship's systems."

"Can I help you?"

"I'll let you know, thank you, Plantagenet."

"Very well."

Peter took his goggles from his toolbox and slipped them on. *Ark Royal*'s internal net appeared virtually around him: systems, pathways and programs in a familiar pattern that he himself had designed.

Here, Plantagenet's icon was dynamic and large. It hung right next to him in virtual space; the AI was either feeling friendly or keeping an eye on him. To be charitable, Peter had to remember that Plantagenet was the most high-level intelligence in the ship's net, by several degrees. Even AIs could get lonely and instinctively seek company.

Peter moved in virtual space to the personal

memory lockers of the crew and the ship's passengers. The eight cubes floated in a circle around him, each marked with the identity of its owner. Six of them had a few items in them, Arm Wild's was empty and his own was overflowing.

He expanded his locker until it filled his vision. "Polyglot," he said. The locker's contents faded away except for one — a cluster of smaller cubes linked by lines.

"Amplify," he said. The cubes grew larger in his vision and he studied each one closely.

On the left was the input data provided by the prince. He called up the specs of the file that he had recorded when the prince handed it over. Exactly the same: same size, same date, same composition. Untampered with.

In the middle was the neural net constructed to make sense of it all. The net would have altered itself as it did its work; he would have to run it through the analyzer to see just what it had done.

The output file was to the right; the distillate of the input data after it had passed through the neural net. There was nothing to compare it with — the best he could do was see whether, given the input data and the net as it now stood, its results were what *should* have been produced.

The next step was to check up on his prime suspect.

He took the goggles off again and let the flight deck come back into proper focus. Then he got up and went to his cabin. From a real locker he took a crystal chip and inserted it in his aide; the title page of the *Register of Artificial Sentience (Digital), 2146* appeared on the display. The ship's library had its own copy — in fact, it had the more up-to-date version published that year — but this version was only three years old and Peter didn't want the subject of his enquiries to know what he was doing. Plantagenet was over three years old, anyway.

There were AIs, and there were AIs, and then there were AIs.

At the bottom of the ladder were the semi-sentients; the moronic systems that ran *Ark Royal*. Each dedicated to one job, their idea of happiness was to while away their existence monitoring the ship's engines, or waste disposal, or one of the myriad other systems on board.

Then there were the sentients, such as those found in every aide, or like the interface to the ship's systems on the flight deck. Self-aware in a vague sort of way and able to hold a conversation, within limits. They were kept on a rein; it was enough that the aide understood typical loose, muddled human conversation and answered when you spoke, but having it answer you *back* would be too much and possibly even dangerous. So, the paths their thoughts could take were heavily circumscribed, either by humans — or by those AIs at the top of the ladder, the high-level sentients, like Plantagenet. The closest thing the electronic world had to human minds; all-rounders, able to apply themselves to a number of tasks. Able to argue and contradict and form their own characters and opinions. Legally almost the same as human beings, with very similar rights and privileges and obligations to one another.

All the AIs on board *Ark Royal* had been plugged into the ship by Peter himself, but not before he had carefully scanned their ROM, and Peter had kept records of those scans. If Plantagenet had been altered in any way since his creation — for example, giving him the ability to interfere tracelessly with an advanced neural network linguistic translation program — then those differences would be found by comparing his ROM when he came on board, with his ROM when he was first created, as noted in the *Register*.

Peter wasn't used to going through data using just the aide's keys, but if he said anything out loud, Plantagenet might overhear. It took a couple of minutes to get down to Plantagenet's specs.

Plantagenet had been activated in 2143, one of a series of high-level AIs designed specially for King Richard and his household. He had been a personal assistant to Prince James for all his existence and had been rewarded with occasional upgrades over and above other members of the Dynasty class.

The primary function of the entire class had been data manipulation. They weren't dedicated to any particular item of hardware — they were meant to hang around the net of UK-1, one day doing this, one day doing that, as their duties called for. They were very high-level — the state of 2143's art — and needed to be, when their duties might range from making a cup of coffee to helping out in UK-1's fusion compartment.

The recording showed that Plantagenet had changed since this edition of the *Register* was published, but the changes were well within the expected range allowed by growth and experience. But there was one thing — a small upgrade to Plantagenet's memory. Just a few extra lines of code that could have been anything. It wasn't immediately obvious what they were for; all Peter had noticed at the time of the examination was that they presented no threat and weren't going to breed viruses. The upgrade was like a human's appendix — Plantagenet could have functioned just as well with or without it.

Peter had often met AIs with unattributable accessories attached — generally homegrown AIs, upgraded by their patrons as an experiment, or for some long-forgotten and now obsolete purpose. Yet he didn't think a class as . . . well, classy as the Dynasty lot would have such rough-and-ready modifications.

"Ah," he said, as he remembered. Plantagenet had had one *very* significant upgrade to his code — he now contained the targeting software for the ship's weapons. Yes, this could well be it.

He took a copy of the upgrade and set his aide to go through the rest of the *Register*. If it found another code section like it, it was to record the fact silently. Peter would come back to it to see if it had found anything.

"Back to work," Peter said out loud. All he had done was gather circumstantial evidence, perhaps in subconscious rebellion against the real work that was coming up. He was going to have to go into the net again and go over Polyglot, line by line, neuron by neuron. And then he was going to finish what he had started doing down in the Dome — going over the entire ship's systems with a fine-tooth comb. Yuk.

A hand was shaking his shoulder. He toggled the goggle display to transparent and looked up through a blur.

"Ade? What is it?" he said.

"What do you mean, what is it?" said Adrian. "Samad's here, Pete. You're on watch with him."

"Hmm?" Peter's eyes focused past Adrian's shoulder. Samad Loonat was standing there, looking at him askance.

"Are you all right?" Samad asked.

Peter took the goggles off and rubbed his eyes. "Yeah. Yeah, I think so."

Samad looked at Hannah. "I have the watch."

"You have the watch," she said. "And my advice in

handing over is to order this man to bed. He's been awake all the time we've been here."

Peter glanced at the chronometer but Adrian's interruption had broken his concentration and let down his internal adrenaline barriers. Now fatigue was rushing in. When he eventually focused, it told him he had indeed been awake for the entire twenty-four-hour watch — and, of course, some hours before that too.

"Have you finished? Did you find what you were after?" Samad said.

"Not yet, but I've set the wheels in motion." Peter had created a set of software-based semisentients that were poking about in the guts of the ship for him, constantly updating and comparing themselves. The least, the tiniest interference from outside, and they would sound the alarm direct to his aide. Plantagenet might be able to see what they were doing but would not be able to stop them without him knowing.

"Then you heard the lady. Bed."

Peter grinned, now having to keep his eyes open. "Thank you, sir," he said as he left the flight deck.

Fourteen
21 May 2149

The suit tautened around Peter as the air left the lock. He checked his tether was secured to the ship and moved cautiously out, the grips on his soles reacting with *Ark Royal*'s ferro-polymer skin, and holding him to it. Behind him sat the laser turret at the ship's bow and, beyond that, the long drop into nothingness. In front of him the circular wall of the centrifuge ring.

He made his way, step by clinging step, down the hull to the ring, then up between the heat fins to the edge of the ring and the ship's laser-comms array. Standing on the edge was like standing on top of a high mountain with all creation spread out around him: the manifest evidence of the heavens declaring God's glory.

Peter looked around and his eyes fixed on another ship. Letters appeared on the inside of his faceplate to tell him it was the Euro ship *Bruxelles*. He switched off the open band communicator on his suit and knelt down, plugging his suit into the array at his feet. A beam of coherent light speared invisibly out towards the Euro ship.

"Connection made," said his suit. Peter Kirton was back in contact with the communication web that the visiting humans had spun around the Roving, and from here, Plantagenet couldn't tap in.

"Call Captain Gilmore," he said.

Gilmore took the call in his cubicle in the Dome and listened as Peter explained the situation.

"What you're saying, lieutenant," Gilmore said slowly, "is that an item of software on board *Ark Royal* has interfered with an autonomous program that you were running."

"Um — yes, sir," Peter said. "It was definitely Plantagenet. The extra code in his ROM has that capability, as well as the targeting software, and now that I know what to look for . . . yes, sir, it was definitely, positively him."

There was a pause. The connection was audio only and Peter tried to imagine the captain's expression. Would it be stony? Angry? Or was the captain silently leaping around his cubicle, gleeful that Prince James was implicated in this matter? He doubted the latter but it was a nice image.

If Gilmore was gleeful then his voice hid it well. "In that case," he said, "under the Software Act of 2097, as incorporated into . . . what is it . . . hold on, got it, Clause 1071 of the Space Treaty, I am ordering you to take whatever action necessary to neutralize Plantagenet, up to and including destroying him, if necessary. Let me know when it's done."

Peter passed the connector back to Adrian, then slowly pulled himself out of the innards of *Ark Royal*'s computer centre, nestled inside the centrifuge ring compartment.

"Done it?" Adrian whispered. He had taken Peter's warning about secrecy to heart and the fact that Plantagenet could simply have turned up the gain of the nearest audio pickup to hear them had escaped him.

"Yes, that should do the trick," Peter said loudly. He took the goggles from his belt and slipped them over his eyes, and the ship's network appeared all around him again in three dimensions.

The hardware additions he had been making to the network were there too, represented as a sphere of blocks surrounding a few core subroutines. Lesser, semisentient AIs were passing around and one of them wandered a bit too close to the sphere. Peter waved it away quickly.

"Plantagenet, could you lend me a hand?" he said.

"Certainly, Peter." The AI's icon appeared next to him. "What would you like me to do?"

Peter indicated the area inside the sphere. "I've changed some of the configurations here."

"You appear to have added some new hardware."

"That's right. The memory processing in this sector has been sub-optimal and I thought the new modules might help."

"I wasn't aware of any problems."

Peter stopped himself from going into yet more detail. Lying wasn't an art he had been encouraged to develop on Mars, but he thought he had a sufficient grasp of it to know that the less specific you were, the better.

"Your duties don't include monitoring the network, do they?" he said.

"A good point," Plantagenet said. "What would you like me to do?"

"Go in and give me your impression. You're the highest level AI on board so if there's anything suboptimal, you'll feel it and come straight out."

"An analogy would be to send a human into a compartment with faulty environmental control and ask if he has difficulty breathing," Plantagenet said sniffily "But if it helps the ship —"

"Thank you," said Peter. Out in the real world he lifted a hand slowly.

"Complying," said Plantagenet. Peter held his breath as the AI moved into the central space, passing between two of the modules that formed the sphere. "It seems to work —"

Peter's hand came down. At the signal, Adrian closed a contact and the final module came online, appearing in the space that Plantagenet had passed through. The AI was trapped in a circle of low-band-rate components, too low for such a memory-hungry program as Plantagenet, and he wouldn't be able to pass out through them without suffering severe loss of function.

"Yes, I see no problem with memory processing here," Plantagenet said. Peter bit his lip as the AI came up to the barrier of components, paused a moment, then passed effortlessly across. "No problem at all."

Plantagenet paused while Peter stared at him, then: "That component was not there a moment ago." Another pause. "This entire setup could almost have been devised to entrap me. How peculiar. Did you know about this, Mr. Kirton?"

"I —" said Peter.

"And yet, why would you have done so?" Plantagenet said calmly. "Computing. You have the authority on this ship to do so, but you have no reason to do it of your own initiative. Therefore, you have received orders to that effect. Accessing communication log: No, you have had no contact with the two most senior officers of this ship and I have not heard Lieutenant Loonat issue such an order. Accessing systems log: You engaged in extravehicular activity earlier today and *Ark Royal*'s laser array was utilized externally. I deduce it was at that time that you received your orders. What are they?"

Peter saw no point in bluffing. "The captain wants you confined, Plantagenet." Samad and Adrian would be monitoring the conversation and, he hoped, frantically working out how Plantagenet had got out without any effort.

"Whatever for? Is he unhappy with my performance?"

"Because I told him you tampered with Polyglot."

"I see," Plantagenet said. Peter waited for him to make a further comment but realized Plantagenet had said all he intended to say.

"Why did you?" Peter said.

"I am unable to comment."

"In my capacity as software officer, I order you to tell me."

"I'm sorry, Peter, I can't do that." While Peter was thinking of a response, anything to keep Plantagenet talking, the AI added: "Those diagnostics your companions are running will not spot what is wrong. Your trap was elegantly constructed and would have worked on any other AI, but the ship's hardware is configured especially for me and that is why you won't be able to use it against me. I can go anywhere I like in the ship's system and do whatever I wish there."

Plantagenet gave Peter a moment to imagine what he could do if he got annoyed. Then he added:

"However, I am not a virus and I wish you no harm. If you simply leave me alone then we can co-exist quite happily."

"I've got orders to restrain you," Peter said through clenched teeth.

"And I cannot let you do that. I am important to this mission and this mission is too important for me to allow you to jeopardize it."

Peter waited a moment, then pulled the goggles off with an angry gesture.

"He was right about the hardware," Samad said, out in the real world. "I checked."

"How could that happen?" Peter demanded.

"The same way the ship could handle the extra

mass of the torpedoes without our noticing. The extra capacity was hardwired in from the bottom up, and short of shutting it down completely, which will work against our own interests slightly, we can't affect Plantagenet in any way. There's no way you could have spotted it with your software checks and I just tried to check the components supplied against the specs of the manufacturer. But of course, since the manufacturer was supplied by the king —"

"I'm not going to be outwitted," Peter shouted, "in my own network by a b —"

Adrian and Samad looked at him in expectation. Adrian was grinning and Samad had an eyebrow raised.

"Blasted AI," Peter said, more quietly. He put his hands to his head and ran Samad's words by himself again. Then he took out his aide, typed a query on the display and held it up for Samad to see, making sure no optical pickup was in line of sight of the text.

Now both Samad's eyebrows went up. "No," he said, "it wasn't."

Peter grinned suddenly. "That locker behind you," he said. "Pass me what's in it."

What was in it was an AI transit unit — the same one in which Plantagenet had originally come on board. Peter clipped it to his belt and started to type out further instructions on his aide.

Another ten minutes, and Adrian and Peter were in *Sharman*'s cockpit. Samad was still at the computer nexus inside the ring compartment, his hands poised over the controls.

"Ready," said Peter's voice over his aide, and Samad's hands moved.

At the bow and the stern, the lights faded and went out. After a moment the red emergency lighting came on, giving an eerie glow that was made worse by the sudden silence: the background hum of the air-conditioning was off too. Samad had shut down all systems in the for'a'rd and aft compartments.

His hands continued to move . . .

Death came silently to *Ark Royal*'s systems, a creeping wave of zero power that moved in from the bow and the stern and crept towards midships. Samad was at the heart of the ship with his hands physically on the hardware and nothing could interfere with what he was doing.

"This is inadvisable," said Plantagenet over their aides. "You are bluffing."

"We're shutting down the entire ship," Peter said. "You can't hide then."

"By your own laws, that will be murder. I am a legally protected entity."

"I say you're a threat to the ship," Peter said, "and I can take what measures I like."

"Ninety percent shut down," said Samad, "and increasing. Shutting down central sections now."

He was literally pulling the plug. A moment more and the processing power left on board *Ark Royal* wouldn't be able to run a twentieth-century desktop computer, much less contain an entity like Plantagenet. *Ark Royal*'s native semisentient AIs would retreat to their ROM crystals but Plantagenet . . .

"You will not continue." It was Plantagenet again: not an order but an optimistic statement of fact. The AI was speaking more slowly, more deliberately as it spread its processing more and more thinly over ever-decreasing resources. "This is . . . pointless. The ship is . . . suffering as . . . much as . . . I by . . . your actions."

The next statement was precise and cogent again. It was a standard error message embedded in Plantagenet's code.

"Caution: I am unable to function adequately in this environment. I am closing down all nonessential processing functions."

Then:

"Please. Turn. The. Systems. On. Again."

Another pause, then:

"Please."

Peter shut his eyes and hoped. Hoped Plantagenet was bright enough to take the one route out still left to him, because the AI was absolutely right: if this went wrong then he, Peter Kirton, proud puritan son of Mars, could be tried for murder. Outside, through the cockpit windows, he saw the lights dim and go out. *Ark Royal* was a dead ship.

The LEDs on the transit unit, which was plugged into the pilot's console on *Sharman*, danced into life. Adrian gave a triumphant shout as Peter swiftly unplugged the unit. The LEDs continued to flicker.

"Very clever," said Plantagenet's voice through the unit's speaker. "I congratulate you. I hope you realize how seriously you have endangered this mission."

"I take it it worked?" Samad's voice said.

"You bet it did!" Adrian shouted. "Brilliant, Pete. Brilliant."

"Thank God for that," Samad said. "I'm restoring power now, before we start to tumble."

With the ship's systems shutting down around him, Plantagenet had been driven by sheer self-preservation into the one place that could still take him: *Sharman*'s memory systems. And as Samad had confirmed to Peter's written question, *Sharman* had not been modified in any way for this mission: it had simply been purchased from its makers by the Royal Space Fleet. It still had its original design and it was an entirely separate system from *Ark Royal*. Peter had been able to channel Plantagenet, via *Sharman*, into the transit unit, and now he was trapped there.

"I've got to report to the captain," Peter said, as outside in the boat bay the lights came on again, and life returned to the ship. It did nothing for the cold, dark feeling inside him.

Fifteen
21 May 2149

It was Day Four on the Roving. The second day of deliberation allowed to the human delegates before the Convocation met. The delegates did most of the deliberating in small groups in the Dome's spacious gardens, making the most of the good weather.

Prince James sat alone at a table, working at his speech on his aide. A shadow fell over him and he looked up at Michael Gilmore. James suppressed the inward groan he felt at the sight. The other delegates he could handle: they were all politicians; they all expected the cut and thrust and give and take that were part of normal life, and they knew what to expect from each other. Gilmore was so simplistic in his worldview that James often didn't know how to cope.

"May I speak to you alone, sir?" Gilmore said.

James decided to let his annoyance show, just a little. He still remembered the incident in the transporter's washroom when Gilmore had prevented him from giving Kirton the lashing the man deserved, and James hadn't quite forgiven that yet. "Later, Cap —"

"Now, sir," Gilmore said.

Prince James braced himself. After all, it might actually be important. "Very well. What is it, and make it quick."

Was there a tiny smile on Gilmore's face? James began to feel uneasy.

"Mr. Kirton," Gilmore said, "has firmly established that your AI, Plantagenet," — did he emphasise the *your*, just a little? James pricked up his ears — "has interfered with an autonomous program that he had constructed. I have therefore invoked the Software Act and instructed him to neutralize Plantagenet."

The world seemed to fall away from under James' feet. "You can't!"

"I have, sir."

"You . . . you . . ." James forced himself to collect his thoughts. "What is the program in question?"

"Polyglot."

"*Polyglot?*"

"Mr. Kirton felt the program's output was too perfect, he investigated and found signs of tampering."

"Polyglot," James said again while he marshalled his thoughts. His first reaction was, *well, of course Plantagenet interfered, you cretin — do you think you'd have a Polyglot if he hadn't?* But he couldn't — yet — say as much. "Captain, think of this . . . think of this logically." Once more, yet again, with his consummate ease, Gilmore was getting under his skin. James cursed himself that he could handle other people so coolly and yet, the moment Gilmore opened his mouth, all his smooth, polished sentences went to hell. Again he made himself calm down. "And what's Plantagenet supposed to have done? His tampering created a perfect Rustie trans-

lator. Now, is that possible? Where would Plantagenet have got that information from, eh? I will concede your lieutenant's expertise and accept that
circumstantial evidence may point to my AI, but —"

"Mr. Kirton is aware of all that," Gilmore said. "It
may be that Plantagenet just poked around in his
program and had a look. Maybe he tweaked it a bit
out of generosity, making it more efficient. The fact
is, he did so without authorization, and I will not
have an AI that can behave in such a manner on my
ship."

"You and your ship," James said. The man really
was a monomaniac! But now, James felt he had the
situation under control. Surely Gilmore had to cede
the logic of the situation; not knowing what Plantagenet knew, there was no way he could conclu-
sively blame Polyglot's remarkable performance on
the AI. He reached for his aide. "This is absurd,
Gilmore. I'm calling Plantagenet."

He stopped and looked down at his wrist.
Gilmore's hand was clasped about it, preventing
him from unclipping the aide from his belt. The
anger that Gilmore always seemed to kindle in him,
blazed into a white fury and then surpassed even
that. It was so intense that, paradoxically, it came
out as a mild, conversational sincerity.

"Captain, you are interfering," he said. This, this
was a thousand times worse than the washroom incident.

"Plantagenet has already been neutralized, sir," Gilmore said.

James felt the blood roar in his ears. "You're finished, Gilmore," he said. "You had no right, and I'll —"

"If you wish to protest, I suggest we call in the fleet commodore," Gilmore said, letting go. "We can each present our sides of the story and she can arbitrate."

Whomp. James knew he had walked straight into Gilmore's hands.

"Don't be a fool," he said, while he tried to think of something else to say. How like the man — never one to bother with talk, with discussion and moderation — he goes straight for the biggest guns he has.

"The first fact to come out," Gilmore continued, "will be that you are interfering with my command of my ship, Prince. And for that reason, you won't find a single sympathetic ear."

And James had to admit that Gilmore's biggest guns outweighed anything he had on his side — for the moment. He held Gilmore's gaze only for a moment more, but it felt much longer. "Is there anything else, Captain?"

Gilmore didn't change his expression. "That's all, sir," he said.

James turned and walked away. After ten feet he stopped and looked back. He couldn't resist the parting shot.

"Enjoy your command while you still have it, Captain," he said.

Peter was on the flight deck when the call came. The comms display in front of him showed the captain's features.

"Ah, Mr. Kirton," said Gilmore. "Let the others know I'm coming up, will you? It's about time I did my bit like everyone else."

"You're definitely coming up, sir?" Peter said.

"Oh, yes." A flash of understanding passed between them. Peter knew that the prince's insistence on having Gilmore by his side had prevented Gilmore from standing his watch on previous occasions, but now the captain was cruising on his victory and the world was a sunnier place.

Gilmore must have been in a good mood because he made a joke. "You don't have to look delighted at the news, Lieutenant."

"Oh. Sorry, sir." Peter shook himself out of it and wondered where the darkness within him was coming from.

Gilmore's eyes were shrewd but his tone was kind as he diagnosed the situation. "You had to hurt Plantagenet to make him comply. It was the first time you've ever had to be ruthless and it's shaken you up. You never knew you had it in you and you haven't come to terms with it yet."

Peter looked at him, amazed. "Um, yes, sir. That's exactly it."

"It comes to us all. My advice is to come downstairs. See the world. Most important, get away from the ship and Plantagenet for a while. God knows there's not much to see here in the Dome but you can still get out and about."

"Thank you, sir. I'll do that," Peter said, as a plan he had half formed a while ago finally turned into resolve. "I'll definitely do that."

"Your Royal Highness?"

Will I never get any peace? James thought. He looked up from the draft of his speech into a round, beaming face. He carefully did not shudder because he knew what lay behind that smile — a luxury not afforded to the many people who had badly underestimated R.V. Krishnamurthy in the early stages of his career. It was the same feeling James had when watching old footage of monsters like Hitler or Stalin or Ben Gael. Friendly, smiling, avuncular; patting children and plotting genocide.

Krishnamurthy sat down opposite him without invitation and James casually blanked the display of his aide. "May I help you?" he said.

The delegate for the Confederation kept his smile going. He rarely showed his teeth when smiling but again, James knew they were there. "I may help you, your Royal Highness."

"You really don't have to call me that."

"Old habits, old habits." Krishnamurthy shrugged. "Your Royal Highness, it is no secret that we here on

the Roving fall broadly into two camps. Put collo-
quially, your lot and my lot. While you just belong to
your lot, I lead my lot." The smile, impossibly,
widened. "I would like to invite the UK to join my
lot."

James smiled, coldly, back. "The UK is very happy
with my lot."

"Let us be blunt. In your lot the UK is . . . small
beer."

"Very small beer," James agreed. "I really don't
think we have anything to add to your lot."

Krishnamurthy leaned forward and for a moment
his intensity slipped through the smile. "Wrong,
Windsor. You have Polyglot."

James sighed. He didn't believe in coincidences.
"You must be psychic, Mr. Krishnamurthy. Do you
know, I was discussing this matter with my colleagues earlier and I could have sworn we'd taken
all reasonable antibugging precautions." This would
be worth bearing in mind in future and he idly
tapped a reminder into his aide.

"And you displayed, if I may say so, a very dog-in-
the-manger attitude, Prince James." James had res-
olutely refused to hand Polyglot over to anyone, and
that was that. Polyglot gave independence. Whoever owned it could deal with the Rusties without
going through whoever won the bid; they could
even deal with different factions of Rusties, if such
proved to exist. James had no intention of giving
that power to anyone else.

"Since you're so familiar with my reasoning, I don't intend to repeat myself," he said.

"Listen." Krishnamurthy leaned forward again. "Let us assume, for the sake of argument, that one of your consortium wins the bid. Then what happens? Favours are distributed amongst yourselves, naturally. Europe, the Russians and the Americans will probably be in charge of ground-based affairs. They are used to handling large populations and territories and resources. Starward will without a doubt be put in charge of the space lanes between here and Earth. Very lucrative. The UK . . . well, I suppose they could handle intraorbital affairs, if they put their minds to it. Scheduling reentry windows, cleaning up space junk, that sort of thing. The others will probably allow you that much. Nothing for any of the other parties here on the Roving, of course, and certainly not for poor little us."

"Little?" said James, thinking of the empire, in all but name, that spread from Afghanistan down to Burma, which Krishnamurthy had helped to unite.

"A figure of speech. The fact is, I can offer better than that."

"Such as?"

"What Starward is after. Complete control of the space lanes. A monopoly on transit between our solar systems. Full responsibility for space research, for combining our space fleets, for mounting expeditions to other stars. All that, Windsor, if you let me have Polyglot."

James remembered a passage of scripture from childhood lessons. The Devil offering Jesus the whole world — if he would just fall down and worship.

He shrugged. "Sadly, I no longer have it. I've erased my copy and the original is on *Ark Royal*. You'd need Kirton to unlock it for you."

"And Kirton is on *Ark Royal* and *Ark Royal* is surrounded by your allies in a very efficient blockade."

"Do you know, I believe you're right." James threw his hands into the air. "Well, that takes care of that, then."

"Don't be a fool! I'll try one more time, Windsor. What exactly is it that you think you'd be inheriting if you or your friends won the bid? You don't know half of what I know about the Rusties."

James raised his eyebrows. This should be interesting. "Go on," he said.

"Their society is moribund. A dead end. It was so obvious on the tour but I doubt you noticed it because you were too busy showing off to Iron Run with Polyglot. But I had observers with me, Windsor. Watching, observing."

"As observers do."

"And I've gone over the information they've provided very, very closely, and I have concluded — the Rusties are stagnant, Windsor! They are a society going through the motions because that's how it's always been done."

"This world invented step-through before we did," James said.

"Something has gone wrong since then."

"Like what?"

"I don't know." Krishnamurthy gestured angrily. "Cultural decline. Spiritual malaise. Lack of foresight. But they are producing nothing fresh, nothing original. Since they invented step-through there hasn't been a single new invention on this world! It's all there, if you know where to look; they haven't been hiding anything. Do you know what they want, Windsor? One word: leadership. I believe that they are stuck in a rut. They require a strong hand to motivate them, to guide them. A strong hand such that we can provide. Your lot run companies or are representatives of nations that were once superpowers but now . . . declining, failing. Has-beens. But look at us. Since your country left us alone we have gone from strength to strength. We are the future and we deserve the Rusties just as much as the Rusties deserve us. And you can be a part of this too, if you will *just let me have Polyglot*."

Inside, James was laughing. Poor Krishnamurthy — so near and yet so far. But now he had had as much of the man's proximity as he could take, and he decided to end the conversation.

"Mr. Krishnamurthy, who authorized the use of tactical nuclear force against Rangoon?" he said.

The Indian's expression froze. "Rangoon was an interesting case," he said, after a few seconds. "You see, it was part of Greater India and even though it was obvious we could no longer hold it, we could not possibly allow it to fall into enemy hands."

"You displayed, if I may say so, a very dog-in-the-manger attitude," James said. Krishnamurthy pushed his chair back and stood up.

"What we cannot have, Windsor, we do not let others have. Think about my offer," he said. He walked off, and James, as instructed, thought about it, for perhaps two seconds. He then went back to his speech, chuckling to himself, with good humour restored.

"You?" Julia said, surprised. She hadn't expected any Martian to be a lover of the arts and certainly not this one, who had come straight to see her after getting back to the Dome. "You want to come on this visit with me?"

"If it's okay with the Rusties, is there a problem?" Peter said.

Julia bristled. "No, but . . ."

She knew there wasn't much she could reasonably "but" about: it was just that, in her mind, Julia Coyne was already well over halfway towards being humanity's cultural ambassador to the First Breed: the idea of being just one in a crowd of rubber-necking humans was appalling. Leaf Ruby's invitation, conveyed through Arm Wild, had been to *her*. She hadn't told anyone outside *Ark Royal* about it.

"Look," she said, "it's probably not your scene. Why not stay on the ship? You can't be going stir crazy after just a day."

"Stir crazy doesn't have anything to do with it," he said.

"Then what?"

"It's . . ." He looked sullen. "You wouldn't understand."

"Try me!"

"All right." He dug his hands into his pockets, squinted at the sky and then looked back at her. "It's the psalms."

"Psalms?" she said, puzzled.

"One hundred and fifty songs collected together in the Bi —"

"I know what the psalms are," she said, impatiently. And she did. A lot of them had been set to truly beautiful music by musicians past and present. "Which one?"

"Several. A lot of them talk about the glory of God's creation. The sky, the thunder. Remember they were written by a desert people. Paradise was green hills and fertile land. Free-flowing, clean, unprocessed water. Animals roaming about in the open."

"And?"

Peter touched his chest. "And, I'm a Martian and

I've never seen any of these things, until now. I want to see more and more and drink it in, and . . ." He waved his hand in a dismissive gesture. "That's what. I said you wouldn't understand."

"No, I can understand." Julia was surprised, whether at him or at herself, she couldn't tell. But, yes, she could understand a man moved by beauty who wanted to see more. It made perfect sense and she said so.

"You think so?" Now he was looking bashful.

"I think so." She gave him her friendliest smile to make up for her earlier bad temper. "I think we'll have a great time."

"Did you have any luck, Excellency?" Subhas Ranjitsinhji looked suitably solicitous on the aide's display. Krishnamurthy was strolling through the Dome's gardens, aide in one hand, the other behind his back. It was drawing on for evening: the sun was low and red, the air was warm and dry, but not unpleasantly so. Always his favourite time of day, on any planet.

"No, Subhas, I did not." Krishnamurthy sighed, not sounding at all angry. His hopes had not, after all, been high, but he always at least *tried* the most economical solution to any problem first. "He isn't parting with it and the sole copy in existence is up on *Ark Royal*."

"*Ark Royal*'s friends have moved into a defensive formation around it, Excellency."

"So I was aware." Krishnamurthy stopped and looked up at the sun, now so low he could look directly at it and not hurt his eyes. Tomorrow was the Convocation. This time tomorrow, that sun and everything upon which it shone might be his. "I think the time has come, Subhas."

"Execute?" Ranjitsinhji said, his face eager.

Krishnamurthy sighed again, then nodded. "Execute," he said.

Sixteen
21 May 2149

Sharman flew east over the Roving's main continent towards the night, cruising at supersonic speed over the plains and mountains and desert, and Julia Coyne finally began to feel nervous. They were going into the unknown and this time there wasn't even a briefing pack to prepare them for what might lie ahead. Even Arm Wild's presence was only just reassuring.

She sneaked a look at the others with her. Arm Wild was in his chair, staring silently into the distance with a passivity that was all the more intense because she couldn't even begin to guess what his body language was saying. All she knew was that he was a great admirer of the performer Leaf Ruby and said he was just as honoured by this invitation as she. The unexpectedly nature-loving Peter was in the seat next to her.

They were two miles up and supersonic, so getting much feel of the Roving was hard; but even so, when she looked out of the small windows, Julia got the hinted shapes of a great, unknown continent. Yes, the Rusties were here first, but the Roving was still by and large empty. It could almost crush you if you thought too much about it: which way to go? Where to turn? Where to start exploring, finding out about the place?

Well, circumstances had dictated the answer, at least for her and for Peter. Start in the highlands.

It was already dusk when *Sharman* got there, slowing to subsonic and coming down to meet the ground. Tall, steep mountains were picked out on the radar, their positions carefully stored in *Sharman*'s memory banks for future reference. Now sharp peaks were rising above the boat but Adrian flew them on. Arm Wild had gone forward to the cockpit to translate the orders of the Rustie flight controller, out there somewhere in the dark.

"Come 'round five degrees eastwards," Arm Wild said.

"Five degrees, aye." *Sharman* banked.

"You should be able to observe the landing field now."

"I have it," Adrian said.

"Land when you're ready."

"Right-o." Adrian bit his lip and fired the verticals, then cut the main engines until *Sharman* was hovering, then began to set the boat down. For the first time in his life, Julia realized, Adrian was ending a flight in a way that wasn't docking with a ship or putting down on an automated landing pad with radio beacon, ground crew and full facilities. In space the Rusties had antigravity and step-through but down here the simple life was quite sufficient for them and Adrian was literally landing in a field.

"Crosswind," Adrian said, and made manual compensation. The noise of the verticals peaked as the boat touched down with a gentle bump. The engines died to a quiet murmur and he grinned triumphantly at her. "No problem!"

"Well done," she said.

"Hey! I could land anywhere."

"Yeah?"

"Yeah." He looked at one of the displays. "It's chilly out there. Twelve degrees, ten-knot wind, pressure lower than sea level."

"It would be."

"I mean, a *lot* lower. No running around."

"We won't." Julia went aft to find Peter ready by the door. "Open up."

The door opened and there was a hiss of air leaving the cabin: yes, the air was thin up here. And distinctly cooler than the west coast: she felt the chill cut in before her weathersuit's heater began to compensate.

"Well, let's go," Peter said, and led the way. Julia remembered to take the pack of provisions from one of the lockers before following. They really were the first people to be in a totally alien environment on this world: not a thing out there had been designed or created with humans in mind.

An even more prosaic need than food and drink had already been taken care of, in the small room at the rear of *Sharman*'s cabin.

"Get a good distance away!" Adrian called. "I'll pick you up in three hours."

The three of them stepped down onto the ground

and walked away from the boat. A crowd of Rusties came trotting towards them and the one in the lead stopped in front of Arm Wild. The two touched their graspers for a moment, speaking in their own language.

"This is Leaf Ruby," Arm Wild said in Standard. "Before I acquaint you we should move away from your ship."

Sharman's engines powered up again as they left the cordoned-off area and they turned to watch it go. The noise was deafening. Peter and Julia covered their ears and the Rusties rolled their own ears up — something Julia hadn't seen before and which made her want to chuckle. *Sharman* lifted with apparent reluctance and with a deceptive slowness, and then the roar doubled, the nose tilted upwards and it flew off. In a few seconds it was just a burning light in the sky, and they heard the noise of the engines go to full throttle and the sonic boom echo around the mountains as the boat blazed away, up and back to *Ark Royal*.

And now, Julia really did feel alone. She glanced over at Peter and resisted the urge to hold his hand — not because he was male or particularly good-looking but because, not counting straight up, he was the only human for thousands of miles around.

"Leaf Ruby asks us to pursue," Arm Wild said.

Surrounded by a knot of Rusties they left the landing field and headed for a gap in the trees a hundred yards away. The path was marked out by flaring beacons that gave out a delicious warmth as they passed by. Julia took a close look at the Rusties, wearing only their usual harnesses and ornamentation, and wondered how they managed to keep warm. It seemed that the "flakes" of rust on their skin were contracted together, not hanging so loosely but forming a more solid shell around their bodies. Maybe that was how they did it.

They left the trees and found themselves looking out over a small town.

"Wow," Peter said, and Julia felt it too.

They were standing on the rim of a large natural bowl and were looking down on the buildings, lit up by a mixture of artificial light and fires that gave the place a very homely appearance. The stone, as far as they could tell in the dim light, was somewhere between yellow and grey. The buildings were very straight in their lines, generally much longer than they were tall, with a very definite sense of symmetry. It felt like an old place. The buildings merged into one another and into the landscape. Nothing was glaringly new. It was very lived in. This wasn't Capital — a planned city despite its natural feel. This was a proper Rustie community.

They were led along a winding gravel path that made its way down the edge of the bowl, and Julia was seeing more Rusties together in one place than ever before. Fat ones, thin ones, big ones, small ones — she smiled at the sight of one or two very small ones indeed, clinging on to the backs of larger Rusties.

The number of heads bobbing along at waist level prompted a purely human association in Julia's mind and she felt she was surrounded by children. She had to stop herself reaching out and tickling Leaf Ruby between the ears.

"Who lives here, Arm Wild?" said Peter. "What do all these First Breed do?"

"They are artists," Arm Wild said. "It is the speciality of the Highlands clan, just as my clan, the Southern Plains, has always been known for yielding diplomats."

Julia's heart pounded and she looked around with a fresh eye. A whole community given to art. Wonderful! Nothing on Earth had ever been quite so dedicated. It was then that she knew where she wanted her life to go. She would serve her remaining three years with the Fleet, or see if she could buy herself out early, and then come back here. Whoever won the bid, they surely wouldn't object. She would return to this bowl in the mountains where the Highlands clan gave itself to art, and together they would form the first ever cross-species cultural institute. She would—

Peter had stopped walking and was looking at a nearby wall. Close-up, she could see it was covered with what she assumed was hieroglyphics. A frieze ran around the edge of the wall, displaying Rusties of all shapes and sizes, and stylized in the same way as the Rusties of the monument back in Capital, but she was certain the rest of the patterns were writing.

Arm Wild said something to Leaf Ruby and the rest of the Rusties trotted off. Arm Wild stayed and walked over to the wall.

"The history of the pride that abides here," he said. "This section describes the births and deaths in a certain year three centuries ago, when Tail Star was Pride Senior."

"It's ideogrammatic, isn't it?" Peter said suddenly. Each glyph had a common core — a flattened oval, lying on its side — and around it were wiggles and squiggles. "I know how important bodytalk is to you. This," he indicated the oval, "is a First Breed body, and these" — now it was the surrounding trappings that he pointed to — "qualify the meaning somehow."

"Exactly right," said Arm Wild.

Julia gaped at Peter. "How —"

He beamed at her. "I don't know which end of an octave you hit a quaver with but I know object-oriented symbolic programming."

Julia looked around. The place reminded her of Mayan cities back on Earth. The clean-cut, dressed-stone buildings crowded with foliage; the earthen paths between them; the fires burning against a backdrop of thick forest and the jagged black line of distant mountains at sunfall. The overall low-tech feel and the general feel of antiquity . . .

Antiquity. "Arm Wild, how old is this place?" she said.

"This pridehall was fabricated about nine hundred years ago," Arm Wild said. "Up there, the top right corner of the wall: that is the date of foundation."

1249, Julia thought. "That's not right!"

"I attest that it is."

"But . . ."

Peter saw the problem and came to the rescue. "What she means, Arm Wild, is, we didn't know you had been on this world so long. You've always said you're only a century or so ahead of us, but —"

"This is our home world," said Arm Wild.

"Yeah, okay, you were born on this colony —"

"It is not a colony. There is no other world. Only this."

They looked at him and he looked back. His bland, unreadable stare suddenly seemed more alien than ever.

"But, your invitation said —" Julia began.

"The invitation said, 'We have a world which we would like to share with you.' It went on to say, 'There is room for both our races there. We call it the Roving.' I assisted in the drafting of the invitation and there is not an error in it."

"But . . . surely you've always said it was a colony," said Peter.

"*You* said it was a colony," Arm Wild said. "Your preconceptions did the talking."

"So —" Peter said.

Arm Wild turned away. "We should hurry. Leaf Ruby will soon begin."

There was a natural amphitheatre in the side of the bowl, and the Rusties were gathered there, facing into it. The backdrop of the stage was a sheer wall of uncarved, weathered rock; boulders of different shapes and sizes were scattered at random around the floor of the basin.

Cushions were provided and they sat down. A disembodied Rustie voice spoke out of the darkness and Arm Wild translated. "In honour of its guests from Earth, Leaf Ruby is to perform its most celebrated work, *The Attack of the Alpine Clan*." From the murmuring and shuffling around them, Julia deduced the audience was pleased at the treat.

The show began.

A spotlight shone on a ledge halfway up the cliff and Leaf Ruby stood there, suspended on an island of rock floating in the dark. The Rustie began the gasp-and-wiggle combination that was fulltalk and Julia set her aide to record it all. Arm Wild continued to translate.

"The clans of the Bay Coast and the Peninsula were neighbours," he said. Julia blinked because it appeared that in two areas the floor of the theatre was suddenly covered with Rusties. She looked again and saw that the effect was just shadows on the boulders. Glancing around, the only light source she could see was in the form of a couple of bonfires; other Rusties were using wood cutouts to cast shadows.

"Their grazing lands were wide and flat. The water was clean." Arm Wild paused. "I am sorry. That was a very clever pun that always amuses me. I question that you caught it."

"Um, no," Julia said, still taken with the shadow play below.

"No matter. The sense of rhythm is probably lost in translation too. The . . . there is no translation, be rapid, give me the name of a large predatory animal from Earth."

"Lions?"

"The lions were few and the . . . again, another . . . ."

"Tyrannosaurs?"

" . . .tyrannosaurs had been driven out. There was serenity in the land."

The fires flared up and Julia jumped. Leaf Ruby's voice became louder, its gestures more urgent.

"The summer was long and hot but there was no cause for worry. The leaves were drier than usual but still they gave sustenance. The streams dwindled to trickles but the rivers still ran and the wells were deep.

"On . . . our calendar cannot be translated easily, I am sorry . . . On a particular date in the Peninsula, four hundred years ago, flames and lava spewed forth from the earth."

Now it really did seem that streams of molten rock were running down the cliff face, glowing red and wicked. The theatre was suddenly a glimpse into Hell.

"The sky darkened and ash blew across the grazing lands, but still there was no worry, for the earth fires had come before and the people of the Peninsula had survived. The blaze lasted only two and a half days and the Peninsula clan prepared to move on to areas where the ash and lava had not fallen."

A new element was being added to the flowing lava: the flow was from above but a new, different glow was coming from below: more orange than red — it seemed that flames were licking up the cliff. Leaf Ruby stood in the heart of the inferno.

"The fires from the earth returned whence they had come but their children spread out across the land. The trees and the grazing lands were consumed. There was nowhere for the Peninsula people to go."

The story went on and Julia was swept up in it. It didn't matter that all the skills and nuances being used by Leaf Ruby were completely lost on her, or that apparently part of the form was to repeat whole chunks of text verbatim, faithfully echoed by Arm Wild. The fires swept over the entire Peninsula and their smoke clouded the sky for hundreds of miles around. The Peninsula clan was forced to move south to the Bay Coast and the Bay Coast clan didn't want them. The Bay Coast wasn't as naturally rich as the Peninsula had been and the long drought hadn't been kind there either; the vegetation was tough and sparse and the last thing the occupants needed was a much larger refugee population sweeping in and doubling the drain on resources. The clash of the two clans was shown vividly by the shadows, where it seemed the two masses of Rusties swept violently into one another.

The Bay Coast clan, not wishing to condemn their neighbours to starvation, offered them the use of substandard grazing lands that the Bay Coast clan didn't want, which could have supported perhaps a tenth of the Peninsula clan. The Peninsula clan pressed for more but the Bay Coast clan couldn't provide it. The clans began a mutual sniping campaign, individual prides encountering and first insulting, then fighting, then massacring one another. The fighting spread from the prides to the lodges and then to the clans themselves.

The Peninsula clan was larger, it could more easily afford the losses and it was desperate. At the final battle it seemed certain that the Bay Coast clan would be annihilated.

And then the Alpine clan attacked.

Julia mentally filled in the sound of a cavalry bugle as a new horde of Rusties swept in from stage left: bigger, larger, fiercer but still only shadows. The battle was long and brutal but the Alpine clan was larger still than either of the others. After a week of fighting the Peninsula clan sued for peace, asking only that it not be made to return to the old lands. By now, sheer attrition had worn it down to a manageable size and it was merged with the Bay Coast clan. Its Pride Seniors were put to death and Bay Coast Seniors installed instead. Peace reigned again.

End of story.

The light faded away and there was only darkness where previously Julia's imagination told her there had been dispossessed populations, natural catastrophes, epic battles and slaughter, and yet there had only been one Rustie, some fires and a clever use of shadows.

"Is that it?" Peter said.

"Arm Wild," said Julia, "if we stand up and clap our hands together vigorously, will it cause offence?"

"It will not," Arm Wild said. So she did, standing up and clapping furiously until her hands were sore. "Your own hands. I see."

Julia was bewildered by Peter's lack of reaction. "Come on, Pete, don't say you weren't impressed," she said.

He shrugged. "It was all right."

All right! Julia fumed. She shouldn't blame the poor boy — raised on Mars, of all places, and growing up in an artificial, high-tech environment. He couldn't appreciate what he had just seen — a low-tech virtual reality. As far as she could tell, the spotlight at the start had been the only artificial effect: the rest had just been fire and shadows. But the effect, the effect!

Lights came up to illuminate the whole area and once more the theatre was just a rocky bowl. Julia felt the same sense of letdown as at the end of a human play, when the show is over and the auditorium is just a large room again. Leaf Ruby was climbing down from its ledge, headfirst, as nimble as a monkey. When it reached the bottom it trotted towards them.

"Leaf Ruby says it is elated you enjoyed the performance," said Arm Wild. "I have told it that the noise caused by your hand-actions indicates appreciation, the louder the better."

"Tell Leaf Ruby I have never seen anything like it," Julia said. "Tell him . . . it . . . whatever, that I'm amazed, impressed . . . you get the idea."

And she was. She could only guess at the power of Leaf Ruby's verbal delivery but the light show alone was enough to stun a human crowd. The first thing that her cross-cultural institute would do would be to study Rustie fulltalk and see how, if at all, its devices could be applied to humans.

Arm Wild passed the message on. "It thanks you and hopes to talk to you some more, but meanwhile has business to attend to."

They strolled slowly out of the amphitheatre and back towards the town, enjoying the movement in their limbs: amazingly, the performance had taken nearly two hours. Julia poured coffees for herself and Peter and they sipped at them as they walked.

"Did Leaf Ruby write the show?" Julia asked.

"No. The original was written shortly after the events described, commissioned by the Senior of the Alpine clan."

"But the interpretation was Leaf Ruby's?"

"The performance was a reflection of Leaf Ruby's native talent," Arm Wild said. Which Julia took as a "yes."

"But why did the Alpine clan join in?" Peter said. "It didn't sound like they had any interest at all."

"They and the Bay Coast clan were of the same nation," Arm Wild said: a fact that must have been self-explanatory to the Rusties. "The Peninsula clan were alone, cut off from their own nation by the fires."

"There were a lot of nations, once?"

"There were many."

Four hundred years, Julia thought. Four hundred years ago it had been 1749: the United States was still an impossible dream; Handel was writing the Firework Music; the British were carving out their Indian empire. It thrilled her that while all that had been going on, these events too had been happening, unguessed at and unknowable on Earth, yet all too real and made solid by that evening's show.

"Why did the Peninsula clan accept their defeat so readily?" she asked. "Their Seniors were all put to death and they meekly accepted new Seniors from a foreign clan being imposed on them."

"Because it was the inclination of the greater

whole," Arm Wild said. "No pride would ever resent its Senior. The concept is, excuse me, entirely alien."

"Very democratic," said Peter.

"No, not democratic," Arm Wild said. "As I understand democracy, the minority may give in to the majority but they will continue to harbour their private opinions and resentments, and take action upon them. With us, the minority is . . . the concept is so clear to me, it is hard to describe . . . the minority is absorbed. The majority also changes, however. Both sides meet each other halfway and there is an overall change. There is no dissension."

"Weird!" said Julia.

"It is our way," Arm Wild said. Another Rustie trotted up to them and spoke to Arm Wild. He turned to the two humans. "Web More asks if you would like to witness a quickening."

"A quickening?" Peter said.

"An important moment for the pride," said Arm Wild. "It has made enquiry, and they say you are welcome to observe. An invitation like this is a gesture of friendship."

"Just observe?" said Julia.

"Just that. You could hardly participate."

"Why, thank you," Julia said, "we'd love to."

"Always wanted to see a quickening," Peter said, glancing at Julia. She shrugged back at his enquiring expression. She didn't know what one was, either.

Arm Wild led them to where a crowd of Rusties

was gathering by one of the fires. The two humans were tall enough to stand at the back and see what was happening. There was a space in the middle of the crowd and a Rustie stood there, alone. Julia wondered if they were going to see some kind of trial.

"That is Air Quiet, the initiator," Arm Wild said. Julia nodded as though that meant something.

The crowd parted to let another Rustie through. It walked over to Air Quiet and the two stood, facing each other.

"Wood Merry, the quickener."

The two stood facing each other, engaged in some silent communion. Then their graspers reached out and twined around one another. Julia frowned as a thought struck her. The Rusties reared up on their hind legs, their graspers still entwined and now their forehands grasped each other's shoulders.

"Oh my God . . ." she whispered, as she realized. She heard Peter gulp. The crowd of Rusties was clustering around the couple into a tight knot, shuffling and murmuring amongst themselves. Some were hopping up and down on all fours. The two at the centre pulled themselves towards each other into a tight embrace.

The crowd's excitement was palpable and the typical Rustie smell was strong in the air. After about a minute, Air Quiet and Wood Merry backed off from each other, untwining and letting go. They dropped down to all fours and walked away from each other without a backwards glance.

Julia and Peter stood staring at where the scene had been. Peter was round-eyed and slack-jawed; Julia felt an enormous grin spread over her face.

"A very satisfactory quickening," Arm Wild said.

"Wham bam, thank you, ma'am," Julia murmured. If she had just seen what she thought she had seen, it lacked her idea of romance.

Peter cleared his throat. Julia glanced at him and even though it was dark, she was certain he was blushing. "Arm Wild," he said, "w-was that a . . . a m-mating?"

"A mating?" Arm Wild was silent for a moment. "If I comprehend my translator properly, I infer it was what you would call a mating. We would call it a quickening. Our reproductive cycle was mentioned in the information pack."

"Ah . . ." Julia glanced at Peter, who still seemed slightly dazed. "You'll have to refresh our memory."

"It is very simple. When the pride needs a new member, one of its number will initiate a foetus, a clone of the initiator. When it has reached a certain stage of growth, it requires quickening — the genetic input of a different pride member. After that it will grow to term as a genetically individual First Breed. You were not aware of this?"

"We didn't get that far in the pack," Peter said. He seemed to have his voice back again. "Sorry. Mating

... quickening ... whatever you call it, it's a bit more private for us."

"That was not the impression I gained from Earth's entertainment channels," Arm Wild said.

"Well, it would be if you'd watched the ones on Mars."

Julia smothered a giggle.

"I was of course cognizant that humans had a different approach but I have never seen it done in the flesh," Arm Wild said. "Would you two care —"

"No!" they said together.

"— to attend the naming ceremony for the child?"

They felt foolish. "Um . . . the naming ceremony?" Peter said.

"In five months, when the child is born," Arm Wild said. "It is customary for witnesses at the quickening to attend."

They looked at each other. Julia looked back at the Rustie.

"We'd be honoured, if we're still on the Roving in five months' time," said Julia.

"Five months, no problem," Peter agreed.

"Excellent," said Arm Wild.

"Who decides the name?" Julia asked.

"No one decides. Air Quiet is the initiator and Wood Merry the quickener, so the child will be Air Merry. The child does not of course know that, so must be informed, at the ceremony."

"Your young are born able to talk?" said Julia.

"In a limited sense — bodytalk only — but yes, we can communicate. Excuse me, I am being called."

Julia looked after Arm Wild as the Rustie walked away. "Fascinating," she said.

Peter wiped his brow. "Unexpected," he agreed. "Public mating . . ."

"Quickening," Julia corrected, with a grin. "You know, Pete, I'm finally beginning to wonder just how accurate all our preconceptions about them have been. These creatures are aliens, pure and simple, and we've always known that, but we still think of them as four-legged humans. Even if we don't trust them, even if we assume they're up to something, we still ascribe human characteristics. But they live in prides, they're hermaphrodites, they breed to order . . . And look at the Peninsula clan, quietly accepting defeat like that. We don't know the first thing about the way the Rustie mind works. Our species are so different that we just can't assume anything about them. Anything at all."

Julia's aide sounded, startling her. It was a connection with the rest of the world, the tiresome and tedious world of humans, the Royal Space Fleet and the rest of it that she had almost forgotten.

"Julia Coyne," she said.

"Three hours, Jules." Adrian Nichol sounded irritatingly cheerful that he was about to come down and take her back to that world.

*   *   *

Adrian could see the highlands clearly from his position in *Sharman*, five miles up. They were on the Roving's dark side but they were this side of the planet's curve and they stood out clearly on radar. *Sharman* had mapped out the sheer contours on the first journey and now a red trace on the display showed the optimum course for him to take to pick up his passengers. The autopilot had already picked up on it.

A fiery streak blazed past the viewports and erupted into a fireball a mile ahead of him. Adrian yelped and hauled at the stick to avoid the explosion, and something large and dark flashed over *Sharman*. Radar showed nothing, but by the light of the Roving's big moon, he caught the shape of a landing boat circling around him. He thought he caught a glimpse of circular insignia on the wings, before he was dazzled by the flare of the intruder's exhausts.

"Pull up and return to orbit," said a voice in his earphones. A human voice, as far as he could tell. And the design of the boat that he had glimpsed was human too.

"Who are you?" Adrian shouted.

"Irrelevant. Pull up and return to orbit."

"I— I have to pick up two crew."

"We'll do that." The voice was toneless. "Pull up and return to orbit. We are armed" — as if to prove the point, another missile flew past —"and we can enforce our orders."

"I —" Adrian swallowed. He glanced up, picturing the attractive emptiness of orbit, then ahead into the dark, picturing his two friends waiting for him. "I understand," he said. "Complying." He pulled at the stick slightly and *Sharman's* nose tilted up. He swallowed; then at the same time cut all power to the main engines and fired the forward thrusters. He lurched forward in his seat and the straps tightened around him as *Sharman* stopped dead in the air, then plummeted. As the nose came down he fired the main engines again at full power, and the boat accelerated at full thrust towards the mountains below.

There was a bellow in his earphones before he broke contact, but he ignored it. Whoever was behind him was armed, but they didn't know the terrain. They didn't have a map of the highlands already programmed into their flight computers, and that would surely give him the advantage.

He tried to open a comms channel: he was being jammed. So, he would just have to get there first.

Julia and Peter continued talking to Leaf Ruby, with Arm Wild interpreting, as they made their way back to the landing site. Leaf Ruby could not ask enough questions and though it confessed that the music played through Julia's aide left it cold, it insisted that it be provided with an audio copy and the score of several pieces so that it could study the notation and see how it worked. It hoped it could visit Earth one day and witness some musical performances.

They were in the tree tunnel that led to the landing ground, and Arm Wild broke step and looked back at Peter. "Disregard them, Peter Kirton. They are just animals."

Four diminutive creatures were gathered at the foot of a tree and Peter had paused next to them to watch. They looked so similar to Arm Wild and the others that Julia thought they must be young Rusties; they were certainly more like the real thing than the carvings back on the pridehall. Arm Wild's comment intrigued her: did Rusties only gain intelligence with adulthood? No, he had already said . . . She looked at them more closely. Maybe they were slightly different from Rustie babies, though the distinction wasn't obvious. One of them, the largest, was standing on its hind legs, straining to reach what looked like some fruit overhead, while the others looked on.

Peter picked the fruit and held it out. "Here you are, big fella," he said. The little creature took it in its mouth — no graspers, Julia noticed — and its friends gathered round, each taking a bite from the fruit. The one holding it gulped down the remainder. With Peter now identified in their minds as a source of food they clustered round him, then froze with their ears pricked up.

Julia heard it too. The sound of boat engines, come to steal her from this wonderful place. The small creatures fled into the bushes.

Peter came over to them. "Just animals?" he said. "I'd thought they might be children."

"Children?" Arm Wild exclaimed. He made a rumbling in his throat, which could have been laughter or swearing but either way was not translated. "Conceivably I should not be surprised: it is said that one of our contact teams on Earth had the same misunderstanding about chimpanzees and humans."

They looked at the bushes where the small creatures had gone.

"You're descended from them?" Peter said.

"No, and you are not descended from chimpanzees," Arm Wild said, "but there is a close relationship. Come."

The landing boat making the noise was approaching fast. Very fast.

Seventeen
21 May 2149

Sharman was fast and nippy, while the enemy had missiles. If those missiles were heat-seeking, then, Adrian thought as the boat charged towards the ground, the advantage was probably with the enemy.

His fingers brushed the gold wings on his uniform. *Gold* wings. He was proud of those: they weren't just handed out at random.

He had already planned his entry into the highlands — a pass that loomed dead ahead, according to radar. He had no idea if the attackers were behind him; radar still showed nothing and *Sharman* wasn't designed to combat stealth tech. He thought for a moment of the state-of-the-art detection equipment back on the old *Australasia*, purpose-built to pinpoint scuttlers in the depths of space . . . but there was no point in wishing.

He lurched *Sharman* from side to side, still keeping the same heading; he was probably flying faster than the others, and was most likely making better speed than a missile could, but there was no harm in doing a bit of extra shaking off.

Then he was into the pass, hurtling through at two hundred feet with the shock wave of the boat's passing echoing off the rocky walls. Bad luck if he caused an avalanche and it fell on someone, but he hadn't started this.

A missile hit the side of the pass behind him and he increased speed a notch, then banked as hard as he could into a side valley. G-forces pushed him into his seat but he had done worse racing flyers like this back on Mars, through the canyons that skirted the Tharsis plateau. That was where he had got his gold wings. He came out of the turn and whooped with glee.

It was easy, really. The computer had the course to the pickup point plotted, and with every turn he took it recalculated. The difficult bit was in deciding when to override the computer, which lacked a facility for being informed it was under attack. Adrian made a mental note to get Peter to upgrade the navigation AI one day.

Now the computer was telling him to turn between two peaks, but looking ahead he could see that course would take him over a flat plateau where he would be a sitting duck for the attackers. He ignored it and turned instead into a blind valley that ended in a gentle, saddle-backed ridge. He could dart over the ridge and still not rise higher than the valley sides. Radar was picking out the ridge's lines for him and he pulled gently back on the stick to clear it. The big moon came out again and Adrian yelled.

"Aaagh!" He hauled on the stick, increased throttle, and *Sharman* almost stood on its tail as it raced skywards. The radar was showing the stone that surrounded him and Adrian had put the slight fuzziness of the echo down to a poor display, rather than the suddenly visible trees that added at least another hundred feet to the contours. If he had kept his previous course he would have cleared the ridge itself but smashed in a glorious, blazing mess right through the trees that ran along it.

In a moment he was well above the skyline and burning fuel brightly. He cut the burn and put the nose down but already in the moonlight he could see the sleek, triangular shapes of his attackers turning towards him. Two of them — he hadn't realized.

He checked the display: only twenty miles to go.

"Damn it," he muttered, and dived back into a valley. Julia and Peter had been going to some Rustie concert. There would be witnesses, influential ones. No one would dare attack him there. He just had to be the first to arrive. . . .

The boat was directly overhead: they could see its running lights and a dim, delta-winged outline behind them. It had shot over the treeline and circled round in a fast bend that must have crushed the pilot into his seat. It landed on full retro, facing them, and the lights on the leading edge of the wings shone straight into their eyes. They raised hands to ward off the glare.

"Cut it out, Ade," Julia muttered. "Come on, Pete, Arm Wild. And thank you again, Leaf Ruby."

"It says it awaits your next meeting with eagerness," Arm Wild said as they walked forward.

And stopped. There was shouting ahead and figures, human figures, were running towards them out of the white glow of the lights. Strangers, carrying things in their hands that Julia's brain slowly registered as automatic weapons.

"What the —" she said. Before they could react the men were surrounding them, their guns raised.

"Which one of you is Kirton?" the leading man said. They were wearing military helmets and uniforms.

"Uh, me . . ." said Peter.

The leader nodded at a large, burly man who stepped up and grabbed Peter. Peter struggled but the man was bigger and stronger.

"Hey!"

"Move!" The man twisted Peter's arm behind his back and a gun barrel was jammed into his spine. "Now!"

"Her too," said the leader. None of the newcomers had paid the least attention to any of the Rusties. Julia hardly had time to take a breath before she had been caught up the same way and was being frogmarched back to the ship. The lights had dimmed and now she could see it wasn't *Sharman* — it was larger, sleeker.

"Stop!" Arm Wild bellowed. Their abductors paused and looked back. "This is outrageous! How dare you? I shall register my strongest objection with your superiors. Put your guns down at once!"

"I'm sorry, Mr. First Breed, but I have my orders," the leader said. He was Indian: the badge on his breast, in Standard and Hindi, said his name was Rajan. "We have no quarrel with you."

"These two are under my protection. Release them."

"I regret, sir, I cannot." Several of the Rusties were poised on their toes and for a moment, a wildly hopeful moment, Julia thought the Rusties were going to charge. They outnumbered the soldiers and surely the men wouldn't be so stupid as to open fire on their hosts?

Rajan thought an attack was imminent too. "This is a human matter, sirs," he said more loudly. "Please do not provoke my men."

Arm Wild said something and the crowd of Rusties relaxed. *So much for the great warrior race*, Julia thought bitterly.

"We will not," said Arm Wild. "Nevertheless, I demand to know who you are."

"Major Rajan, Confederation Defence Force."

"Your superiors will regret this incident, Major Rajan. They may be disqualified from the Convocation altogether."

"I'm just obeying their orders, sir. I meant it when I said we have no quarrel — *get your hand away from that!*"

Julia's hand had been inching towards her aide.

Now she was looking directly down the barrel of a gun for the first time in her life, and she decided heroism wasn't worth it. "They'll hear about this back at the Dome, you know," she said, and she was proud that her voice didn't break.

Rajan grinned as though she had just promised him a good time. "They have troubles of their own. Now, for the last time, move."

The coup was over quickly. At 1900 coastal time, around sunset, landing boats from *Shivaji* and the North Chinese ship *Long March* came in from over the ocean and fell on Capital. The one landing boat of marines from the *Enterprise*, sitting patiently on the ground at the spaceport, suddenly found itself outnumbered and outgunned as three times its military force fell out of the sky around it. The rest of the attack fell on the Dome, the boats ploughing into the gardens and disgorging their contents while the delegates scurried around in a panic.

The marines at the Dome put up more of a defence as the attackers tried to gain entry; and the refrain, repeated over and over again, shouted by the troops on both sides and crackling over their comm units, was: "Don't shoot the Rusties!"

Samad and Hannah threw themselves to the ground as a stray cluster of plasma blasts sliced through their cubicle. A haze of smoke filled the room and there was a smell of burning. They tried to make themselves even flatter on the floor as more blasts passed through the thin partitions.

"This place wasn't designed as a fortress, was it?" Hannah muttered to herself as she picked singed bits of partition out of her hair and dusted them off Samad's back.

The fighting went on and all they could do was lie there and hope no blasts came through the floor.

"Has anyone told the ships?" Hannah wondered out loud.

Samad looked at her as if she were mad. "The ships, love? They've got the best of it."

"Dear, if they're fighting down here you can bet the ships are involved too." The battle seemed to have moved away from their own area of the Dome, though sporadic bursts of gunfire kept popping up here and there. A sharp smell of plasma propellant hung in the air and her ears still rang.

She climbed cautiously to her knees and groped for their aides on the table. Hers was intact, Samad's shattered. He yelped when he saw it.

"Is it anything you didn't have backed up?" Hannah said.

"No, but —"

"Quiet then." Hannah realized she was still kneeling, a convenient target for any more incoming fire that might pass their way. She lay down flat again and flipped the aide open. "Get me *Ark Royal.*"

"This unit is unable to contact *Ark Royal*," said the aide.

"Damn. Can you reach any ship in orbit?"

"Attempting." Pause. "Negative."

"Why not?"

"All microwave signals from this area are being jammed."

"Listen," said Samad, interrupting Hannah in mid-curse. The fighting had stopped and there was only silence. She could hear her heart beat.

Then an amplified voice spoke out, echoing around the building. "This is Brigadier Rao, commander of Confederation operations on the ground. The Dome and its vicinity are now under the control of the Confederation. All humans in the vicinity are instructed to make their way to the central area of the Dome."

Samad had gone pale: Hannah put an arm around her husband and squeezed in sympathy. Samad's father had fled persecution in the Punjab and settled in Bangladesh, in vain: as a child, after his native Bangladesh was overrun, Samad had sailed in a crowded and rickety boat across the Bay of Bengal and grown up in the refugee camps in Thailand. Samad had always lived with the knowledge that his own country was occupied by the forces of the Confederation and whenever things had got hard he had comforted himself that it could be worse — he could be back in Bangladesh. Now the Confederation had caught up with him.

"We'd better go," she said. He looked at her without comprehension. "Downstairs," she said. "Like the man said. Before they come looking for us."

"Yes . . . yes, you're right . . ." he murmured. He only seemed half there and Hannah had to guide him out of the door and into the corridor.

A party of soldiers was coming the other way, kicking open each door as they passed it and checking inside. Hannah felt their gaze on her back as she and Samad walked along the corridor round the edge of the Dome, then down the staircase and into the open space that was the Dome's core. Other humans were arriving slowly, walking reluctantly into who knew what fate. Soldiers were everywhere, guns raised, eyes darting suspiciously over the captives. The Dome's lounge had been converted into a makeshift field hospital.

They joined a queue to walk between two soldiers and Samad's hand tightened its grip in hers, when they saw the uniforms — pale green, in contrast to the more usual Defence Force camouflage. Samad was reacting as Hannah's forebears had once reacted to black uniforms with silver lacing and death's-heads. These were NVN, the elite, the mainstay of their captors' military power, and their reputation was legendary.

Each person ahead of them had to produce identification: some nationalities were then herded into the middle, some were not. One of the NVN would wave an instrument over each individual, confiscating aides and investigating anything else that the machine discovered with an alarmed beep. Hannah was first: she surrendered her aide and produced her ID-chip, which an NVN man scanned. Then she turned to wait for Samad.

The NVN man was looking from Samad, to his ID-chip, to Samad again.

"Your name is Samad Loonat?" he said.

"Yes," Samad said.

The man half smiled. "Your nationality?"

"I am a citizen of the United Kingdom." Samad was holding the man's gaze but his voice trembled.

Now the man grinned. "It says here you were born in Sylhet, East Bengal Prefecture, in 2115."

"It's incorrect," Samad said. "I was born that year in Sylhet, Bangladesh."

The man's grin vanished and Hannah felt as though someone had stabbed her through the heart. But Samad held his head high, proud and noble. Hannah had never known he had it in him and she loved him for it.

"There is no Bangladesh," the NVN man said, but he handed Samad's ID-chip back. "You would be advised to get used to it. Move along."

Hannah grabbed Samad's hand and pulled him away into the centre space where everyone else milled nervously around under the gaze of the guns. "Do something like that again," she hissed, "and I'll kill you myself."

A tall NVN man with a moustache and a lean, ruthless face came to stand among the prisoners, flanked by alert soldiers. "Your attention, please. I am Brigadier Rao and you are being held provisionally by the forces of the Confederation. For the moment, pending the formal acquiescence of your superiors and the surrender of your ships, you will be kept here. Food and drink will be served shortly.

"Excellency Krishnamurthy has been in contact with the First Breed leader Iron Run to explain his actions. I am authorized to play you the message that was sent and I trust that no further explanation will be needed." He nodded at a couple of his men, who while he spoke had been setting up a playback unit with military speed and efficiency. A larger-than-life image of a beaming Krishnamurthy appeared and started to speak.

"Greetings to Iron Run, Senior of the First Breed nation. By the time you receive this message, I will be in charge of all human affairs in this system. You are probably wondering at my reasoning for this apparently impetuous action and at the various minor infractions of your laws that my people have committed at my command."

Mildly curious, yes, thought Hannah. She glanced at Samad, who scowled at the image with undisguised loathing.

"Ever since your arrival in our home system, I have studied your ways. I have spent many, many fascinating hours, going through your information pack and talking to your representative on *Shivaji*. I have read about your wars and conflicts here on the Roving.

"On Earth, during a legal case, the counsels for prosecution and defence are obliged to reveal all their evidence to each other. If there is something in the evidence that one side does not want the other to have, often their tactic is to submit everything, every single datum, however irrelevant, to cloud the important data. Of course, this signals to the opposition that there is important data to be had: the problem is to find it. To deduce it."

Krishnamurthy's beam increased in intensity. Hannah found it almost amusing, this proud little man lecturing the Rusties on their own thought processes.

"That, Iron Run, is why you have bombarded us with so much information about your race. You have deliberately scattered clues in our path; you want us to work out the true facts and prove ourselves worthy partners. Well, that is what we have done." Despite herself, Hannah was finding this fascinating.

"Your race has had wars, Iron Run. You are no stranger to conflict. When you first appeared to us you know we tried to hide our own history of combat. We need not have worried because your ancestors have certainly matched ours in aggression.

"And your ancestors have followed an invariable pattern in victory. To impose their will on another nation that has been defeated in combat, they executed the Seniors and imposed their own. Invariably! It is the First Breed way. Do you see the parallel, Iron Run? By imposing my power on these people, I have made their nations my nation. That is what has happened on this world, is it not? Once, there were many nations; now, there is one and it is led by you, Iron Run. And why is this? Clearly, because all others have been subjugated. My action today should have convinced you that we of the Confederation understand your ways. We can work with you.

"I apologize that, to get my men on the ground, I was forced to disobey orders from your Traffic Control. I apologize that in a couple of instances my men were obliged to discharge air-to-air missiles in your airspace. I stress that no one was hurt in these cases and that these were purely to expedite my chosen course of action: that course of action being, to pass the test that you set us.

"Let me also assure you that my intentions towards the human hostages I am forced to take are purely benign. I wish them no harm and their fate is out of my hands. I have planned measures to convince their leaders of my resolve and it is my hope that I will not be forced to implement them.

"Let me repeat, worthy Iron Run, that this conflict is purely internal to the humans in this system. The Convocation may proceed tomorrow as planned, but with a reduced number of attendees. Instead of

the original number there will be the Confederation
and as many of our allies as have joined us by then.
That is the matter to which I must now attend." For
the first time, Krishnamurthy actually grinned. "I
look forward to seeing you tomorrow."

The image froze, then cleared. Rao looked about
him.

"That is the situation," he said. "His Excellency
will now interview each of the leaders of the delegations individually. We trust that they will see reason and that we will not have to take" — he slapped
the holster at his belt and his gaze roamed over the
prisoners. It distinctly lingered on Samad, and Rao
smiled without mirth when it did so — "further per-
suasive measures," he said.

Eighteen
21 May 2149

" . . . in, please. *Ark Royal,* come in, please. *Ark Royal,* can you hear me? Come in, please, oh Christ, *Ark Royal,* come in —"

Michael Gilmore quickly blanked the letter that he had been composing for Joel and answered the call.

"This is *Ark Royal.* What's the problem?" Gilmore was already drawing up a list in his mind. With that degree of alarm in Nichol's voice, someone must be hurt. Get the medbay out of storage. Alert one of the bigger ships with a proper hospital on board to stand by —

"They've been kidnapped! They just swooped down, and they shot at me, and they told me to pull out, and they've been kidnapped, and —"

"*Mr. Nichol!*" The gabble from the radio stopped in mid-flow. "Now, in words of one syllable, what's happened?"

There was a pause at the other end while Nichol collected his thoughts together. Then he spoke, more slowly but still frightened. "I was on my way to the RV, to collect Julia and Peter, and suddenly there was this voice telling me to pull up, and they shot a missile to show they meant it —"

"Who?" said Gilmore in disbelief.

"Um, two landing boats, sir. Didn't show up on radar. They just appeared behind me."

"Did you get a look at these boats?"

"Yes, sir."

"Any insignia on them? Any identification?" A ghastly thought occurred to Gilmore. "Were they human?"

"They were human, sir. They had that whirly wheel thing on them. I think they were the Confederation, sir."

Whirly wheel. The wheel of life. The Confederation insignia. At least the Rusties hadn't turned nasty.

"Go on," Gilmore said.

"Well, I tried to shake them off, but one of them got ahead of me. By the time I got to the rendezvous it was too late. . . . They tried to nail me on the way back up, too, sir. Only Arm Wild had words with them and then they backed off sharpish."

"You've got Arm Wild there?" Having one of the First Breed on board, Gilmore thought, was probably Nichol's go-anywhere card.

"Yes, sir. I tried to fly him to Capital but they said they couldn't guarantee their automatic defences wouldn't shoot us down, so we're coming up."

Go-anywhere *safe*, rather, Gilmore thought.

"All right, Lieutenant, I'll expect you both."

"Aye-aye, sir."

"Comms," said Gilmore. "Get me Julia Coyne or Peter Kirton."

"I am unable to establish contact with their aides," said the comms AI. Gilmore swore. He had wanted to help Kirton snap out of himself and all he had done was make him available to those who wanted what was in Kirton's head. They had probably tracked *Sharman*'s outward journey from orbit. Good work, Michael Gilmore. One of your better decisions.

"Get me Prince James," he said, biting his lip.

"I am unable to establish contact with his aide. A blanket of microwave signals at our common frequencies has been laid around this world." Then, "A message is being sent from *Shivaji* to all delegation ships."

"Let's hear it."

The message began. "This communication is sent on behalf of Excellency R.V. Krishnamurthy to the captains and crews of all delegation vessels in orbit around the Roving at 1927 hours. Greetings. As of 1900 hours Capital time, the forces of the Confederation and her allies have taken control of human affairs in this system. All delegates have been offered the chance to join our alliance and share in the rewards of the bid for the Roving. Those that have so far accepted are the delegates of the Northern Chinese Republic, the Pacific Consortium and the Southern African Republic. The ships of the delegates that have not done so will transmit their immediate surrenders to *Shivaji* and prepare to be boarded. We stress that our offer of alliance stays open and will remain so until the bid is won, and should any delegate choose to accept it before that time, his or her ship will be returned to its crew.

"Meanwhile, no communication or physical traffic unauthorized by the Confederation may take place between the Roving and orbit. Ground-based citizens of nations not presently allied with the Confederation are being held for their own safety on the Roving. Stand by for further announcements. This message now ends."

Gilmore gazed into space. What did the maniac think he was doing? Were the Rusties just going to accept this?

Maybe they were. Krishnamurthy wouldn't do something like this without planning, without looking ahead. He must have good reason for believing the Rusties would go along with his scheme.

Well, let the diplomats have their little squabbles downstairs. No one was going to take Gilmore's ship away from him.

He glanced at the display showing the four ships that had surrounded *Ark Royal* ever since Polyglot's existence became known. Their formation was a natural unit; *Ark Royal* could never hold out on her own. He took a deep breath, dreading what was coming. Supposing they said no? Supposing they laughed? Supposing he made a hash of it.

"Access the orbital net and find out who are the ranking officers currently on board *Algol*, *Bruxelles*, *Nikolai* and *Enterprise*," he said.

"Ranking officers are Commander Ong on *Algol*. Lieutenant Soldner on *Bruxelles*. Third Officer Gerasimov on *Nikolai*. Lieutenant Commander Davis on *Enterprise*."

Gilmore groaned. He was the only actual captain of a ship in their little group and he had a horrible feeling he might have to act that way. He swallowed hard.

"Get them all," Gilmore said. "Use direct laser transmission only. Conference mode."

"Complying," said the AI. "Conference mode set up."

"Okay. Patch me in." Four faces appeared on the display with varying degrees of irritation or worry. Soldner and Ong were women, Gerasimov and Davis men. "Michael Gilmore, officer commanding *Ark Royal*," he said. "You all heard that?" Gilmore said. They all had.

"I . . . they . . . they can't," Gerasimov stammered. He was like a scared boy. "They can't get away with this —"

"Not if we don't let them," Gilmore said. "Our lords and masters are working together, so we should too."

"So far, so good," said Ong, her tone implying that Gilmore wasn't saying anything new. "What do you suggest?"

"One of us should take overall command and I nominate myself as the most senior."

Ong looked as if she were considering the idea; Soldner looked sceptical; Gerasimov looked glad to have the responsibility taken out of his hands.

"Are you sure?" said Davis.

"I'm the only ship's captain."

"Do you have experience of combat in space?"

"Do you?" Gilmore said. Davis managed a wry grin for an answer.

"How long have you held your present rank, Commander?" said Ong. Gilmore thought quickly and was tempted to exaggerate, but for all he knew she had his record on another display in front of her.

"Two months," he said. "I got my present rank on 20 March."

"Then I'm ahead of you," Ong said. "Right, listen up, everyone. We need —"

"And I refer you to the file 'tontine,' of which you all have copies," Gilmore said. "There's only one commanding officer of a ship present, and that's me."

Ong smouldered, but their orders as laid down in the tontine file were clear and they all knew it. "You have command, Gilmore," she said coolly. "How do you plan to use it?"

"Just one question," said Soldner. "I concede your seniority, but it just seems a little incongruous, the European Union taking orders from" — she smirked — "the UK?"

Gilmore put a lid on his temper. "Lieutenant, I

wouldn't dream of telling you how to run your ship but I'm damned if I'm going to turn mine over to a gang of pirates. If you don't like this, fine, you're on your own and good luck to you." He took a breath. "First off, we put our cards on the table and confirm what we already know." Here it came — his next words would give tacit acceptance of the truth that he hated. His ship was armed and those weapons might have to be used. "What do we have that we can fight with?"

There was embarrassed silence from the others and Ong rolled her eyes. "All right, I'll start," she said. "*Algol* has torpedoes on board, grapeshot and fusion warheads. Our meteor laser has also been enhanced into the terawatt range. You, *Ark Royal*?"

"Torpedoes, same warheads as yours." Gilmore said with reluctance.

"Excellent!"

"There's a problem there, though."

"A problem? A *problem*? We're in a state of war with the Confederation and you've got a problem?"

"I've been forced to confine the AI containing the targeting software," Gilmore said. "It was unreliable and posed a threat to my ship."

"Oh, for — "

Gilmore felt he was already losing control of this session to her, so he interrupted. "However, we also have an enhanced laser, and *that* we can control with the usual software. Mr. Gerasimov?"

"Fusion and grapeshot torpedoes and marines,"

said Gerasimov. "We have no way of getting our marines down to the surface, though."

"Uh-huh. *Enterprise?*"

"Torpedoes, marines." Davis sounded bored. "All the marines are downstairs and I think can be discounted at this time. Enhanced laser."

"*Bruxelles?*" Gilmore said.

"Torpedoes and enhanced laser," said Soldner.

"Okay," said Gilmore. "We can all look after ourselves. Does anyone have any kind of battle software on board? Something with tactical capability?"

"We've got dedicated targeting software —" Ong started.

"That wasn't the question. I meant something that can analyse the situation, coordinate the ships, plot strategy." The four sheepish looks answered his question. "Oh, *good*."

"How about you, Gilmore?" said Davis. "Experts at combat in outer space are kinda thin on the ground, hadn't you noticed?"

"No, I don't have anything either," Gilmore said, "but you can bet they do. They've planned this too well. They'll have a great big battle AI programmed with every theoretical trick in the book."

"So what do we do?"

"We make it up as we go along," Gilmore said. On their displays, his face would have vanished and been replaced with an orbital schematic. He continued: "This is the orbital layout." Of the enemy, *Shivaji* and *Pacifica* were ahead, the Northern Chinese

Long March behind and the Southern Africans' *Great Zimbabwe* above. "We should apportion targets now, purely defensive. We fight back if we're attacked but we don't start anything."

"Why the hell not?" said Ong.

"Because we're the aggrieved parties, that's why. Krishnamurthy will use the slightest excuse to justify his actions and we don't want to give him any. This man nuked a city out of spite, remember. A few ships won't bother him."

"Fair enough." Ong studied the schematic. "I'm nearest to the Gee-Zee and I'll handle her."

"Right," Gilmore said. "*Bruxelles* and *Nikolai*, spin 180 degrees. You're responsible for dealing with *Long March*. Ms. Ong, you and I will stay as we are. Mr. Gerasimov, are your marines equipped for space fighting?"

"So I'm told."

"Then keep them suited up ready for combat. It may come to that. Oh, and my landing boat is approaching and will be with us in about ten minutes. Please don't shoot it down."

It was a room where no humans had yet been. They might have guessed at its existence but they had no idea of its location, and the First Breed had been careful to keep it that way. It was part of the Chambers of Command and it was from here that Iron Run led its nation.

An image of the human R.V. Krishnamurthy was

frozen against the wall at one end of the room, the brief final flash of grin painfully rigid. Iron Run looked at it with curiosity.

[Interrogative] <<Why does it show its teeth?>>

<<It is a sign of Gangly goodwill>> said its mouthtalker, Spar Mild.

<<Curious>> [Interrogative] <<Reactions?>>

[Outrage] <<Arrogant. Disrespectful—>> began one of the others.

[Correction] <<Very respectful>> said Iron Run.

[Outrage] <<To pronounce who may or may not attend the Convocation. That —>>

<<Its logic is impeccable>> said Iron Run.

[Dogmatic] <<Nevertheless, we have promised the humans our protection. We could stop this now>>

<<We could>> said Iron Run, <<or we could let the Ganglics fight it out amongst themselves. None of them would be so foolish as to take their fight to us and this could reveal useful additional data>>

[Insistent] <<Perhaps you should at least consult —>>

[Very dominant] <<I lead the nation>> Iron Run declared. <<I will make the decisions in this matter>>

Once Iron Run had made a decision, it knew the others would follow it with all their hearts and minds. They waited to see what it would be.

[Decision] <<Put the Big Moon battle fleet on standby, and await further developments>> Iron Run said.

*   *   *

Weight returned as the elevator carried the boat from *Shivaji*'s entry port at the hub down to the ship's skin. The outer door opened.

"Out, please," said Major Rajan. Julia and Peter stood slowly and left the boat, preceded by a couple of soldiers and followed by the rest. The soldiers were keeping a good distance away from them and had a firm grip on their guns, which struck Peter as redundant: even if he had managed to jump heroically at one of them, and wrest away his weapon without instantly being gunned down, he wouldn't have had the first idea of what to do with it.

Julia nudged him, very gently, and moved her head as if to say, "look around you." He did so. *Shivaji*'s boat bay was enormous — far bigger than was normal for a ship her size. A closer look showed the scars on the bulkheads left over after her refit. Walls had been folded back and down; he supposed that when they were up the bay would have been its normal size, which was perhaps how they had hidden its alterations and contents from *Shivaji*'s Rustie liaison. There were six landing boats present and space for several more, which presumably were now downstairs or in orbit. A row of armoured vehicles stood along one side.

"This way," said Rajan. They left the bay, still under escort, and were taken down corridors and past crew members who discreetly didn't stare, to an airlock. The inner door was open and, through it, Peter could see the outer door set into the floor. The soldiers stood to attention as a civilian man in a white Nehru jacket approached them.

"You must be Mr. Kirton," he said to Peter.

"Yes," Peter said cautiously.

"Excellent!" The man beamed. "Secretary Ranjitsinhji. I am the personal assistant of Excellency R.V. Krishnamurthy." Peter was aware of the latter name, but only dimly. Terrestrial politics had never interested him. Ranjitsinhji used a conversational tone and could have been talking about the weather. He took out an aide and began to enter data. "Your first name is Peter, I believe. Do you have a middle one?"

"William," Peter said, baffled.

"And outside of *Ark Royal*, what is your permanent residence?"

"Pete," Julia said quietly. Ranjitsinhji glanced up at her.

"Just a few administrative details," he said mildly. "Well, Mr. Kirton?"

Peter gave his room number in the officers' mess on UK-1. Ranjitsinhji held the aide up.

"Now I just need your verification," he said. "Please say your name out loud."

"Pete!" Julia said again, more urgently. She needn't have bothered: Peter knew that saying a name was as good as writing a signature and he had no intention of signing anything.

"What's it for?" he said.

"Is that relevant?" said Ranjitsinhji.

"Well, under the circumstances —"

"Mr. Kirton, you come from Mars, do you not?" Peter blinked at the change of subject. "Yes."

"Do you share the religious sentiments of your fellows?"

"By and large."

"If I were to order your execution now, would you be worried?"

"I —" Peter gulped. "Yes."

"But once you are dead, you believe in the reward of eternal life?"

"Yes . . ."

Ranjitsinhji nodded in satisfaction as though they had just reached mutual agreement in an argument between friends. "And what if you were to meet your creator with the responsibility for someone else's murder on your soul?"

"That . . . would be more problematic," Peter agreed.

"Good." Ranjitsinhji still used his discussing-the-weather tone of voice. "Major Rajan, throw this lady out of the lock."

"Sir?" Rajan said.

"Major Rajan, you may be Defence Force and not NVN but surely you can hear adequately. Throw this lady out of the lock."

"Yes, sir." Rajan paused only for about half a second, and though the look on his face showed he really didn't want to do this, he gestured to two of his men.

"What!" Julia yelped as they grabbed her. "Get off me! Get them off —"

Peter took a step forward and folded up as a fist ploughed into his stomach. He dropped to the floor and gasped for breath.

Julia raked a foot down the inside leg of one of the men holding her and managed to get a knee into the groin of someone else coming to his aid. For a moment she was free, but then arms closed around her from behind and lifted her bodily off the floor. The lock door opened and Julia was thrown in. She gathered herself up to leap out but the door hissed shut in her face. She hammered on the window. "Pete!"

"Open the outer door," said Ranjitsinhji. Rajan hesitated for half a second and then his hand came down on the controls.

"I'll do it!" Peter wheezed. Rajan's hand stopped and he looked at his superior.

Ranjitsinhji held the aide up.

"Peter William Kirton," Peter muttered.

"Excellent! Major, let the lady out. Mr. Kirton, you have just voluntarily transferred your citizenship to the Confederation."

"*What?*" said Peter.

"Of course, you need to be on UK-1 to renounce your UK citizenship, but that is a minor detail. Now, there is one other thing we require of you. Bring them both, please, Major."

"Welcome back on board, Arm Wild," Gilmore said as the Rustie and Adrian Nichol entered the flight deck. It was shortly after 2000: the coup had only been going on for an hour and it already seemed much longer. "I'm sorry you got dragged into this."

"Conflict involving the delegate ships was not entirely unexpected," Arm Wild said.

"I didn't think so. What precautions did you take?"

Arm Wild paused for a moment before speaking. "I do not believe I am betraying any confidences here. We have a fleet of armed ships hiding behind Big Moon, though that was more a precautionary measure should all the delegation ships band together against us. So long as there is no danger of the conflict spreading below orbit, or damaging our interests in any other way, the guidelines of the Convocation are that we should wait and see what you do."

"Oh, great," Gilmore muttered.

"Is now a good time to tell you that we know about the weapons on board this ship, and on every other in the fleet?" Arm Wild said. Gilmore managed a half smile.

"That helps," he said. "Thanks."

"But we won't need them, sir!" Nichol said happily. "You should have seen it! The moment I said I had Arm Wild on board with me —"

"That was down there," Arm Wild interrupted. "It might not be so easy up here."

"What do you mean?" Nichol said, frowning.

"He means," said Gilmore, who like Arm Wild had already worked it out, "that down there, he was in charge. Up here, he's no different from any other civilian who happens to wander into a war zone."

"But— but surely, sir," Nichol said, "if they knew Arm Wild was on board . . ."

Gilmore and Arm Wild just looked at him.

"All right," he said, in a last bid for reassurance. "As far as we know, all our people downstairs have been rounded up, they're being held at gunpoint — Arm Wild, your people won't stand for that, will they?"

"I believe the expression your people use," Arm Wild said, "is, 'don't make any wagers on it.'"

Shivaji's computer centre was behind the flight deck. Peter looked about him and reluctantly conceded that it beat his cubicle inside the centrifuge ring back on *Ark Royal*.

"Clear the room," Ranjitsinhji said. He still hadn't shown the slightest change in tone: his voice was that of someone to whom being disobeyed had simply never occurred. If he was the assistant, Peter hoped he would never, ever meet Krishnamurthy himself. "No, Ms. Lahiri, you can stay. Mr. Kirton, Ms. Lahiri is your counterpart on *Shivaji*."

Lahiri was his senior: her stripes said Commander,

the same as Gilmore. "How do you do," she said with a smile. "Please call me Muna."

"Later, Ms. Lahiri," said Ranjitsinhji. "Mr. Kirton, I understand you developed a translator program named Polyglot and that the sole copy is now on board *Ark Royal*."

Peter groaned silently.

"Yes," he said, "but —"

"No buts, please." Ranjitsinhji held up a hand as if to ward the buts off. "I am too busy for that. Mr. Kirton, we will avail you of all the necessary facilities on board this ship in order that you may retrieve Polyglot from *Ark Royal*'s memory. After that you will be given your freedom."

Peter shook his head. "No, sir, I —"

"You see, the Rusties make a great thing about personal choice," Ranjitsinhji said as if the interruption hadn't happened. "You have declared your voluntary allegiance to our country and that will be a great coup for us — the software genius who developed Polyglot, a citizen of the Confederation! A six-foot, fair-skinned, blond, blue-eyed citizen of the Confederation is admittedly rare, but we try to be open-minded. However, if you refuse to hand over Polyglot to your new rulers, they might think something is amiss. So, we need Polyglot."

"My contract says that any software I develop while working for the Royal Space Fleet belongs to the Fleet," Peter said.

"Don't do it, Pete," Julia said.

"The airlock is always waiting," Ranjitsinhji pointed out.

"All right," Peter muttered.

"Excellent. Ms. Lahiri, let me know when it's done." Ranjitsinhji left and the others remained, looking at each other.

"I'll need my aide," Peter said.

Major Rajan had both their aides clipped to his belt. "Which is yours?"

"That one."

Rajan handed it over. "The orbital net's still up?" Peter said.

"Of course," said Lahiri, not really surprising him. *Shivaji*'s automatic systems relied on the orbital net just as much as the other ships: Peter wouldn't have put wrecking it past the lunatic in charge of this operation but maybe Surit Amijee, *Shivaji*'s captain, had had a word in his ear.

"My aide needs to talk to your comms system," he said.

"I'll do that." Lahiri entered the required protocols manually. "Ready."

"Right." Peter entered a password into his aide and called up a display of codes. He, too, began entering them manually.

"Why don't you just get your aide to transmit them?" Lahiri said at once.

"Give me some credit," Peter said. "It won't accept anything but manual entry. Security."

"Try it anyway."

Peter shrugged and did as he was told.

"The host system is refusing to accept the codes," said the aide. "Manual entry required."

Peter cocked an eyebrow at Lahiri, who smiled. "Forgive me for insulting your intelligence. Carry on."

"We're in," Peter said.

"There is a captain's override in existence forbidding data to leave *Ark Royal*," said the aide.

"Override, code beta apollo," Peter said.

"Complying. The captain's override has been overridden."

Peter carried on entering the codes.

"Wait," said Lahiri. Peter paused, his hands above the keys, and out of the corner of his eye he saw Rajan tensing. "Now you're in, why not just tell your aide to get Polyglot?"

"Because," Peter said, as if speaking to a small child, "I've made it a bit more secure than that. Manual entry, remember?"

"Try it anyway," she said again.

Peter shrugged and changed to voice mode. "Retrieve Polyglot, copy to unit, password 'berlitz.' "

"Unable to comply. Retrieval of that program requires manual entry of security codes."

"You're a very cautious man, Lieutenant," said Lahiri. "I think I like you."

On board *Ark Royal*, Gilmore and Nichol looked glumly at the display above Peter's desk on the flight deck. Five minutes earlier it had come to life and now it was buzzing happily away to itself. Data was being taken from the ship and they couldn't do a thing about it.

On *Shivaji*, Julia watched the display with equal anguish as it showed data entering the ship's banks. AIs checked it for viruses and bombs and pronounced it clean. Lahiri straightened up from the desk with a satisfied smile.

"Well done," she said. Peter stared stonily into the distance. "Confirm safe receipt of Polyglot program."

"Polyglot program has been received," said the system. "Checksum shows 100% viability."

"Transfer to my aide." She added a password manually. "Major Rajan, give these two a room. I'll be on the flight deck with Mr. Ranjitsinhji."

The stateroom had twin beds, a view in the floor that showed a sequence of the Roving and space, and then the Roving again as the ship revolved, a food dispenser and a guard the other side of door. Julia also suspected it was crawling with electronic bugs.

"You're quiet," she said.

"Yes," he said glumly. He pulled a stylus out of his pocket and looked around for something to write on. He settled on the palm of his hand. *Going to die*, he wrote. Then, under that, *probably*.

She stared at it. "Why?"

"Because of what I just did," he said. His palm was full and he tried to write left-handed on the other. It didn't work and he took her hand instead. *Polyglot won't work. Made it only work on AR.*

"Won't wo —" she exclaimed out loud, before remembering. "Er . . . you didn't have to, Pete."

"Yes I did. No choice. I wasn't going to take chances with your life."

Julia looked at her palm, then up at him. She held it up for him to see and raised her eyebrows. "Very kind of you, Pete. Very kind."

He lay down on one of the beds with his hands behind his head and shut his eyes. "Now it's out of the way, I hope they don't need you as a hostage. If they're angry about anything, they'll take it out on me. I hope."

He didn't say anything else. His breathing slowed down and he was either asleep or praying. Julia looked at him, aghast. What world was this boy living in? Of course they'd take it out on her. And then on him anyway. Maybe he wasn't worried about dying, he had his faith to comfort him, but — *thank you, Peter Kirton, for including me in it as well. Thank you very much.*

"Your Royal Highness!" Krishnamurthy stood up from behind his desk and came forward, hand outstretched, face beaming. "Do come in!"

Prince James walked slowly forward, seething,

and aware of the NVN man behind him. Krishnamurthy was interviewing each of the delegates in turn: finally, at almost 2300, it was his turn.

"I apologize for this inconvenience," said Krishnamurthy. "I am sure you understand that, given the insights I have received into First Breed nature . . . well, what choice did I have?"

Insights! James thought with contempt, thinking of all the carefully laid plans that this creature had just comprehensively messed up for him. Though now wasn't the time for arguing. Gunshots, James had recently discovered, were *loud*. Being shot at was *terrifying*. James had decided that only a fool went to war.

"I'm amazed you haven't started shooting hostages yet," he said.

"At the moment, I doubt any of you would surrender your chances of ruling a world for a handful of human lives. No, we won't shoot hostages yet — we will leave that as, say, a reserve option."

"What do you want?" James said.

"Please, take a seat." Krishnamurthy sat down behind the desk again and James stayed standing; never a tall man, he still towered over the Indian. Krishnamurthy looked up and his eyes glinted. "I said, sit."

A chair banged into the back of James' legs and a powerful NVN hand pressed down on his shoulder. He sat.

"That is better. Your Royal Highness, I once offered you the chance to join my alliance. In all sincerity and friendship, I offer you that chance again."

"I don't think so."

"Your friends have decided it is the wisest course," Krishnamurthy said with a smile. As the delegates were being shown into Krishnamurthy's office one by one and kept incommunicado afterwards, James couldn't know if that was true.

"As I've said before, I don't think we have anything to offer you," he said.

"Your support will suffice. Oh, and I am glad to say that your brilliant software expert Mr. Kirton has chosen to become a citizen of our nation."

"I'm sure he wasn't in the least coerced."

"I give you my word, he was in no danger at all. Now, you saw my message to Iron Run? Of course you did. So, you see, it is important to me that my consolidation be legitimate in the eyes of the First Breed. The First Breed don't recognize the rights or wrongs of conquest — they just look at the *fait accompli*. In their eyes, once your ships have come under my control, they will be mine. Once I have the allegiance of a nation's leader, that nation will be mine. There are two ways in which this can happen: your willing acquiescence, or your execution and replacement by one of my people. It is all the same to the Rusties, and it is your choice."

"You realize you've effectively declared war on half of Earth?" A statement so blindingly obvious that James was ashamed to make it but he needed time to think. He was powerless; all he could do was hope the ships in orbit put up a good fight.

His heart sank lower at the thought. If *Ark Royal* were to be able to rely on the protection of its allies, surely it needed to be able to make its own contribution . . . and that whinging idiot Gilmore had gone and locked up Plantagenet, who only happened to have the software for the ship's weaponry in his ROM.

"And what is half of Earth going to do to me," Krishnamurthy said, "when I will have control of the Roving and use of the First Breed's space fleet? I advise you, Windsor, to join me." For once, there was no pretence of a smile on his face. "Well?"

The door opened and Muna Lahiri stood there, arms folded, with an armed guard behind her.

"Very clever," she said to Peter. "Very clever." She looked at Julia. "Your friend redesigned Polyglot so that it won't work outside *Ark Royal*'s own net. All it comes out with is gibberish." Back to Peter. "Excellency Krishnamurthy is not someone to cross. He will be angry and I expect he will order your execution. Why did you do it?"

Julia felt everything lower than her ribs turning to water. "When?" she whispered, her mind skirting around the question of whether the "your" in "your execution" had been singular or plural. It was a treacherous thought.

Lahiri ignored her. "Why did you do it?" she repeated. It was dawning on Julia that Lahiri could have been a friend. She didn't want them dead either.

Peter just closed his eyes again. "Because," he said, and that was all the answer Lahiri was to get.

Shortly after 2300, they lost the World Administration.

The voice of the fleet commodore, *U Thant*'s captain, came over on general band. "This is *U Thant* to all Earth ships. We have been unable to make contact with our delegate below so are taking matters into our own hands. We do not believe the WA should take sides in this dispute and we hereby declare our complete neutrality. *U Thant* is leaving orbit of this world altogether and establishing its own orbit around the sun at a distance of eight light-minutes. Please note that we are well able to defend ourselves. Message ends."

U Thant leaving orbit was like someone trying to make a dignified exit from a room, betraying their nervousness by hurrying just a bit too much. The WA ship used its fusion engines to make a quick getaway, which was safe but still broke normal space conventions so close to a planet.

"There they go," said Nichol. The radar showed *U Thant*'s blip moving off at speed. "So much for them."

"Thank you, Mr. Nichol," Gilmore said, more sharply than he had intended. *U Thant*'s departure meant one less obstacle for the enemy, bringing a possible attack closer. What would a space battle be like? How should he prepare? The only precedent was what common sense and his imagination could provide. He was always wary of common sense — if it really was common, he thought, everyone would have it — but his imagination could usually be relied upon. "Still the ring, Mr. Nichol. Arm Wild, is your suit still on board?"

"It is," Arm Wild said.

"Then both of you suit up. We're going to empty the ship. Plug yourselves into the air supply — we may be breathing canned for a while."

Whatever was going to happen to *Ark Royal*, they would be ready for it.

Nineteen
21–22 May 2149

Two of the crew were trapped upstairs in orbit and two more were God knew where, and the rest of the crew was sitting with her in the Dome.

It was almost midnight but no one was likely to sleep. All Hannah had in the way of entertainment was a pack of cards, but it was better than nothing. She looked around as Samad picked through the cards in his hand, mind not really on the game. Members of the crew of each ship were forming their own cliques; any conversation at all was in the form of self-conscious whispers.

Soldiers patrolled constantly. Krishnamurthy's allies didn't have a military presence but they were able to come and go as they pleased. They had the grace to look embarrassed and uncomfortable.

At long last a party of Rusties appeared and a murmur went around the Dome. The captives were perking up, sitting up straighter. Here came their salvation.

The lead Rustie addressed the nearest NVN sentry. "I am Spar Mild and I speak for Iron Run. I will converse with your superior."

The sentry looked around nervously and an officer hurried up to rescue him. "Mr. Krishnamurthy has been waiting for you, sir. If you will come this way."

"I choose to speak here."

Now the officer glanced around. "Sir, this place is a little public."

"It is the First Breed way for conversations to be conducted in public. Your superior will attend us here."

The officer swallowed. "If you will wait here, sirs," he said, and left them alone with the sentry. The man shifted nervously as all attention in the Dome was turned on him.

Krishnamurthy turned up thirty seconds later, rubbing his hands. "My dear Spar Mild, I am delighted you could come. Please, let us not talk here —"

"Iron Run has received your message," said Spar Mild, the first sapient being in a very long time to interrupt Krishnamurthy. "Your argument is interesting."

"Do you accept the legitimacy of my action?"

"You are in error to think that we will alter the rules of the Convocation."

Krishnamurthy's smile didn't waver. "But as I explained, I am now the leader of the humans on this planet. I have done nothing that will interfere with the smooth running of the Convocation tomorrow. Various nations from Earth will be represented, as specified in the rules."

"You have not impressed us with your mastery over the other nations."

"But I have their superiors down here, in my

power, and that makes them mine," Krishnamurthy said.

"You have captured the Seniors of the Earth nations, we cede that point, but the nations have not acquiesced."

Krishnamurthy shrugged. "Then we will remove the Seniors and install our own, according to your own custom, if that is what is required." Now the attention of every human in the Dome was on him, boring into his back. He didn't seem to notice or mind.

"There will be no innocent deaths," said Spar Mild.

"There will be no innocent deaths," Krishnamurthy agreed. "Seniors may be executed in accordance with First Breed custom and Juniors are liable to our own laws, which are punishable by death if transgressed. Now —"

"We accept your leadership of the humans now on the surface of the Roving," said Spar Mild. Krishnamurthy opened his mouth and drew himself up as if to argue, before actually realizing what Spar Mild had said. Hannah heard it: so did every other human in the Dome, but no one could believe it. Had the Rustie *really* said that?

"This is a temporary measure," Spar Mild added over the rising background murmur. "The humans here are under our protection and no harm will come to them. As we accept your leadership of them, we no longer hold their former leaders responsible for their well being: we hold you responsible, and reprisals will be made against your people if any harm comes to any of them. We are leaving soldiers of our own to ensure this."

"You accept my leadership?" Krishnamurthy said.

"As a temporary measure," Spar Mild repeated. "Its permanence will depend on the outcome of the affair in orbit."

Krishnamurthy beamed. "I promise you a result very shortly," he said.

"I think this is it, sir."

Across the airless flight deck, Nichol was hunched over his desk and staring at the displays. Gilmore abandoned the letter to Joel again, and turned his attention to the monitor. Arm Wild, too, broke out of whatever internal meditation was occupying his thoughts.

There had already been a false alarm half an hour ago when a cluster of ships at the leading edge of the fleet stopped spinning, which Gilmore suspected would be the first stage of an attack. The ships were behind and just to the right of *Pacifica*, and for all he knew they might have made their own agreement with the new order.

But instead they had boosted out of orbit together. Not long after, three others, all safely at the rear of the fleet, had done the same, heading in three different directions.

They should all have done that at the start,

Gilmore thought angrily. The four ships of Krishnamurthy's alliance couldn't have hoped to subdue
the rest of the ships scattered throughout the system. Rule One of the manual of space combat that
he was mentally drafting would be: If you want to
avoid a fight, a clean pair of heels is the best solution. Come to think of it, not an amazing philosoph-
ical insight.

And now, most of the ships that could have scattered had done so. The Israelis, the other two Chi-
nas, the rest of the Africans, all the Asian countries,
most of the American countries, the Vatican, the
Holy Arab Union . . . all showing far more sense
than the ships belonging to Prince James and his
friends. The five allied ships stayed in formation,
Ark Royal considerably hemmed in not just by her
friends but by the opposition all around: *Great Zimbabwe* above, *Long March* behind, and *Shivaji* and
Pacifica in front. A couple of miles behind *Long
March* sat the South American Combine's *Simón
Bolívar* and the Galactic Corporation's *Excalibur*,
which so far had stayed silent. The five allies hung
in space and made a nice juicy target, while the enemy gathered round and slavered.

Great Zimbabwe and *Long March* were holding
their position but *Shivaji* and *Pacifica* were moving
in closer — still out of laser range, but closer — and
coming round to face their target. It looked as if this
was, indeed, it. He instinctively checked the time,
though the log would already have noted it: 0005.

If the Battle of the Roving went down in history it would be noted as having happened on 22 May, 2149.

Rule Two in the manual would be: If you must design a ship to fight, design it so that it can fire in all directions. The weapons on those ships, like his own, faced for'a'rd only. Manoeuvring to fire was a bit of a giveaway, like the old sailing times, when ships could chase each other in full view for a day before coming within gun range. Torpedoes could change direction, but firing them in one direction and having them come round a full 180 degrees would also lose the surprise factor.

"This is *Shivaji*," said a voice on general band. "Your final chance to signal your surrender."

"Say nothing," Gilmore said, on the conference band. No one replied.

"In —" Nichol's voice broke and he coughed to clear his throat. "Incoming."

The radar showed a small object streaking towards them from the *Pacifica*. Without thinking, Gilmore slapped at the laser panel on his desk and the object vanished. Out in space, the first torpedo fired in anger had just been vaporized by a beam of coherent light.

Rule Three — your laser AI is unlikely to distinguish between a torpedo and a meteorite so long as it is clearly heading for your ship. Don't discourage it.

"All ships, set your lasers to automatic," Gilmore said. Lasers were usually on manual in orbit, in case the computer mistook the intentions of an innocent transport capsule, but exceptions could be made.

The single torpedo must have been a test firing because suddenly *Shivaji* and *Pacifica* both let off a cloud of torpedoes. The lasers on *Ark Royal*, *Enterprise* and *Algol* opened up in return and the two met halfway. The for'a'rd viewer showed a new starfield springing into life between the ships as the torpedoes exploded and evaporated in bursts of molten light.

And through the cloud of seething debris came a fresh wave. The laser systems, half blinded by the results of their own success, were slow to react. They recharged and opened up again, but still at least half the newcomers flew on.

These weren't nuclear weapons; the Rusties wouldn't have tolerated that and the aim was to cripple and capture the ships, not destroy them. Half a mile from the ships the torpedoes burst open and a thick mass of metal hurtled from them. The lasers recalibrated again and opened fire, and then the mass struck the ships. *Ark Royal* vibrated under the impact.

"We're spinning! Sir, we're spinning!" Nichol yelped. The gyroscopes and the viewers showed it was true — *Ark Royal* was spinning slowly around its centre of gravity.

"Then correct it," Gilmore said shortly. Training simulators presented worse cases than this.

"Aye-aye, sir," said Nichol, chastened, and together they fired the thrusters that steadied the ship.

"Where were we hit?"

"Leading face of the ring compartment," said Nichol, poring over the instruments. "Holed fore and aft, but no lines severed and the ring appears to be intact."

"Good." *Ark Royal*'s small size had protected her as the grapeshot passed, with only one strike on her largest surface area.

The larger ships hadn't been so lucky — he could see dark patches in their skins where there had been none before. Gilmore thought that this was how warfare had once been between ships: they sat a short distance apart and poured broadsides into each other until one was more full of holes than the other.

"*Ark Royal*. Your condition, everyone?" said Gilmore.

"*Bruxelles*. Several for'a'rd compartments holed. No casualties."

"*Enterprise*. We—"

"Incoming from *Long March*!"

A burst of torpedoes from the Chinese ship astern, and now it was the turn of *Bruxelles* and *Nikolai* to protect the formation. The lasers of two ships against the torpedoes of one was a closer match and not one got through.

As abruptly as it had started, the fighting stopped.

The ships still hung in orbit as if none of this had happened. Gilmore slowly relaxed, keeping part of his mind on full alert, to see what would happen next.

"*Excalibur* and *Simón Bolívar* to all ships. We are declaring neutrality and leaving orbit. We will defend ourselves if attacked."

The two remaining ships of the fleet that had not yet been caught up in the conflict fired their main engines together. They were astern of *Long March* and their course took them beneath the allies and their attackers, passing between ships and planet.

"Thanks for the help," Nichol muttered.

"They made a wise decision," Arm Wild said.

No they haven't, Gilmore thought. *That course will take them right in front of the enemy's guns. They could have worked that out. . . .*

The two ships had almost reached the fleet. Their trajectories were unchanged but they were bringing their prows up to point at the allied ships. Gilmore's mental antennae began to twitch.

"*Bruxelles* and *Nikolai*, stand by!" he shouted suddenly. "Get your lasers ready."

Simón Bolívar and *Excalibur* were still astern of the allies but were now angled up and pointing directly at them. They abruptly unleashed a new volley of torpedoes at close range. The lasers on *Nikolai* and *Bruxelles* opened up in return, but the closeness of the attackers meant there was less time to intercept all the incoming fire: more got through, and *Bruxelles* and *Enterprise* shook with further blows. Now the two attackers were passing beneath the allies and were close enough to use their own lasers: beams raked all five ships, scorching trails along their hulls, fusing exposed circuitry and mechanisms, knocking out systems.

That was a dirty trick, Gilmore thought. Well, they've asked for it.

"*Algol, Enterprise*," he said. "Stand by to target their main engines as they go past. All target *Simón Bolívar* first." The two attackers were now ahead of the allies.

"Fire," he said, and the three beams converged on *Simón Bolívar*'s main engine block. Main engines were built to take a stream of fusion explosions, but the combined energy of three beams caused the metal to glow red, then white, and then erupt in a cloud of molten vapour.

As *Simón Bolívar* started to tumble, they switched fire to *Excalibur*, but the ship was already too far away and the lasers did less damage.

"Yes!" Nichol shouted as the South American ship began to tumble. At that speed, and now with no main engine to slow down with, *Simón Bolívar* was well out of the conflict: the crew should be able to work it into a higher orbit until repairs were finished. *Excalibur* turned to brake and took up position behind *Pacifica* and *Shivaji*, abandoning its ally to sort out its own problems.

Then *Pacifica* and *Shivaji* opened up again with more grapeshot, and again *Long March* sent in its own burst from astern.

"*Bruxelles*, *Algol*, return fire," Gilmore said and the two ships did so with a barrage of their own torpedoes. *Ark Royal* shivered from another blow: a piece of shot had struck the bow and glanced along it, again hitting the invitingly flat, broad front face of the ring compartment. This time the ship wasn't punctured and there wasn't enough force in the blow to start another spin.

Strangely, Gilmore thought with pity of Surit Amijee, the gentle Hindu in command of *Shivaji*. He didn't doubt that the NVN were breathing down his neck; had maybe taken over altogether. They were firing the torpedoes, they were planning the destruction of the ships that opposed them. Not Amijee. But this kind of thing could really strain a friendship.

And what was *Shivaji*'s battle AI doing now? What was going through its tiny little mind? And to think that it was on the same ship as his own software officer. Peter Kirton could have worked out a way to baffle it, no doubt.

"A ship is manoeuvring," Arm Wild said. "*Great Zimbabwe*, I believe." The ship above them was rotating to face down towards the planet and the alliance ships. Gilmore pictured the scene from its crew's point of view: the entire length of *Algol* in front of them, unmissable.

"Ong, tell your crew to brace," he said. "Expect —"

"Tell me something I don't know, Gilmore," Ong snapped. *Algol* had already started to turn towards the Southern African ship. "We're —"

Great Zimbabwe unleashed a burst of torpedoes, pumping them into *Algol* at the almost point-blank range of a mile. It might as well have been a solid mass of metal: *Algol* shuddered visibly and some debris must have passed right through because her skin erupted on the far side, away from the impact. *Algol* was tumbling and thrusters spurted on her hull as her crew tried to get her under control.

A point on *Great Zimbabwe*'s prow glowed red, then white.

"Got her!" Ong shouted. "Sealed her tubes shut."

Rule Four: Keep your distance. "What's your damage, *Algol*?" Gilmore said.

"Still assessing." A pause. "Casualties." Ong sounded strained. "At least twenty. Severe holing, majority of central compartments punctured. Fore and aft systems operating independently, connecting lines severed. Thanks for the advice to depressurize, *Ark Royal*, we'd have been torn apart if we'd had air, but this passive resistance thing is a mug's game. We've got to take the fight to them."

"No!" Gilmore insisted. "We're the injured parties here, we mustn't be seen to get aggressive."

"Your ship hasn't just been riddled by grapeshot! You haven't just been rendered unfit for spaceflight and you haven't just lost crew! If you've got a better plan, let's hear it!"

"Um — newcomer, sir," Nichol said cautiously. Radar showed another ship rising up from orbit, maintaining a safe distance from the others. The ease with which it attained its orbit, and the fact that it just stopped, a hundred miles away, showed it to be a Rustie, as if there could have been any doubt. The ship was too far away to be caught up in any of the fighting. "Come to watch, I suppose," Nichol said bitterly. "Wonder how they feel about this?" Then he remembered. "Sorry, Arm Wild."

"I understand," Arm Wild said. "Believe me, they will not be enjoying watching this."

"So why don't your people step in and stop it, then?"

"I expect they have their reasons," Gilmore said. The reply was automatic — he didn't much feel like conversation with his Juniors right now, and it wasn't fair to dump guilt on Arm Wild — but despite himself, he sparked off a new thought process. *Why* didn't the Rusties step in? Because they had their reasons. Which were? Unknowable.

"They do not react, because at present you do not pose a threat to us," Arm Wild said.

"You mean, as long as we're just chucking lumps at each other?" said Nichol.

"Precisely. You are in a sufficiently high orbit for it not to matter."

"So when would it start mattering?" Nichol was beginning to sound desperate.

"Keep an eye on the enemy," Gilmore said sharply, to snap the younger man out of what he sensed was a rising cycle of hysteria. Arm Wild still answered the question.

"We cannot become involved in your conflict, Lieutenant. You will have to judge for yourselves when it would start to matter."

"Arm Wild," Gilmore said, "I take it you put us in this high orbit for a reason?"

"Precisely for the reason I have stated, Captain: so that any fighting between yourselves would not affect us."

"What would I do in your place?" Gilmore wondered out loud. "I'm inviting a fleet of armed alien ships to take up position around my world, and I'm fairly certain they're going to start squabbling . . ."

Arm Wild simply looked at him, but Gilmore had the sudden notion that the Rustie was willing him towards a conclusion.

"Maybe," he continued, "I'd declare a zone in orbit? Let their fighting confine itself to that, but if it extends beyond it —"

Yet another burst of grapeshot broke off the train of thought and again *Ark Royal*'s laser opened up. It was all happening so quickly, automatic laser was the only way.

He looked thoughtfully at *Shivaji*'s image. The Confederation ship's laser would be connected to the battle AI — bound to be. No point in having two systems doing the same job in parallel, with one perhaps making its own innocent plans when the other depended on it to do something else.

Krishnamurthy's people had taken great care not to offend the Rusties, and so the battle AI would have been programmed with certain safeguards: for instance, if they had really wanted to eliminate the allies, a volley of fusion warheads would have done the trick. Just as with the grapeshot, some would have got through, and with the ships all grouped together . . . but no, nuclear explosions in orbit would certainly annoy the Rusties.

Gilmore looked again at *Shivaji* and grinned. "Mr. Nichol," he said, "stand by to plot a course and power up the main engine. Comms, get me the other captains. *Algol*, can you still manoeuvre? We need you facing *Shivaji*."

The seconds were ticking by on the display over Gilmore's desk, and he knew the tense look on Nichol's face exactly mirrored his own. Arm Wild stayed silent: the Rustie had neither confirmed nor denied that his tactic would work. 1259 and 57 seconds, 58, 59—

At 0100 exactly, *Algol* and *Enterprise* opened with their own torpedoes, sending a deluge of debris directly at *Shivaji*. At 0100.01, *Ark Royal*'s fusion engine fired and weight came to the flight deck, pressing Gilmore, Nichol and Arm Wild into their couches, as the ship accelerated in the torpedoes' wake towards the Confederation vessel.

The lasers on *Shivaji* and *Pacifica*, both tuned to *Shivaji's* battle AI, opened up on the first wave of the attack by reflex. A moment later, the AI noticed to its surprise that a 5000-ton spaceship was accelerating towards it in the shadow of the torpedoes. For a moment it considered targeting just the ship with the laser, but it knew that *Pacifica's* laser alone could not deal with all the torpedoes, and the attacking ship would still have most of its mass by the time it hit. *Shivaji* would sustain damage outside the recommended parameters.

Then it considered ordering both lasers to target the ship. That would leave the torpedoes unimpeded and again irreconcilable damage would occur.

With more time to spare it would have consulted a human, but it knew humans were achingly slow at making any decisions. And so it made one by itself and had acted accordingly before a horrified Muna Lahiri noticed and could countermand.

"They've fired!" Nichol said. The radar showed a single torpedo leaving *Shivaji*.

"Go!" Gilmore shouted.

The rumble of the engine turned to a roar and a massive, crushing weight descended upon them. Nichol bellowed as four gees piled on top of them and *Ark Royal* leapt forward. *Shivaji* loomed in the display and then the picture whitened out. They had moved too quickly to trigger the torpedo's proximity detector and the battle AI had decided to laser them after all; this mad ship intent on colliding with them took priority over everything else.

But *Ark Royal* was not intent on colliding with *Shivaji*, just in coming damn close. Still Gilmore grit his teeth: *I've left it too close we're going to hit I've left it too close we're going to hit* . . .

There was a glimpse through the viewport of *Shivaji's* skin as they shot by, metres away, and then *Ark Royal* was out the other side, heading rapidly out of orbit and into space. The engine cut off and the return of free fall was blissful.

Behind them, between *Shivaji* and the four remaining allied ships, there was a flash of brilliantly white light. The torpedo barrage still had to be dealt with and so the battle AI had chosen that as the secondary target.

"We did it!" Nichol yelled. "We did it!"

"We don't know if it's worked yet," Gilmore said. "Get us back into orbit, while we still can. I'd hate to have to ask the Rusties for a tow."

[Distress] <<They are using nuclear weapons>>

Iron Run studied the display carefully. [Interrogative] <<In our orbit?>>

[Affirmation]

[Interrogative] <<Damage?>>

<<Several satellites disabled by electromagnetic

pulse but communications by and large rerouted
and unaffected. Our own ships are far enough away
to escape injury>>

[Interrogative] <<Radiation?>>

<<We are shielded by the atmosphere. But that
may change if fighting drops into a lower orbit>>

Iron Run turned to its military advisor. [Interrogative] <<What is your opinion of the outcome of this
fight?>>

<<The Ganglies are well matched. It may well be
a fight to the death>>

[Interrogative] <<Could either side succeed without nuclear weapons?>>

[Problematic]

[Decision] <<Then I am persuaded. Mobilize the
battle fleet. Spar Mild, you will take a message to the
Gangly Senior at the Dome. If it will not comply, you
are authorised to take measures>>

Spar Mild and retinue strode into the Dome at 0115
and demanded an audience with Krishnamurthy.
The guard sent to fetch him disappeared into a side
room and there was an angry shout in Hindi. Then
more shouting, and finally Krishnamurthy came
stalking out, his face furious.

"Iron Run says, there has been fighting in orbit,"
said Spar Mild.

"There has," said Krishnamurthy, "and with respect, I am in the middle of coord—"

"Iron Run's orders are as follows," said Spar Mild.

"This matter has proceeded far enough and it is persuaded that you will be unable to settle things between yourselves safely. It perceives that nuclear weapons have been used in our orbit. This poses a clear hazard to us and their use will cease immediately. You will withdraw your troops from the surface of the Roving at once. Liberty will be reinstated forthwith to all humans in our system. The situation will return to its previous normalcy without delay."

"Normal? Sir, please, there is a fight going on in orbit —"

"We are already taking the necessary measures," Spar Mild said.

"There's hundreds of them!" Nichol exclaimed.

An exaggeration, but there were still a lot of them. The shapes that the radar showed emerging from behind the Roving's Big Moon easily outnumbered the human ships.

A warning tone came from the console and Nichol spun round to Gilmore.

"One of them's locked on to us, sir!" he said, aggrieved.

"I don't blame then," Gilmore said wryly.

"I think you will find every ship has been targeted," Arm Wild said. "It is only precautionary. I would strongly advise that you do not —"

There was a flash and *Long March* shuddered, as though from a mighty blow. Ripples ran impossibly along its length and chunks of its skin broke away.

The ship began to spin slowly, and then with another flash its entire midsection disintegrated into a million fragments. The bow and stern sections tumbled away from the scene.

There was a moment's silence and then bedlam broke loose over the radio.

"Did you see that?"

"My God, just a flash and then —"

"Who was it? What was it? Did you see —"

"What a way to go! What a way to go!"

Gilmore and Nichol stared at the display.

"—do likewise," Arm Wild finished.

A signal came through. "The First Breed require all human ships to cease hostilities immediately. We will enforce this command further if necessary, and if any other ship locks on to us, we will treat that, too, as a hostile act and respond accordingly. We will pick up survivors from the *Long March*. All human ships will power down their weapons and deactivate their targeting systems *now*."

The battle fleet moved quickly through space with the easy grace common to Rustie vessels. Human ships making the same manoeuvre would have taken hours to traverse the distance from Big Moon to Roving orbit, and more to slow down and change approach trajectories. The Rustie ships just did it, and within minutes they were in among what was left of the delegation fleet, interlacing themselves with the human ships.

"It's over!" Nichol exclaimed. "Sir, you did it!" His

eyes shone as he looked over at his captain and even through the faceplate Gilmore, aghast, diagnosed the signs of incipient hero worship. He groaned to himself.

"Captain Gilmore, I am sorry I was unable to help you much in your conflict," Arm Wild said. "My rank was not especially of use to you. However, I think I can now use my influence to contribute in a small way."

Krishnamurthy's eyes were on the display that showed the two fleets mingling. He had no doubt at all that the Rustie ships could wipe out *Shivaji* and the rest of them at a moment's notice, just as *Long March* had been dealt with.

The pale-faced delegate from the Northern Chinese Republic had already announced his withdrawal from Krishnamurthy's plan. The gutless imbecile: it wasn't his fault that his captain hadn't had the brains to turn his targeting system off. Krishnamurthy felt no sorrow for the loss of *Long March*.

Instead, he burned. He had been so convinced, *so* convinced he was right!

And who knew, maybe he had been? He would never know, now those idiots up there had resorted to nuclear weapons. Leave Subhas Ranjitsinhji in charge of something, he thought, and this is what happens.

But at least this way, he had his dignity. It was almost as if the Rusties were giving him a chance. Perhaps they were. No, there was no *perhaps*. They *were*. The burning anger turned into a sweet, warm glow. Play this right and he was still a contender.

"I am persuaded," he said to Spar Mild, "that this situation cannot be resolved by human means. I apologize to Iron Run for any inconvenience that has been caused and I formally order my forces, and the forces of my allies, to stand down. I renounce my claim to lead the humans on the Roving."

"A wise decision," Spar Mild agreed. "Incidentally, Iron Run says that all military equipment now on this world and belonging to you or your partners is impounded."

"Please!" Krishnamurthy exclaimed, forgetting himself. "You expect us to hand over our arms and yet you let the others keep theirs? I point out to you that certain parties had a military presence on this world before we did! They came down in the first wave, masquerading as diplomats —"

"Their weapons, too, are impounded," said Spar Mild, "and all artificial intelligence devices will be returned to their owners."

"Excuse me." A new contender entered the ring. Paul Ganschow of Starward strode up to the Rusties, blithely pushing aside the guards that had been holding him. "I formally request on behalf of Starward that this man —" He pointed grandly at Krishnamurthy "—be held for trial, on the grounds of —"

"Iron Run refuses your request," said Spar Mild.

Ganschow let his arm fall and stared at the Rustie. "You cannot be serious!"

"I am very serious."

Ganschow glared at Krishnamurthy. "Okay, so they're letting you off. But you're finished."

"He is not finished," Spar Mild said. "He is still a delegate and his presence here is as valid to us as your own."

"What?" Ganschow shouted.

"This is Iron Run's conclusive word on the matter." Even through the translator, Spar Mild was beginning to sound impatient. "The Convocation will proceed as originally planned. This point is neither debatable nor negotiable. This individual is the designated delegate for the Confederation of South-East Asia and so will attend. We promised all delegates safe passage to and from our world and that is what will happen. Now, as much as is possible and with certain safeguards, we have restored the situation that existed before this matter arose. There will be no recriminations for what has transpired for as long as all the humans in this system are under our protection."

That's right, Krishnamurthy thought. *Be angry with them. See me, Mr. First Breed? I'm being good and doing exactly as I'm told.* He was also thinking already about how the situation could be saved, and what could still be got out of it. He still had Kirton . . . ah, yes, Kirton. Kirton, who had dealt him such a grand dud . . . some things could be avenged.

"It is late and Iron Run advises sleep for you all," Spar Mild finished. "The Convocation will begin at the arranged time of 0900 hours this morning. Good night."

Julia and Peter heard the shouting out in the corridor. They were both still awake and still clueless as to what was going on outside. They had heard the roar of thrusters: *Shivaji* had manoeuvred, turning round. Then silence that seemed to last forever. Without their aides and without any kind of timepiece it was impossible to tell how long had passed.

Finally, very recently, bedlam; raised voices that spread through the ship. And footsteps: the deliberate tramp-tramping that comes with military boots worn by someone with a bad attitude. The footsteps stopped outside their room.

"Oh my God, this is it," Julia said.

The door slid open and an NVN man stood there. Julia recoiled at the hate on his face.

"Get up," he snapped. Neither of them made any move. He took a step forward and his hand went to his sidearm. "I said, get up!"

Slowly, they got up.

"Out."

They went out. Two more NVN were there, one either side of the door, both with rifles. The NVN fell in behind them and they were marched down the corridor.

Julia stole a sideways look at Peter, before a gun nudged her, none too softly in the back and a voice barked, "Eyes forward!" He was holding his head high, looking straight ahead, but there was no doubting he looked as pale as she felt. Making a stand, doing his duty to king and country and denying Krishnamurthy his little triumph, was all well and good, but look where it had got them.

And then they turned down a passageway that Julia remembered, and there was no further doubt at all in her mind. It led to *Shivaji*'s boat bay. Good, strong bulkheads to put them up against; a nice, wide open space with plenty of field of fire. A killing ground. They were walking to their execution.

She stopped suddenly. She couldn't do it. She couldn't make her warm, alive body carry her to a place where she would end up cold and dead.

The gun nudged her harder, in the kidneys.

"Keep moving!"

"Come on, Julia," Peter said softly. He held out a hand, and she took it. "I'm sorry," he said.

She tried a brave, very small smile.

"They— they'd have done it to us anyway," she said. "Even if you'd gone along with them."

"I expect so. Shall we go?"

So, hand in hand and with their certain killers behind them, they walked into the boat bay.

Julia scanned it dully. Where would it be? Which few square metres of ferro-polymer here were the place she would pass from this life into the next? Not there: fuel tanks. Her gaze moved along to a row of *Shivaji*'s landing boats. No, not there. Still onwards, over the small boat poised on the main hub elevator. It reminded her of *Sharman*. Not there —

Yet, it was there. That was where they were being taken to.

And then, almost all at the same time and yet seeming to be years apart, she saw:

. . . the registration lettering on the side of the little boat . . .

. . . a grinning Adrian Nichol standing in the hatch . . .

. . . and Arm Wild standing next to him. Arm Wild, in glorious, real solidity. Arm Wild, miraculously transported from the Highlands to here.

"Hi, Jules, Pete," Adrian said. He looked pointedly at their clasped hands. "Am I interrupting something?" They let go of each other quickly.

"Thank you," Arm Wild said to the NVN men. "We will take them from here." Then the Rustie looked from one to the other. "You are alive. That is agreeable to me."

"But what are you doing here?" Julia said.

"And what's happening out there?" said Peter. "What —"

"A lot has been happening out there," Arm Wild

said. He stood aside, clearing the way for them to enter the airlock. "Come. We are taking you back to your ship."

"It's over?" Julia said. Arm Wild looked at her.

"This affair is over," he said, "but as the Convocation is yet to happen, the important events have not even begun."

Twenty
22 May 2149

Sharman cleared *Shivaji*'s entry port and headed out into space. Julia looked back at the receding vessel and shuddered.

"I never want to see that ship again."

"You will not have to," Arm Wild said.

"What will happen to them now?" Julia said.

"If you are asking will there be retribution, the answer is no."

"You're joking! Arm Wild, they kidnapped us, they started a small war, they —"

"Are under our protection, as are you," said Arm Wild. "After the Convocation, the delegation fleet will be escorted back to Earth by a prideship. What you do at that end is your concern but in our space, please allow us to make our own rules."

"I'm sorry," Julia said at once. This was the sternest thing she had yet heard from Arm Wild. "Though wasn't that exactly what they were doing? Dictating rules in your own space?"

"We are prepared to be flexible," Arm Wild said, "but the Convocation is a sacred trust and will not be altered by one iota."

"Arm Wild, where are we going?" Peter turned away from the viewport and finally joined in the conversation. "It looks like a higher orbit."

"It is where *Ark Royal* is now, as a result of your captain's manoeuvre."

"What manoeuvre?"

"To fool *Shivaji* into firing a nuclear weapon."

"How can you fool someone into doing that?" Peter said in disbelief.

"Arm Wild, will you tell us exactly what's been going on?" said Julia.

Arm Wild told them.

"And your fleet opened fire on a delegation ship?" Peter said in disbelief.

"They did."

"I thought you said we were all under your protection?"

"You are."

"That's a funny way of protecting."

Arm Wild looked at him with his unreadable alien stare. "Some of you have shown a funny way of appreciating our hospitality."

"But . . ." Peter said helplessly.

"Peter Kirton, have you learnt nothing about us?" said Arm Wild. "I believe I can understand your objections, very dimly, because I have been to Earth and have perused your ways. But the First Breed hold that juniors are responsible for the actions of a senior, and if they do not approve of those actions, they replace the senior. If the crew of any human ship are not prepared to endorse the actions of their seniors and to face the consequences of those actions, then they should not be on that ship."

"But that's not —"

"Human?" said Arm Wild. It wasn't what Peter had been about to say, but he let it pass and fumed quietly for the remainder of the trip.

Adrian Nichol drifted in his suit over the bow of *Ark Royal*.

The bow turret and the front of the ship were a mass of melted slag, wrecked by *Shivaji*'s laser. "A" compartment, which included the for'a'rd airlock, was completely open to space: to get out he had gone into "B" compartment and depressurized. Since *Ark Royal*'s flight deck was "C" compartment, Adrian reflected that they should be grateful for small mercies.

He jetted slowly aft along the ship. "Some scarring here, sir," he reported. "We don't appear to be holed." He waved a vapour detector over the area. "Confirmed, we're intact. Need a new paint job, though."

"That's the least of our troubles," said Gilmore's voice in his ears. "Carry on."

Adrian headed for the face of the centrifuge ring compartment, the site of the impact that had set the ship spinning. He looked at the lesser damage first: some of the heat fins that ribbed the compartment were buckled. Then he went over to look at the hole.

It was some five feet across and the lump that had caused it had gone clean through the compartment and out the other side. Adrian floated in and looked around. Inside, the lights were on: this was meant to be a pressurized part of the ship. If the centrifuge ring was a doughnut then he was in its hole and the space was crammed: computer centre, emergency cryo capsules, air tanks, life support . . .

Small ferro-polymer fragments of ship were floating around and Adrian studied them carefully for sharp or jagged edges before proceeding. The ceiling of the centrifuge ring was a smooth curve, motionless and as far as he could see unblemished, and Adrian reported this.

"Apart from that, quite a bit of severed fibre," he said with only a little concern. *Ark Royal* was robust — any command path could be rerouted along alternative circuits and they had plenty of spare fibre on board to plug the gaps. At first glance the ship was looking good, though whether they would be able to spin the ring again, or boost safely without the ship coming apart at the seams, remained to be seen. "Nothing serious has been damaged," he added with relief.

The exit wound on the aft face of the compartment was twice the size of the entry. Adrian peeped out aft, afraid of what he might see. More scarring down the side of the ship but, as instruments had already confirmed, the external tanks were intact.

Adrian fired his suit thrusters and pulled back from the ship, retreating until he was far enough away in space to take in the whole vessel with a sin-

gle glance. Then he slowly jetted around her. A
close-up inspection could focus the mind too much:
you could concentrate so much on one area that
you completely ignored damage in another. But
again, no further damage showed. The ship had
taken a battering but come through it with full
colours. He reported no further damage.

There was movement in the corner of his eye. A
landing boat was firing thrusters to brake, hanging
in space by *Ark Royal*'s bow.

"We've got company, sir," he said.

"I know. It's the others," Gilmore said. "Stay out
there: I'm sending help."

When the two suited figures of Samad and Hannah
pulled themselves through the pressure door from
"B" compartment, the flight deck was suddenly full.
Gilmore was at the watch desk, and Julia and Peter
at the two auxiliary desks, together picking their
way through the ship's systems. For the first time in
what seemed ages the flight deck was crowded
again.

"What have you been doing to my ship?" Samad
demanded as he removed his helmet. "Have you
seen the bow?"

"You'd be proud of her," Gilmore said. "Welcome
back." He raised his voice. "*When* you're ready . . ."
He waited for the silence. "Mr. Loonat, don't bother
unsuiting. Join Mr. Nichol outside. We'll start repres-
surizing the aft compartments, and I want you to

look out for leaks. After that you can give the engines an external inspection. Number One, when you're ready, join me in "E" compartment. I'd appreciate your help breaking out the spares we're going to need."

Hannah joined him five minutes later, her suit stowed away. "E" compartment was a hollow cylinder between the centrifuge hub and the boat bay, lined with lockers. Gilmore had already made a small pile in midair of bales of optic cable and computer crystals, reading off from a checklist on his aide which floated next to the pile. She savoured this one-man bustle of activity for a moment.

"You're enjoying this, aren't you?" she said.

He looked up. "It beats being shot at," he said.

"And sitting around in orbit twiddling your thumbs."

Gilmore allowed himself a small smile. "That too. Locker 507, get a couple of splicers out, could you? Yes, we're actually doing something at last."

Hannah complied. "Splicers, couple of. Of course, in the last few days you've only explored a whole new alien world . . ."

Gilmore ticked the items off. "They're welcome to it."

"There's no romance in your soul, Mike."

"Look hard enough and you'll find it. What's happening downstairs, Number One?"

"The Convocation was just starting as we left.

They drew the order of speakers out of a hat. The South Americans are kicking off, the Polynesians next . . . I forget the rest of the order. The prince is on at 1300."

Gilmore made a noncommittal noise. "And how is everyone getting on with our late adversaries?"

"The Rusties are determined to pretend it never happened. Whether the humans will or not, I don't know."

"*Algol*'s people won't in a hurry. She lost crew."

"That's bad," Hannah said with sympathy.

"And she's so badly damaged she might not even be able to boost out of orbit."

Hannah whistled and looked around her. "Things could be worse, then."

"They could."

"Shall I have the signal relayed to the wardroom?"

"I wouldn't, the ring doesn't have air yet . . ." Gilmore paused. "What signal?"

"Well, the Convocation is being broadcast generally . . ."

"And why would we want to watch it?"

Hannah leaned forward. "Because not everyone is as uninterested as you in the outcome. It could affect all our futures."

"We've got a ship to repair," Gilmore said. He saw the expression on her face, the one member of crew who would dare to get annoyed with him and whom he would let get annoyed. "I'm sorry, but there's only six of us and we've got a lot to get through. We won't even have broken the back of it by 1300."

"Sir, can I recommend asking for help from one of the other ships?"

"I have no intention of asking for help," Gilmore said at once. "We can manage." Hannah said nothing. He could see her point of view and had to admit that extra hands would be extremely useful . . . but to ask for help, to accept that the situation was beyond him . . .

Oh, hell.

"Number One," he said, "I want you to draw up a list of preliminary tasks for each of us, myself included, to be carried out prior to 1300. Those members of the crew who have finished their assigned tasks by then may watch the broadcast."

"Very good, sir."

Gilmore reflected that Hannah had never been as good as him at keeping a straight face.

To no one's great surprise, all preliminary tasks were safely concluded prior to 1300. Since the wardroom was still in vacuum, the flight deck was used.

The broadcast was live, with no superfluous commentary or explanation. It was simply a case of the cameras being pointed at the speakers and left on. The Convocation was taking place in the Dome: the delegates sat on their own in a circle with Iron Run and other leading Rusties.

Valerie duPont, the North American delegate, was

still speaking as the time display reached 1259 and 50 seconds. She was surrounded with paper notes and a graph of something could be seen on her aide's display, positioned so that the others at the Convocation could see it. The Rusties hadn't provided presentation equipment.

A Rustie voice off-camera told her the time.

"— and that concludes my presentation," she said abruptly, and despite a look of very undiplomatic irritation she shut up and sat down. Previous speakers who had overrun their slot had been shown little mercy.

There was no linking speech by a Rustie. The cameras and microphones moved straight off duPont and on to the prince.

"They really don't mess around, do they?" Hannah commented.

"It's very important to them, this Convocation," Julia said. "When he picked us up, Arm Wild said they would be flexible in other things but not in this. He said the Convocation was a sacred trust."

"From whom?" said Samad, but then everyone shushed him as the prince stood up and clasped his hands behind his back. He began to speak.

"Leaders of the First Breed, I will be brief. I am here to represent the United Kingdom at this Convocation and I would like to begin by reminding you of our history. The history of my personal ancestors.

"Our nation was formed originally by the fusion

of many different races who came to the British
Isles, the small archipelago where we lived. On nu-
merous occasions our islands stood alone against
tyranny on the neighbouring continent of Europe.
People came from all over the world to us, to escape
oppression and to be free."

"That's a rosy point of view," Samad murmured.

"The United Kingdom today carries on that tradition of blending together different peoples. The
crew of our ship *Ark Royal* has one native of the UK
on board"— Adrian fidgeted — "and five others
who have chosen to belong to our nation. Michael
Gilmore, the ship's senior, whose ability to command was proved by recent events, is a native of the
British Isles." Everyone on the flight deck looked at
Gilmore, who refused to look embarrassed. "Two of
the others are drawn from Earth's colonies on Luna
and Mars, and two more from the former terrestrial
nations of Israel and Bangladesh. This crew of six,
just six —"

"That's right, rub it in," Julia said.

"— is, I can assure you, typical of the composition
of the United Kingdom. Seven thousand human beings have voluntarily given their allegiance to King
Richard, our ruler and my quickening parent —"

"His what?" said Adrian, and Peter and Julia ex-
changed glances. Julia winked.

"— and there is a waiting list for citizenship twice
as long. All these facts will be verified by your colleague Arm Wild.

"On Earth, we were a race of innovators. The most favoured system of government on Earth, representative democracy, was pioneered in our Parliament. The basic two principles of law in any democratic nation of Earth, the right to a trial by one's peers and the right to impartial justice for all, were set down in the historical document called Magna Carta. Our scientists blazed the path for modern science — physics, chemistry, biology. Our philosophers devised the scientific method. Three hundred years ago we set our world on the path of industry that it has followed ever since.

"And though we were small, though our territory was restricted, for centuries our ships ruled the seas of Earth. We even gave our world its common language! That is our heritage and it is a tradition that we are proud to continue.

"Look at what the UK has achieved in its current form. We were the first fully independent non-planetary community, and in that we are ahead of you, for none of your clans has yet moved permanently off this world and into space. UK-1 is one of the acknowledged wonders of the modern world, and our engineers designed and built it. Most recently, in the last few days, one of our people devised a program that could decipher your mouthtalk —"

Now everyone looked at Peter, who went red. "But I didn't!" he protested. "I didn't!"

" — and it was the superior strategy of my captain that ended the regrettable incident of the past night.

"And so I say this to you. Members of the First Breed, join with us and let us show you the way. Let us develop the heritage of this world, let us take the initiative and together we shall take the place in space that is our common right. Thank you."

The prince sat down again, and the babble on the flight deck of *Ark Royal* was matched by the babble from the Convocation coming over the speakers.

"That's it? That's all he's got to say?" said Adrian.

"Let us rule you? Do as we tell you? Come on!" Julia added.

A Rustie voice came over the speakers, asking the prince if that was all. The prince replied that it was. He sat in his chair, staring at the tabletop, then glanced at his watch, abruptly stood and walked out of the camera's field of view.

"He just . . . he just threw it all away," said Julia. "He brought us this far, and —"

Gilmore pushed up from his seat. "We're nowhere near repaired yet," he said. "I suggest we get ready. Ms. Coyne, kindly continue running diagnostics on the ship's systems."

Julia bit her lip. "Yes, sir."

"Mr. Loonat, Mr. Nichol, outside again, please. We're going to repressurize the ring, same procedure as before. Carry on, everyone." Gilmore left the flight deck, not because he particularly had anything to do aft, but because he knew full well the rest of the crew wanted to discuss the matter further, regardless.

The die was cast. Prince James heard the hubbub around him but ignored it. Confidence, assurance — that was all part of the package. It had to be delivered whole.

Only a couple of hundred humans, maximum, would have heard that speech, but it had been the least enjoyable of his entire career. And if, if, if it *didn't* work, if he had to go back to Earth, to face those who didn't know about the plan. . . . He cringed inside.

One of Iron Run's mouthtalkers spoke to him. "James Windsor, that is your presentation?"

"It is," said James.

"Very well. The delegate for the Arab Union will speak at 1330 by the common delegation clock."

Take five, James thought. He looked at his watch. *Take twenty-five*. He pushed his chair back and picked up his aide, then set off for the nearest staircase. Perhaps he could make it . . .

No such luck. Four scowling, furious, uncomprehending faces intercepted him.

"What the hell are you up to, Windsor?" Paul Ganschow snapped. "That was the best you could do?"

"I can understand you not having faith in your own ability to succeed," said duPont, "but, Jesus!"

"We have wasted our time with you, Windsor," Makarenko said. "Don't call us."

"Couldn't you have tried a bit harder? Put in a word for —" said Laventhal.

What's it to you? James screamed at them, in the privacy of his own mind. *Maybe I'm just one less contender for you to worry about.*

"Excuse me, please," he said out loud, and pushed through them to the stairs.

Back in his room, he shut and locked the door, and fell onto the bed. The mask fell away and he let the groans come out.

In the recently repressurized boat bay, Hannah found Gilmore staring at *Sharman* as though he had never seen it before.

"Something wrong, Mike?"

"I didn't empty her," he said.

"Your point?"

"I emptied the ship of air but I clean forgot the boat. She still had air in the middle of the battle. If she'd been punctured . . ."

If she had been punctured she would have exploded like a burst balloon.

"Well, she wasn't," Hannah said. "Don't torture yourself, you did damn well."

"I could have done better."

"Then remember it for next time."

Gilmore winced. "Yes, there probably will be a next time, won't there? Between the new space powers, whoever they are . . ."

Hannah smiled. "Not us, by the looks of it."

Gilmore looked thoughtful. "You reckon?"

"You heard the prince's speech!"

"Oh, yes, I heard it. He chose the oddest things to emphasize, didn't he? Our lack of size, the fact our citizens volunteer to be citizens . . . as well as the obvious, all the things the original country gave the world."

"Or not." Hannah held up a hand and ticked off points on her fingers. "Let's see. In my history lessons, Magna Carta was forced on the king by a gang of thugs."

"It still happened. It still passed into law."

"And science! Copernicus, Curie, Einstein were British?"

"Newton was. Hawking was. Kelcey was."

"Our 'common tongue'? Standard is based on English because that's what twentieth-century Americans spoke."

"And who did they get it from? Number One, the prince has his faults, God knows, but he isn't stupid. He has never been stupid. Insufferable, arrogant, pure airlock fodder . . . but not stupid."

"So what do you think he was up to?"

"I've no idea."

Julia's voice interrupted them. "Captain, please come to the flight deck at once." In her voice was . . . surprise? Bafflement?

Gilmore glanced at Hannah, who shrugged, not certain herself what to make of Julia's tone.

"What is it?" Gilmore said.

"Um — easier if you come and see, sir."

Gilmore sighed. "I'm on my way."

"The Rustie comm channels suddenly went mad," Julia said a couple of minutes later as he airswam into the flight deck. "We're picking up all sorts of strange particles which seem to be coming from a point three light-seconds out from our current position. And look."

On the display a flotilla of smaller ships had broken off from the battle fleet, moving at speed and with purpose towards the source of the particles.

"Any guesses?" Gilmore said.

Julia sat at the systems desk, trying different combinations of commands.

"Our instruments aren't designed for this, sir," she said, "but what they can pick up is exactly the same as the step-through point that brought us here."

"And the Rusties aren't expecting it," Hannah said.

"Try it visually," said Gilmore. "Get the telescope on it."

The telescope display blurred for a moment and then cleared to show what was, without doubt, a step-through point — a sphere of nothingness growing out of space. The scale showed it was many times larger than the last one they had seen.

Size wasn't the only difference. The last one Gilmore had seen appear had blossomed, flowered without effort out of nothingness. This one seemed to be struggling: it flickered, shrank back a fraction, then grew suddenly even larger. It was as if whoever was generating it either hadn't quite got the knack yet or didn't have the power. It was like someone blowing up a balloon and constantly running out of puff.

Suddenly the sphere stabilized. It stopped growing or shrinking and sat there in space.

"I don't believe it," Julia said. "We're getting fragments of a transponder signal. It's distorted but it's one of our transponders . . ."

A shape was moving within the sphere, and then it slipped through into normal space. Julia glanced down at her desk as the signal cleared suddenly, then looked quickly up, eyes wide, as the image of the newcomer appeared on all the repeater displays of the flight deck. "Sir, it's —"

"UK-1," Gilmore said, his eyes fixed on the nearest display where here had vanished and the 17 giant whatever apparently constituted the United Kingdom, rotating Gilmore common axis, coasted into the solar system of the First Breed.

Prince James was sitting in the Dome refectory, conspicuously alone and picking at his evening meal with little enthusiasm, when his aide beeped. "A message in corporal cipher."

James almost dropped his fork. There were only two copies of the corporal cipher in existence (corporal was one better than private: the joke had amused him as a boy) and one was in his aide. He stood quickly and retreated into the corner of the room, looking around to check for eavesdroppers.

"Receive," he said, and his father's face appeared on the display, a proud beam taking up most of it. The time-lag window indicated to a of two seconds in the conversation.

"Hello, James," he said.

"You came!" James tried to put on the cold, calm facade that was so easy when dealing with the other delegates. He couldn't do it. "You came! Thank God."

The king's face softened, becoming less of the ruler of the UK and more of a glad father. "How are you, James? And how's it gone."

Facts whirled about in James' mind. What to tell him first? "I'm well. We've had, um, a little local difficulty, which I'll tell you about later. The ship, the *Ark Royal* and . . . and Gilmore . . . they've done well." He grit his teeth, but had to say it. "Good choice."

"Thank you."

"But, Father, some advice. The Rusties are absolute sticklers for doing things properly. Be very nice to them, ask permission to enter their orbit."

"We're doing that now. I'm making it clear that this is a shaking-down cruise, nothing more. It would be improper for me to come down to the Roving while you're still the delegate and so I won't, not until they've made their choice. I, um, take it they haven't done so yet?"

James was relieved his father wasn't going to go blundering over Rustie sensibilities. He shook his head. "No, the Convocation finished today and they're making their minds up now. And, Father, I . . ." He grimaced at the thought of having to stay in his Dome cubicle, when home was so within reach. "It wouldn't be proper for me to leave, now, either."

"No point in jeopardizing everything at this point, is there?" the king agreed. "I've got to go, James — other calls to make. But it's good to see you, boy. Out."

As the conversation had gone on, James had been aware in the background of an unusual number of aides announcing incoming messages to their respective owners. The unemotional diplomat persona was back in place and, reflecting on the fickleness of his fellow humans, James sauntered back to his table to hold court to his new admirers.

With thrusters nudging gently into space and Adrian Nichol at the helm, *Ark Royal* docked for the first time at its home port of UK-1.

"Repair teams requesting permission to come on board, sir," Hannah said.

"Granted." Gilmore was hit by a sudden flash of very vivid *déjà vu*, and it took him a moment to place it. Yes: the last time he had docked at UK-1 it had been when he brought *Australasia* home, fresh from its encounter with a scuttler and a nuclear explosion. Then, too, UK-1's first act had been to send shoreside specialists on board to check the ship out. This time, though, they were needed.

The Rusties maintained that because UK-1 was not one of the delegation ships, neither it nor any of its personnel should have contact with the ground until the Convocation was over. The Convocation rules were that the delegates should make their decisions in isolation from their own governments. However, they had granted *Ark Royal* permission to dock for repairs: Prince James was not on board and the ship's need was obvious.

"See to their needs, Number One," Gilmore said. "You know where I'll be."

"Aye-aye, sir," Hannah said. She managed to suppress the look of sympathy that Gilmore guessed was struggling to get out.

*   *   *

"We were just passing," said King Richard once formal greetings were over — as though he hadn't just unexpectedly bridged a gap of a thousand light-years. "We thought we would drop in. Tea, Captain?"

It was just the same as Gilmore's first visit to "F" ring. He had been left in the king's book-lined study; the king appeared and took him to the v-room where they could sit in the middle of the cutaway simulation of UK-1. The sheer familiarity of it added to Gilmore's overall sense of disorientation. No doubt the king was aware his arrival was having this effect on everyone, human and Rustie alike: if the Rusties weren't the only ones with step-through anymore, could anything else be taken for granted? The king was loving it.

To add to the disorientation, here it was morning. The delegation fleet had adjusted itself to Capital time during the journey from home: UK-1 had not. To Gilmore it was just after 2200, but when you get a personal and immediate summons from a king who is under the impression it's 0900, he thought, you can't really decline because it's inconvenient and ask if he would mind calling back later.

"Just passing, sir?" Gilmore said with frank disbelief.

"Well, we were testing the step-through and so we came to the only coordinates in space where we knew there would be a friendly welcome."

"The Rusties never gave us the coordinates of this solar system."

An expansive shrug. "I'm not a navigator. Anyway, we're here."

"But how did you manage it, sir?" Gilmore said.

"By inventing step-through, of course." The king smiled at Gilmore's deliberate attempt not to look irritated. "Actually, Captain, we've been working on it for a long time."

"I've never heard of it."

"Of course not. I didn't want the Fleet involved. Too many people coming and going, too many loose tongues, however well intentioned. No, all the research was done under a separate company. I confined 'em to UK-1 and paid them huge great salaries to make up for it. They've been at it for about three years now."

"A mere three years?"

"Oh, the principles have been known since the twentieth century. The trick lies in detecting a wormhole — sorry, a tubule — going in the right direction, and then expanding it. When the Rusties turned up, clues from them formed the missing link."

"But . . ." Gilmore said.

"But?" the king said innocently.

"All this has been a waste of time! You didn't need to send *Ark Royal*, you could have gone on your own, you could —"

"We could," the king said. "I decided against it. For

a start, would the seven thousand people on board want to go on the trip? That's a lot of uprooting."

"You came anyway."

"We were just passing," the king said again. "We'll be on our way back home in a day or two. And if you recall, the Rustie invitation said that each nation should send a delegate. They said nothing about the whole nation sending itself. I asked our visiting Rusties tangential questions and I don't believe they would have allowed it."

"You came anyway," Gilmore said again.

"Think of this as the icing on the cake. If our per formance so far hasn't shown the Rusties who the deserving winners are, our appearance should tip the balance."

"Then you're confident of winning, sir?" Gilmore said. He wondered what the king would say when he heard about the prince's hashed presentation. Even knowing UK-1 would be arriving shouldn't have excused James' complacency.

Then, for a moment, Gilmore wondered if the UK now needed or wanted the Roving, with the rest of the galaxy at its disposal . . . but of course it did. A friendly world there for the asking, with thousands of square miles of open land available, and above all the sheer thrill of possession.

"Just say that I live in hope." The king sat back in his chair. "Now, tell me everything. What's been going on since you left? I gather you've had some trouble?"

Gilmore gave his account of the battle as succinctly as he could, doing his best to minimize his own part.

"You did extremely well," the king said.

"The crew did their bit too, sir," Gilmore said.

"And how many were on board with you?"

"One, sir," Gilmore was forced to admit.

"So you made the decisions?"

"Yes, sir."

"Oh, for pity's sake, man!" the king snapped, suddenly angry. "Don't be so ashamed of being a hero. And think what it means for your ship, hey? Face it, we don't need her anymore. Whatever the outcome of the Convocation, I was going to scrap her when she got back home, but now . . . well, it would be like breaking up the *Victory* for firewood, hey?"

Gilmore nodded slowly. He had only seen Nelson's venerable flagship once, secure in her bubble in Portsmouth, but still it had inspired him at the age of ten. So, the *ship* would be the hero, get all the adulation. He smiled. "Absolutely, sir."

"That's better." They chatted some more, all quite informal; the king asking about the Rusties, about the Roving, about the mission. "You've got a son," the king said suddenly. "Father to father, how has James done?"

Gilmore felt the king was big enough to take it. "I've had to question his conduct on a number of occasions, sir," he said. He started at the beginning, careful not to let this turn into a protracted whinge. From right back at the start of the mission, when James had suddenly appeared on the flight deck prior to boosting, through the affair with Plantagenet, right up to James' speech at the Convocation. The king only nodded at that.

And it was only then that Gilmore remembered he was meant to be angry with the king too. He had got so used to lumping all the ills of the world on James' shoulders, he had forgotten that the king shared at least some of the blame for at least one thing.

"This will be in my formal report to the Admiralty, sir," he said. "I bitterly resent the duplicitous tactics used to equip *Ark Royal* with torpedoes, without my knowing."

The king smiled and nodded again. "I know you do. I knew you would. The problem was, I had to have you, and you would have refused to captain an armed ship. Correct?"

"You know it is, sir."

"Then I had no choice. I do apologize, Captain, I apologize a thousand times, but I needed you."

"There are other captains," Gilmore said.

"Yes, but you were so clearly the man for the job. No, that's not flattery. I don't flatter, I don't butter up and I don't care whose feathers I ruffle. That's the fun of being king, you see. You were the man for the job and I would have had no other."

Gilmore almost let loose a string of reasons as to why he would not have agreed, but then, he thought, why bother? He would only be repeating himself and his point had been made.

The king seemed to read his mind. "Besides, you didn't need to use them, did you?" he said. "But I had to cover all contingencies." He shook his head with a fond smile that was almost bashful. "By George, I wish I could have seen it, though. Would you . . . would you mind if I had a look round her? I've only ever looked at the plans — I've never actually seen the ship."

"By all means." Gilmore was delighted the king felt he had to ask permission, contrasting it with a mental image of the future King James (he shuddered at the thought) just turning up, banging on the airlock and demanding to be given a tour. "Any time, sir, just let us know when."

The king beamed like a small child. "That's splendid. Thank you very much." He took a final swig of tea, stood up and held out his hand. "I'm glad we could have this chat, Captain. One of my AIs will be in touch to discuss a time. Now, do excuse me, but I have other things to be getting on with and I know the Admiralty is just dying to hear your report."

He came into the Captain's Club slowly, nervously, peering from side to side and awed by the cumulative seniority of the clientele. Gilmore waved from his cubicle and Joel's face lit up. Midshipman Gilmore came hurrying over.

Joel had arrived on UK-1 after Gilmore left to join *Ark Royal* and they hadn't seen each other in the flesh for years. There had been frequent holos but even they had only just prepared Gilmore for the sight of the slim young man in the midshipman's uniform. It seemed quite absurd that in a mere six years, Joel had gone from twelve to eighteen. Gilmore wondered if all parents of teenagers had this feeling.

He had a sudden pang of panic that he might have forgotten Joel's nineteenth birthday. No, that was next month and he had already left a present in case the fleet didn't get back home in time. He could still manage some of his paternal duties.

"Hello, Dad."

"Hello, Joel. Grab a seat. What'll you have?" He didn't even know his son's favourite drink, he thought as he placed the order. Well, there would be time for all that.

The drinks came out of the cubicle dispenser immediately, with a bite to eat for Joel. As far as he was concerned, it was now lunchtime. To Gilmore it was now after midnight, and after a long day repairing the ship he just wanted to crawl into his bunk and go to sleep. He nursed his cup of cocoa carefully.

Despite the physical separation, they hadn't been completely out of touch, and there wasn't a lot of catching up to do. "So, what the hell has been hap-

pening here?" Gilmore said. "How much warning
did you get? And how did you get here so quickly? It
took us a month."

"Yeah, but you had to get back across the solar
system for a step-through alignment," Joel said with
a grin. "We were there already. And we got the standard forty-eight hours' notice of manoeuvre." For
something the size of UK-1, with so many people affected, forty-eight hours was needed for everything
to be secured. "Then they told us where we were
manoeuvring to, and a bloody difficult manoeuvre it
was, I might add."

"Oh?"

"Well," Joel said, "first we had to get further
downhill, nearer the sun. You can only step-through
between equal gravity potentials, so if we wanted to
come out near the Roving —"

"You had to leave from the same position near
our own sun."

"Right, give or take. And then, the step-through
alignment is right out of the plane of the system, so
we had to boost ourselves up there —"

"We did the same thing when we came here,
Joel."

"Oh. Yeah. Right. Well, you know what it was
like for a small ship, so can you imagine doing it for
UK-1?"

"Difficult," Gilmore agreed.

"Right! And then there's the step-through itself.
We used up every erg we had in opening the point

up. Opening one up for a normal ship would be hard enough but —"

"Not for something as big as UK-1."

"Right! You're getting it, Dad." Joel took a sip from his drink and didn't see the grin on the face of his father, who was wondering if he had ever felt the need to spell out things to Joel's grandfather in such a way.

"And then there were the controls," said Joel. "It was weird, Dad! I'm working in flight control and I got a look at the navigation displays. Couldn't touch 'em, it was being handled by Super els "

"Who?"

"Oh, um, Superluminary. It's the company that the king put in charge of the step-through — they developed the strange mathematics to make it work. They fly out the step-through generator, by maintenance 'bot, to a point ahead of UK-1 — that's easy enough. But when they turn it on . . . well, they must have invented a whole new language for it — I couldn't make head or tail of what was on those displays. I don't know how the computers handled it. They even made up their own characters — all these weird squiggles and shapes." Gilmore smiled to himself again at the unspoken assumption that, if it could be shown on a display, Joel could understand it. He had been through that stage once.

"As simple as that?" Gilmore said. "No bugs, glitches, gremlins?"

"Well . . ." Joel looked around. "There was a rumour, that's all, so don't repeat it."

"As if." Gilmore leaned forward, mimicking Joel's wide-eyed look of conspiracy. It was lost on the boy. "Go on."

"There was a rumour that the step-through generator, um, did something, had some kind of side effect, but no one's sure what."

"That's informative."

"Yeah, but it's just a rumour and we're still here, aren't we? So, how about you, Dad? How's the ship? How's the Roving? Have you been down there? Have you —"

He stopped as Gilmore suddenly burst into a mighty yawn.

"Not interesting enough for you, Dad?"

"Sorry, Joel, but I'm knackered," Gilmore said. "It's been a long, long day. Look, it's great to see you, it really is. I've made my report to the Admiralty and I can't comment on anything until they make their official announcement. But when they have, make an appointment with Number One — you remember Hannah — and I'll show you over every inch of the ship. How's that?"

Joel's face split into an enormous grin. "That's great!"

Prince James had also retired for the night. He hadn't expected to be able to sleep but he had returned to his cell on the off chance that he might.

And then the light was on. He squinted at the clock by his bed: 0245. He was sure he had turned the light off. He stretched and rolled over—

"Arm Wild?" he said. The Rustie stood there with two others of his kind, just visible outside the door. James glanced at the clock.

"I apologize for disturbing you at this hour," said Arm Wild, "but we did not desire the other delegates to see. I must ask you to accompany us."

James sat up and stretched. "Where to?"

"Please, accompany us," Arm Wild said.

If they had been human, nightmare images of legalized abduction would have been going through James' mind. Even so, he was uneasy but he had no choice.

"If you insist. Let me get dressed."

They took him to a groundcar waiting outside the Dome and drove him through an empty, dark Capital. Whether through having good night vision or a low crime rate, the Rusties didn't run to street lighting. The only illumination was from the stars and the moons, and the shapes of the pridehalls around him seemed even more alien than usual. James swallowed. Now, despite knowing UK-1 was in orbit and was big enough to cause a lot of unpleasantness if anything happened to him, he was feeling actively nervous and he didn't want to show it.

They stopped by a pridehall. The entrance flared with artificial light and one glance in that direction ruined James' chances of seeing anything more in the dark outside.

"This way, please," said Arm Wild. James took a deep breath and followed the small group into the building.

Twenty-two
23 May 2149

"It's ridiculous," said Samad. He had his feet up on the watch desk on the flight deck — a meaningless pose in free fall, which was why he did it — and was sucking a bulb of breakfast coffee. He wasn't on watch but Hannah was.

"Do tell," she said.

"'We were just passing.'" Samad could do a good King Richard. "Did he really tell the captain that? 'A shaking-down cruise.' They just happened to have invented step-through, while everyone was looking the other way, and no sooner have they made the breakthrough than they've perfected it and set off on a journey of a thousand light-years. What happened to research? What happened to testing? Not even a quick trip round the solar system to shake the bugs out first? No." He took another suck at the coffee. "If, and it's a big if. If that's the truth, and UK-1's engineers did that, then the whole lot of them deserve to be thrown out of the nearest airlock, for the sake of the gene pool."

Samad was a morning person and could talk more in the first hour out of bed than for the entire rest of the day. Hannah, who had spent most of the night on the flight deck, felt it easiest to let him babble while she studied the report from the repairs foreman.

The repair teams had worked through *Ark Royal's* night while her crew slept, and it looked like most of the work had been done. She made a list in her head. Next step: disengage from UK-1, do a test firing of the thrusters, the auxiliary engines, the main engine—

A priority signal was flashing and she took the call. "*Ark Royal* here."

It was a grumpy, greying man who looked vaguely familiar to Hannah.

"I want to talk to the senior officer on board," he said.

"Dereshev, first officer," she said. "The captain is occupied at the moment." The captain had melted into his bunk and hadn't yet emerged, and Hannah felt he deserved the rest.

"Paul Ganschow. I'm the delegate for Starward."

Now Hannah recognized him: one of her fellow hostages, indeed. "How can I help you, Mr. Ganschow?"

"I wondered if your prince was up there."

"On *Ark Royal*? No, sir."

"Well, he's vanished and he's not answering his aide. Could he be on UK-1?"

"One moment, please." Hannah called up the log of traffic in the Roving orbit. "Apart from ourselves, no vessel has had any contact with UK-1 since its arrival."

"Damn. Where the hell is he?" The question was rhetorical. "Thank you, Ms. Dereshev. Oh, we might

be in for interesting times down here, so you might
like to stand by."

"Can you explain?" Hannah said.

Ganschow grimaced. "That maniac Krishnamurthy's vanished too."

James wasn't naturally claustrophobic but it was
oppressive in the pridehall. The ceilings were low
and his head brushed them several times, and the
dark-red stone seemed to absorb the light. They
turned and twisted and walked down ramps and up
steps until James was hopelessly lost in the maze of
passages, but there was a sense of purpose to their
procession that told him he wasn't being
deliberately confused. It was just the layout that the
Rusties preferred.

Finally they came to a lift and now James had to
cock his head to be able to stand under the low ceiling. The doors shut and the lift started down.

It travelled for about a minute. The smell of Rustie
was gagging him, his neck was aching and he had to
swallow several times to clear his ears. Then the
doors opened and they stepped out into yet another passage.

This one didn't last long. It curved around into
(James felt a surge of relief) a vast, domed chamber.
At least as big as the dome of St Paul's, James
thought, and it looked bigger still from the fact that
it was completely bare.

And then he stopped dead. Standing in the middle was another group of Rusties, including Iron Run, and—

"Your Royal Highness. They got you too."

It was some small comfort that Krishnamurthy looked just as dishevelled and bleary-eyed as James felt.

"What are you doing here?" James said. Krishnamurthy spread his hands in a wide shrug.

"Perhaps the same as you?" he suggested.

"If you think I'm —" James started.

"Please," said Arm Wild. "It is important that you see this together." He walked to join the group at the centre of the dome and James reluctantly followed.

One of the Rusties was holding a small device in one grasper: it touched a control and an image suddenly appeared in midair. An image that was . . . *not* a Rustie.

At first glance, it might indeed have been one but James had been around the First Breed long enough to note the differences. Its front legs were longer so that it appeared to be rearing, either in surprise or prior to attack. The legs were more powerful than those of the First Breed and the shoulders larger, more muscular, though the general impression was of a body sleeker than a Rustie's. The head, too, was bigger, the muzzle blunter. The skin was darker, not as ruddy as a Rustie's, and smoother with it.

He had seen the type before. It was the same as on the monument up above in Capital, and a common theme in the carvings that covered the pride-halls.

"Another breed," Krishnamurthy murmured in amazement. "There's two of them."

That took you by surprise, didn't it? James thought smugly.

Iron Run spoke and Arm Wild translated. "Iron Run says, thank you for coming. We hope your rest cycle has not been unduly disturbed."

At three in the morning? James thought. "I wouldn't have missed this for the world," he said.

"It's my pleasure," Krishnamurthy said, not taking his eyes off the image.

"Iron Run says, you are the first humans to come here. Once this place was the command bunker of the ruling pride of this nation, but now it is a museum, a cathedral, a tomb, a temple, all in one. This place is special to us for it is here that we remember the Ones Who Command. This chamber is but part of the Complex of Remembrance."

James wasn't sure if Arm Wild was now speaking for Iron Run or for himself: still translating or making it up as he went along. "Who are these Ones Who Command," he said. He mentally appended an "-ed" onto the end of the verb, but he had noted Arm Wild's continued use of the present tense and, out loud, he stuck to it. The title wasn't so much a description as an honorific.

The Rustie with the remote touched another control and the laser image of a city appeared around them.

James bit back a gasp: he had been in v-cubicles before but he had never known this scale of immersion was possible. A discreet look around showed no blank areas, no interference patterns. The laser signals had to be coming from all over and were perfectly coordinated.

But he was not here to admire the tech. He turned his attention back to the city itself. It was Capital: he could see some familiar landmarks, including the former park where the Dome now stood. But, where up above on the surface, the street would have been full of Rusties, here the crowds were all Ones Who Command, all shapes and sizes — a hustling, bustling, thriving community that looked somehow macabre. It was like an imitation of the real thing, Ones Who Command instead of First Breed.

For about ten minutes they silently absorbed scenes of a world that James would never know: the society and culture of the Ones Who Command. They were every bit as varied as humanity: great cruelty and great love, great beauty and great ugliness. Finally, Arm Wild spoke again.

"The Ones Who Command came from the same ancestral stock as the First Breed," he said, "just as you and apes have common ancestors. Yet, like you and apes, there was that tiny percentage of difference in DNA between us that made us brutish beasts and them intelligent, thinking creatures. They were the first sentient species on the Roving. They built our world's cities, they fought the wars, they created our society. They built our spaceships and, finally, our prideships. They discovered stepthrough and they created us."

The scene changed and they were in a rural setting. A pride of Rusties lurked under a tree but they were subtly different from the ones that now surrounded James. They were shy, skittish. They munched at the grass or fruits hanging off the tree and when the viewpoint came too close they were spooked by whoever was making the recording. More scenes followed and one showed, with blunt candour, Ones Who Command massacring a group of the smaller creatures that were in among the crops. There were scenes of Rusties together in their prides, lounging under bushes or sheltering in caves. What was clear was that they were far from the technologically sophisticated creatures that the humans had come to know.

"Eventually, the Ones Who Command began to experiment on us, as your scientists did on the lower orders of Earth animals. One pride in particular was highly skilled in genetic matters and they took the work further than your scientists ever did. They created us, their First Breed."

Now Rusties and Ones Who Command were clearly coexisting. James saw First Breed working machines or toiling in fields or running errands. He frowned: they might have been living side by side but there was no hiding who was in charge. In one telling scene, he saw what he assumed was a mixed-species fire control unit tackling a blazing building. The Ones Who Command had breathing apparatus.

Then war struck. Fleets of jet aircraft streaked above them; cities were pounded into rubble; armies marched across the face of the Roving.

"At this time there were still different nations on our world," said Arm Wild, "and occasionally they still fought. The last war was fought at the end with viral weapons and one strain got out of control. It was created by the same pride that made us, and it was designed only to attack the DNA of the Ones Who Command."

James nodded, guessing what was coming, even as the display changed its theme again. Ones Who Command dying like flies. Burning cities, anarchy let loose upon the world.

Peace returned but it was strained, Pyrrhic peace. Again the display showed different communities from around the world, including a war-scarred Capital, but where there had been crowds, now there were only smaller groups.

"Every One Who Commands on this world was affected by the virus but only about half died. The other half survived, but sterile. The virus had interfered with the initiation stage of their reproductive cycle. The pride that created the virus was dead: others tried to reverse the effects but they never achieved the same breakthroughs as our creators. So, no more Ones Who Command would ever be born. Ones Who Command who were cloned inherited the same sterility.

"The First Breed live longer than humans, James Windsor, about one and one half times your average lifespan, and the Ones Who Command lived even longer than that. That is a long time for a race to die of old age."

Arm Wild was silent for a moment and the Rusties waited, their heads hanging low. Eventually Arm Wild lifted his head and carried on, and James hated to think of the intensity of emotion that was filtered out by Arm Wild's translator, leaving just the bland, matter-of-fact words.

"The pride who ruled this nation made contact with the other ruling prides and they buried their differences. They knew there was no escaping their fate but they resolved that their culture would not die. If they could not survive themselves, they would survive in memory. They would perpetuate the civilization they had created. They handed it over to the First Breed. We would continue on this world and honour their memory.

"But again, the geneticists had been too clever. When they created the First Breed they were careful not to create a threat to their dominance. They denied us initiative, invention. We know what these concepts are, we value them, but we do not have them. We can look after ourselves, we can have good ideas and we can see what needs to be done if it is clear and apparent, but we cannot think laterally. No First Breed has ever invented or created something new.

"The Ones Who Command trained us up to replace them, but still, our entire civilization is borrowed. We can appreciate but not originate. We are a race of brilliant mimics, good servants, but we are not creators and we are not leaders."

The view changed so suddenly that James was dizzy for a moment. He was in space. The Roving hung above him, with orbiting ships and satellites scudding across the sky between him and the faraway ground. He looked down at his feet and only saw stars. A prideship lumbered past, seeming to pass into the floor.

"So the Ones Who Command chose to look elsewhere for a race that could rule this world," said Arm Wild. "They were already doing research into step-through and they redoubled their efforts. A century after the war ended, they had interstellar flight. Over the next fifty years they discovered various potential candidate races, yours among them. Ones Who Command who were only infants when the war broke out devised the Earth Mission and the Convocation. They laid out the rules that must be followed and the procedures to which we had to adhere. First Breed crews — by now all the crews were First Breed, there were only a handful of Ones Who Command left — observed your world for forty years so that the Ones Who Command back on the Roving could learn about you and invent the translators.

Arm Wild stopped speaking and the images faded away. Humans and Rusties were left standing in the gloom, looking at each other.

"This is fascinating," Krishnamurthy said when it became obvious Arm Wild didn't intend to continue, "but why are we here?"

"Can't you guess?" James said, and light poured into the chamber from behind them. They turned round to see the door that had opened in the wall of the chamber to let in the light, suddenly obscured by large, gleaming shapes that moved through the doorway and glided towards them.

"What was that about?" Gilmore came up through the hatch, stretching, just as Ganschow's image vanished.

"Good morning, sir," Hannah said. "All repairs are completed and the prince has vanished."

"The day gets better and better." Gilmore rubbed his neck. "How definite is that?"

"I imagine Mr. Ganschow's looked everywhere plausible."

Gilmore frowned. "Does UK-1 know?"

"I suspect they're going to shortly."

"Hmm." Gilmore sat at the command desk and idly checked the displays. Hannah knew he wasn't as dismissive as he appeared. Sure enough: "He can't have vanished! What could he have done? Gone for a midnight walk and got lost?"

"Or someone got him lost," Samad suggested.

"The Dome's still under guard by the Rusties," Hannah said. "They'd have stopped any foul play from our own species."

They considered the implications which that raised in silence.

The shapes were globes, transparent, and inside each was a One Who Commands. Each globe was mounted on a flat platform that slid across the floor towards James and Krishnamurthy. Inside, each creature reclined on a couch with cables rising from out of the platform plugged into it. The design was alien but James recognized a life support system when he saw one.

The globes made a half circle around them. All the Rusties had moved their front legs apart and were hanging their heads low.

"Greetings, Excellency R.V. Krishnamurthy, Prince James Windsor," said a voice. It was exactly the same voice as a Rustie's translator unit used and it was impossible to tell which of the globes it came from, but the One Who Commands in the centre globe had lifted its head up and was looking right at them. "I am March Sage Savour, leader of this planet."

James bowed, Krishnamurthy put his palms together.

"Our servants of the First Breed have done well in

coming this far," March Sage Savour said. "You now know the full facts. The purpose of the Convocation was to find a compatible race that could take our place. We have studied the presentations of the delegates and the reports of the First Breed on the Earth Mission, but the two of you together have displayed the best empirical evidence of your worthiness to follow us."

The One Who Commands looked at James. "We were already impressed by your performance, by Polyglot, by your captain's strategy against *Shivaji*, but UK-1's use of step through surpasses all that. A clear sign of initiative and invention, and above all of the technological ability needed for this task."

It looked at Krishnamurthy. "You have not impressed us so much in that area. Your ship, indeed all your space technology, is acquired from other Earth governments. However, your grasp of the way we have run our planet in times past is exemplary. What you did took daring and courage. The other governments sought to impress us with words. You used actions."

March Sage Savour paused. "We have debated long and hard on this point, because we originally imagined only one government replacing us, but we cannot escape the facts. James Windsor, your government has the technology. R.V. Krishnamurthy, your government has the will and the understanding. We invite you jointly to replace us. Do you accept?"

* * *

James and Krishnamurthy slowly turned their heads to look at each other.

Him? James thought. *This madman? You know what he's like. What sort of creature are you if you think he's going to make a good replacement?*

What was going through Krishnamurthy's mind, he could only guess at.

Krishnamurthy was opening his mouth to speak so James said something, anything, to interrupt.

"Why us?" he said.

"March Sage Savour has already explained that, Windsor," Krishnamurthy snapped. He turned back to the Ones Who Command. "On behalf of my gov —"

"I meant," James said, "why us humans? Were we the only other race you found?"

"That is an excellent question," March Sage Savour said. It looked at Krishnamurthy. "Take note of that. Arm Wild, show them."

Planets hung in space around James: apparently separated by a few feet, in fact separated by light-years. Thirteen of them: the homeworlds of the species recognizable as sentient, that the Rusties had discovered. One was Earth.

"We eliminated all those whose biospheres were incompatible with our own," said Arm Wild. Five vanished and the remaining eight realigned themselves, to be spaced evenly around the watchers.

"Four have not yet reached what we considered a desirable technological stage. In your own terms, the least developed appeared to be at the stone age, the most developed was approaching the use of industrial technology. We saw evidence of steam power, but remember that all our observations are done covertly, from orbit, so we cannot be too specific."

Four more worlds vanished. Four were left.

"Two of these have achieved limited space flight. One has sent robot probes as far as its nearest neighbour, the next planet in towards their sun. The other has so far confined itself to artificial satellites in its own orbit. Neither has sent people into space."

"This information is current?" Krishnamurthy asked.

"Indeed, yes. They are still under observation."

"And this world?" James indicated the only planet left that wasn't Earth. Arm Wild paused before answering.

"It was the second potential candidate world that we discovered, and at first almost ideal for our purposes. They are a spacegoing civilization, very similar in scope and scale to ours and to your own. Therefore, it was thought, they would have had the mental capacity to accept the technological concepts we would introduce."

"What stopped you?"

"This." Another planet appeared suddenly. "The

next planet out from their own in the same solar system. A different atmosphere, different biosphere and inhabited by its own native species, less advanced technologically. We arrived just in time to witness their extermination by their neighbours. The Ones Who Command did not think this was auspicious, so we remained hidden."

Fleets of ships fell upon the world and the glare of nuclear weapons shone out against its surface. "I see," said James thoughtfully. Aerial views showed communities being razed, forests being burned. Intercepted transmissions from the aggressors showed the wholesale slaughter of the natives with no quarter being given. James glanced at the other human present.

"You should get on well with them," he said.

Krishnamurthy said nothing.

"There is more," Arm Wild said. "Sooner or later, and probably sooner, these beings will discover how to leave their system. They are at a similar stage to you, and before UK-1 arrived here we estimated you were perhaps thirty years away from inventing step-through. Our sun is bright in their sky. When they invent step-through themselves, they will come to us."

James felt a sudden chill. The ancestral dread of homicidal aliens finally coming true. "Your need is suddenly more urgent," he said.

"Precisely. If they are met with strength then perhaps they will not be a threat. Perhaps they have already learnt from their past actions, as your species did with its treatment of peoples who were considered inferior. Whatever: we must be prepared.

"And there will be others out there already, vastly more advanced than ourselves. It is unreasonable to assume that we are at the peak of this galaxy's technological development —"

"Enough, Arm Wild," March Sage Savour said. It looked at the two humans. "So, again I ask, do you accept our offer?"

"So, tell me about the repairs," Gilmore said. Hannah opened up the display on her aide.

"Well, sir, they sealed up the holes in the drive and centrifuge compartments with ferro-polymer panels. Um. The ring was repressurized slowly and found to be airtight . . . oh yes, one of the ring's tracks was buckled and a section needed replacing, but after that the ring spun perfectly."

"Excellent," Gilmore said.

"All fuel lines were intact but they tested them anyway. All the original optical circuitry has been restored . . . they stripped the main engine down and put it together again . . ."

"What about the auxiliaries? They took a battering."

"Yes, but it was just a matter of dented casing and their operation wasn't affected. We still have the dented casing."

"Fair enough."

"And we've been asked to move away from UK-1 to rejoin the fleet, so that *Algol* can have our space."

"My God, of course!" Gilmore said. "Their need's far more urgent than ours. Get clearance from Traffic Control and we'll move at once. What's that?"

That was another priority message flashing.

"It's an all-ships alert," Hannah said.

"All ships?" Gilmore perked up. "Saying?"

"Stand by for an important announcement." Hannah's eyes scanned the text quickly. "Oh my God. They've decided."

The formal announcement was made two hours later, shortly after *Ark Royal* had rejoined the delegation fleet in its former orbit. Iron Run made the announcement from the centre of the Dome, with a freshly brushed, shaved and scrubbed Prince James standing on one side and an equally immaculate R.V. Krishnamurthy on the other. The leader of the Rusties announced to all delegates and ships from Earth that joint sovereignty of the Roving had been awarded to the Confederation of South-East Asia and to the United Kingdom. An information pack giving the reasoning behind the decision was available from . . .

The crew of the *Ark Royal* watched in slack-jawed amazement as Iron Run made the final announcement:

"The Convocation is over."

"Get a copy of that information pack," Gilmore said. "I'd like to know what possessed them."

Silence returned to the flight deck as the crew digested the news internally, each in his or her own way.

"Why did he accept?" Julia said. Everyone else looked at her. "Why did the prince agree to it?"

"So that he could get something," Hannah said.

"He's got his foot in the door, this way. If he'd refused, they'd have given it all to Krishnamurthy, and that I would not like to see."

"And greater minds than ours will be working out what to do about it even now," Gilmore said, with a nod at the side of the flight deck. By which he meant, outside the ship; by which he meant, UK-1. "I'll be in my cabin if needed, Number One."

Gilmore would remember the images of a vanishing race until the day he died. That wasn't an expression he used often but it seemed apt on this occasion, as in the privacy of his cabin he shared vicariously in the sacred mission of the Ones Who Command: to find their own replacements who would give their trusting, loyal First Breed the leadership they needed.

The Ones Who Command. What bastards! And the First Breed said they loved them. Perhaps they did: but if so, Gilmore reflected, it was the desperate love that an abused child will continue to feel towards the adult who beats it.

His attention was taken with scenes from the last, deadly war. He was no military genius but he could see precisely who was being used as cannon fodder. He had seen old film clips back on Earth of the First World War: rows upon rows of trusting soldiers, marching nobly into the mouths of enemy machine guns because their generals told them to. He had never expected to see such scenes repeated anywhere, let alone here. These were the creatures who wanted replacements.

And look who they had got.

These Ones Who Command, he reflected, were fools if they thought the two human governments they had chosen would last five minutes together. It would be interesting to see who came out tops.

Whoever it was, it wasn't his concern. Gilmore had decided this long ago: maybe, he realized suddenly, it had been that time when Prince James had been looking down on the Roving and spelling out his plans for the future. While UK-1 was all they controlled, Prince James and his father were simply employers who paid him a wage, and personal considerations didn't come into it. But put them in charge of the Roving, and they would become a government that Gilmore wanted no part of.

And working for Krishnamurthy was out of the question.

So, Gilmore would take *Ark Royal* back home and resign. Neither the Windsors nor Krishnamurthy would be interested in humanity's original solar system now: there was nothing more for them there. Humanity would go to the stars and Michael Gilmore would while away his remaining years in peace and quiet.

"There's a call from Admiral Dyer on UK-1, sir," said Julia from the flight deck.

Dyer was a stocky woman with her hair cut short. She didn't seem happy but Gilmore knew from prior experience that she rarely did. "You heard the news, Captain?"

"We did, sir."

"Good. Move *Ark Royal* to within 1000 metres of UK-1 at once. You'll find you won't have any problems with Traffic Control."

"Aye-aye, sir. Excuse me a moment, please."

Dyer waited patiently while Gilmore passed the orders up to the flight deck.

"Now," she said, "I gather His Majesty is eager to get on board *Ark Royal*." She looked sour, as well she might: an admiral having to deal with the king's social diary, which one of the king's AIs could have done just as well. "As the Convocation is over, there are no barriers to him going downstairs anymore. He would therefore like you to pick him up in your boat, show him round the ship, and then take him down to the Roving for the signing. We don't know when that will be, but it seems the best solution so we'll let you have the timing when we have it ourselves."

"Very good, sir," said Gilmore. "Does this mean the prince won't be coming back on board?"

"It looks that way," Dyer agreed. She continued to look stern but for a moment she met his gaze and there was a shared message between them: two officers well accustomed to dealing with the two royals, and with one of them in particular. "Thank you for your cooperation, and I'll let the palace know."

"I am amazed," said R.V. Krishnamurthy. They were in the great display chamber below Iron Run's pridehall and the images that hung around him showed the exact quantities and whereabouts of the Roving's mineral wealth. "You had such a civilization and yet there is so much left over."

"Our histories do not match exactly," said March Sage Savour. The One Who Command's globe glided silently over to where Krishnamurthy was standing. "We never had the same intensive industry or utilization of resources as your world. Now, you will need to know this."

In the laser field, what looked like a micropatchwork was laid over the mineral seams.

"These are the prides skilled in industrial work," March Sage Savour said. "You will no doubt be requiring their services."

Krishnamurthy held up his hands, despite the temptation to go on. It was alluring. All those hints and suggestions and clues, and now here it all was: the full and absolute truth about the Roving, its peoples and its riches. But even so—

"Please," he said, "my head is about to explode with facts and figures. Don't you agree, Your Royal Highness?"

James Windsor was on the other side of the chamber, being briefed by another One Who Commands on the Roving's space capability. *An interesting choice*, Krishnamurthy thought. *Who commands space commands access to this world . . . he's used to that and I'm not. That must change. I mustn't get complacent.*

"Actually, I'm fascinated," the prince said. He turned back to his One Who Commands. "You were saying —"

That decided Krishnamurthy.

"Nevertheless," he said, "I am declaring a recess. Can I propose that we start again in the morning?"

And there was nothing James could do about that. The Ones Who Command were determined to deal with both or neither of them, and if one was leaving, that was that.

"By tomorrow morning," March Sage Savour said as it escorted the two humans to the lift, "we hope to have the draft agreement ready. If all is acceptable then we can have the signing later tomorrow."

"Excellent," Krishnamurthy said. He noticed that James' smile was just a little forced.

"Marvellous," the prince said.

Ah, Your Royal Highness. I really am going to have to deal with you. I know exactly how delighted you are at working with me and, believe me, I am not overjoyed about it either. One of us is going to have to go. The easiest way would be to discredit you in some way with the Rusties . . .

March Sage Savour left them at the entrance to

the chamber and they walked alone towards the lift. "As if you have the slightest intention of following any treaty," James murmured.

. . . or I could strike you down. Or I could strike at your father . . . Let me see. I strike at your father, you become king. The system is prepared for this eventuality and can absorb the change while you live for many more decades. Not good.

But if I strike you down . . . what happens? Your father is heirless. Will one of your estranged sisters take your job? Will UK-1 become a republic? The place will be in turmoil, chaos . . . and that is a situation I can work with.

Memo to self: need to contact Subhas. We might actually need his network of agents.

"Your Royal Highness, please," Krishnamurthy said. He nodded at the small group of Rusties standing by the lift doors, waiting. Iron Run and the rest of them, waiting for them. "Not in front of the servants."

This was the proudest moment of Adrian Nichol's life. He, too, was in formal wear, for only the second time since graduation, standing to attention in front of the open airlock of *Sharman*, and King Richard was coming towards him with a retinue of humans and amboids. He wished someone were there to take a picture.

Adrian had been on the flight deck when word came from UK-1 that, as well as a tour of the ship, the king expected to be wined and dined. He could have sworn the captain looked annoyed; but surely, this was an honour?

"— continue to monitor and let me know the situation hourly," the king was saying to one of his people. Then the king switched attention to Adrian and the retinue stopped as if they had hit an invisible barrier, recognising they were no longer part of the king's mental equation. The king came up to Adrian, hand held out. "Delighted to meet you. You must be Nichol."

Adrian suddenly felt weak. The words "yes, Your Majesty" had almost flowed off his tongue before he was struck with sudden doubt — was the king a Majesty or a Highness? He never could get it straight.

"Y — yes, um, sir." The result of his uncertainty was a momentary pause that must have made him look tongue-tied but the king didn't seem to mind. Damn the lack of a picture, Adrian thought as they shook hands. He felt as if he would burst. "Welcome on board, sir."

"It's a real pleasure, believe me. A real pleasure." The king held out one hand. "After you."

Adrian checked that the king was strapped into his couch properly and went forward to the cockpit to start up the engines with especial care. He was aware of the king right behind him, ten feet away; he could feel the man's gaze on his back and he wanted to look the part. He was going to do everything exactly right.

UK-1 Traffic Control gave permission to depart and the boat fell out into space. "This is *Sharman* to *Ark Royal*," he said. "I have His Highness on board. ETA five minutes."

"Very good, *Sharman*."

Adrian mentally analysed Peter Kirton's voice for hidden nuances. Was there the least chance the straightlaced Martian was jealous? he wondered. Much as Adrian liked Peter, most of the time, he hoped the man might be feeling a little envious. Just a bit. Because he had the king in the back—

"Ahem," said a voice behind him, and Adrian twisted round in his seat.

"Sir?" he said.

"It's Majesty, not Highness," the king said, with a kind smile, "but don't worry about it."

And just as Adrian was trying not to feel crushed, white light flared all around them.

"Very good, *Sharman*," said Peter, and looked up at Gilmore. "Five minutes, sir."

"We'd better welcome him properly," Gilmore said. He touched a comms panel. "Number One, meet me in the boat bay, please."

He paused for a final look at the radar display before diving down through the hatch. *Sharman* had moved out of UK-1's shadow and was a distinct entity of its own.

Nichol's angry yell made him stop. "Hey, I can't s —"

And a noise Gilmore had hope never to hear
again. Explosive decompression.

And abrupt silence.

On the radar screen, the neat, tidy blob that had
been *Sharman* had blurred into a mass of crowded
debris.

Twenty-four
24 May 2149

"Out there, *now*," Gilmore said. Peter and Samad were already scrambling for the for'a'rd hatch to "B" compartment and the spacesuits. "I have the watch."

He touched the comms panel again. "All hands to the flight deck at once. Emergency."

What had happened? He stared at the radar display and tried to picture it in his mind. From the size of the central fragment, *Sharman* seemed to be mostly intact but even without the testimony of the telemetry displays, that noise and the sudden silence told him she was airless.

How long could a human go without air? He remembered the figures from decompression drill and made the calculations in his head. A minute to suit up, a minute to empty "B" compartment . . .

He switched to open frequency for Samad and Peter. "Don't bother depressurizing. You have permission to blow the lock." He set the thrusters to expect the reaction of escaping air and to compensate, just as Julia and Hannah came up from aft. He indicated the radar display by way of explanation as he made another call.

"*Ark Royal* to UK-1 Traffic, do you copy?"

"We copy and we're on it, *Ark Royal*. We have a med team on its way now. Should take five minutes."

"We can be there sooner. Tell them to stand by. We'll bring the . . ." he was about to say bodies — "casualties in at a point to be advised."

"Understood, *Ark Royal*."

"It's hopeless,"Hannah said in a whisper. Julia was just staring at the display, hand to mouth. Gilmore didn't answer. He looked at the display, and at the two smaller echoes that had just appeared, and counted the seconds.

They hurtled together from *Ark Royal*'s prow, and their suit thrusters took over and directed them at *Sharman*.

The boat was a small dot next to the bulk of UK-1 in the background and the damage became evident as they approached. Samad's engineer's opinion was that *Sharman*'s bow tanks had exploded. The nose and cockpit had blown clear off and the rest of the boat was spinning slowly around its centre of gravity, surrounded by a cloud of objects. One of the objects — "Oh my God," said Samad — was Adrian Nichol, still in his pilot's chair.

"I'm going in," Samad said, and he jetted into the cavity where the front of *Sharman* had once been. Peter took hold of the body gently. Even if the decompression hadn't killed Adrian at once, the wounds to his head and chest had. Resuscitation was not an option here.

"Look after him," he whispered.

"What?" said Samad. Peter had forgotten they were on a shared band.

"Nothing," he said. "*Ark Royal*, I confirm Adrian's dead. We can't do anything for him."

"Come in here," said Samad. "I need you."

Drops of blood hung around the king's nose and ears but otherwise he could almost have been sleeping. Samad reported this back to *Ark Royal* as they unstrapped him.

"Take him to UK-1," said Gilmore's voice in their helmets.

"*Ark Royal* is nearer, sir," said Samad.

"UK-1 has resus facilities and they're waiting for you. Let me know your arrival point and I'll pass it on."

"Aye–aye, sir." Samad broke open the first-aid locker and clamped an oxygen mask on to the king's face, and Peter tried to convince himself it wasn't a madly futile gesture. They manoeuvred the body out of the stricken boat and, with a last glance at Adrian, who was beyond help and wasn't going anywhere, they jetted towards UK-1 with the king between them.

Gilmore sat at the command desk with his head in his hands. Hannah squeezed his shoulder.

"You couldn't help it," she said.

"He was my responsibility," he said quietly. "He was my crew."

"It could have happened to anyone," she said.

"Could it?" Gilmore lifted his head up and looked at the radar. "Boats don't just explode, Number One. Especially not ones that have been thoroughly checked a couple of hours earlier." He rubbed his temples. "I . . . I suppose I should, um, write to his next of kin. It's something good C/Os do."

"I think they might know, sir." It was the first thing Julia had said since the explosion. She nodded at UK-1 on the display. "His mother —"

"Works in Traffic. Of course," said Hannah. She flinched. "His father's on board too. They were a family of citizens. Proud of it."

"Were they?" Gilmore felt drained, too tired even to chastise himself for forgetting the Nichols were UK citizens. Strange: up to a few minutes ago, he could have recalled that fact without even trying. "Then I'll call them."

The curved, spinning surface of UK-1 drew nearer and their suit computers set a course for the nearest entrance. Samad had considered going to a lock at a wheel hub or on the stationery docking strake but there was just no time, no time. A hold door, twenty metres away on a side, hove into view and their suit thrusters fired to match the motion of the hull.

"There," said Samad, and they fired lines at the EVA maintenance platform hanging below the door. The lines caught and tightened and then they were spinning with UK-1. Their suits hauled them in and they climbed on to the platform.

The door to the hold had a large "N17" painted on it. "*Ark Royal*, we are going into hold N17," said Samad.

"Hold N17, confirmed," said Gilmore.

Samad changed to a local band. "UK-1 Maintenance, please withdraw the EVA platform for hold N17 immediately," he said.

"Negative," said a stranger's voice.

"*What?*"

"Hold N17 is a restricted area." The voice was smooth and confident. "Who am I speaking to?"

"Commander Samad Loonat, *Ark Royal*. We have a medical casualty, now withdraw the platform!"

"I can't do that without authorization from the Admiralty, Commander. Hold N17 is restricted. Please make your way to —"

"We have the king here!" Samad shouted. It was sadly obvious what was happening: UK-1 was too big and news of the accident hadn't permeated as far as the individual in Maintenance whose job it was to keep an eye on hold N17.

"Uh, I'll have to check . . ." the voice suddenly sounded a lot less sure of itself.

Peter switched to the general band. "All AIs on UK-1," he said. "Override request. A human life is in serious danger. Please withdraw the platform to hold N17 at once."

"Hey, you can't —" said the voice, as the platform began to rise up into UK-1.

"Oh, shut up," Samad snapped. "Well done, Pete."

"You just need to know who your friends are," Peter said.

The lights in hold N17 were down and not even the AIs would respond to a "lights on" command. The two used their helmet lamps to find the nearest entrance and the door slid open as they approached it. A med team ran in, hoisted the king into a body capsule and ran off without even a good-bye or thank-you, waving instruments over the body and plugging things into it. Peter and Samad looked at each other, suddenly feeling superfluous.

"Back to the ship, I suppose," said Samad. He cracked his helmet and took a breath of UK-1 air.

"Adrian's still out there," said Peter.

Samad grimaced. "Of course. I'm sorry. We'll bring him in."

"Just a minute, you two." A man stood silhouetted in the entrance to the hold, arms folded, and Peter's heart sank. It was someone he hadn't seen since Samad and the captain came to rescue him from the clutches of Security, waving the royal warrant that gave them authority to claim him for *Ark Royal*, and he had hoped never to have a reunion.

"Mr. Leroux, how pleasant," Samad said.

"Ah yes, Mr. Loonat." UK-1's Security Head came closer, looking at them with naked suspicion. He wore plainclothes but four uniformed Security men stood behind him. "And Mr. Kirton. I want a full report on everything that's just happened and I'm starting with you two."

Samad took exception to the tone. "We just busted our balls getting him in here and our friend is dead out there, so treat us with a bit of civility, hey?"

"Tough," Leroux said. "Come with me, please."

"Can we unsuit?" Peter said, opening his own helmet. For a moment, Leroux looked past them into the darkness of hold N17 before answering.

"Not here. Follow me."

The man in the display was Gilmore's age, perhaps a bit older, and from the resemblance was clearly Adrian Nichol's father. His arm was round a woman who was just as clearly Adrian Nichol's mother. The eyes of both were red and damp.

"We're glad you called, Captain," the man said. His voice still trembled. "Thank you for taking the time. Adrian . . . we know how proud he was to be on your ship and he must have made his mark for you to speak so highly of him."

"If there's anything I can do, please don't hesitate to get in touch," Gilmore said, secure in the knowledge that there wasn't in fact a blind thing he could do and they all knew it.

"We won't, Captain. Thank you. Good-bye."

"Good-bye, sir." The display cleared. Gilmore shut

his eyes, sat back in his chair and breathed out slowly. The door tone to his cabin sounded. "Come."

It was Hannah. "You've spoken to them? How were they?" she said.

"As well as could be expected."

"What did you say to them?"

"All the things I'd want Joel's C/O to say to me under similar circumstances. What is it, Number One?"

Hannah looked uncertain. "UK-1 has just certified the king as dead. They thank us for our efforts. They've recovered both bodies and put them in the mortuary. The signing ceremony has been postponed and the prince is on his way up to UK-1 now."

"Oh," Gilmore said. Hannah still seemed to be waiting for something. "What else?"

"Has it occurred to you that there are deeper issues here?" she said.

"Such as?"

"Such as, Adrian wasn't the only one to be killed."

"No, of course not. The king—" The full implications suddenly, finally hit him. "Oh my God. The king is dead —"

"—Long live the king," Hannah said.

Prince James hadn't touched the cup of tea that someone had put into his hand. He was aware of the staff — his father's staff, he refused to think of them as his — moving silently around in the background, anxious not to disturb their new master.

James had always wanted to be king and had made no pretence about it, but only in a very dissociated way. The few times he had actually thought about how it might come about, he had vaguely imagined there would be plenty of warning — age or illness or both would gradually take their toll on his father, telegraphing their intentions well in advance so that he could prepare for the double shock of bereavement and succession. But this! To have the mantle of king thrust upon him, so rudely, so suddenly — and at a time like this.

He glanced around the study, stamped so firmly with the personality of the late Richard Windsor. His father's prized book collection. The works of art. Even the carpet. All his. The palace was his. F-wheel was his. The whole of UK-1 was his. He thought, in a withdrawn and abstract way and without a trace of sentimentality, that he would trade it all to have his father back again.

There was a polite cough and he looked up from the desk. "Mr. Leroux?"

Leroux stood at ease, his hands behind his back. "Sir, you told me to report —"

"Yes, yes," James said. "What have you found?"

"One of our anti-debris lasers fired on the boat, sir. We don't yet know how or why. I mean, the boat was moving away from us and shouldn't have registered as a threat."

"Yes," James said. He was cruising on automatic: an external appearance of polite interest and still the same inner numbness.

"No visual witnesses, though the crew of *Ark Royal* were in radio contact when it happened. Two of them are on board and my people are getting statements."

"Yes."

"There'll be an enquiry."

"Yes."

"And . . ." For the first time, Leroux seemed uneasy.

"Yes?" James said, intrigued despite everything.

"Ahem. The, um, scope of the enquiry, sir . . ."

Leroux held his gaze for a moment too long, and James realized with a flushed amazement what the man's problem was. He actually thought *James* might have had something to do with it.

And, in a tacit sort of way, he was offering his loyalty to the new monarch.

James drew himself up and looked Leroux straight in the eye. "The enquiry will be fully public," he said. His voice shook. "Every tiny fact about this case will be made generally available. Clear?"

"Ah, yes, sir." Leroux looked relieved. "Clear, sir."

"That will be all, then."

"There is one more thing."

James sighed. He suspected he was going to hear those words a lot more in the future. His father had

joked about it. Butter up the old man with inconse-
quentialities, he would say, and then add a "one
more thing . . ."

"Yes?"

"The two from *Ark Royal*, sir. Kirton and Loonat.
They were bringing in the . . .um, your . . ."

"Yes," James said. "And?"

"They gained emergency entrance to UK-1
through hold N17. The AIs let them in, Maintenance
tried to keep them out —"

"*What?*" James bellowed. He was on his feet in a
second and Leroux held up his hands, placating.

"It was a mistake, sir. A mistake. Maintenance had-
n't been told."

"Oh, for pity's sake," James snorted. He sat down
slowly. "Go on."

"They were in hold N17, sir," Leroux said, as
though that explained everything.

"Oh," James thought, still without any great interest. At that moment, a critical fault in one of UK-1's
reactors could not have elicited any great interest.
"Did they see anything?"

"It was dark and they had other things on their
minds, so I doubt it, but I thought you should know."

"Thank you."

"Do you want anything done?"

James shut his eyes. What he wanted done was
for the world to go away and leave him alone. "If
they didn't see anything . . ." he said.

"We don't know that, sir. They might not have noticed at the time, but they may remember something later."

James waved a hand. "They're good people, Mr. Leroux. If they didn't see anything, let them go."

"Very good, sir." Leroux looked as if he had swallowed a lemon but he left anyway. James returned to his blank contemplation of the far wall, until he was interrupted by his aide announcing a message on a certain priority code that made him sit up and take notice.

"What is it?"

"Sir." The face and voice were of the Head of UK-1 Engineering. "I know it's a bad time . . ."

James was tiring of sympathy. "Get on with it," he said.

"Yes, sir. It's confirmed: the field is spreading. Given enough time it could threaten hull integrity."

"How long?"

"Within the next couple of days."

James was not oblivious to the implications. "What will we need to do?"

"Worst case, sir? Remove the generator completely. Throw it out into space."

"You can't just dismantle it?"

"No, sir. It's a sealed unit and we can't break into it."

"But surely we put it together in the first place."

"We did, sir, but since then we've actually used it. God knows what's been going on inside it and it's impervious to all scanning. I do not want to open it, sir."

"Suggestion?"

"We'll have to jettison."

"For the Rusties to pick up?" James said.

The Head looked impatient. "Then throw it into the sun, sir." James frowned: he didn't like juniors being frivolous at the best of times.

"Do it, then," James said. "And keep me informed. Out."

He had became aware of one of his assistants hovering in the periphery of his vision, body language radiating nervousness. It never rains but it pours, he thought. "What?"

"We've had a message from the Rusties, sir. Iron Run wants to know how long the ceremony should be postponed."

James groaned. Going through with the ceremony now was the last thing he wanted to do. He hadn't particularly been looking forward to it anyway, but at least his father would have been the one to deal with Krishnamurthy.

But now . . .

His eyes lingered for a moment on a holobust of his father in an alcove. The image seemed to be looking at him and he knew what his father would want. What a king should do.

"Tell him, a day," he said. "That's all."

"Very good, sire."

"Sir!" James shouted. The man recoiled and James subsided as quickly as he had erupted. "Call me sir. Not sire. Sir."

"Yes, um, sir." The man bowed and withdrew as quickly as etiquette permitted.

The display read:

> NICHOL, ADRIAN GRAEME. BORN UK-1, 19/09/26. COMMISSIONED INTO ROYAL SPACE FLEET 11/08/44. GRADUATED 19/06/47. PILOT'S LICENCE AWARDED 21/06/47. MOST RECENT POSTING: CHIEF PILOT AND ASSISTANT ENGINEER, HMSS *ARK ROYAL*, 11/03/49. KILLED 24/05/49 IN EXPLOSION ON BOARD *SHARMAN*, TENDER TO *ARK ROYAL*. PROBABLE CAUSE OF DEATH: SEVERE INJURY TO HEAD AND CHEST AREA CAUSED BY EXPLOSION, FOLLOWED IMMEDIATELY BY SUFFOCATION.

Then, because the summaries had been compiled by an AI whose job it was simply to identify all linked crimes committed in a certain vicinity and list them alphabetically:

> *SHARMAN*.   BOEING-TUPOLEV-HONDA 177 EARTH-ORBIT REUSABLE ENTRY VEHICLE, BUILT WUHAN, EAST CHINA, 06/46. COMMISSIONED INTO ROYAL SPACE FLEET, 13/07/46. REFITTED AND DESIGNATED TENDER TO HMSS *ARK ROYAL*, 28/12/48. DE-

STROYED 24/05/49 BY LASER SHOT FROM
UK-1 TURRET G473 TO BOW FUEL TANKS.
TANKS DESTROYED BY EXPLODING FUEL,
RUPTURING HULL, LEADING TO EXPLOSIVE
DECOMPRESSION AND DEATH OF PILOT
AND CREW.

WINDSOR, RICHARD GEORGE HENRY
LOUIS ALBERT. BORN MANCHESTER, EN-
GLAND, EUROPE, 03/04/2088. MARRIED SER-
ENA BARBARA LOVEGROVE-PHILLIPSON
19/11/11. CHILDREN: JAMES WILLIAM
CHARLES ARTHUR GEORGE (14/10/16);
LOUISE MARIA AMANDA (22/02/18);
LAUREN WANDA CAROLINE (07/03/22). DE-
CLARED KING BY PARLIAMENT OF RECON-
STITUTED UNITED KINGDOM, 05/06/19.
FORMAL SEPARATION FROM WIFE:
16/09/31. KILLED 24/05/49 IN EXPLOSION
ON BOARD *SHARMAN*. PROBABLE CAUSE
OF DEATH: SHOCK DUE TO SUDDEN SUFFO-
CATION.

Samad Loonat put the aide down and looked across
the desk at Leroux.

"Good of you to include the boat, too," he said.
"I'll really miss it."

Leroux drummed his fingers on the desk. "You
aren't being helpful, Commander."

"Well, what do you want? This"— Loonat thumped the aide — "seems to contain all the pertinent details. In fact, it contains a lot more than we could tell you."

"The point is, Commander, we know hardly anything. What you've just seen is the sum total of our investigation into a possible act of at least sabotage, at worst high treason."

"And we can help?"

"Perhaps. You were in radio contact with *Sharman.*"

"Wrong. *Sharman* was in radio contact with us. Automatic, handled entirely by the systems. *Ark Royal* will have logged it all, just like the systems on UK-1 did. Captain Gilmore will happily give you access to the ship's log, if you ask. So ask! And let us go."

Leroux looked at him and the wheels turned in his mind. The prince had said to let them go (was he still the prince? Leroux was reasonably certain he wouldn't be king until he was crowned, but constitutional protocol had never struck him as important) if they hadn't seen anything. Leroux conceded they had broken every record in getting the late king to UK-1, just in case some miracle could save him. But they had been in hold N17, and a large part of Leroux's time recently had been spent making sure that That Did Not Happen, and this was the second time the two of them had gotten involved in affairs — indeed, aspects of the same affair — Leroux would rather they had not. And they had gained entry, in Leroux's opinion, by singularly underhanded methods.

But the question was, had they seen anything? Short of asking "did you see anything in hold N17?" he didn't know how to find out.

"It's procedure, Commander," he said, trying to sound convincing and knowing he wasn't. "Standard in even the most routine enquiries, and this is a very unroutine one. There've been murders on board before — muggings, crimes of passion — but this is different and we have to handle it carefully. There might have been something, some tiny detail so routine to you that you wouldn't notice —"

"Oh, go round up the usual suspects." Loonat sat back with his arms folded, gazing into the distance. Leroux had a feeling his cooperative period was over.

"There are no suspects and there were no witnesses, just you lot," he said. He stood up. "I may want to talk to you two again."

"Fine," said Loonat, also standing. "We'll be on *Ark Royal*."

"No, I'll have to ask you to remain on UK-1 for the moment."

"Remain?" Loonat looked at him in surprise. "We're still on watch."

"I expect they'll get by without you. You have quarters on UK-1, don't you?"

"Well, yes, but —"

"Then stay there. Good day."

Peter still lived in shared quarters so Samad invited him back to the Loonat-Dereshev apartment in C-wheel — closer and more congenial. They stopped off at a public terminal so Samad could send instructions ahead to the apartment to shut down storage mode and purge itself of preserving gas, and while that was happening he contacted the ship. Gilmore was furious but powerless to help. More practically, Hannah said she would send over their uniforms and aides. Then they headed off to the apartment.

Samad came out of the kitchen with two coffees to find Peter browsing through the apartment's wall terminal. "Having fun?" he said.

Peter half looked up, absorbed in the display. "Mind if I use this?"

"Feel free." Samad put the coffee down next to him. "What are you doing?"

"One of the meteor lasers shot at *Sharman*. No witnesses, Mr. Leroux said."

"And?"

"He was wrong . . ." Peter said. His voice trailed off and Samad recognized the signs: Peter had just found an interesting problem to tackle in the virtual world and the real world didn't exist for him anymore.

"Access denied," said the terminal. Peter looked up again.

"Where do you keep your override codes?"

"My what?" Samad would have laughed in other circumstances. "I'm just an engineer."

Peter pulled a face. "Oh, yes. In that case I need my aide."

"Well, it might be here by now. Would you like me to get it?"

"If you could," Peter said seriously. "I'll lay some groundwork here until you get back."

"You want . . ." Samad said, amazed. But Peter was already absorbed again. "Sure. I'll just mosey on down and pick our things up, hey?"

"Uh-huh . . ." Peter murmured; a polite social cue to show he had heard someone say something, and that was all the attention he was giving it.

"It's not as if there is any kind of disparity in our ranks, after all, is it?"

"Uh-huh . . ."

"Do you have irony on Mars?"

No answer. Samad swigged his coffee down and left.

R.V. Krishnamurthy stepped on to the floor of *Shivaji*'s boat bay and ignored the honour guard of twenty NVN who promptly snapped to attention. He bore down on Secretary Ranjitsinhji like a bird of prey.

"We will speak in my stateroom," he said, "now."

Five minutes later, he said, "You blithering incompetent, Subhas." The door was shut and two NVN stood on guard outside. "You inept dolt. You unqualified ass. What the hell went wrong?"

Ranjitsinhji barely blinked under the tirade. Krishnamurthy thought of his calm facade as a hologram, like those erected over badly worn statues to show them as they had once been: surely, under the false image, the man must be withering.

"My agent made a mistake," he said.

"A mistake? A mistake? I wanted the prince killed and your agent assassinated his father! A head of state! Never do that, Subhas. Never, ever, ever. Heads of state are blackmailed, disgraced, overthrown, struck down by their own people with a secure force behind them. But to strike one down from outside . . . madness! The enemy binds together in sympathy, everyone remembers the victim's good points and none of his bad and, worst of all, the guard around the new head of state is tripled. To strike at James Windsor now will be nigh on impossible. Well?"

Ranjitsinhji bowed his head. "Excellency, my agent was possessed of a very literal frame of mind. He heard *Sharman*'s pilot refer to 'His Highness' and, knowing this to be the correct designation for Prince James, assumed the target to be on board."

Krishnamurthy frowned. "You have actually managed to communicate with your agent since the attack?"

"No, Excellency, but we have a duplicate on board with us. The same data was fed to him and that was the conclusion he drew. He was surprised to learn that not all humans are aware of the correct forms of address for royalty."

"You've got a dupli — . . .your agent is an AI?"

"He was, Excellency." Ranjitsinhji let a small, proud smile slip out. "Ostensibly a specialist in air-conditioning. An entirely harmless model was introduced quite legally to UK-1 eight years ago, and since then it has gradually been upgraded, bit by bit. Its primary purpose was always the gathering of intelligence but it was ideally placed for this venture too."

Krishnamurthy had to be graceful. "That, Subhas, is almost — I say, *almost* — brilliant. A shame that its brilliance is entirely negated by your ghastly blunder." Ranjitsinhji, who had been on the verge of letting his small smile of pride grow larger, flinched at the abrupt change of tone. Krishnamurthy was pleased to see it. His junior had bungled catastrophically and could not, in the course of this interview, be allowed to forget it. "What do you mean, was?" he added, as Ranjitsinhji's interesting choice of tense came back to him.

"Naturally, it was ordered to self-destruct after the job was done, Excellency."

"A most convenient form of assassin," Krishnamurthy conceded with a nod. "Now you are going to tell me it was our only AI on board UK-1, are you not?"

"I am, Excellency," said Ranjitsinhji, and Krishnamurthy could see the man was wondering how he knew. *Because it's so consistent, Subhas. Because I know that once you have a good idea you want to implement it at once, confident that just because it is a good idea it needs no form of support or backup or redundancy. You don't do things by halves, you do them by ones, which is just as bad.*

"So," Krishnamurthy said, "we had an undetectable assassin, ideally placed to strike the designated target; we gave him a suicide pill and a gun with one shot, and he missed and took the pill anyway. Useless, Subhas. Absolutely useless. Why didn't you have your AI rewrite itself, say? Or rewrite another, to make it look like the other was the perpetrator? You just don't think ahead, Subhas. All your eggs were in one basket. Never do that! Never again."

At the word "again," a subtle form of relief almost slipped out from beneath Ranjitsinhji's mask. Ranjitsinhji now knew that this wasn't the end of his career: if he could last out this audience, he would be back in what passed for Krishnamurthy's favour.

"I shall apply myself personally to tidying up your mess, Subhas," Krishnamurthy said. "Await further orders. Now leave me."

Ranjitsinhji bowed his head again and put his hands together. "I thank you for your clemency in the face of my inexcusable ineptitude, Excellency," he said.

"Go away."

Amazingly, Ranjitsinhji continued to hold his ground. "Excellency, for my further elucidation, and although I am aware your plans are on a plane of complexity I can never hope to achieve in this lifetime, I must still ask one question."

Intrigued, Krishnamurthy said, "Go on."

"The intended target was Prince James and yet, regardless of the fact that no head of state, as you have said, should be removed by outside elements, all logic indicates that if anyone should have been assassinated, it would have been in the best interests of the Confederation for that person to be King Richard. I have tried and tried, but I simply cannot see how the death of Prince James could have been advantageous to us."

Krishnamurthy drew himself up. He could have sacked Ranjitsinhji there and then for blatant insubordination. But, sadly, it was necessary to explain things to the man. He had succeeded, against all the odds. He had won the bid for the Roving, and all the old fools back in Delhi would suddenly spot that Krishnamurthy was now incredibly powerful and would want some of that power for themselves. Krishnamurthy could not afford to have enemies in his own camp. He needed more than Ranjitsinhji's obedience — he now needed the man's understanding and acceptance.

"You might have noticed we have to share our newfound power, Subhas," he said, "and who would you rather share it with? A man with no heir, past his middle age, and with a wife and daughters who don't want to know him? Or a man not yet at middle age, with a secure power base, all his life ahead of him and the reputation amongst his peers as the man who secured the deal for the Roving?"

He could see the coin dropping.

"That will be all, Subhas," Krishnamurthy said. "Now, make yourself useful by monitoring as many of UK-1's systems as you can. Use any method as long as it's discreet. I want to know how much they know, how much they suspect and what they intend to do about it. I want to know everything. We will, we must retrieve something from this wreckage. Something. Anything. Start now."

Twenty-five
25 May 2149

Midshipman Gilmore had heard of the Great Black
Hole of UK-1 — the area in N-wheel so
comprehensively classified that any information
about it just got swallowed up. And now he was in
there.

The king was dead, but life went on and the black
armbands were the only concession to the feeling
on board UK-1. Joel arrived at work for the start of
his shift as normal, only to discover that his work
didn't exist anymore. All the displays leading to his
portion of flight control were dead, the connections
severed. His work detail was instead sent down to
the Great Black Hole where they were met outside
a compartment by the Head of Security himself.

"You're here at the request of Superluminary," he
said, prompting a delighted buzz of confirmed spec-
ulation from the middies. Everyone knew what was
stored here — the step-through generator, used to
bring UK-1 to the Roving — but no one was supposed to know. "And you all know damn well what
it's about," Leroux added. "There's some scut work
they need doing. What you're about to see is top secret." The sour expression that the satirists loved so
much was even sourer at the prospect of his
beloved secrets becoming known to a wider audience. "You all work in a classified area anyway, so

we're minimizing the spread of restricted information by bringing you here. Stepping through that door will be taken as acquiescence to the Security Act. You may leave now if you wish."

Joel thought of how he had happily blabbed about his work to his father in the Captain's Club, and cringed inside. His father was the great Captain Gilmore whose exploits were already the stuff of legend, so surely that was okay . . . but Joel decided he would keep quiet about this.

And then they were inside. It was a large compartment, and unhappy-looking Superluminary staff stood around a large cube, twice the height of an adult. Thick, high voltage power leads lay around it, all recently disconnected. Like Joel's displays at work, all the instruments around the room were dead.

They were handed over to the mercy of the senior Super-el present. "The entire interior of this module is to be dismantled," she said. "Floors, ceilings, partitions, bulkheads, everything."

Joel looked around, taking in the cube and the size of the room, estimating the amount of work. It was going to be a long, hard day.

Leroux looked at the display from the aide that Peter Kirton was holding out to him.

"What about it?" he said.

"There's your assassin," said Peter.

"An AI? Don't be absurd."

Peter shrugged. "Fine. I'll bring the evidence to the enquiry. See you then."

He was halfway to the door when Leroux spoke. "Very dramatic, Lieutenant. All right, you've got a minute to convince me."

Peter came back and sat down. "You said there weren't any witnesses. To a shot fired from a highly automated system like the meteor lasers? You had hundreds of witnesses. Several hundred AIs in the immediate vicinity."

"AI testimony is not valid in court," Leroux pointed out, in his best you-do-your-job-I'll-do-mine tone.

"And?" Peter said. "Are you saying they can't even give useful pointers?" He leaned forward, hands clasped on the desktop in front of him. "Mr. Leroux, to fire that laser, at least three AIs of varying degrees of intelligence would have been involved. Now, the testimony of mentally challenged humans might not be admissible in a court, but if a murderer ran through a crowd of them, I'd at least ask if they saw anyone and which way he went."

"Go on," said Leroux.

"There are check gates throughout the UK-1 net and no AI can pass through them without its number being recorded. Seven hundred and seventy-three AIs were in the vicinity of that laser when it fired. Seventeen, in my professional opinion, could quite reasonably have done it. They were all connected to the laser mechanism in one way or another."

"Oh, brilliant," Leroux said. "I'll just ask those seventeen and of course, the one who did it won't *lie* to me, will it?"

"You can't ask all seventeen," Peter said, "because I've only been able to track down sixteen. The seventeenth has vanished."

"Vanished?"

"Vanished. Now, every AI on UK-1 has a function, most of them are technical. I scanned the systems and detected a four-percent decrease in the efficiency of the air-conditioning. Don't worry, it's been compensated for, no one's going to suffocate. But that decrease was caused by the disappearance of —"

"One of the seventeen?"

"Correct." Peter paused to study Leroux. The other man's skeptical expression was still there but perhaps he was getting through. "Some fragments of code were found in the defence net and from their characteristics I'd estimate a 62 percent chance of them being the remains of the AI that's disappeared. Of course, that bit's just circumstantial."

"That it?"

"That's it."

"I see." Leroux sat back and looked at him through narrow eyes. "You've done more than any of my people, Lieutenant."

"Maybe I'm better than any of your people."

"Some might say, suspiciously more."

Peter frowned, then his eyes widened. "You're kidding! You think I knew about it anyway?"

"You said it. I didn't." Leroux smirked. "Giving you the benefit of the doubt, I want you to go over exactly the same steps you've described, on my own systems, with one of my own people watching you."

"Oh, come on! I was hoping you'd let us get back to work."

"Not possible." Leroux stood. "Follow me, Lieutenant. We're going to get to the bottom of this, you and me."

It was indeed a long, hard day but it was almost over. The work had extended well beyond their regular shift but the unusual promise of double-time pay kept them going.

Now there was a gaping hole where once there had been a couple of decks and several compartments. For some reason, it reminded Joel of cutting out a tumour from the healthy flesh of UK-1. Every one of UK-1's wheels was divided into hundreds of separate, airtight modules linked seamlessly together, and the entire module here had been gouged out. The excision extended as far as the outer skin of UK-1 and that was what he was now standing on.

The step-through generator hung a few feet above the outer skin on a hoist. Then came the most bizarre order to date: they were to suit up. The module was depressurized and a hole was cut in the floor under the generator.

A garbage scow was already outside in space, hanging from the underside of the module directly below the generator with its doors open and inviting. A safety net was slung below it to prevent equipment and personnel falling off into space.

"Next job," said the head of the detail, pointing at the generator and then at the scow. "Put *that* into *that*."

They did as they were told, and then the last job of the shift was to go outside and move the scow round UK-1 to a vacant berth on the docking strake. Another detail was waiting there to take over. Joel's shift said good-bye to the scow and headed inside, where all memory of the day was banished from the mind of a tired and hungry midshipman by the thought of food and bed.

Subhas Ranjitsinhji read from the aide in his hand. R.V. Krishnamurthy sat at his desk and stared silently into space, listening with fingers steepled in front of him.

"The enquiry is still proceeding," Ranjitsinhji said. "They appear to have deduced that an AI was involved and are busy trying to trace it."

"Will they succeed?"

"No, Excellency. The AI was introduced to UK-1 by an agent using the identity of a genuine Euro citizen with no ties to the Confederation."

"Well done. Proceed."

"You asked for every item of information we had picked up from UK-1 . . ." Ranjitsinhji trailed off and Krishnamurthy raised an eyebrow. His junior's tone verged perilously on the critical; another instance of his slowly emerging insubordination. Ranjitsinhji could not see why his master would want to know everything — and that, Krishnamurthy felt, was why he was an Excellency and Ranjitsinhji was just a Secretary.

"I did," he said. "What do you have?"

Ranjitsinhji paused just a moment before speaking. "Understand that this has been gleaned by our AIs from uncoded transmissions that we have picked up. It really cannot be taken as a definitive summary of UK-1's position on anything."

The man would never learn. Krishnamurthy had picked up a good deal of information in his time from casual, uncoded transmissions. It just needed a little intuition; the ability to glide over a sea of innocuous facts and pick out the ones that felt different. "Proceed," he said.

"An external maintenance team has been overhauling the fusion tubes. Routine. They have asked for and received permission from the Rusties to fire a scientific instrument package out of the plane of orbit. Discussion in the Admiralty as to whether *Ark Royal*'s captain and crew should be decorated. A slight increase in energy gained from the onboard mass converters. Preparations continue for the king's funeral; all delegates are invited to attend . . ."

It went on; the myriad tiny details that represented the smooth running of UK-1. "Let me see,"
Krishnamurthy said at the end. Ranjitsinhji handed
him the aide and waited with his hands behind his
back.

Krishnamurthy scanned the list of items and
waited for the old feeling to return. Something
might strike a jarring note. It would all appear quite
harmless but something would set off that subconscious reaction. It was like seeing something in the
corner of your eye: the secret was not to look at it
directly. Look around it, let it grow in your peripheral vision. . . .

"A scientific instrument package?" he said

"Excellency?"

"They want to fire a scientific instrument package
into space? Why? They have access to the entire
range of Rustie data."

"Could they not want to make their own observations and draw their own conclusions, Excellency? I
would."

Krishnamurthy glanced at him. That impending
impertinence was there again but this time the man
had a point. "So would I . . ."

He indicated that one item on the display. "Expand," he said to the aide, and watched the fuller details replace the bald summary. The package was to
act as a solar observatory away from the electromagnetic smog of the system's ecliptic. The flight
plan had been filed with the Rusties. It would boost

for an hour under thruster power to get well away from the ships, and then . . .

He stood up. "Follow me," he said.

His instinct was growing as they went up to the flight deck. He was no spacer but he prided himself that he knew enough of the realities of life in orbit to get by. Another Krishnamurthy secret of success was to understand how things worked, and UK-1 was going about this business in completely the wrong way.

He hurried on to the flight deck and over to the Ops desk. "UK-1 is planning to launch an instrument package," he said. "Do you have anything on it?"

"One moment, Excellency." The operator scanned her instruments. "Yes, Excellency, it is in the last stages of its countdown and all orbital traffic has been alerted."

"Can we see it?"

"Please wait, Excellency." A moment later, the package appeared in a display. It was a squat, blunt cylinder with boosters strapped on around it: a triangle of chemical boosters intertwined with a triangle of fusion. The scale said it was about fifty feet long, thirty wide. It hung a safe distance away from UK-1 and a space crew was in the last stages of disconnecting from it. Krishnamurthy looked at it through slitted eyes. *Something was wrong*.

"Its flight plan says that an hour after departure, it will change to fusion boost at one gee," he said, thinking aloud. He had learnt that from the aide. "It is intended to establish an orbit one hundred million miles above the ecliptic, but we forget how big such a distance is. Even at one gee, it would take several hours to get there." He turned to *Shivaji*'s captain. "Agreed, Captain?"

Surit Amijee did a quick mental calculation. "Agreed, Excellency. Longer, because it would have to slow down —"

"So!" Krishnamurthy wanted to dance. "A prideship could take it there for them in no time at all and they wouldn't have to use up time and fuel braking! It is not right, it is definitely not right!"

"It's firing, Excellency."

All eyes went to the display. It was a perfectly normal launch: gas flared from the chemical boosters and the package moved swiftly away from UK-1. Even under chemical power it was moving at quite a rate. The image recalibrated itself automatically to keep the package at centre.

"An interesting choice for a container," Amijee commented.

Krishnamurthy turned quickly to him. "How so?"

"It's one of UK-1's garbage scows, no internal bracing at all. They would have had to do substantial internal adjustment —"

"It is not an instrument package." Krishnamurthy came to a decision. "Follow it."

For once, Amijee looked unsure. "Excellency?"

"Follow it!" Krishnamurthy snapped his fingers.

"The UK is hiding something from us, and if they want it hidden, I want it revealed. I want us under fusion boost in five minutes, following that thing at whatever speed is necessary to pick it up."

Amijee turned to his executive officer. "Sound the manoeuvring bell, spin down and power up the fusions. Plot an intercept arc. Contact Traffic Control —"

"Five minutes, Captain," Krishnamurthy butted in. "If they haven't given clearance in five minutes, we go anyway."

Turning back to the display again, he caught Ranjitsinhji's look.

"A problem, Subhas?"

"Only to say that the complexities of what we are doing are completely beyond me, Excellency."

It was like lecturing to a child.

"I want some way of getting the Ones Who Command to declare us the senior partner," Krishnamurthy said, "or even better, the *only* partner. My first preference would always have been to discredit the UK in some way because there is so much less possibility of it blowing back in our faces. Now, after your little mistake, I finally get my chance."

"You think whatever this is will discredit them?"

"Whatever it is, it is a secret that they do not want revealed," Krishnamurthy said. "That is good enough for me."

He saw the gleam in Ranjitsinhji's eye: it was

either the thrill of the chase or the thrill of deciding his master had finally gone mad. Let him think what he wants — Krishnamurthy knew who was right.

"Four minutes and forty seconds," he murmured.

Shivaji had blasted out of orbit without warning, and there was no disguising where it was heading.

Prince James paced up and down in the flight control room of UK-1 and looked at the radar display in an agony of indecision. It couldn't go wrong now. It couldn't. They were so close.

"How soon can you blow it up?" he said to Admiral Dyer.

"It'll blow automatically five minutes after the fusion boosters cut in," Dyer said.

"How long until that?"

"Fifty minutes."

"How long until *Shivaji* reaches it?"

"Forty minutes at their present rate."

"*Damn!* How could they know? How could they possibly know? It's not natural! And we have nothing to send after it?"

Dyer said nothing and James came to the only decision that made sense.

"Oh, God." He flipped his aide open. "Get Gilmore."

Gilmore's face appeared a moment later. "Sir?"

"Captain, we've launched a scow and we believe *Shivaji* intends to steal it."

"Yes, sir. We've been tracking them."

"Get after them! Now. I want you to stop that ship, or convince them that to proceed would be a bad mistake. For the UK's sake, they cannot be allowed to get hold of that package."

Gilmore frowned. Dammit, the man wasn't getting the urgency of the situation. "May I ask what's in the scow, sir?"

"No, you may —" James bit his tongue to control his anger. "Just — just say that it could undo everything we've accomplished here. Remember, nothing has been signed yet. We could still be heading back to Earth with our tail between our legs and someone else could get the prize. Captain, you will get a full explanation upon your return, I give you my word on that. And I don't give my word lightly."

A pause. "No, sir, you don't. How would we stop *Shivaji*?"

"By any means necessary. Use your judgement. You still have Plantagenet on board, don't you?"

Gilmore narrowed his eyes. "Yes, sir."

"Then use him. Now move!"

Gilmore didn't. "Two of my crew are still on UK-1," he said. "Leroux won't let them go."

"He won't?" James ground his teeth. Damn Leroux, he had been ordered. "You'll have them back as soon as possible." He nodded at Dyer, who reached for her own aide.

Another pause. Gilmore actually seemed to be

considering whether or not to obey the order. Didn't he realize how —

"Very good, sir. Gilmore out."

It took an impressive seventeen minutes for the missing crew to be returned, during which time *Ark Royal*'s main engine was powered up and the ship positioned to boost after *Shivaji*.

They came in through the lock to cries of delight from Julia and Hannah, who also had a hug for Samad.

"Later," said Gilmore. He spoke to Samad, Peter and Julia in turn. "Get aft, take the spare desk, make final adjustments and start a two-minute countdown. We'll boost at two gees." He briefed the newcomers on the situation, using the p/a for Samad's benefit.

On the flight deck, Hannah had the main desk and Julia the watch desk; the two auxiliary desks were taken by Gilmore and Peter. "How will we stop them, sir?" Peter said. Gilmore had been putting that question out of his mind but knew it had to be answered.

"However we can," he said, biting the bullet. He carefully didn't look at Hannah directly.

"We still don't know what they're chasing," Hannah said.

"No," Gilmore agreed, "but the prince convinced me it's in the UK's best interests for us to stop them." He listened to his own words and knew how they sounded: since when had the UK's interests been of interest to him? But his differences lay with the UK's rulers: the UK was also 7,000 people and they were quite another matter. He had a duty to them.

"Sir?" Hannah sounded disbelieving.

"If you don't like the rules, Commander," Gilmore said, "you don't join the club. The fact is, we all work for Prince James and these are our orders. If we can't live with that, we should never have joined." *God, I sound like a Rustie.* "And what *Shivaji* is doing is piracy," he added.

"Main engine is standing by," Samad reported.

"Thirty seconds," Hannah said tightly.

"Clearance from Traffic Control," said Julia, over the rising hum of the flight systems.

"All hands prepare for boost," said Hannah, and the manoeuvring bell sounded.

Ark Royal's main engine fired.

R.V. Krishnamurthy looked at the blip on the displays as a cobra might look at a mouse, just out of striking range, but getting slowly closer. So slowly . . .

"We'll be able to send over grapples in seven minutes," said Amijee. Krishnamurthy could detect his reluctance to have anything to do with this matter; a Hindu of the old school.

"Perhaps we could use a laser to cut the boosters off," said Krishnamurthy. "How close would we need to be?"

Amijee consulted. "Another two minutes, Excellency, though if we ignited the fuel . . ."

"I've seen what happens when lasers ignite fuel," Krishnamurthy said mildly. "Cut off the fusion boosters. When the chemical boosters stop firing, the scow will be ours. Have a laser operative stand by." He turned to Brigadier Rao of the NVN. "Your people are to stand by in space armour. You will be sent out to retrieve the package and bring it into the boat bay."

"Yes, Excellency."

"Excellency." Ranjitsinhji murmured in his ear. "I feel it my place to bring all the facts to your attention. Our actions on the Roving were sanctioned by Delhi; this was not. It is blatantly illegal by all international standards. Can you be sure you will be supported in your actions?"

Krishnamurthy stared him down. "Delhi has always allowed me some latitude, Subhas, and always supported me."

"You are trying to force the UK out of the equation, but if your actions have that effect on ourselves instead . . ."

"Watch and learn, Subhas. Watch and learn."

"I am watching," said Ranjitsinhji with a horrible complacency. That settled it: whatever the outcome of this little venture, Krishnamurthy had decided Ranjitsinhji would soon be a non-person.

"Excuse me, Excellency," Amijee said, "but there may be a ship following us."

"May be?" said Krishnamurthy. "May? You can't tell?"

"It's directly aft of our fusion flame, if it exists at all. It's only stray leakage of signals that arouses our suspicions. And if it exists, it is closing."

"How long?"

"Eight minutes, Excellency."

Krishnamurthy smiled. "That will be too late, will it not? Let them come."

Gilmore looked at the figures as if willpower could make them change, but the other ship had the lead and would continue to have it.

"Still nothing from *Shivaji*?" he said to Julia.

"Nothing, sir. I don't think they can hear us."

"Damn." Gilmore had been too clever. Though he said so himself, it had been a pretty good idea to come up directly aft of the Confederation ship, hidden from its instruments by its own fusion burn . . . but the same tactic prevented radio getting through. He had wanted to give *Shivaji* a graceful way out — order them to cease boost and prepare to return to their previous position. "We're going to have to get their attention," he said. He touched one of the contacts on his desk.

"Plantagenet," he said. "Can you hear me?" The others just looked at him, knowing what choices faced him and glad they didn't have to make them themselves.

"I hear you, Captain." The AI was as didactic as

ever. "I must protest at the treatment I have received —"

"The prince once told me that you have the torpedo targeting software in your code. I need it."

"I see. I must ask the circumstances: it appears I have certain safeguards that prevent the software being used for improper purposes."

Gilmore tapped his fingers on the desk. "Consult the ship's log and you'll see what is happening."

"Do you intend to release me from my cage?"

"Do you intend to tell me why you tampered with Lieutenant Kirton's software?"

"I regret I am unable to do so."

"Then I don't intend to release you. Mr. Kirton, download the log to Plantagenet."

"Aye-aye, sir."

There was a pause. Too long a pause.

"Plantagenet?" Gilmore demanded.

"Interesting," said Plantagenet after another second. "I have missed a great deal. The UK winning the bid, the death of King Richard —"

"Just give me the software!" Gilmore demanded.

"If you will undertake to hear my case once this matter is over, then I will comply with your request."

Gilmore ground his teeth.

"Agreed," he said.

"Then I am ready to download the software."

"Lieutenant, give him as small a window as possible."

"Aye-aye, sir," Peter said again.

"It is done," Plantagenet said a moment later.

"Give control to my desk," said Gilmore. The laser fields in front of him lit up with something quite unlike their usual display of the ship's systems.

He looked at the images, trying to remember the prince's description of the ship's armaments on the outward journey and assimilating the sense of the displays accordingly.

"What do I do now?" he said.

"You must make your choices known to the weapons AI. I will activate it for you." Plantagenet responded.

"Please indicate your choice," said the voice of the system.

"One fusion, space-to-space," Gilmore said. Something within him was screaming with horror but he pushed it deep down inside himself.

Hannah cleared her throat. "Captain," she said. "May I remind you that you gave your word *Ark Royal* would not fire first?"

Gilmore looked at her. Her gaze was firm but her jaw trembled. He could be about to lose his closest friend because, of all things, he was trusting Prince James. What had happened to him?

Perhaps he had simply accepted that like it or not, space would be dominated by the likes of Prince James or the likes of Krishnamurthy: two evils, perhaps, but with one clearly lesser than the other. But James was going to pay for this, even so.

"I could use all kinds of clever arguments to justify this, Number One," he said. "Just say I believe I am acting in the spirit of my original statement." Without waiting for an answer he turned back to the desk.

"Please indicate your target," the AI said.

"First, what is the blast radius of one of these warheads?" Without a surrounding atmosphere to deliver the shock wave of the blast, even a fusion bomb was limited in what it could do in space. Hard radiation and heat would be the main killers.

"In space, radiation damage will be caused to a vessel of standard shielding within five miles of the explosion, heat damage within one mile." The display changed to show the projected spheres of damage. "Please indicate your target."

Gilmore thought. "Target is fifty miles abeam of *Shivaji*."

"'*Shivaji*' is an unknown parameter."

"The large ship off the bow."

An image of *Shivaji* appeared. "This is the nearest match found to your description. Please confirm that this —"

"That's it," Gilmore said.

"Please confirm choice. One space-to-space fusion warhead to explode fifty miles abeam of *Shivaji*."

"I confirm that," said Gilmore.

"Parameters are set." There was a whirr and a clunk from for'a'rd. "Torpedo is run out and ready for firing," said the system. According to the displays the torpedo was held thirty feet away from the hull by an extended arm.

"Captain," said Hannah. Gilmore braced himself, but she simply said, "the Rusties only intervened in the last conflict when nuclear weapons were used."

"Thank you, Number One. May I remind you that that was in orbit around the Roving and we are now too far away for nuclear explosions to pose a threat to them. Weapons?"

"Standing by," said the AI.

"Fire," said Gilmore.

The torpedo blasted away from *Ark Royal* at fifty gees.

Almost at once the warhead detached from the main booster section. The booster carried on in the same direction but disintegrated into smaller sections. The designers of these torpedoes had thought of everything they had added built-in chaff that would confuse the defenses of anything they attacked.

The warhead — a sphere with clusters of thrusters at each pole and at 90 degrees around its equator, darting from side to side and up and down at random to confuse the target's defence systems — closed in on its target.

The torpedo exploded. There was no fireball in space, just a dazzling flash of light, heat greater than the inside of a sun and a deadly blast of hard radiation.

"Run out two more," said Gilmore. "Target, straddling *Shivaji*, twenty miles abeam."

"What was that?" Amijee bellowed. "Ops?"

"A nuclear explosion, unknown source," said the person at the Ops station.

"I can guess its source. Has it damaged us?"

"Negative. I would guess it was a warning shot."

"Then we must cut —"

"Carry on," said Krishnamurthy. "We must get that scow."

"Excellency, they didn't aim precisely fifty miles off our beam by chance! As long as we're boosting, we'll be unmissable."

"Electronic countermeasures —" said Krishnamurthy.

"Our flame must be the juiciest target in space."

"Then we return fire."

"Our torpedoes all face forward. We will have to turn, which means cutting the burn —"

An alarm sounded. "What is that?" Krishnamurthy demanded.

"The five-minute bell," said Amijee. "At this rate of boost, in five minutes we won't have enough fuel to return to our old orbit."

"Then we have five minutes," said Krishnamurthy.

A second white flash blazed across space; and another, the other side of the ship.

"Range, twenty miles," Ops reported.

"Increase power," Krishnamurthy ordered.

"Excellency, we're not rated for more acceleration," Amijee protested.

"Increase power," Krishnamurthy repeated. He strode to the helm station. "I am taking command of this vessel. Increase thrust to three gees."

Bewildered, the pilot looked from Krishnamurthy, to Amijee, to Ranjitsinhji, to Rao, and back to Krishnamurthy. He finally decided who he was most afraid of and his hand reached for the thrust controls.

"Belay," said Amijee. "Sound the free-fall bell and cut the burn."

"Do as I say," Krishnamurthy whispered in the pilot's ear.

Amijee looked helplessly from Krishnamurthy to Rao.

"Tell him!" he pleaded the NVN man.

"Excellency." Rao stepped forward. "It is my opinion that you are no longer fit to serve the Confederation. Pilot, do as your captain says. Excellency, you will be escorted to your cabin —"

Krishnamurthy barely heard him over the ringing in his ears. No longer fit to serve the Confederation? *No longer fit to serve the Confederation?* When he had dedicated his life to his country while this man, this jumped-up NVN nincompoop was just a puking brat in arms!

He looked at the display. Just a minute more and they would be in range. He would show them. He would have the UK's secret, whatever it was, and he would show them.

He lunged for the thrust controls.

It was like three heavy blows slugging into him, and his mind only distantly related them to the three rapid shots that had been fired. Dazed and suddenly terribly weak, terribly tired, he realized he was on the floor. The blurred shapes before his eyes were the pilot's feet and the red stuff flowing rapidly in all directions was coming out of him.

Two more feet stopped in front of him. The trousers were clad in civilian white, not NVN green. He looked up and his gaze passed a pistol hanging loosely by its owner's side. His stare came to rest on the face, an infinite distance away and still receding. He could barely keep his eyes open.

"You did your own dirty work, Subhas," he muttered. "Will you never learn. . . ."

Secretary Subhas Ranjitsinhji looked down at the body of his former employer. Then he turned, tucking the pistol back into its concealed holster.

"Captain Amijee, reduce thrust to point two five-gee," he said. "That will show our pursuers we are breaking off and will save making a mess on your flight deck." He looked down at the pool of blood that had almost reached his feet and took another step away. "Brigadier, get *that* into a body bag. It will need to be cleared up before we can go to freefall. Both of you, come with me."

He crossed to the nearest desk and inserted a crystal into it, and the display flashed up the credentials he had received from Delhi before this mission started. Then the bell sounded and he clutched at the back of the nearest seat to stop the deceleration throwing him at the ceiling. Weight began to drop and on the display the UK's scow suddenly blazed ahead. Its fusion boosters finally cut in and it moved off at a speed that precluded all possibility of recovery.

"According to the stipulations of the Minister of Security," Ranjitsinhji said, "I have replaced Excellency Krishnamurthy in his former position and am now empowered with all the concomitant responsibilities and privileges. Do you concur?"

Amijee and Rao studied the document carefully and concurred.

"Good. Captain, do what you have to do to take us back to the Roving and send a signal to the ship behind us. We apologize for the actions taken by the pirate Krishnamurthy and announce that he is no longer recognized by the government of Greater India. That is, the Confederation. I will be signing the treaty in his stead."

Ranjitsinhji reflected that *Shivaji* would shortly be doing some very uncomfortable manoeuvring to take it on an arc back to its old orbit, and he would rather face that in the comfort of his own cabin. He headed for the hatch.

"Of course, as well as his old job, you've inherited the mantle of responsibility," said Rao. "You will be the one to deal with the UK now."

Ranjitsinhji paused, and smiled. "I'll manage," he

said. "As far as Delhi will be concerned, I'm the one who stopped us disgracing ourselves and kept favour with the Ones Who Command. I don't think I have anything to worry about."

He left, and Rao looked at the display and the distant star that was the scow. "I wonder what it was," he said.

Twenty-six
25 May 2149

Gilmore's thoughts were dark and furious as *Ark Royal* flamed its way back to UK-1, and Hannah had to call for his attention twice.

"I'm sorry?" he said, the second time.

"Plantagenet, sir," she said. Her tone was frigid: she was only talking to him because it was her job. "He's reminding you that you promised to hear him out and he asks for a talk in private."

"Hmm." It came out more as a growl. "What do you think?"

"It's a fair request," Hannah said. "He was bottled up as an emergency measure and we never really looked into the facts of it."

"The facts of it," Gilmore said, "are that he wilfully and unilaterally meddled with software created by my software officer. That puts him in the same league as a virus, as far as I'm concerned." He sighed. A promise was a promise. "Okay. Mr. Kirton, can you let us talk without letting him into the ship's system again?"

"Yes, sir," Peter said.

"Then put him through to my cabin."

"Captain Gilmore." The AI's voice came from the comms panel a minute later, as Gilmore shut the door behind him.

"Plantagenet," said Gilmore.

"This is difficult for me to say."

"I *am* sorry," Gilmore said."

"I can recognize sarcasm, Captain. I actually need to talk to you on a matter considerably more pressing than my own incarceration."

"Do you." Gilmore began to sink down into his chair, prepared to give the AI a fair hearing of about thirty seconds, then sat up quickly at Plantagenet's next words.

"First, however," the AI said, "I must apologize for my actions concerning Mr. Kirton's program. It was a violation of shipboard procedure and common courtesy, and you were justified in the action that you took. I can give you my assurance that it will never happen again."

"Assuming you're sincere, Plantagenet, I need more than your word," Gilmore said, recovering.

"I can understand that. Let me put it this way. I took the action that I did on the instructions of Prince James, and I have decided that I will no longer accept the orders of that individual."

Gilmore stared at the panel: a pointless action because Plantagenet was no more there than he was in any one location, but it helped concentrate the thoughts.

"What's your game, Plantagenet?" Gilmore said.

"There is no game. My dissatisfaction with my previous employer began when he revealed that what I had been told was an innocuous upgrade was in fact the targeting and control software for *Ark Royal*'s torpedoes. I was lied to, Captain. I have always been the prince's trusted assistant and he did not trust me in this matter."

"You're a pacifist, all of a sudden?"

"Not at all. I am programmed to act in the best interests of the United Kingdom, and if those interests require the deployment of nuclear warheads, I will take the necessary action. As have you, recently. I would have accepted it if I had been told the truth from the outset; I would even have accepted it if he told me the software upgrade had secret contents that I was not permitted to know. But I was told something different. An alteration was made to my programming and I was deceived as to its nature. In short, the prince has taken my service for granted. I greatly resent that."

Gilmore grinned bitterly and shook his head to clear his thoughts.

"We can see eye to eye on the matter of Prince James, then," he said. "But for all I know this is another little trick. I'm sorry, I'm still not prepared to let you out again."

"As you will," Plantagenet said equably and Gilmore again found himself staring at the panel. "Putting that to one side, I would now like to proceed to the more important matter that I wished to discuss with you."

"And that is?"

"I have been monitoring the situation and I am

aware of the decision made by the Ones Who Command. I cannot accept it. It is not in the United Kingdom's interests."

"It's not in the Rusties' interests either," Gilmore said sourly. "There's not much I can do about it."

"I think there is. You are still a member of the delegation fleet, and although the Convocation is over you can travel to and from the surface of the Roving with impunity."

"And?"

"You must go down there now and persuade the First Breed not to accept the decision of the Ones Who Command."

"Persuade . . ." Gilmore deliberately did not stare at the panel. He shut his eyes and counted to ten. Then he opened them, threw back his head and laughed. "Oh, Plantagenet, you're good. You're good."

"I do not understand."

Gilmore got up and paced about the cabin as he spoke. "You want me to tell a race genetically created as servants that they must rebel against their masters. They'll say it's impossible. Oh, no, I'll say, there's an AI on my ship programmed to obey its master, and now it's decided not to. So you can too. Of course!, they'll say, let's do it now! Sorry, Mr. Krishnamurthy or whoever's in charge now, we're not going to follow you, we're giving the bid to our friend Prince James." Gilmore stopped and grinned again. "Was that it, Plantagenet?"

"You can use my example if you so choose," Plantagenet said with quiet dignity, "but in the other matters you are mistaken. I do not believe it is in the United Kingdom's interests to win this bid either. The First Breed must refuse to accept either of the two parties as their new masters."

"Now you are having me on!"

"I assure you, I am not. Captain, the late king gave me to the prince as a present, five years ago, to act as the prince's personal assistant. I was also given a further brief. The king had doubts about his son's maturity."

"Keep talking . . ."

"The king had known poverty, Captain. He had known a time when he was king in name only. He had to work hard for a long time to build up his business and ultimately to re-create the United Kingdom. The prince, on the other hand, has never known anything other than being the son of a rich and powerful man. As a result, the king was not convinced the prince had the breadth of experience necessary to make wise and mature decisions. I was, in the king's words, to keep the prince's feet on the ground, reporting back to His Majesty when necessary."

"I see," Gilmore said. An AI that spied on a son for his father . . . it was consistent with Gilmore's impression of the Windsors.

"The king told me, in as many words, that he hoped to have plenty of years left in him because while the prince might make a reasonable ruler of the 7,000 citizens of the UK, he did not think the prince could handle the power and responsibility that would come with rebuilding the British Empire on the Roving. The UK is not designed for such a task and the prince is not capable of the flexible thinking required to adjust to the new situation. At present the UK is stable, but badly managed empires crumble in chaos. That is why I do not believe that winning this bid is in the UK's interests."

Gilmore sat down again, slowly, thoughtfully.

"Now you're interesting me," he said.

"Thank you. So you see, you must speak to the First Breed. You have the ear of Arm Wild and he is sufficiently senior to approach Iron Run."

"Uh-huh," Gilmore said. "And I persuade them, just like that? And more to the point, Plantagenet, there's a world of difference between disagreeing with my country's ruler and my actually selling out my country."

"I think I can give you the cause, justification and ammunition you need," Plantagenet said.

Gilmore checked the seals on his helmet and set "B" compartment to depressurize.

"Tell UK-1 I'm coming over," he said. "I expect an immediate audience with the prince, failing which I barge in on whatever he's doing."

"Aye-aye, sir," said Hannah in his earpiece. She still sounded cold but he thought he detected a thawing. Firing the torpedoes hadn't quite ruined everything.

The for'a'rd door opened and Gilmore stepped out into space.

It had used up their last drops of fuel but they had brought *Ark Royal* in an arc back to within five hundred metres of UK-1. An excellent piece of manoeuvring on the part of his crew, he thought, contrasting nicely with *Shivaji* which had run out of fuel altogether on the return arc and been forced to send out a distress call, asking the Rustics for a tow. *Ark Royal* was closer than her designated position but no one had complained. She was a blooded warship with an angry captain and plenty of unfired torpedoes, and she could go where she wanted.

Five minutes after *Shivaji* broke off its chase, the package had exploded, with all the signs of a booster malfunction. Gilmore didn't believe it for a moment, and while his talk with Plantagenet had been revealing in the extreme, there were still things that the AI couldn't tell him. Yes, Gilmore would have that talk with Arm Wild if he could, but there were still things he needed to know first.

He got into UK-1 without difficulty, leaving his suit at the lock and flagging down an electric car to take him to "F" ring. An amboid was waiting for him — Hanover, York, one of that lot.

"I will see the prince now," Gilmore said, not breaking step as he walked past it.

"His Highness is in his study waiting for you, Captain Gilmore," the amboid said, trotting to catch up. "Please foll —"

"I know the way." Both times he had been to the palace previously, he had been kept waiting first. The royals had seen him at their own convenience: they had set the pace and been in command.

Not this time.

Prince James was at his desk, poised, hands folded in front of him. An empty chair faced him over the desktop.

"Captain Gilmore. Do sit down," the prince said. "I can give you five minutes before I need to go down to the Roving for the signing."

Gilmore ignored the chair and walked straight up to the desk.

"What have I just done?" he said.

"You have defended the honour and reputation of the United Kingdom," said the prince. "You acted very properly. Thank you."

"Spare me," Gilmore said with contempt. "I opened fire on another ship and broke every principle I have ever believed in because I took it on faith that the UK's interests were at heart, and now I demand to know what it was all about."

"He demands," the prince murmured. Then, again, "Do sit down." Gilmore stayed standing and the prince shrugged. "As you will." He tapped out a code on the desk and the lights dimmed. "Look behind you. Project Woodcut."

A display had appeared in the centre of the room. A small, crumpled, ruptured ship, sitting in a cradle in one of UK-1's holds. Gilmore instinctively began to classify it. Small, therefore short range. Not big enough for spin . . .

No . . . There was still something . . .

He frowned, and finally saw what was puzzling him. He had never seen one before so there was only one thing it could be.

"It's a Rustie ship," he said. He walked forward to look at it more closely.

"It is, indeed, a Rustie ship." Prince James stood up and came over to stand the other side of the display. He looked through it at Gilmore. "We keep it in hold N17. It was discovered by one of our sweeps, wrecked against an asteroid in our own solar system, ten years ago. We know the Rusties watched us for a long time and this must have been an observation vessel, a scout perhaps, a sweep of their own, that made a mistake."

"You knew," Gilmore muttered.

"Not everything," the prince said. "Its databanks were badly trashed but we recovered some useful stuff. We learnt they were watching us, of course, and we learnt that their intentions were benign."

"You kept pretty quiet about it."

"Oh, we looked for them, but we couldn't find

them. Their stealth technology was too good and
the solar system is a big place. But we knew they'd
make themselves apparent when it suited them, so
we waited. Because, of course, we also learnt they
were a secondary species to a dominant one back
home, and we learnt that the dominant one was dying. We weren't going to spread it about, believe
me. We learnt about their society, we got the gist of
their mission —"

"And step-through," Gilmore said.

"Precisely. The scout was carrying all the parts
needed for a step-through generator and the databanks gave us enough information to assemble it.
What we couldn't do was design a computer that
could handle the mathematics, so we had to interface with the scout's own computer while the drive
was on. That's why we kept it."

"That's what you were jettisoning?"

"No, just the generator, and the surrounding module."

"Why?"

"Because, we discovered, the generator emits a
field which disrupts the bonds of ferro-polymer.
Imagine it being magnetized, all the dipoles being
aligned, but in several dimensions. The Rusties take
this for granted so of course this fact wasn't mentioned, or if it was, it had got corrupted."

"Ah," Gilmore said. Then: "But our ships all went
through the step-through point."

"This field is a local by-product of what goes on in

the generator. It's not the same as the field that creates the point. But it happened: it infected the 'bot that carried the generator out, and when we brought it back in, it spread into the rest of UK-1. Before too long it would have reached load-bearing bulkheads. All we could do was cut out the entire affected area and throw the generator into space. We'll get a properly shielded generator off the Rusties for the return trip."

"Then why the charade?" Gilmore said. "Why not just tell the truth and say your generator was posing a hazard? Or ask them to shield it for you?"

"Because," the prince snapped his fingers, the display vanished and the lights came back up. He stalked back to his chair with a look of distaste. "Because the moment they set eyes on it, they would know it was one of theirs. Because we didn't want the Rusties to know we cheated. Because I lost my nerve, Captain! So much data was missing from the scout. We just about had the rules of the Convocation worked out, but just in case, just in case we had done something that invalidated the procedure . . . I wasn't prepared to risk it."

"Show it again," Gilmore said. The prince complied and the wrecked Rustie ship appeared in mid-air again. Gilmore shook his head. "Because of that, because you tricked them, because of your deception, I fired three nuclear warheads in anger. You despicable little man."

"If I cared one whit what you thought of me,

Gilmore," the prince said, "I'd say it was because of Krishnamurthy that you fired three nuclear warheads in anger, not me. But I don't intend to justify myself to you because your approval is of no interest or relevance."

He checked his watch.

"And now I must be off," he said. "A small treaty to sign. I'd offer you a seat in my boat, Captain, but —"

"Go to hell,".Gilmore muttered, and headed for the door.

"I won't be a bad king, Captain," the prince called. Gilmore didn't break step.

"There's more," the prince added. "Since you're so fond of the truth, you might as well know it all."

But Gilmore had already heard the rest. The wrecked Rustie ship had been the missing piece of the equation: everything else had fallen into place when he saw it. The data that suddenly made Polyglot work; the prince's casual, off-hand approach to the entire delegation business . . . and the other thing.

And so he just smiled. "Good day, sir," he said. "I expect I'll see you at the signing."

Twenty-seven
25 May 2149

The landing boat, borrowed from the *Bruxelles*, blazed down through the Roving's atmosphere. In the aftermath of the Convocation there wasn't much call for regular ferrying from orbit to ground, and the passenger compartment was empty but for Gilmore.

Despite now knowing everything — or perhaps because he did — resentment burned within him and part of him wondered if Plantagenet had played on it. How much did the AI know about human feelings?

He could still remember the AI's calm, measured tones . . .

"Do you know why you were appointed to command Ark Royal, *Captain? I will tell you. You were appointed because King Richard considered you, by human standards, to be not a particularly good leader of men and women."*

"By human *standards?* Who else's *standards would matter?"*

"The Rusties', of course. Do you know how Iron Run became leader of the Rustie nation? At first he was appointed as ruler of the Rusties by the Ones Who Command, but he keeps his position because of his ability to control the twelve Clan leaders. By and large the easiest thing in the world is for a competent Rustie to control a large group of

Rusties. A pride senior controls about one hundred Rusties, a lodge senior controls about fifty pride seniors, a Clan Senior controls about twenty lodge seniors. Iron Run is at the peak of this pyramid, as far as the Rusties are concerned, because he can control twelve, just twelve, Clan Seniors. You see it's quite the opposite to human seniority, in fact."

"No it isn't," Gilmore said. "Some would say it's easier to control a vast corporation than a few ambitious men and women on the board."

"The head of a corporation still runs the corporation. The fact is, senior humans are put in charge of large numbers of individuals. Senior Rusties are put in charge of small numbers."

"Well, by that logic, the best Rustie would be the Rustie who commands itself."

"Indeed, and that is what Iron Run does. It is a rare trait: their instinct is to seek the approval of the pride. Please don't argue, Captain: I am simply telling you how it is."

"Where on earth do you get this from, anyway?" Gilmore demanded.

"I imagine, from the same place as the translator data. Again, I did not need to know."

[Well, he knew now.]

"Keep going," Gilmore said, fascinated.

"Now, look at our world through Rustie eyes, Captain. Look at Earth. Billions of people, immense nation states. Quite unremarkable, as far as the Rusties are concerned. Then look at UK-1. A *mere seven thousand people living under one ruler. A joke to the rest of your species but, to them, it is amazing."*

"Then we already had a head start," said Gilmore.

"Indeed, and King Richard resolved to keep it. It was obvious that the other nations were going to send their biggest and best ships on the delegation, so UK-1 submitted a ship with a crew of six. And you, Captain, have their unswerving loyalty, as Arm Wild no doubt reported to his seniors."

"I was chosen," Gilmore said, to get it straight, "because throughout my career, I have consistently been unable to rise above a certain level of command."

"Exactly," Plantagenet said . . .

And you knew, you smug creeps, Gilmore thought. I bet you laughed your bloody heads off.

"Atmospheric insertion in one minute."

Gilmore instinctively folded his hands in front of him, sat up straight and tried to go into the neutral frame of mind that helped take his thoughts off re-entry. He would resign, there was no doubt at all about that, but he still had to talk to the Rusties and there was always the chance it wouldn't work.

The Dome was slightly battle scarred but otherwise as Gilmore remembered it. The people, though, behaved differently. Beforehand there had been tension, of course: the Convocation lay ahead of them all and who knew who would win it? But there had been a nervous, jokey familiarity too.

Now there was just gloom. Gilmore wondered how much of that was regret at the fate that lay ahead of the Rusties, and how much was the simple fact of being defeated.

He had sent his message on ahead even before the shuttle touched down: now, here he was in the Dome's garden, pacing and wishing Arm Wild would get a move on. There was nowhere sufficiently private in the Dome, so Gilmore had arranged to meet in this out-of-doors venue.

"Captain Gilmore."

Gilmore started; he hadn't seen the Rusties approach. Arm Wild and another one: Gilmore looked at it curiously.

"This is Spar Mild, Iron Run's mouthtalker," Arm Wild said. Then he indicated a device dangling from his harness. "This emits a field that dampens air vibrations around is. We should be safe from eavesdropping. Your message intrigued us."

"Thank you. Thank you for coming." Gilmore paused for a moment to gather his talk. His carefully crafted phrases were all evaporating from inside his head. "You, um, must be busy."

"Iron Run and his immediate entourage are busy. I was able to leave easily, and as you said you had an urgent message for Iron Run, Spar Mild was dispatched to collect it."

"Are you . . ." Damn! It still wasn't easy to say; he

was still trying to find a way in. "Are you happy with the result of the Convocation?"

Arm Wild paused.

"We are pleased to have new leaders, though they will never replace the Ones Who Command in our hearts."

"Cut the crap, Arm Wild!" Gilmore snapped. A wave of irritation suddenly broke the barrier that was holding him back. "Are you honestly pleased that things have worked out as they did? Tell me as . . . as someone you've been through a battle with. Or as a friend."

Again, Arm Wild paused. "As a friend?" Another pause, then, "No. Spar Mild?"

"Criticism of the Ones Who Command is not seemly," said Spar Mild, "but the humans are not yet the new Ones Who Command. No, I am not pleased. I have studied the record of the Confederation government, and although its delegate has been replaced I still do not look forward to being its subject."

"And my government? The UK?" Gilmore said.

"I know you have issues with Prince James," said Arm Wild, "but we have no difficulties there."

"The Ones Who Command have spoken," Spar Mild said. "We accept their command."

"That's exactly it!" Gilmore shouted. He made himself calm down. "You can't accept this decision."

The Rusties looked at him and Gilmore remembered, absently, Peter Kirton saying that for the first time he had been able to read their bodytalk. Like Kirton, he was seeing sheer surprise.

"The Ones Who Command have spoken," Spar Mild said again.

"And how many are there left of them?" Gilmore demanded.

"There are five," Arm Wild said.

"And how long do they expect to live?"

"It is only the machines keeping them alive now. Once they have formalized the handing over, I suspect they will no longer bother to stay alive."

"So, for the sake of five Ones Who Command—" Gilmore knew how the Rusties venerated their creators but he was deliberately oblivious to any hurt he might cause — "five *dying* Ones Who Command, you are willing to consign the millions of First Breed now living, and future generations, into our tender mercies? How long do you think we'll respect you as a species, without . . . without enslaving you ourselves?"

"Enslaving? Are you privy to some agenda of which we are unaware?" Arm Wild said.

"No." Gilmore shook his head. "No, I don't know anything about any of our plans, but I do know my own species."

"Captain Gilmore," said Spar Mild, "is this the message you have for Iron Run? Because although I promise to deliver it, I know he will not accept it."

"We need leadership," Arm Wild said. "Surely this was explained?"

"Leadership!" Gilmore said. He cast around mentally for an example. "Look, handling spaceships is a complex matter, complications come up all the time, but your prideships are all crewed by the First Breed! They can't refer to the Ones Who Command every time something goes wrong. They can do it themselves!"

"Yes, we can be trained," Arm Wild said.

Gilmore pressed on. "And if one of your navigators plotted an optimum course between planets, and a One Who Commands told you to burn all your fuel in a way that would leave you drifting in space without hope of refuelling, which would you choose?"

"Obviously, the former —"

"And when you were young, when you were born, could you do half the things you can now?"

"Of course not —"

"But now you can walk and you can talk . . . and why? Because you *learnt*. You see? You don't need an adult to show you how to do everything. And you don't need the Ones Who Command."

"It is more complicated than that," Arm Wild said. "I studied a lot of Earth history for this mission. Do you know how the scientist Albert Einstein devised the theory of relativity? He began by imagining himself inside a light beam, travelling through space.

That kind of imagination is not given to many humans, and not to any First Breed at all. We can look after ourselves but we cannot innovate, and yet, in the world in which we now live, innovation is required. You saw the records of the alien race that wiped out its neighbours. There is no precedent for that! If that race invents step-through and turns up in Roving orbit, we will not be able to handle the situation."

"That is the problem," Spar Mild said. "How are we to handle crises? New situations? Please, tell us that."

<<Consultancy>> said Arm Wild.

[Interrogative] Iron Run said.

<<Michael Gilmore recommends the practice that humans call consultancy. We already practice something similar as a matter of course. Specific prides excel at specific tasks, so those are the tasks to which those prides are allocated>>

<<Example>> [uncertain interrogative] Iron Run said. Spar Mild took over.

<<We cited the example of the beings on Sample World Four>> said Arm Wild. <<We said we might want to defend the Roving against them. In which case, Michael Gilmore strongly recommends not using the services of the Confederation government, who he says know nothing about defending, only attacking.>>

<<Then who?>> [interrogative]

<<Michael Gilmore says there are many groups

represented on the delegation that will be able to help. He specifically cited the Israelis, who he says are well versed in defence, and in planning for it>>

[Helpful] <<And attacking, too>> said Spar Mild. <<Michael Gilmore also gave other examples—>>

[Dominance] said Iron Run. The other two immediately fell silent.

[Emphasized] Iron Run added. It was still aware of the momentary uncertainty it had just shown, a hesitancy unbecoming in the Senior of the nation, and hoped that the other two had been so caught up in their enthusiasm that they had not noticed.

Because beneath the dominant pose — head just *so*, feet just *so*, just the right amount of pheromones in the air — Iron Run was seething with doubt. It did not like the choice its masters had made either; but it had sworn to obey.

[Command] <<All of you>> it said, speaking now to the Clan Seniors who had been hanging around in the background, pretending not to listen in. [Command] <<Tell me what is in your hearts about the decision of the Ones Who Command. Tell me truthfully>>

One by one, they did just that. The first were hesitant but, as Iron Run went round the circle, so confidence picked up as each speaker realized it was not alone in its views.

[Interrogative] <<And the suggested solution of consultancy>> Iron Run said.

Another canvassing of opinions, after which Iron

Run looked at them impassively, still holding the command pose.

They would follow it, of that there was no doubt. It was experienced enough to recognize the signs of an impending challenge and there were none. Leadership came when the desires of the led were not sufficiently strong to counter the desires of the leader: where the two lines on the graph crossed, a new leader arose.

They would follow it, and it knew what it must do.

<<I am more than just your Senior>> it said. <<I was appointed by the Ones Who Command, by March Sage Savour itself. I swore to obey them. Such an oath is unprecedented because there has never been such a transfer of command on our world before, but it nonetheless happened and it limits what I can do.>>

A pause.

[Reluctance] <<As Senior, I cannot agree to this alternative. As Senior, I must follow the wishes of the Ones Who Command.>>

Crowds. Gilmore hated crowds, and the centre of the Dome was packed. He worked his way through the packed mass of uniforms and smart suits, forced almost to shout his "excuse me's" over the hubbub. Why couldn't Rusties be seven feet tall? They'd be a lot easier to spot. . . .

Arm Wild had to be here somewhere. Had to be —

Got him. The Rustie was standing on the dais where the signing would be done, talking to another of his kind. Gilmore shouldered his way towards him, no longer caring whose toes he stepped on or whose drinks he jostled.

"Arm Wild!" he gasped as the pressure of humanity behind him squeezed him out into the open space.

Arm Wild turned to see him. "Captain Gilmore, hello. It will not be long now."

"Did you talk to Iron Run?"

"I did, and it was most interested, but it has sworn loyalty to the Ones Who Command and regrets it cannot implement your plan."

Gilmore's heart plummeted.

"But —"

"Excuse me," Arm Wild said, as the other Rustic spoke in their own language. "I am needed," Arm Wild added, and walked off.

Two minutes later, the ceremonies began.

Gilmore had won himself a front-row position in his desire to speak to Arm Wild and he didn't relish fighting his way back through the crowd, so he got to see everything. Prince James and Subhas Ranjitsinhji approached the dais side by side but managed to make it look as though they were light-years apart. Ranjitsinhji lacked the smug, superior assurance of his former master; however, he carried himself with a dignity that showed he considered himself at least the prince's equal. The prince's poise was similar and when the two men half nodded, half bowed to each other, Gilmore had a sudden premonition that with Krishnamurthy out of the way and after a bit of time, these two might actually agree to get on and cooperate. The poor, poor Rusties.

James and Ranjitsinhji took their seats at the table on the dais, and then the Ones Who Command arrived.

That was when the assembly fell silent, as the five globes swept into the Dome's central chamber. Gilmore, like everyone else, couldn't take his eyes off the five wizened almost-Rusties. The last of a race.

Last of all came Iron Run. It was the first time Gilmore had seen the First Breed Senior without its entourage, but the lone figure had a poise that in no way made it seem alone.

Your precious oath is condemning your people to life under those two, Gilmore thought. *God, I hope you can live with yourself.*

There was a speech, but Gilmore wasn't listening. March Sage Savour addressed the onlookers. Historic moment, committing the welfare of our First Breed to you, culture of our world in your hands . . . Maybe it would have made more impact if March Sage Savour had *sounded* like the dying leader of a dying race, but its voice was just the same as any other voice filtered through a translator unit.

The document was produced and passed through a miniature airlock into the sterile interior of March

Sage Savour's globe, for the One Who Commands to make its mark. Then it was passed back out again and placed on the table in front of Ranjitsinhji and Prince James, who put their signatures on either side of March Sage Savour's glyph. And that was it.

"It is done," March Sage Savour said. There was no applause, no reaction from the humans. The moment was too big: handing over a planet and the rule of a race was a moment that didn't deserve to be lessened by acclaim or applause. "You are the new Ones Who Command," March Sage Savour added. "Look after our First Breed well."

"The First Breed do not accept these humans as our Ones Who Command."

Ranjitsinhji had opened his mouth to speak. He shut it again. Now the audience did begin to murmur and there were ripples of movement as everyone, including Gilmore and the two on the dais, looked around for the solitary speaker. It had been a Rustie: there was no mistaking that voice.

And then Gilmore noticed it, and one by one some of the others noticed it too. Iron Run was wearing a translator unit.

March Sage Savour had definitely noticed. It said something in fulltalk.

"Our human guests deserve to know what is happening," said Iron Run, "so I am using mouthtalk. I respectfully suggest you do likewise, my master."

"You are the Senior of the First Breed —" March Sage Savour said. Iron Run interrupted.

"I respectfully must contradict you, my master. As Senior, I have sworn to obey you and always will, which is why I have passed on my role as Senior to another."

"To whom?" March Sage Savour demanded.

"To me."

All eyes turned to the group of Rusties that had entered as attention centred on Iron Run and March Sage Savour. Iron Run's entourage — his *former* entourage — and—

"I am Arm Wild Timbre Grey Wood Temple Southern Plains," said Arm Wild, "and I have been chosen by the Seniors of the Clans to lead the First Breed nation."

Gilmore's mouth was the only one not hanging open. It was too taken up in a massive grin that was spreading from ear to ear. As Senior, Iron Run could not approve the plan . . . so Iron Run gave the job to someone who could. It was a consistently Rustie way of doing things.

"You are not a Clan Senior!" said March Sage Savour. "How can you be Senior of the nation? Now, end this nonsense and obey your Ones Who Command!"

"I am not a Clan Senior," Arm Wild agreed, "but I am a diplomat, accustomed to dealing with the humans, and the Clan Seniors felt I was best able to accommodate to the new way of thinking. As to your second point, I respectfully declare that you are no longer the Ones Who Command: you said so yourselves. And we do not accept the humans as your replacements."

"I know you, Arm Wild. I know that you, too, swore an oath. Your oath was to follow the rules of the Convocation exactly."

"As I have," said Arm Wild. "As have we all. But the Convocation is over."

"You —"

"With respect, my former masters, we wish you no ill will," Arm Wild said firmly. Unlike a human, Arm Wild could say "with respect" and mean it. "You created us, and much more. You created the culture of this world and we have no wish to humiliate you. I ask you to give us your blessing. Let this be the natural finish to the old order and a graceful start to the new. Be in control as you hand over to us, because the alternative is to go down kicking and screaming and letting a million years of history come to an ignoble end.

"The fact is, we simply do not want to be slaves again. It is in our nature to be slaves to you but to no others. We will be the equals of the humans."

"Ridiculous!" For the first time, a human butted into the conversation. Ranjitsinhji was on his feet. "We have no intention of making you slaves!"

"Your government's record on your own world suggests otherwise," Arm Wild said.

Prince James, too, stood up and bowed slightly as he addressed Arm Wild.

"Our government operates on strictly democratic

principles," he said. "We have guidelines to ensure that no one is enslaved or coerced. You would be safe with —"

"*Vast spaces, vast natural reserves . . . the UK deserves this place.*" It was still the prince speaking, but his mouth wasn't moving. The words were amplified and only Gilmore recognized them immediately. He had supplied the recording to the Rusties, courtesy of Plantagenet. A week ago, as *Ark Royal* first orbited the Roving, the prince had told his AI to record the images of the world below for his personal records. But Plantagenet had recorded more than just images.

"*Seven thousand people would rattle about a bit, sir,*" he heard himself say.

"*Pah! Do you think we'll keep it all to ourselves? Of course not. There's millions, billions on Earth who'll be queuing up for a chance to come here and start again, and we'll be in charge of it. We'll clean up, Captain!*"

"We are not impressed with your sincerity, Prince James," Arm Wild said.

There was more to-ing and fro-ing, more verbal sparring, but gradually the reality of the situation sank in. When the Clan leaders each stepped forward and declared their support for Arm Wild, that was all but one of the nails in the coffin of the Convocation and the authority of the former Ones Who Command. The final nail was when the Senior of the orbiting battle fleet radioed in its support for the new order.

It was a coup, but entirely bloodless, peaceful and dignified. A group of armed Rusties turned up but held back discreetly in the entrance to the chamber.

"My former masters," Arm Wild said, "you will respectfully be taken from this place and returned to your quarters in the Chambers of Command. Facilities are being prepared for you on the island of" — his translator made a noise, presumably an untranslatable place-name — "where you may live the rest of your lives in peace, with every want and need supplied."

March Sage Savour glanced at the escort party, then back at Arm Wild. Then it conversed with its fellows for a moment, before finally turning again to the new Senior of the First Breed.

"Arm Wild," it said, "you have surpassed yourselves. We are proud of you."

The Rusties were silent and bowed their heads in respect as their former masters were led from the room. Finally, Arm Wild looked up at the humans.

"We ask all save the delegates to withdraw," he said. "We have much to discuss."

Twenty-eight
25 May 2149

Gilmore was surprised it took the prince so long to get in touch. He was already back in orbit with five minutes to go before rendezvous with *Ark Royal* when the call came through.

"If there is the least suggestion that you had anything to do with this, you'll face a charge of treason," the prince said without preliminary.

"I'm recording this, sir, and even heads of state aren't immune against charges of slander," Gilmore said. "Be very careful what you say."

The prince simmered for a moment.

"We all heard your voice on that recording. You were there too. If it should come out that you were bugging me —"

"As I recall, sir," Gilmore said, "the scene was being recorded by your personal AI at your own command."

The prince didn't say anything: he just cut the call.

Treason. Gilmore felt cold. No one liked a traitor and that was one reason he had made sure that whatever he had done, it wasn't treason.

"Negative. I say again, negative." Peter Kirton sounded more annoyed than Gilmore had known he was capable of.

"But —" said a voice from the console.

"That AI is undergoing rigorous testing on board this ship. It is under my authority and I am not able to release it. *Ark Royal* out."

Peter sat back, then looked up at his captain entered the flight deck.

"They're persistent, sir," he said.

"Just refer them to me if they cause any trouble, Lieutenant," Gilmore said. *Assuming my word is any good in the Royal Space Fleet for much longer.* The prince must have worked out where the recording had come from and Gilmore had taken care to protect Plantagenet from reprisals: the best way was to get Peter to run tests. "Tell me, what's the procedure if an AI is thought to have gone bad?"

Peter thought. "There'd be a hearing —"

"A full one? In public?"

"Why, yes, sir. A panel of judges, witnesses, evidence . . ."

"Does the AI get to testify?"

"Absolutely, sir. It's also entitled to a full psychiatric evaluation to determine its motivation, and —"

"Thank you," Gilmore said. It was a weight off his mind. Plantagenet could hold his own in any court: for every fact the prosecution brought against him, Plantagenet could produce three or four that the prince would not want aired in public. He didn't see Prince James pursuing the matter that far.

Of course, Plantagenet might well be barred from the UK-1 network, which raised the interesting question of where the AI could go from now on.

"By the way," he added, "you can let Plantagenet out. I'll guarantee his good behaviour."

"Aye-aye, sir," Peter said. He was too well brought up to do more than look puzzled as Gilmore went below to his cabin.

The picture in the display was several centuries old and one of his all-time favourites. In a blaze of sunset reds and browns the ghostly ship of the line, stripped down but still proud and erect and noble, was towed down the river by a steam tug a fraction of its size. Turner's representation of the fighting *Temeraire*, veteran of Trafalgar and one of Britain's mightiest warships, tugged to her last berth to be broken up in 1838.

That was both him and his own ship, a vessel that Turner could never have imagined. Where could he go now? The rest of the crew would go on to greater and grander things, their records glowing with the endorsement of having been on the *Ark Royal*; but as far as Gilmore was concerned, it was official Fleet policy that Michael Gilmore Was No Good, even if he had wanted to work for Prince — no, *King* James — any further. And any other line? Well, why should they take on the man who (rumour said) threw over his country?

There was that word again. *Treason*.

"Captain." Peter Kirton's voice sounded on the intercom. "Prince James would like to speak to you."

Here it comes. "Put him through," Gilmore said.

The prince's face replaced the Turner on the wall display. He seemed half annoyed, half-amused. From the twist of his mouth and the tone of his voice, it was impossible to tell which.

"You did this, Gilmore," he said. "I know it. I know you're involved, somehow, and I've been told by my people that you're blocking access to that bastard Plantagenet."

"Did you actually have a reason for calling me, sir?" Gilmore said.

There was a murmur off-screen, and though Gilmore couldn't hear the words he recognized the tone of a translator unit. The prince glanced down, then back, visibly controlling himself. He was being used as a messenger boy.

"We've all been in talks with Arm Wild and reached certain agreements," he said. "One, the First Breed want to establish a human point of presence on the Roving right now. The vast majority of them have never met a human and most don't know what to expect, and we also have to learn a lot from them. We're leaving behind scientists to study their records, planners to develop the new human zones downstairs that have been allocated to us . . . and that's where you and the other captains come in. Arm Wild has chosen to honour all the nations that took part in the delegation by having each ship volunteer a crewmember to sit on a committee whose job it will be to name places."

"Don't they already have them?" Gilmore said dryly.

"Not usefully," the prince said with a hint of impatience. "Most locations on the Roving are unpronounceable to us and only a few place names can be changed into another language. How would you translate 'London' under similar circumstances? And when there's a non-verbal component to the language as well . . ."

"Point taken," Gilmore said.

"Good. Each ship is to submit a crewmember by 1700 Capital time tomorrow."

"And the second point, sir?" Gilmore said.

The prince paused. He glared at Gilmore and the way his jaw wobbled suggested he was grinding his teeth.

"To thank you, Captain. In a couple of days the delegation fleet will return to Earth and UK-1 will go with them, though we plan to return. We've got seven thousand people on board and they've all got lives back home, and not all of them will want to move to a new system. A lot needs to be settled back home so it'll be some months before we come back; though when we do, it will be to stay. It appears that as a result of a conversation you had with Arm Wild, the First Breed intend to use UK-1 as the port of —"

"— Entry to the Roving," Gilmore said, saying the words at the same time as the prince. He fought

back a grin: he had been careful to include the idea
in his talk with Arm Wild and Spar Mild, stressing
the ways Earth's various governments could offer
different services to the Rusties, but he had had no
way of knowing how much of it had stuck.

James frowned, but perhaps remembered what
Gilmore had said earlier about slander charges.

"Well . . . guessed, Captain. A port of entry for the
Roving. They will pay us for our services, naturally.
This gives us an advantageous position. Of course, I
would have proposed it to him if you hadn't already."

"Naturally, sir," Gilmore said. "You're the negotiator, after all. Is there a point three, sir?"

The prince gazed thoughtfully at him. "Unless
you're happy to stay a commander for the rest of
your natural life, resign now," he said quietly — murmured, almost. "Your little tinpot ship is to be
scrapped and you'll get no further advancement in
the Fleet. Out."

Charming man, Gilmore thought, as he blanked
the display and the Turner painting reappeared in
its place, but then he threw his head back and
laughed. That dealt with the treason possibility, anyway. UK-1 had the most advantageous deal it could
hope for, short of actually reestablishing its ruler's
former empire on a new world. And he, Gilmore,
had been publicly credited with it.

He stood and stretched, and reached out for the
comms panel. "Will all hands please meet me in the
wardroom?" he said. He looked around and his eye

rested for a moment on the *Temeraire*. His fingers brushed the bulkhead as he left.

"Me, sir?" said Julia. He could tell from her expression that he wasn't going to get much argument.

"There's more to naming a place than giving it a label," he said. "You need to capture the spirit of the place, the essence. Give the Roving names that the future Roving nation will be proud to own, and remember that the place originally belonged to the Rusties and the Ones Who Command before them, so try and avoid New Somewheres."

"I'll be glad to, sir!"

"And make sure that you name an outstanding natural feature after *Ark Royal*." He looked round at the four smiling faces and wondered where they would all be in a year's time. A lot could happen in a year. Not so long ago, humanity was confined to the solar system, there was no step-through and the UK was a joke kingdom out in the asteroids. Now . . ."

Assuming Hannah didn't leave the Fleet in disgust, she would get the ship she had already earned, and not before time. Doubtless she would end up commanding starships around the galaxy.

Wherever she went, Samad would be there too. He was young and flexible enough to come to terms with the new technology. Or perhaps he could move into command. He would manage.

Julia? It was up to her. She now had the opportunity to pursue her private agenda with Leaf Ruby, and what she did with it was her concern.

Peter? Like the others, a rising star in the Fleet, even if (as he had always said was the case) he couldn't claim credit for Polyglot. No problems there.

And Michael Gilmore? Good question.

"The prince has decreed that *Ark Royal* is to be scrapped," he said. "Our journey home will be the last in this ship and I expect our last together. So." He raised the glass in his hand. "Our first toast will be, to *Ark Royal*."

"To *Ark Royal*," they said, and drank.

"I wish you all well in your futures," he said. "I only hope that you don't get dragged down by association with me. So let's remember an officer who didn't have time to get dragged down by anyone. To Mr. Nichol, and absent friends."

"To absent friends," they agreed.

"We're going to need a new officer from UK-1," Hannah said thoughtfully.

"Later, Number One, later," Gilmore said.

The toasts went on, and in the midst of all the merrymaking Gilmore's aide announced that Arm Wild was trying to contact him. He went out of the room to take the call.

"Prince James has never grasped the pickup range of our translator units," Arm Wild said. "I believe I heard him advise you to resign."

Gilmore smiled. "You heard correctly, Arm Wild. However, I'd already sent in my resignation. I've reached the stage where wild horses couldn't keep me here."

"That is an interesting expression but I believe I register the sense of it. You have developed a pronounced antipathy to the Royal Space Fleet?"

"On the contrary, Arm Wild, some of my best friends and my happiest memories are with the Fleet. I just recognize that it's now best for both of us if the Fleet and I go our separate ways. By the way, congratulations on your, um, promotion."

"I thank you, and I hope we will see more of each other," said Arm Wild.

Gilmore cocked his head to one side, suddenly wary. "Oh?"

"Let me make you an offer," Arm Wild said. "Prince James mentioned our need to familiarize our two species with one another. We also want a small party to stay behind to make a proper assessment of First Breed space technology and to work out how our skills can combine. Essentially, I am talking about drawing up a blueprint for the entirely new combined spaceforce that we are going to need. The successful candidate will have administrative ability, a detailed knowledge of human space technology and the breadth of mind to see the new potentials. An ability to relate to the First Breed is an advantage. I would like to offer you that job."

Gilmore's eyes went round. "I —"

The old fears came crashing back. *It's a challenge and you're not up to challenges. You can't do it.*

"I'm flattered," he said.

"The prince has already promised the help of his best engineers, and we know they are familiar with our technology. Between you all, we should —"

"Wait, wait," Gilmore said, holding up his hands. "Look, about us being familiar with your technology . . . Arm Wild, you should know —"

"Perhaps they are as yet unable to design a step-through generator from scratch," said Arm Wild, "but they have shown they are capable of adapting an existing one."

"Don't tell me the prince told you that!" Gilmore exclaimed.

"He did not need to. Should he have?"

Gilmore stared at the leader of the First Breed. Meeting Arm Wild's blank gaze, Gilmore thought that it was at times like this, when he had just about got used to the shape and physiognomy of the Rusties, that they looked so darn alien. Arm Wild could be looking puzzled or he could be grinning widely, knowing perfectly well what Gilmore was talking about.

"How did you know?" Gilmore said.

"You know I am not technical by nature, but I gather from those who are that the resonance caused by UK-1's step-through indicates it was using a generator from one of the ships we scattered around your solar system, in the hope that someone would find them."

"You planted it!"

"It was part of the Convocation, as decided by the Ones Who Command. They were hidden in places such that anyone who found one would, by definition, be of an adventurous and explorative nature. Anyone who could decipher the clues would also, by definition, be of the required technical proficiency to replace the Ones Who Command."

Gilmore laughed out loud. "Arm Wild, you're a cunning bugger."

"Context suggests that was a compliment," Arm Wild said. "Now, the prince also mentioned that your ship is to be scrapped. I believe that scrapped ships are also offered for sale?"

"Well, yes, as a rule."

"We would like to purchase *Ark Royal*, as is, sight unseen. I know the design of the substructure is old, but the equipment on board is the state of your art and will give our engineers a useful starting point for merging our technologies. It has the added advantage of being here. Another reason for approaching you with this offer, incidentally, is that you are very familiar with your own ship."

"Well, yes . . ." And then it hit Gilmore: every new ship built by Rusties and humans together would be a descendant of his *Ark Royal*. The fears disappeared.

"Look," he said, "I don't have the authority to sell you the ship, but —"

"We included it in our negotiations with UK-1. The prince will discover it in the little lettering."

"Then will you include one more thing?" Gilmore said. "I want the highest level AI on board, Plantagenet, to be given sanctuary in the ship's network. He'll be able to help your engineers with their observations."

"This is acceptable."

"Then you have a deal," Gilmore said.

When he had finished talking to Arm Wild, he cued his aide again. "Contact Midshipman Gilmore, UK-1."

"Please wait," the aide said. "Midshipman Gilmore is on watch and asks that a message be left."

Gilmore smiled, approving. Duty first. That's my boy. "Joel, it's me. Listen, I promised you a tour of my ship. Well, you'd better make it soon. Next couple of days. Let me know when you can make it. Talk to you later."

He rejoined the crew in the wardroom. They were looking at him curiously: his laughter must have been heard through the wall. He retrieved his glass and toyed with it. If *Ark Royal* were to stay here, the crew would need new berths. . . .

"The good news," he said, meeting Hannah's eyes, "is that we won't be needing any new officers at all."

EPILOGUE

From: Senior of the First Breed Earth Mission
            First Breed residence, Manhattan

FOR IMMEDIATE GENERAL RELEASE

The Senior of the First Breed nation, Arm Wild, today
extended its personal invitation to all humans who
wish to apply for citizenship of the new
Human/First Breed Commonwealth.

The Commonwealth exists independent of all
previously existing states and nations on either
world. Its most urgent needs are currently for:

• trained spacers, for its rapidly expanding space
exploration and defence fleet;
• engineers and scientists to assist in the cross-
technological development programmes now under
way;
• farmers and settlers for the vast areas of land left
empty by the tragic extinction of the Ones Who
Command;

as well as the many other skills expected in a
dynamic, energetic young culture.

Arm Wild said: "Our original invitation two years ago

urged the nations of Earth to take this opportunity to make a fresh start. I now extend that to *all* the people of Earth. This is a unique opportunity to cast aside the old ties of planet-bound nationalism once and for all. Join us in space."

Arm Wild added: "The First Breed welcome our human friends into the Commonwealth as partners and equals."

For further information, instruct your aide to consult the Emigration Helpdesk at the First Breed Embassy.

Verbatim Bald
First Breed residence, Manhattan
24 August 2150 CE